THE SECOND BAT GUANO WAR

ALSO BY J.M. PORUP

Novels
The United States of Air
The Second Bat Guano War
Death on Taurus

Plays
Ariadne's Lament and Two Other Shorts
Very Skinny People
Thy Fearful Symmetry

Travel Guidebooks
Lonely Planet Colombia
Lonely Planet Venezuela
Lonely Planet Dominican Republic & Haiti
Lonely Planet South America on a Shoestring
Lonely Planet Caribbean Islands

Nonfiction
Colombia's Diversity Problem: a Speech on Tourism

Diet/Self-Help
Food-Free At Last: How I Learned To Eat Air [*]

[*] with Dr. Robert Jones, MD, PhD, DDS, ODD

THE SECOND BAT GUANO WAR

BY
J.M. PORUP

THE SECOND BAT GUANO WAR

Published by J.M. Porup
ISBN: 978-0-9880069-9-7
First Edition: December 2012

www.JMPorup.com

for Anna-Sofia

a nightmare I dreamed up
before you were even a glimmer

Timon: What wouldst thou do with the world,
                Apemantus, if it lay in thy power?

Apemantus: Give it to the beasts,
                to be rid of the men.

—Shakespeare, *Timon of Athens,* Act IV, scene iii

1

SOMEONE WAS CALLING MY NAME. THE SOUND was distorted, a foghorn of death and regret. Jackhammers pounded inside of my skull, a reminder of yesterday's excess.

"Horse."

There it was again. I pinched the bridge of my nose, trying to dull the pain behind my eyes. Who was talking to me? I peered out at my class through grease-smeared lenses. My students avoided my gaze. Can't say that I blamed them. They were criminals, all of them, the oozing pus of this chancre of a city. But who was I to judge? I'm no better than they are.

No. I'm worse.

"Horse, *please!*"

The voice called me again. Whoever it was, why couldn't they leave me alone? Couldn't they see I was trying to teach English?

"Oh my God, what is that?" said Paco the pickpocket. "Is that a UFO?" He thrust a finger skyward at some plaster dripping from the ceiling.

"Excellent, Paco." A noise was coming from my throat. Was that me talking?

"And then I steal them."

"Steal *from* them. Yes. Very good."

Six months ago I caught Paco with his hand in my pocket. My friend Pitt wanted to crack the boy's skull open against a nearby dumpster, then leave him in it. I gave him my business card instead.

"English for Criminals." Word got around. If you wanted to learn English in Lima, and from a teacher who wouldn't rat you out (and who happily accepted, in lieu of cash, cocaine by the ounce, *pisco* by the case, or sexual favors in half-hour increments as payment), then I was your man.

The class was no longer looking at me. I followed their gaze. A blonde stood in the doorway of my grungy classroom, a long cherry fingernail up her nose. She cleared her throat. She was tall, a good six foot something, a Valkyrie towering over my Napoleonic shortness. She had a whiplash-inducing figure, but on closer inspection the sands were draining from her hourglass, as things began to sag and bulge in all the wrong places. She wore a black leather miniskirt and a turquoise tube top, which would have looked good on her twenty years ago; her breasts were in open revolt against gravity, a testament to the efforts of a talented plastic surgeon. If you didn't look too closely at the crow's-feet around her eyes, you might think she was still in her thirties. That is, if you dynamited your way through several geologic layers of makeup, first.

Every pair of eyes swiveled to examine the blonde's crevices and curves, calculating their odds. Including, I was sorry to see, Juanita, the only female in the class, who carried a slim switchblade parked between her breasts and always paid me promptly, and in cash.

The fingernail slithered out of the blonde's nostril, tried in vain to hide itself under a breast. She stepped forward. "Horse?"

I turned back to my class. Maybe if I imagined she wasn't there, she'd go away.

"Now, Major." I addressed the class's sole member of Lima's finest. He'd busted me with a kilo of coke, which, I might add, really was for personal consumption. I gave him free English lessons in exchange for keeping me out of jail. At first his presence had inhibited conversation. But the major was too drunk most days to remember his own name, much less those of the others, and tales of illegal exploits soon flowed freely once again.

Today was one of the cop's more lucid days.

"Major Villega," I continued, ignoring the blonde's urgent stare, "when you catch the thief, what do you say to the gringo?"

He grinned, his rotting teeth glittering with saliva, grotesque belly spilling sideways over his belt. "I say, 'Hello, pretty lady, you wan' make fuck wit' me?'"

The blonde's pale complexion, covered as it was in the fine powder that settles on everything in this city, colored a violent shade of pink. Even her makeup wasn't enough to hide her discomfort. The students pounded their desks and laughed, slapped each other on the back.

Besides Paco and Major Villega, there was Luis, an earring snatcher who paid me in blood-stained gold; Álvarita, a transgender whore who sucked cock in the park, then robbed her johns with a knife to their balls as they came; Lucho the *taxista,* who was always there to give a horny gringa the ride of her life; Andrès, a Hilton bellboy who was also the de facto concierge—*cocaine? chicas? concert tickets? I get for you, don't worry;* Ricardo, a script kiddie who wanted to know the value of the secrets he stole; and half a dozen other creeps, lowlifes and riffraff, the scum who make up most of this foul city.

"Horse, please," she said. "It's about Pitt."

I sighed. "You have to call me that? The name is Horace. And what about him?"

She tiptoed into the room, teetering on her high heels. "Can I talk to you?" She lowered her voice, glanced at the class. "Alone?"

"El profesor tiene cojones, amigo!" The class whooped and high-fived. "Who's your lady friend, man?"

"That's enough." I looked at the clock. Five to. "Same time Wednesday. Your homework," —I held up my arms to stifle the groans— "excuses and apologies. I want to see some creativity this time!" I shouted as their chairs scraped against the rotting wooden floor. I had given them a long list of possible excuses, ways to convince a gringo victim not to turn them in: sob stories of nonexistent baby sisters in need of operations, kidnapped cousins forced into slavery and cannibalism in the high Andes, malnutrition in the slums. I wanted them to think for themselves, though; it wasn't good enough to just memorize my list. They needed to be ready to improvise.

As Paco walked by I grabbed his arm. I held out my hand.

He grinned. He pulled my wallet from his pocket and laid it on my palm. "You alright, Horse. You cut me slack."

Getting people to call me by my given name was a lost

cause. Once they'd seen my camel toe, the nickname stuck.

I slapped him on the shoulder. "See you, Paco."

The last of the men trooped down the stairs, leaving me alone with the blonde. I walked down the peeling linoleum hallway, past the overflowing toilet with no door to a small room with a bed, fridge and stove. My flip-flops threw up puffs of dust. Her spike heels echoed behind me as they punctured divots in the underlying floorboards.

I dropped my glasses on top of the television before turning around. She looked better out of focus. Less tempting, too. I avoided pretty girls as a rule. I threw myself ass first onto the bed and sank almost to the floor, the ancient metal springs creaking to support my modest weight.

"What do you want, Lynn?"

We had met in a bar in Barranco. The Rat's Nest. Three levels of debauchery, each more wicked than the last. We'd ground against each other to the *reggaetón,* then paid for one of the stand-up booths in the corner. I'd penetrated her without a condom. She didn't object. I don't think she cared much either.

It became a regular afternoon liaison. I knew she was married. I knew she had kids. My age. I knew I could do better. I didn't want to. Being with her was the same sadness I got from lying with whores, only more intense. I was a worthless piece of shit and deserved no better.

"Pitt's missing," she said.

She crunched her way over to the bedroom window, looked down at the courtyard. I lived over a butcher shop. Most days it served as an impromptu abattoir. If it moved and you could eat it, they'd kill it, skin it and pack it for you.

From my bedroom window you could watch the meatpackers in their gore-flecked vestments making sausage, mixing flyblown offal with wheelbarrows of sawdust. The reek infiltrated my room through cracks in the glass.

"What else is new."

I pulled a half-empty bottle of *pisco* from under the bed. I unscrewed the top and threw it across the room at the swarming mass of cockroaches that lived in the corner, scuttling their grandparents' carcasses in its wake. I took a long swallow, grunted, held the bottle out to her. She took it and drank.

She said, "I haven't seen him for a month."

"So put the goon squad on the case. What're you asking me for?"

"They can't know about this, Horse."

"You mean the embassy, or—"

"Neither."

I shrugged. She took another swallow of *pisco* and offered me the bottle. I waved it away. I reached under my pillow and pulled out a travel soap dish. One of several I kept about the place. Pried off the lid, took a big pinch of cocaine between my thumb and forefinger, and snorted it. I held out the soap dish to her.

She looked at the coke and delicately scratched the inside of her nose again, as though considering today's required dosage. Paced to the end of the small room, her heels sinking into decades of dirt. Her leather mini creaked with the movement. She clutched her forearms under her breasts, bit her lip.

"You don't care, do you," she said.

"Not really, no."

"And if he's lying in a gutter somewhere?"

"It was me," I said, and snorted another pinch of coke, "I wouldn't want to be disturbed."

"The two of you are friends."

"*Were*. And he'd do the same for me."

The coke hit me. My head went numb. Anesthetic for the memories. Instead of live-action replays of my crime on endless loop, it froze for an instant in gruesome caricature.

I put the soap dish on my pillow and stood up. Her breasts were at eye level. I put my hands on her hips and craned my neck. She didn't move.

"I told you," I said. "It's over."

Turned out she wasn't just the mother of my best friend. Correction, *former* best friend. She was also the wife of my one-time employer, Pitt's adoptive father. The two of them, father and son, had a license to kill—for their country; for sport; for any minor transgression, real or imagined; whenever they felt the urge. So hell yeah, I broke things off with Lynn. For our own good, I told her. And I meant it. But doing what was good for me was something alien to all my being, and again and again we came together in furtive intercourse, hating each other and loathing our own weakness.

She laid her hands on my chest. "I didn't come here for that."

"Then what did you come for?"

She unbuttoned the top of my shirt. "Maybe I could have a glass of water?"

I slid my hands down past her muffin top and clutched her cottage cheese buttocks, pulled her pelvis against me. "You came here for a glass of water?"

Her voice was soft, wounded. "Please."

I went to the sink and filled the kettle with water, trying not to inhale the stench from the tap. Even I couldn't handle that. Drinking water in this town was a shortcut to unhappy bowels. The best you could do was boil it. It still tasted like sulfur. No doubt I would drink my fill from hell's reeking pits soon enough.

"Since when do you drink water?" I asked.

I carried the kettle to the stove and lit the gas burner with a match. I put the kettle on to boil.

"Since this." She held out a piece of paper.

"Which is?"

"Read it."

I took the paper. "You know I can't read without my glasses."

"Dammit, Horse. It's an email from Pitt."

"What does it say?"

"'I've found a way to end the guilt.'"

Muhammad Ali connected with a solid right hook. My world spun. I held on to the table for support. Since when did Pitt feel guilt?

Conscience is overrated, bro. All it'll do is get you killed by people like me.

"The words," I said. "The exact words."

She spotted my glasses on top of the broken television. There was a hole in the screen where I had kicked it in some months ago. On the whole I found I preferred watching dust gather on the gaping shards to the usual cable fare. She grabbed my glasses and forced them onto my face.

"Not so rough," I said, adjusting the frames. I straightened the printout and squinted to focus. I recognized Pitt's email address. The message was dated a week ago.

"End the guilt."

Those three little words ripped open a wound no balm could heal. They weren't Pitt's words, either. And that meant—*No. Don't go there. Don't even think about it.* I put the paper on the table and a cockroach scuttled down the table leg and across the floor.

Lynn impaled the insect on the heel of her shoe. "You got a real cockroach problem, you know that?"

She lifted her foot. A pile of twitching goo stuck to the tip of her heel. I snagged a tissue and bent down, running my fingertips along her calf, the sheer black stocking an electric separation between us. I held her foot steady and wiped the goo from her shoe.

"I'd say it's the cockroaches who have a real human problem."

I went to the window and opened it just enough to flick the tissue-wrapped bug outside. It landed in a passing wheelbarrow of red-black flesh. A butcher with a shovel scooped it into the meat grinder.

The thick gravy of Lima's filthy air spilled into the room and I choked. Cold and disgusting. I took a deep breath, held it in my lungs. Perfect. I picked up the pack of Hamiltons on my desk. Nasty local cigarette. No filter. Stuck three in my mouth and set them all on fire, the match trembling in front of my face. I sucked in the hot smoke. The flavor of cheap tobacco mingled with the taste of exhaust.

The *pisco* and coke were no longer enough. What was

Pitt trying to tell me? I ripped open my shirt and hunted for a patch of skin not covered in scar tissue. A futile quest. Over the course of the last year I had pockmarked my entire body from the neck down with multiple layers of cigarette burns.

Lynn came up behind me and wrapped her arms around my chest, pinning my elbows at my side. Her breasts made divots in my shoulder blades. I could smell her perfume. *Musk of Horny Woman.* By Calvin Klein.

"It's not your fault," she said.

I struggled to break free but she held me tight. "The *fuck* you know."

"Could happen to anyone."

"Well it didn't, did it? It happened to me."

"It's OK to cry."

"Fuck you," I said. I elbowed her in the stomach and she let go.

There. Found a spot. I extinguished all three burning cigarettes under my armpit. The smell of burning flesh wafted up between us. I put the cigarettes back in my mouth and lit them again, puffing to get them nice and hot.

She clutched her navel. She said, "I need to know."

"Where the door is? Right behind you."

"What it means. 'End the guilt'? What guilt? What has he done?"

She had no idea. I wasn't about to enlighten her. "Maybe he killed a cockroach."

A sharp blow knocked the cigarettes from my hand.

"Damn you, Horse. I need your help!" Her face grew red. Brine leaked from the corners of her eyes. She reached for my crotch.

"Let him go," I said. I held her breast firm in my hand. "He's an asshole, same as me."

"My son is not an asshole," she said, shimmying out of her tube top.

"But you'll admit that I am?"

She grinned through her tears. "You're my kind of asshole." She unbuckled my belt. The kettle began to scream.

"BROS FOREVER, DUDE?"

We were sitting on our longboards in the waves off Huanchaco, a short hour flight north of Lima. Pitt's fist hovered in midair, waiting. His smile was full of teeth, his green eyes the color of the sea. A halo of early morning sun surrounded his head.

A blond god with a deep tan wanted to fist bump.

I pushed his fist with mine. "Bros forever."

A wave was coming fast. A big one. It threw us apart and we scrambled to cling to our boards.

"Longest left hand point break in the world," Pitt shouted over the noise of the sea and the caw of the gulls. A shark-tooth necklace danced on his chest, triangles of white on his black wetsuit.

We paddled out into the deep, our arms sweeping the lengths of our longboards, pushing through the ocean waves. A kilometer out, we pressed our chests against the waxed boards.

In the distance the gray, dead Peruvian coast watched us, a cemetery waiting patiently to be filled. We aimed our boards at the white church on the hill. Reed boats lined the foreshore,

tiny handmade kayaks with curved prows like a jester's slippers. The hour of fishing was over. Now was the hour of surf.

"Just get me back to shore," I gulped, spitting salt water.
Another wave lifted us in a heavy swell, dropped us again.
The sun peeked over the eastern horizon, but in the west dark
clouds hovered.

"Surfing's better than sex," he shouted.

"How's that?" I asked.

"Better than drugs! Better than anything!"

"Oh yeah?" I retorted. "What happens when you're back
on land?"

He laughed. "That assumes you make it back!"

He slipped off his board into the water. He grabbed the
end of my surfboard and paddled toward shore.

"The fuck you doing?"

"When I say go, get up, OK?"

Another wave swelled. Without warning, a sudden shove
launched me into the air—*what happened to "When I say go"?
But no time to dispute the point now*—and I leaped onto the
board, and for what seemed like eternity the only thing that
mattered was staying upright.

I had gone surfing once or twice on a high school trip
to Tijuana. My memory of the lessons was rather hazy, no
doubt due to the quantities of liquor, pot and mescaline I had
consumed that weekend, but somehow my feet remembered,
my body understood, and the wave picked me up into the
air, my arms out, body tense, and bore me toward the shore
faster than I had ever gone before.

The sand got closer, the wave got higher, I began to panic.
Now what? How do I make it stop? How do I get off this

thing?

The wave collapsed. My feet left the board and I fell into the surf, crashing sideways into the surfboard, my chest flattened against the hard surface. Pain blossomed in my ribs. *Gather ye rosebuds,* I thought. I stood in waist-high water, but the following wave knocked me over.

I swallowed sea water. Coughed, spat brine. I grabbed hold of the board again, ignoring the pain in my side, and floated into shore on the next wave. When I felt my knees hit sand, I picked up the board and walked out of the surf.

Pitt rode the crest of a monster wave. Must have been three meters, easy. He slid down into the curve beneath the wave, darting sideways through the tube as it collapsed behind him. It looked as though he'd make it all the way to shore, cruising along on the final efforts of the wave, when the sea decided it had seen enough insolence for one day, and crashed down around him.

He tumbled out of the water, staggering with his board under his arm, feet struggling through the outgoing tide. He pumped his fist in the air. "Wipe out!"

I waited until he got within non-shouting range. "I think I prefer cocaine."

"That's why we brought a kilo, didn't we?"

He grinned, the sand and the sea streaming from his hair, the sun peeking through the gathering clouds to bathe us in its flickering warmth. That grin that said all was right with the world, there could be no wrong, happiness was as simple as a dip in the ocean or a trip to the brothel, and misery too complex to understand. I envied him.

I stuck my fist out. "Bros forever?"

"Dude," he said, and punched my fist so hard it hurt. "Bros forever."

Welcome to Happy Frying Pan Store.

So proclaimed the sign in Spanish, English and Chinese. Although I don't know Chinese. Maybe it said Buy Cocaine Cheap Shop in that oriental chicken scratch.

Pitt had wanted coke for our trip up the coast. Insisted on meeting my dealer in person.

"Never know what they cut it with," he complained.

"The stuff you're snorting now is finest high-mountain nose candy," I said. "Besides, I'm one of Hak Po's best customers."

But he insisted, so I let him tag along. He waited for me after class, and we took a bus deep into the warehouse and factory district adjoining Lima's million-strong Chinatown.

I pushed open the front door. The bell tinkled. A Chinese boy of about twenty lounged behind the counter, picking his fingernails with a knife. He was missing an eye. The remaining orb appraised us quickly: gringos in the wrong part of town.

"You like fry pan?" he asked in pidgin English. "Very good fry pan." Piles of cast-iron skillets lay stacked around the shop.

I chuckled and leaned on the counter. "You must be new. We're here to see the boss."

He held my gaze, his one eye unblinking. "Name?"

"Horace. But people call me Horse. As in hung like a."

The boy closed the hasp of his knife and retreated through

a hanging bead doorway.

Pitt hefted a frying pan. He ran a finger through a thick layer of dust. "Your drug dealer runs a frying pan factory?"

I shrugged. "Good a cover as any, I suppose."

A wizened yellow gnome of a man shuffled through the bead door. The ever-present Cubs cap perched high on his head, exposing his wispy baldness. His sallow face puckered in a grin when he saw me.

"Hak Po!" I said. I hacked up some phlegm and spat on the floor.

"How's my leetle Horsie?" he asked, dangling a finger at crotch level.

We shook hands and laughed.

"Friend I want you to meet," I said.

He glided around the counter, his black slippers skating across the dust-covered floor. He looked Pitt up and down.

Pitt grinned and held out his hand. "Horse says you're the best."

Hak Po looked at the hand but did not take it. "Where I see your face before?"

Pitt's eyes flickered my way. "I don't know. My first time here."

"You stay." He pointed at me. "You come."

Hak Po shuffle-glided back behind the counter and the little-used cash register.

Pitt went to follow, but I put a hand on his chest. "Sorry, dude," I said. "I love you like a brother, but if Hak Po says stay, you stay. Besides," I said. "Maybe you can find a nice frying pan for your mother or something."

"Fat chance I'd ever see *her* cooking," he laughed. "But

you go on. Don't worry about it."

I stepped around the counter and through the bead door. Hak led me along a dark corridor into the factory. Great cauldrons of liquid iron belched and hissed steam. Workers poured the molten lava into frying pan molds, then plunged the newly created cookware into cold water to temper them. Steam rose in clouds. The din was terrible.

I'd asked him once, my nose full of coke, "Wouldn't it be cheaper to import cast-iron cookware from China?"

He had grinned up at me, a spoonful of cocaine ringing the edge of his nose. "I like make fry pan. What wrong with that? You insult my profession, something?"

"No," I'd said. "Fry pan good. You good fry pan man."

"Yes," he'd said, snorting his uncut powdered joy. "I very good fry pan man."

Hak Po's office was a small room just off the factory floor. He let me go first. I squeezed through a gauntlet of four filing cabinets and climbed over his desk to take a chair. You didn't want to slip; Hak Po, as his name suggested, was a spitter, and the floor was covered in a slick coating of slime.

Hak took a seat and unlocked a filing cabinet. He took out a kilo bag of cocaine and placed it on the desk. I tossed an envelope full of used fifties into his "in" tray and reached for the coke. He stopped me with an open hand.

"Tell me something, Horse, please."

I was itching to get some of that powder in my nose. "Sure, Hak. Anything."

"How long you know friend?"

I shrugged. "Couple months. Long enough. Why?"

"I know I see him somewhere. No remember where." He

waggled a finger in the air. "He bad man."

I laughed. "As am I. As are you."

A grunt. "True. But some are more bad than others. You stay away him, hear?"

"Sure, Hak," I said. "Whatever you say."

He let me taste the coke. It was good. The closest to forgetting I was ever likely to find. I stood and climbed past him over the desk.

A yellow hand pinched my calf. "You watch yourself now, Horse. You hear? I no like lose good customer."

I'd been warned. I should have known better. Alarm bells had gone off the day I met Pitt, but I ignored them.

I was in the Rat's Nest trying to pick a fight with a pacifist fucking general in the Marine Corps. I'd heard an aircraft carrier was in harbor down at Callao, and I went looking for the biggest, meanest-looking grunt I could find.

I believed in America. Its ideals. But those ideals had become so warped and mangled that nothing was left of them but hypocrisy and lies. The mere thought of living in America again made me sick to my stomach. Better an honest hellhole like Lima than the plastic smile and the knife in the back you'll get at home. *Don't you tread on me, motherfucker.*

"You oughtta be ashamed of yourself," I told him. "Killing innocent women and children for a living." I spat on his uniform.

He wiped the loogie from his jacket and stood up. "I've met your kind before," he sneered. "Traitors like you in every port in the world. Not good enough for your own country." He turned to go. "You're not worth the time it takes to piss on."

"Well God bless America and pass the apple pie," I said, and took a swing at him.

He blocked the blow easily, and sent a devastating punch my way. I closed my eyes and waited for impact, savoring in advance the coming stars. They never came. I peeked. His fist hovered in midair inches from my nose.

A crunching sound of broken bone. The man howled in pain. His forearm bent over the bar at an unnatural angle.

"Bye-bye," a new voice said, and a man took the general's barstool. He looked far too young and blond and happy to be sitting there in that filthy bar, chuckling to himself as the marine limped from the room, clutching his broken arm to his chest.

"The fuck are you doing?" I shouted over the noise of the bar.

"Saving your ass by the looks of things," he said. "Name's Pitt. Buy you a drink?" To the barman: *"Dos cervezas, por favor."*

"Make mine a bottle of *pisco*," I hollered. "And who are you to get involved?"

Pitt cracked his knuckles. "That guy was going to beat you up."

"Yes. I know. That was the point?"

The *pisco* came. Pitt poured me a shot. I took the bottle and drained it in one long swallow.

"Thirsty," he said, and rested his chin on his fist. "You want another or should I just tape a 'Rob Me' sign to your forehead?"

"Fuck off, will you?" I said. "You've already ruined my evening." I looked around the room. None of the other crew off the USS *Asswipe* seemed inclined to brawl. Not with Pitt at my side. I slid off my barstool, feeling unsteady. "Now I'll have to go somewhere else to get beaten up."

Pitt drank his beer and laughed. "You are weird, dude. Why on earth do you want to get beaten up?"

My liquor tolerance was pretty high but even I was struggling to process an entire bottle of *pisco*. The stuff was raw local brandy, as nasty as it gets. I held on to the bar to steady myself. "Because I deserve it," I said to a puddle of beer on the bar. I sat down and covered my face with my hands.

He slapped me on the back. "What can you possibly have done to deserve that?"

So I told him. I tell everyone. I love to watch their faces change. The horror when they hear what I have done.

When I was finished, he just laughed. "Dude," he said, "that's nothing. Don't be such a fucking wuss. How can you feel guilty about something as stupid as that?"

The world was spinning now. "Wouldn't you?" I managed to croak. I reached for my soap dish to righten the good ship Horsie.

"I do that kind of shit before breakfast sometimes," he said. "And I sleep like a baby. Um, sorry," he said, catching my expression of pain. "You know what I mean."

"Tell me about it," I said, snorting cocaine up my nose until my septum bled. "Tell me all about your pre-breakfast guilt-free ways."

"I'm CIA," he said breezily. "An enforcer. Part of the Dissent Suppression Unit."

"And I'm the King of Spain. I dub thee, Sir Stranger Who Must Now Fuck Off." And I collapsed into giggles.

He pinched my neck. A sharp pain shot down my spine. "I kill people for a living, dickwad," he said. "You hear about the murders in Iquitos last week?"

I squawked an affirmative, his hand still on my neck.

"That was me. Strangled three dissidents with their own intestines. Roasted their nuts over an open fire. They were tasty." He smacked his lips close to mine. "Fucking villagers didn't want us drilling for oil. Thought it might ruin their precious fucking habitat. Guess what?" He laughed beer smell in my face. "We run this country. We don't put up with that shit from nobody. You get in our way, you object to our policy, you protest our raping your country for money? Dead. Tortured. Disappeared."

He let go of my neck, and I sat back, rubbing my spine.

"Decapitate dissent," he said. "That's what I do. Literally. Kill the leaders, and the sheep will follow." He ticked off on his fingers. "Union organizers. Indigenous leaders. Hoity-toity academics who can't be blackmailed or bullied. Artists. Writers. Opposition politicians. We make them go away." He thumped his chest. "And I am a one-man disappearing team. I will kill, torture, maim, rape, sodomize, cannibalize and terrorize until you fucking obey, you stupid fucking Peruvians." He leaned back in his chair with a smile. He drank his beer, then held it to his cheek and grinned broadly. "But after a hard day's work, it's time for an ice-cold Bud. Don't you agree?"

I stared at him. It was bizarre. This golden boy, this Greek god spewing such filth...he didn't look like he was joking. "If that's the case, how come you're telling me all this? Isn't that, you know, like, classified?"

"You wearing a wire?"

"No."

"Good. Because if you were I'd have to kill you." He swigged his beer and grinned again.

From the depths of my soul came a reply: "You are either a liar or a psychopath."

He swallowed suds and wagged a finger. "Sociopath, actually. Company shrink said so."

Turned out he wasn't a liar.

3

THE SIGN SAID NO SMOKING. I LIT A CIGARETTE.

Two blue leather sofas glistened at right angles in the waiting room. Paintings of mountains long since gouged flat regarded me mournfully from the wall. Above them blazoned the coat of arms of Anglo-Dutch Mining, Ltd.: two unicorns rampant over a field of poppies. Four clocks ticked in unison, alerting the visitor to the current hour in London, Johannesburg, Melbourne and Lima.

Behind the yacht of a reception desk, its skipper, a twenty-something albino with her hair in a bun, tapped daintily at a computer. Her unfettered nipples ogled me through a tight red twinset. She glanced up from time to time, caught me staring at her. Those pink eyes made me think of rats. She'd greeted me with a polite *"buenos días,"* but switched to English when she heard my gringo accent. "Hey, you a Merkan?" she twanged. The South Florida accent made me want to hurl. "How's it going? How do you like Peru?" She giggled. "Isn't it just wonderful down here?"

Santana's "American Woman" played in my head on endless loop. I blew smoke at the ceiling.

"You need to put that out." She snapped her pale fingers at the sign.

The imperial finger snap made me want to wrench her arm from its socket and beat her over the head with it. My first wife used to do the same. Fuck her. And fuck her whole half of the species, especially the American ones.

At our son's second birthday party Mrs. Bossy had snapped her fingers in my face and announced in front of all the company that she was divorcing me and suing for child support. Oh—and that the child wasn't mine, but my best friend Larry's.

"Child support?" I'd asked my lawyer. "Is she joking?"

"Nope," he'd said with a chuckle. "According to the law, you got two years to order a paternity test. After that, doesn't matter if it's yours or not." He aimed his pencil at my head. "You're on the line for the next sixteen years, bucko."

I heaved myself from my seat with a squish of leather and approached the yacht, cigarette between my lips. Ash dribbled onto the spotless marble. I exhaled smoke through my nose.

"I can suck myself off," I said. "Wanna see?"

"I'm *sorry?*"

You better be, cunt, I thought. *You and all your kind.*

"I need to see Sergio. You want to see me do it. Get your girlfriends, make some popcorn."

"*What?* I—*no.*" Her ghostly face flushed crimson. "Are you crazy? I *told* you, Mr. Salazar is in a—"

"You'll regret it if you don't." I unzipped my jeans, tooth by tooth. The noise echoed in the sterile waiting room.

She closed her mouth. Glanced at my crotch. Picked up the phone.

Fucking slut.

***

That morning I sat in bed for a long while, smoking cigarettes. Lynn had spent the night. A first. Went to great lengths to change my mind. Didn't even complain when the cockroaches crawled into bed with us. When I woke up screaming, rats clawing at a baby in my arms, she hushed me, stroked my face, held me against a silicon breast. I wondered what she'd tell her husband. I spent the night fucking your former agent's brains out. Why? So he'd help me find my son. You remember him. Pitt?

Pitt, I thought. *Goddamn Pitt.* Only friend I'd had down here in Lima. Or thought I had. *Serves him right. After what he did? No. He can get fucked.*

I extinguished the cigarette against my left nipple. Lit another. "End the guilt." That's what the email had said. Pitt had found a way to end the guilt. Pitt! With a conscience! Just the idea made me want to laugh.

He was everything I hated in the world. So why did I love him so much? Even now, after he betrayed me. How can you love someone you hate?

Maybe because, compared to him, I felt like a good person. He was a reminder that there were worse people in the world than myself. Truth be told I was jealous of his lack of conscience. What freedom he must feel! Not to be weighed down by ten tons of baggage like me.

Why had a murderous sociopath like Pitt wanted to hang around a sad sack of shit like me? God only knows. A source for his coke, I suppose. Although cocaine wasn't exactly hard to come by in Peru. Hell, the country produced more of the stuff nowadays than Colombia did. Pitt had used me, of course. *Of course.* On my first, last and only mission for the CIA, thank God. But I could think of a dozen other people with the right access for that op. Why did he pick me?

I guess I was his audience. He liked to get high before going on a killing spree, murdering dissidents and protestors, whatever he did for a living. Then he'd fly into town and we'd go out drinking and whoring. He'd tell me about his latest atrocities.

His stories always made me feel better.

Pitt was one sick, twisted fuck. If his conscience had suddenly clicked on, then he was staggering around with a helluva load.

I burned another cigarette into the multilayered scar that covered my body. Winced in joy at the pain. I could still smell Lynn's aging pussy in the sheets. The crusty spot where we'd ground together scratched against my thigh. I touched the divot in the lumpy pillow at my side.

No. I had to find Pitt. Had to find out what he meant by "end the guilt." But not for her. For me. I wanted to know what he meant.

Had to know.

The glass security door clicked open. A bulldozer of a Latino plowed into the waiting room. He wore a sky-blue bulletproof vest over flowing robes of yellow and scarlet, like Buddhist monks wear in Tibet. One arm rested on the shotgun draped across his chest. His head gleamed from a recent encounter with a razor, and he stank of cheap aftershave.

He put his palms together, bowed to me. "*Shanti*," he said. "Peace." He straightened up and his voice coarsened. "You got something to say?"

"To Sergio, yes."

"*Shanti*," he said again. "We are one. Mr. Salazar and me."

"And *I*. One what?"

"He see what I see. Hear what I hear."

"*Sees* what you see. *Hears* what you hear." I ground out my cigarette on the marble countertop. "And if that's the case, he must be blind, deaf and stupid. C'mon."

I held out my arms and spread my legs. The guard's lips puckered. He swung a fist at my face. I flinched. He patted my cheek. Laughed.

"It is lucky for you that I am a pacifist." His hands fondled me in all the wrong places. "What is this?"

He held up a rusty hammer with a rubber grip. I'd filched it from the butcher's shop downstairs and washed the blood off. I'd seen them using it the day before to make their cat'n'dog patties.

"A gift for Sergio," I said. "Something I thought he might like."

The man grinned, but did not return the hammer. He gripped it low at his side, tense, as though expecting me to make a move. The receptionist buzzed the security door. The bulldozer *del día* charged through, held the door open for me.

"Nice meeting you," the receptionist said. She undid her hair, let it fall to her chest. Her nipples peeked through the cascade of white.

"Nice tits," I said.

She laughed. "Let me know, I'll get the popcorn ready."

She slid a business card across the counter.

I picked up the card. Her horny pink rat's eyes devoured my disgusting exterior. When did I last take a shower? Much less wash my clothes. Why would any woman want to be with me, unless I paid her? For that matter, why did Lynn? Beat the hell out of me. I tore the card in half, then half again, and let the pieces flutter to the floor.

"You do that," I said.

The glass door clicked shut. The air quality inside the office was good. Too good. My lungs didn't know what to do. I coughed, tasted Lima traffic on my tongue. I spat on a plastic plant.

"Wait here." My escort pointed to an unoccupied cubicle. He fiddled with a security panel and disappeared through a door.

I sat down. How long had it been since I'd last seen Sergio? Couple of months? No. Longer. More recent than my last shower, anyway. Our paths had crossed a couple of times, but he was more Pitt's friend than mine. That, and Pitt's boss. At least the one Pitt told people about.

Sergio's a nothing. A nobody. My dad and I run this country. And we run Anglo-Dutch Mining, too.

Blue canvas fuzz lined the wall. In nearby cubicles phones rang. Bodiless voices answered. Unseen fingers typed on unseen keyboards. Ambitious tongues, sharpened for the kill, slurped on half-empty mugs of coffee. I clutched my stomach, suddenly nauseous.

Cubicle slavery, American-style. You couldn't escape it, no matter how far you flew. My first wife had tried to keep me in my job. When I refused to pay child support, she garnished my paycheck. I quit my job. Withdrew all my cash. Strapped it to my thighs, bought a one-way ticket to Buenos Aires. They stopped me at the airport and took my passport. Confiscated the money, gave it to her and her brat.

I would be a slave to no man. And no fucking woman, either. So I did what anyone would have done in my situation. I fled across the Rio Grande into Mexico. Passed wetbacks going north. "Are you crazy?" I shouted. "Go home! Freedom lies the other way!" But they ignored me, and plodded onward to their new careers as America's de facto slaves.

I hitchhiked my way south, teaching English along the way. Picked up a fake passport, good enough to get me through Central America. Somehow wound up in Peru.

I met Kate. Things were looking up. Life was getting good again. We had a dream and we were building it, piece by piece. Until the evil God who runs the universe intervened, and decided I'd had my fill of happiness.

A man in polyester pants walked by, humming to himself. He propped a cardboard box on one hip, tapped a security code into a nearby panel and walked through the same door as the bulldozer. I could stand no more of this office bondage. Minions, be damned! I caught the door before it shut, pushed my way into the room.

Fifteen men in tailored suits looked up from their laptops. Their pasty faces drooped, puffy with excess. I recognized three of them from the brothel circuit. Glasses and watches and tie pins glittered under the fluorescent lights, battle regalia of the modern warrior.

The man with the cardboard box turned, opened his mouth and put the box down in midair. The box fell, exploding in a shower of manila folders. He scrambled to pick them up. Bulldozer grabbed me by the collar of my dirty brown sweater. I spotted Sergio at the end of the conference table. His dark Andean complexion and gray ponytail were hard to miss.

"Sergio!" I waved. "So good to see you again!"

"You know this man?" asked a portly gent in a three-piece suit, caressing his pinstripes.

Sergio removed a white handkerchief from the breast pocket of his gray alpaca suit. He patted his forehead. "I can't be expected to know every homeless in Lima, now can I?"

Dipstick here's a useful puppet. Looks Indian enough to keep the locals happy. In private he takes orders like everyone else. Hello, I'm Sergio! I'm a sock puppet! Will you be my friend?

The bulldozer tightened his grip and yanked me toward the door. "*Shanti*," he grunted. "This hurts me more than it does you."

"The bathhouse," I said, ignoring the guard's feverish cultic pantings. "You don't remember, Sergio? You and me, the three Brazilians? That amazing daisy chain?"

"My dear boy, this city is not the place to be telling lies." Sergio nodded to my escort, who reached for the door handle. "Libel law in Peru may not be very strong, it is true, but then neither is the criminal code." He put his hands together and cracked his knuckles. "You don't want to know how much Shanti here bench-presses."

"You mean that's his *name?*" I said, and regretted it. Shanti gripped me around the waist, lifted me off the ground and heaved me from the room. I clung to the door frame. "Alright," I said, "stop pretending you don't know me, and

I'll stop pretending we're lovers."

"What is this about?" The portly gent stroked his waddle.

"The disappearance of Pitt Watters," I said. "And will you get this goon off me?" Shanti was even now prying my fingers one by one from the door frame, mumbling prayers of penance as he did so.

Sergio lifted his chin and the brutal bending stopped.

The man at his side said, "Pitt what? What who?" Fingers pinched loose neck fat now, measuring and testing its elasticity. The other men sat silently, watching me.

"Pitt Watters," I said again. "Your employee? The American ambassador's son?"

I remember the first time I met Sergio. Pitt and I had arranged to go to a new strip club. Something New, Pitt called it, in his never-ending quest for novel and peculiar pleasures.

Life is pleasure, he'd hoot after his third hooker for the night. *So what if it kills you? Quality, not quantity! Who wants to get old and wrinkly, anyway?*

I got to the club first. A leather-clad dominatrix led me to a table, cracked a whip in the air to attract the waitress's attention.

The waitress came over, swinging her hips from side to side, her body encased from nipples to knees in latex. They didn't have any *pisco,* so I ordered a bottle of cheap Scotch and some ice. I shoved a wad of play money down her cleavage, told her to show my friends the table when they arrived. When she'd gone, I slipped into the bathroom and snorted coke off a urine-stained toilet seat.

I emerged to find Pitt in a manly embrace with a guy in a Phantom of the Opera mask. They assailed each other with mutual toasts of brotherly love: elbows wide, chins high, white teeth glistening, glasses sloshing with drink. The look of pure friendship Pitt beamed at his new companion made my stomach twist in acid convulsions. And what was with the mask?

"Horse!" Pitt yelled across the room, motioned me over. Half the assembled perverts turned to look. "Friend of mine!" he shouted in the man's ear, despite a lull in the music. His voice rang hollow in the cavernous space.

"You say so. You Sergio?" I filled my glass, nibbled at my Scotch.

"Guilty as charged." He stabbed an open hand at my abdomen, tilted his head so that his voice drooled from his nostrils. "They call me The Silver Fox."

I took his hand. It was moist, like a tepid vanilla pudding. "Most people just call me an asshole."

A brown finger flecked with long black hairs pointed at my head. Sergio's mouth opened in a soundless laugh.

"What's with the mask?" I asked.

He winked at me. "Let's just say, a man in my position does not wish to be identified."

I regarded him calmly. "Did your momma drop you on your head, or were you born that way?"

"What way?"

I dangled my Scotch from a limp wrist. "The mask only covers half your face?"

He laid a hand on my arm. "My friend, you would be surprised what this mask hides."

He was short and dark. Bolivian dark. Fifty-something, gray ponytail that lingered halfway down his back. A scar snaked across one hand, disappeared under the cuff of his white silk shirt. He was tie-less, and wore a wool suit, the same shade as his hair, buttoned tight against his paunch. He stooped as he sat, shoulders hunched, like a gnarled tree, warped by wind and rain, unable to stand straight.

Pitt caressed my shoulder, gave a squeeze. "Daddy bought him a pretty accent, don't you think?"

Sergio's nasal passages echoed with the studied irreverence of Eton and Oxford. In his face you could barely note his father's blood, the millionaire Russian Jew who'd sired him off an itinerant Bolivian maid. The Russian took care of his flock of bastard children, Pitt had said, and Sergio had done well. As South American executive of Anglo-Dutch Mining, Sergio was considered by many the next logical choice for CEO of the South Africa-based mining conglomerate.

And Pitt, as chief engineer at Anglo-Dutch's lithium mine in Bolivia, was acknowledged as Sergio's heir apparent.

I looked around the club for faces I might know. When gringos meet in Latin dens of vice, there is instant camaraderie. Men whose names I didn't know, histories I didn't share, with whom I'd never exchanged a word, would look up from haggling with the girl at their side and lift a chin, an eyebrow, a salute of mutual appreciation that said: I found freedom too. Aren't we both glad we left?

But there were no other gringos here today, except for the three of us, so I communed with my liquid friend from Scotland. Pitt elbowed me in the ribs. Sergio was saying something.

"What do you do?"

"English teacher," I grunted.

Sergio stroked his upper lip. "I see."

"Do you?" I drained my glass, felt the liquor burn its way into my body.

"It's honest work."

"Honest?" I said. "I teach English to criminals so they can cheat tourists. You call that honest?"

Sergio's pudding hand wobbled, threatening to spill his drink. "Not for you to judge your clients, if what you offer them is honest."

BDSM was not my thing, and people who lie to themselves pissed me off. *What I do is wrong. Don't lie to me about my crimes. Don't lie to yourself.* I tapped Pitt on the elbow, opened my mouth to suggest we move on, but just then the lights dimmed and a woman strode onto the stage.

Peruvian strip clubs aren't the same as American ones, with their no-touching bullshit. Here that was the point. The stripping was merely advertising for the services offered out back, in the row of small rooms that invariably smelled of disinfectant, maintained by an army of maids. I often wondered about the maids. No matter how many brothels Pitt and I visited, banging away in adjacent rooms, the walls thin enough to hear each other come, I never saw the ones who cleaned up the mess.

"Who deserves some pain?" asked the MC, a thin, dark-skinned woman with bleach-blonde hair. She wore a tangerine bra, panty and garter set, and every pair of eyes gobbled up the sliver of fabric between her thighs. Her pear-shaped breasts hung pendulous, ripe fruit ready to be plucked. I settled into my chair. Perhaps I'd stick around, after all.

Two women dressed in leather unitards and black spike-heeled boots carried an apparatus onto the stage. It looked like a bizarre exercise machine. Wrist restraints hung from above, ankle restraints protruded from below. Another woman stepped from the shadows, her eyes masked. The whip she trailed in one hand curled around the points of her six-inch stiletto heels. She lifted her arm, cracked the whip against the stage floor. The sound of leather on wood echoed in the lofty space. The audience shifted in their seats.

"No one here's been naughty?" purred the tangerine-pantied MC. "No one here's a—" and she breathed the words, almost a sigh, "—a bad boy?"

Sergio thrust his arm in the air, fingers spread wide, hand twitching, a first grader eager to please. *Pick me! Pick me!* A spotlight swung around from the ceiling, engulfed our table. I shielded my eyes with my palm.

Sergio stepped across Pitt's lap, walked down the aisle and hopped onto the stage. The light followed him. The MC smiled her kindergartner grin, helped him shrug the jacket from his shoulders. Two women in leather unitards laid light fingertips on his biceps, directed him where to stand. He faced the audience. They smiled and spun him back the other way. The audience tittered.

The woman on his right lowered the restraints from above, attached them to his wrists. The other nudged his feet apart and strapped in his ankles. They cranked the restraints tight, so that his arms and legs were fully extended, a man frozen in the middle of a jumping jack.

A crack of the whip made me flinch in my chair. The

dominatrix stepped forward. She curled her fingers around the back of his shirt collar, looked over her shoulder at the audience, and grinned. With one fierce movement she ripped the garment from his body. The sleeves hung loose from his arms. The crowd murmured when they saw his back. White scar tissue formed deep rivulets from neck to waist. I stifled a gasp. It reminded me of looking in the bathroom mirror. At thousands of small white circles cratering my own flesh.

I leaned sideways toward Pitt. "This place wasn't your idea then."

"I thought you might enjoy it," he whispered.

"You thought *what?*"

Pitt gestured around at the club. "All your guilty conscience crap. Isn't this what you're after?"

I sighed. I had tried to explain the concept of a conscience to him hundreds of times in the few months we had known each other, but had long since given up. "I don't want pleasure through pain," I said. "I want *pain* through pain. There's a difference?"

"I dunno," he said, sipping his Scotch. He nodded at Sergio on stage. "Those scars don't look like much fun to me."

A crack of the whip demanded silence. The audience held its breath. The dominatrix began to work. Quick nips elicited gasps from Sergio. Red welts formed—low down on his love handles, high up on his shoulders. Her aim was flawless: she never hit the same place twice. She paused, posed for the audience: demure.

Sergio twitched. "What are you doing? Why are you stopping?"

Beneath the mask, a smile flickered on her lips. She cast

her eyes at the floor.

Sergio heaved at the restraints, arched his back. "Do it!" he screamed at the ceiling. "Don't stop! Please!"

The next blow hit him square in the middle of his back, all her strength aiming the whip at his spine. The skin broke. Sergio groaned.

I fidgeted in my seat. The dominatrix slashed at his back with her whip, taking ten-second breaks between each blow. Sergio's noises of satisfaction became whimpers. Blood smeared, splattered with each stroke, trickled along the scarred waterways of his back into the seat of his pants. The remnants of his shirt turned scarlet.

"Oh God," he panted, his head on his chest, "give it to me. All of it. All that I deserve."

I swallowed my glass of Scotch. It tasted bad. I had never felt less aroused. Maybe Pitt was right. Was this what I was like? But I didn't enjoy the pain. Pain hurt. I'm not some kind of pervert. Pain was what I deserved.

All that I deserve.

But that's what he'd just said. It wasn't the same. It couldn't be. I fingered the two bits of paper in my pocket. I carried them with me everywhere. A picture and a post-card. I took out the postcard, bent it to catch the light. The front showed a photo of Lake Titicaca. I flipped it over to the handwritten scrawl on the back, even though I had long since memorized it. Pitt snatched the card from my hands.

"Hey!" I shouted, and reached for it.

He held it overhead. "Who's this from?"

"From Kate. Give that back!"

"Who's Kate?" His eyes scanned the note.

"My wife."

"Your *what?*"

I grabbed for the postcard again, but he held it out of reach. "My almost-wife. Or never-wife, as she called herself. We were engaged."

"And what's this—'End the guilt'? What is that all about, man?"

I slugged him as hard as I could. He bent over, and I retrieved the note.

He chuckled through his pain. "How can you even think about getting married, bro?" He flung an arm at the stage. "There's so many *chicas* here in need of good gringo loving. How can you pick just one?"

A security guard with a hand cannon on his hip appeared at the table. "Gentlemen," he said. "Is everything alright?"

"Fine." I put on my innocent gringo grin. The guard reluctantly strolled away. I said to Pitt, "You're an asshole, you know that?"

His laughter faded quickly. "Of course I'm an asshole. How many times I got to tell you?"

"Yeah, well. You don't have to be that way with me." I took out my lighter and flicked it on and off. On and off. On and off.

"My shrink says I'm numb to the world. A real insensitive blockhead."

I nodded. "It's alright, man. I've been hanging on to this goddamn thing for too long anyway. Maybe I can learn a thing or two from an insensitive blockhead like you." *Lighten the ten-ton load on my shoulders by half an ounce.* I held the lighter to a corner of the postcard. It caught fire.

"What are you doing?" He snatched it from me and smushed it out in the wet circles that coated our table. "Why don't you go to her? It sounds like she's found a better way to cope than you."

I shook my head. "She's a reminder of my crime. I could never find peace with her." I stood. "Come on."

Sergio moaned his pleasure. While the dominatrix continued to whip him, a whore knelt before him and loosened the zipper constraining the bulge in his pants.

Pitt followed me to the exit. He still held the postcard in his hand. "Sure you don't want this?"

"You keep it," I said. "Burn it. Wipe your ass with it. Just so I never see it again." I burst out into the foul air, the streets swarming with human vermin. "Now let's get a move on. The night is young, and so are we, and we have our bodies to destroy."

Sergio said, "We'll finish after lunch."

He unbridged his fingertips, bent a smile from his crowbar of a frown. He flicked his ponytail off his shoulder and stood, buttoning his suit jacket. He led the way out of the conference room. I followed, Shanti right behind me, three ugly ducklings in a row.

No sooner had he closed the glass door to his office than he grabbed a hairbrush and faced me, brandishing it like a rapier. "What would Ambo say?"

Ambo was Pitt's father, the American ambassador to Peru. One drunk luncheon by the beach Pitt had dubbed him "Ambo," and despite the frequent paternal threats of physical violence, the nickname stuck.

I shrugged. Outside the floor-to-ceiling windows, Shanti's broad shoulders rolled and flexed, as though preparing for round two. I said, "Ambo doesn't know."

"Yes, well. You say that now. He has ways of finding out."

The room was simple. Spartan. No. Not even. It was actively uncomfortable. There were no chairs for guests. Papers lay scattered across a beat-up metal desk, the kind I had in my own classroom. A broken fold-out chair served as Sergio's throne. In the corner stood a cheap plywood cabinet. A heavy lock dangled from its latches.

Sergio ripped a black hair tie from his ponytail and flicked his hair over his head, a sixteen-year-old girl in the throes of pre-prom grooming.

I said, "You must have some idea where he is."

"I assure you, it is a mystery to us both." He attacked his hair, scraped the brush from neck to forehead.

I sat on the edge of his desk. "But you have an idea."

Sergio tossed his hair back. It surrounded his head in a cloud of gray. He pointed the brush at me. "Pitt resigned effective immediately."

"What do you mean, 'resigned'?" I asked. "Why would he resign? This place was perfect cover."

"Never showed for work. That's all I know."

Pitt worked a fly-in, fly-out schedule. Two weeks in the *altiplano* at the mine. Then a week in Lima raising hell. Among other things.

"That's *all* you know," I said. I crossed my arms and stared down my nose.

"My dear boy, I assure you it is."

I went to the door and opened it. "Thug dude. Hammer back?"

Shanti bent his yellow-and-scarlet frame into the room. Sergio looked up at the man through a haze of hair. "What's it for?"

"New trick you, uh, might enjoy," I said.

"Oh, darling." He nodded to the bulldozer. "Let him have it."

I took the hammer, closed the door and walked over to the cabinet. With both hands I smashed the hammer down on the padlock. The latches ripped from their flimsy moorings and crashed at my feet.

The office door opened. I dropped the hammer to the floor and flung open the cabinet's plywood doors. Strong hands encircled my wrists and drew my elbows back at a painful angle.

Inside the cabinet, five shirts dangled from paper-shrouded hangers, draped in dry cleaner's plastic. Five suits of various shades of gray jostled for space. At the bottom, a pair of black shoes, a tin of shoe polish, a dirty rag. A tie rack spat fistfuls of colorful silk.

Sergio poked at a hole in my filthy brown sweater. "Looking to improve our wardrobe?"

"What are you afraid of?" I asked. "Since when do you use bodyguards?"

"I've told you what I know," he said. "Now get out."

Shanti frogmarched me to the door.

"Be sure to check behind the suits," I said. "You'll find it worth your while."

A vase beside me shattered, spilling a dozen plastic birds

of paradise at my feet. A hairbrush bounced off my shoe. "Bloody hell. I'm going to have to move them now."

"Move what?" I asked. "Good help hard to find?"

A sharp hiss of breath. Sergio said, "Let him go."

Shanti released my arms. He put his palms together, bowed. "Forgive me," he said. "Peace be unto you. I'll be outside if you need me."

Sergio massaged the bridge of his nose between thumb and forefinger. He sighed. "I'm sure you will."

I returned to the cabinet, pushed the shirts and suits out of the way. Venetian blinds fluttered and whirred, as Sergio sought escape from the prying eyes of his employees. The back of the cabinet had no obvious cracks.

"Must you do this?" he asked.

"I can break it if you want."

He felt under the pile of silk. A button clicked. The back of the cabinet slid down.

To one side, a variety of dildos and butt plugs. A Fleshlight. Hanging from one hook, a small whip; on another, a cat-o'-nine-tails. A third hook sat empty. I lifted the cat. From each of the nine ends hung a twisted spike of barbed wire. Dried blood and chunks of gore caked the spikes.

"Something missing on that hook," I said.

"On back order. Are we satisfied?"

I studied the empty space. Blood stains marred the plywood where another implement had hung. "Tell you what," I said. "Be bad enough, I might just use this on you."

Sergio shuddered. "Don't say that."

I lifted the cat, slashed it down on his desk with a loud crack. Sergio jumped across the room. Slammed the door shut as Shanti began to enter.

"Not now," he wailed. "Don't come in unless I call you, understand?" He locked the door, rested his weight against the frame. The blinds crackled.

I held the cat to my nose. It smelled of blood and sweat and sex. I stifled the urge to vomit. "You were telling me why Pitt resigned."

Sergio lifted a trembling hand to his lips, wiped a strand of saliva from his chin. "He sent me a note, you see," he said, not looking at me. "Pitt did."

"Still got it?"

His open palms trembled in front of him, a saint beseeching the empty heavens for salvation. "I don't understand what it means."

I lifted the cat in the air. "You got it or don't you?"

His head twitched sideways, unable to look away from the cat. "No," he mumbled. "I threw it away."

"What'd it say?"

His entire body spasmed now, his eyes fixed on those barbed spikes. "My dear boy, I don't understand what it means. Or didn't. Not at the time. I swear. Some rubbish about ending his guilt."

Ending his guilt... Was BDSM Pitt's solution? Had he changed his mind? Hard to believe. If that was his answer, he was barking up the wrong tree. Still...

I pointed to the cabinet, the empty hook.

Sergio pressed his knees together, like he had to go to the bathroom. Confessed with a jerk of his head. "He stole my favorite cat."

"Stole it? Why would he bother?"

"These cats are handmade in a factory in Tibet by Buddhist monks. They are rare, and exceedingly valuable."

"So?" I said. "Pitt's got money. You know he does."

"Online purchases can be traced. You know this as well as I do." He glared at me. "So much more subtle than you. At least *he* picked the lock. Broke in when I was gone."

"But pain is not his scene. You know it's not. How can you be sure it was him?"

Sergio said nothing, swung his head from side to side. I cracked the cat on his desk again.

The little man hopped like a puppet on a string. "How could I possibly? It was only when he disappeared that I knew."

"Knew what?"

He bit his lip. His eyes darted around the room, looking for some escape from his perversion, finding none.

I lifted the cat again. "Knew what?"

He tiptoed across the room, leaned into me. God, what a smell. He'd shat himself. The stink made me choke. He whispered into my ear, "Bat guano."

"Bat—"

"Shh!" He clamped a hand over my mouth.

I held up an open palm, nodded. He withdrew his hand. I mouthed the words: *Bat guano?*

"Yes," he whispered.

"What about it?"

"Go ask Ambo."

I slashed the cat down on the desk, the metal frame booming with the impact. "I'm asking you, slave."

"Oh God, oh please." A turd slid from his pant leg onto his shoe. He pressed his palms together between his thighs. "I'd tell you if I knew. I swear I would."

"What else?"

"Pitt was involved. He was key."

"Then it wasn't you who made him vanish."

"Me?" His face exploded in outrage. "I'm a businessman who dabbles, not the other way around."

"The dabblers are the best," Pitt had said that day on the beach, the ocean waves rolling into shore, as though to punctuate his point. *"You pay them with the thrill. They're desperate for action. You give them less than what they want. Keep them hungry. Wanting more."*

"I see." I put the cat on his desk. He eyed the blood-encrusted barbed wire.

He said, "One thing more."

I raised my eyebrows.

"The whole plan fails without him."

"What makes you say that?" I asked.

"Ambo's looking for him."

"Is he now."

"Since a month ago."

A month ago. A month head start. Hadn't even mentioned it to Lynn. And if he didn't want his mother to know... The thought erupted in my brain. Pitt had gone rogue. I walked to the door, unlocked it.

"Wait!" he screamed, dialed down the volume mid-word. He picked up the cat and held it out.

I said, "Any idea where to find him?"

"Ask his wife. She might know."

For the second time that day I did a double take. "His *what?*"

"Five years, four kids. House in San Isidro. Didn't you know?"

"You're shitting me."

Sergio shrugged, bounced on his toes, the cat held out in one hand. A second turd stained his other shoe. "Maybe you don't know your friend as well as you thought."

My mouth hung open. I stared at the wall. His *wife.*

Unbidden, Sergio set the cat down and scribbled on a sticky note. The pen clattered on the desk. He slapped the yellow square to my chest.

"The address."

I read it. Closed my mouth. Peeled the note off my sweater and shoved it in my pocket. I opened the door.

"Wait!" Sergio pawed at my elbow and pointed at the cat on his desk. "You promised," he whispered.

I thought about it. Give him a whipping. What he deserved. But what about me? What do I deserve? I can't even save myself. How was I supposed to save him? I'd punished myself for a year now. Three times over I'd burned my body from neck to toes. How much was enough? When will I have paid the penalty? The rest of my life? Tomorrow? Next week, next year? Will I ever be free to live again?

"No," I said, loud enough for the cubicle-dwellers nearby to hear, "I won't give you a blowjob. That's disgusting."

The door clicked shut. The bodyguard and I ignored each other. I walked toward the exit. Through the glass wall I heard the slashing sound of leather and metal on flesh, followed by a soft, high-pitched groan. Two overweight expatriate engineers discussing basketball scores sat up straight, frowned. It was the sound of pain. Of well-deserved punishment.

Or was it merely masochistic pleasure?

I STARED AT THE ADDRESS SERGIO GAVE ME.
Three stories of moldy stone cast menacing shadows on the
sidewalk below. A pair of gargoyles hissed their disapproval
from above. Black mildew crept down from the gutters. I
rang the doorbell.

I'd stopped off at an internet café to look up bat guano.
There'd been a war over the stuff. In the 1880s. Apparently it
made great fertilizer. Farmers paid big money for it, before
they invented the synthetic variety. Peru and Bolivia fought
Chile, some dispute over tariffs. That was back when Bolivia
still had a coastline. Although what a war over bat guano
had to do with Pitt, much less his wife, was beyond me.

A woman in a *niqab* answered the door. Black silk covered
her from head to toe. Only her eyes were visible. I looked at
my yellow sticky note, then at the address. They were the
same. I crumpled the note. Sergio had been a real bad boy
this time.

"Sorry," I said in Spanish. "My mistake." I turned to go.

The woman rested her head against the door frame, a
buzzard eyeing the final moments of dying roadkill. She
said, "You're at the right address." She spoke in English, the

accent a clear, unmistakable Boston twang.

Her face was a mere strip of white behind the silken armor, her eyes blue balls of fire. Another cock-hungry American whore. I knew her type. But what was the deal with the sheet?

"Your name Pitt?"

She laughed. "No, silly."

"Well then." I stepped backward down the stairs.

"My husband's name is, though."

I lost my footing, banged my knee. *"You're* Pitt's wife?"

She shifted in the doorway. The silk stretched tight across her body. Was she wearing any clothing underneath?

"You with the company?" she asked. Her eyes darting below my belt.

"Yes," I said. "I mean no. That is, I'm a friend of Pitt's. I need to find him." *Damn. That came out kinda lame. You got a horsie, act like it for chrissakes.*

She cocked those balls of fire sideways, as though taking aim with a shotgun. "Since when did Pitt have friends?"

I lifted my eyebrows in self-defense. "Since when did Pitt have a wife?"

A child's voice broke the spell. "Who is it, Mommy?"

She shouted over her shoulder, "Friend of Daddy's!"

"But Daddy doesn't have any friends!"

She held out a hand, exposing a slender wrist. I snorted at the sight, a bull aroused by a moving cape. The hand was soft, and the touch of her skin sent a jolt of fire to my groin. Resisting this woman was going to be tough.

She squeezed my fingers. "Janine. Janine Watters."

"Horse."

"What, like the animal?"

"It's Horace, actually. But people call me Horse. As in hung like a."

"Are you really?" she asked, her voice a throaty purr.

"You're nice to me, you might find out."

She laughed. "You better come in."

As I walked past, she pressed her breasts against my arm. They quivered, nipples like pebbles under the thin silk.

Toy with her, I told myself, ignoring the bulge in my pants. *That's all. You don't need to add "cheating on your best friend's wife" to your list of sins.* Of course, he wasn't my best friend anymore. And fucking his mother wasn't exactly high on the list of noble activities. *Crap.* I adjusted myself as subtly as I could. Which for me was difficult.

I stepped into the main room of the house, a large atrium. Unlike the mortuary facade, the interior overflowed with life: primeval ferns hung from hooks along the walls, dripping their damp and steamy essence on the tile floor. The walls of the house were clad in teak. A pyramid skylight caught the weak sun. Mirrors of varying shapes and sizes hung from impossible angles, scattering light into the far corners of the building. The second and third floors loomed above me, balconies encircling the space below.

"Your fly is open, by the way."

"Is it?" She caught me off guard. I yanked at my zipper. I must have forgotten to close it after talking to the albino receptionist.

She padded barefoot ahead of me. "Don't want your horsie popping out now, do we?"

A long table stretched down the center of the atrium. Beneath it, three young children played with an orange

tabby. An infant cried in a nearby crib. The newfound agony of its existence shattered in mournful echoes against the
wood-paneled walls.

"Pieu, pieu, pieu! You're dead!"

The oldest child, a pretty black boy of six or seven, had dis-
covered me, and was assassinating me with a Lego automatic.

I nodded. "Sometimes I wish I was."

"Were."

"I'm sorry?"

"Sometimes you wish you were. Mommy taught me that."
He glowed up at Janine. "Right, Mommy?"

She patted his shoulder. "Good boy, Jerome. Go play with
your brother and sister, OK?"

Thus dispatched, the errant space fighter detached itself
from the mothership, ran in circles about the great hall, firing
imaginary projectiles at all manner of objects, stationary and
otherwise, and pronounced them dead on sight.

The infant renewed its complaint with mounting volume.
Her cries were knives in my ears. Against my will, my feet
carried me to the crib. I bent over the railing. Red-faced,
screaming, the little one beat her tiny fists against the mattress. Six months old or so. Same age as Lili...

"What's her name?" I asked.

Janine stood at my side. "Esmeralda."

I sniffed. "I think she needs her diaper changed."

"I'm a bad mother and a lousy wife," she said, and crossed
her arms. "Anything else you want to know?"

"Whoa," I said, hands out. "I didn't mean it like that."

"Then how did you mean it?"

"I just hate to see a baby cry is all."

"Fine." Janine shrugged. "You wanna change her?"

The little girl looked so much like my own. "Would you mind?"

"Whatever turns you on."

I hadn't touched a baby since La Paz. Something drew me to her. Because she was Pitt's? Because she needed a fresh diaper? Or because she suffered, and there was something I could do to make it better? Her tears were for the whole world, even if she didn't know it yet.

Janine looked on with amusement. When I finished, her only comment was, "You've done that before."

I wiped my hands and dried the baby's face. Her crying subsided. I chucked Esmeralda under the chin. She gurgled happily and squeezed my finger.

"Some grip," I said.

"Yeah, well, she'll need it to keep herself a husband."

Janine walked over to a black leather sofa, her silk bustling with the movement. She sat down. The leather creaked. She patted the seat next to her.

I remained standing. "You mind I ask you something?"

"Go right ahead."

"I didn't know Pitt was a Muslim," I said.

"He's not."

"But you are?"

"Catholic, actually." She laughed, a bitter sound. "You mean the sheet."

I eased myself onto the sofa. She snuggled against me. Pitt had married Mrs. Mile-a-Minute. I put my arm around her. I could smell her, a brassy mixture of sex and sweat. An exercise bicycle stood near a shuttered window, a damp towel draped across the handlebars. From under her *niqab,* a buzzing noise whirred and throbbed, like a cell phone on vibrate.

"Pitt is often away."

"Yes?" I said, jarred from my reverie.

"I find I have a certain...effect on men."

"I know what you mean," I said. "I have a similar effect on women."

She tilted her chin up at me. "Do you?"

I brought my lips close to hers. "You tell me."

An instant before our lips touched, she turned away. "I'm not being vain," she said. "I'm just saying. I want to be faithful. You understand?"

I sat back. So tiresome, these games. "I thought you said you were a lousy wife."

"Oh, I am."

An awkward silence fell between us, two satellites circling the planet Pitt, and abruptly sent crashing together. She ground her hips into the sofa. The buzzing noise continued.

"You need to get that?" I asked.

She nodded. "Just let me turn it off."

One arm disappeared under her robes. She lifted her butt. The buzzing got louder. Her arm emerged from a sleeve bearing a two-pronged violet vibrator. She plunked it on the coffee table. Flipped a switch. The buzzing ceased.

"Sometimes it goes on all by itself," she explained.

The dildo stank with juices from both holes. "Does it," I said.

"So." She clapped her hands together. "You're yes-no-sort-of-with-the-company." Her eyes twinkled. I could hear her mocking grin.

I wrenched my gaze away from the soaking sex toy. "Which company would that be?"

"Anglo-Dutch. Who else?" She propped her hidden chin on one hand. Her blank stare convinced me she knew nothing of Pitt's clandestine calling.

"No," I said. "We used to work together, but not anymore. We're just friends."

Janine laughed, long peals of ejaculating merriment.

"What's so funny?"

"Guess how long I've known Pitt."

"No idea."

"Senior year at Vassar."

"Which is?"

"Eight years. I tell you where we met you'll laugh."

"Try me."

"A strip club."

"Really," I said.

"Stuffed a hundred-dollar bill inside my thong."

"And that was that."

"It was."

I put a hand on her knee. "I'd like to stuff more than that inside your thong."

She leaned into me, trailed a thumbnail along my thigh. A bolt of lightning stiffened my back, cracked my neck sideways. I pulled away.

Down, boy. Down!

"And in all that time," she continued, delighting in my torment, "I have never known him to have a friend of any kind."

"No?" I struggled to keep my voice steady.

"Drinking buddies, maybe. Work mates, sure. Fellow

students. Roommates." She observed me from behind her veil, her eyes the inscrutable blue of a Siberian husky. She withdrew her fingernail from my leg, and I sighed, a victim of the Inquisition released momentarily from torment. "But never a friend."

I snorted, coughed up a wad of traffic-tasting phlegm. I swallowed it. "We aren't friends."

"But you are. I can tell."

"That is," I said, and held out an open palm, "we aren't anymore."

"I see," she said. And looked at me.

I felt compelled to complete the thought. "He used me."

"Of course."

"He does that, does he?"

"But here you are, looking for him. Why is that?"

"I—" The words caught in my throat.

Why *was* I looking for him? End the guilt, of course. Find out what he meant. And then? Once I find him and we're standing face to face? Tell him to go to hell. What else was there? This wasn't about him. It was about me. I was a self-centered bastard and didn't care who knew it, and this woman's questions were getting on my nerves.

She said, "You love him, don't you."

"I *what?*"

"You love him. You love Pitt."

"I'm not gay."

"I never said you were."

Love. Love was giving your girl the big beefy injection. Cooing over tiny humans caused by said beefy injection. Bald, half-naked cults that meditated on the Ganges. You might as well go catch a fucking cloud.

"Fuck love," I said. "You just met me. What do you know."

"Where did you meet him?"

I'd had enough of this game. She didn't know anything. And even if she did—there had to be some easier way to find Pitt. I got up. "You don't know where he is, just say so." I walked toward the door.

"You didn't even think to ask?"

My stride faltered. "So you know where I can find him?"

She giggled and clasped her knees. "No idea."

"Well then." I made a beeline to the exit.

She called after me, "No one else is going to care."

That struck home. I stopped. Beneath the table, the oldest child was demonstrating to the others how to pick up the cat by the tail. The cat made no complaint.

"No one likes me," I said. "I am not a nice man."

"I'm sure you're not."

"I'm an asshole. Scum."

"If you say so."

I sighed. "But Pitt liked me. Or pretended to."

Get out of my head! I wanted to scream. Now who was toying with who?

"Why would he pretend?" she asked.

"I have been disappointed too many times by too many people." I thought of La Paz. What happened to Lili. People I had trusted wrongly. Dozens of them in my past. But for reasons I could not fathom, Horse the Master Cynic got suckered in again and again, and every time the betrayal felt like the first time.

I ran a hand across my face. "But with Pitt, it was like..."

I shrugged, began again. "The one time, the only time I ever—"

"Loved another human being."

"*Used* me. I was nothing to him. Nothing." I paced the room. I raised a clenched fist, nearly crashed it into a mirror hanging from a nearby staircase. "A tool."

"Maybe," she said. "I wouldn't be too sure."

"And you know what the worst thing is?" I rushed on before she could stop me. "I knew it was going to happen. I could see it coming a mile away. It was like watching a train wreck and being unable to stop it. I mean the man told me the day we met, for chrissakes."

"Told you what?"

If she didn't know, I wasn't going to be the one to break the news. "The kind of man he is."

"And now you want to find him."

I ran my fingers through my hair. "Yes."

"*Need* to find him."

I hung my head. "Yes."

"I understand."

I studied her. Was this part of her seduction? Turn shrink and psych me out? She wanted to fuck my mind as well as my body. That is *verboten* in Horse Land.

"Do you?"

"I am his..." she paused, bit her lip. "That is, in my dark moments, when he is not around, I call myself his secret shadow."

"Meaning what?"

"I have done him wrong." She laughed, and the sound seemed to conceal great sadness. "A lousy wife, remember?"

She gestured at the children, none of whose various skin tones matched Pitt's striking blond Nordic features. "I take what scraps of love I can, and for that I am grateful."

I sat down next to her again. "Has he called? An email? Letter, anything?"

"Sergio called from Anglo-Dutch. 'On special assignment' was all he said."

I exhaled through my nose. Lit a cigarette. A cloud of smoke rose in the air. Maybe it would be enough to keep her at arm's length. Doubtful.

"Nothing else?"

"His Highness came by."

"Ambo."

She laughed and sucked in a lungful of secondhand smoke. "Pitt taught you that too."

"And?"

"Said the mining company wouldn't talk to him. Wanted to know had I heard from Pitt."

"Had you?"

"No. But then I don't usually. Ambo asked me to call if I heard anything."

"So Pitt said nothing, where he might have gone?"

The children under the table were inserting matches in the cat's anus. The animal arched its tail to allow for greater access.

Janine sat back against the sofa. She laid one forearm across her belly, tightening the thin silk across her breasts. "He had to go find himself," she said softly. "I had to let him go."

"Go where?" My anger was seeping away, replaced by

frustration.

"Does it matter?"

I took a long drag on the cigarette, let the cancerous smoke trickle from my lungs.

One child, the oldest again, scraped a match against the box. It failed to light. He scraped it again. The third time it caught. The cat looked around, curious, nosed the boy's hand. The child held the flame to the match heads. There was a flash of sulfur, and the cat's tail caught fire. The animal yowled and ran across the room, the movement fanning the flames that spread across its body.

Janine reached behind the sofa and came up with a fire extinguisher. She tracked the cat, like shooting skeet, and let go a blast of white powder that coated the animal in white sugar frosting. Snookums dove under a recliner, trying to escape its tiny tormentors. The fire extinguisher returned to its appointed post behind the sofa with a hollow clunk.

"Come on," she said. "I want to show you something."

She walked to a corner of the house, strode down a narrow corridor. She unlocked a side room. I followed after her, and she closed the door.

An unmade king-size bed sprawled across the empty room. Bookshelves overflowed, their contents in disarray. Empty beer bottles stood on a nightstand. A rolltop desk sat open in a corner, its pigeonholes stuffed with papers. One corner of the room was coated in dry vomit. The stink of stomach acid and rotting, half-digested bits of food filled the room.

"Tell me something, Horse," she said.

She unlatched the chain that held the veil across her face. She dangled the silk between two fingers. Let it slip to the floor. If her eyes were astonishing, her face doubled the effect. Angular features formed the platinum setting those burnings balls of sapphire deserved.

I shuddered. I put the cigarette in the corner of my mouth and ran a thumb along the bookshelf. Plato. Nietzsche. Sartre. Augustine. Camus.

I said, "Shoot."

"Am I beautiful?"

I pulled out a well-thumbed copy of Kierkegaard's *Sickness Unto Death.* "Didn't know Pitt was into philosophy."

She clucked her tongue. "He's not."

"No?"

"Or wasn't. Until recently."

"What happened?"

She sighed. "I was a philosophy major. About a month ago he asked to borrow all my books from college."

I laughed. "Pitt can barely read."

She shook her head, the blue fire keeping me in its sights. "Pitt always tells people that. He's a speed reader. Could do it faster than anyone I've ever met. Went through all my books in a week."

"Any idea why?"

She shrugged. "Afterward, he got drunk and puked in the corner."

"I can see that."

Her lips lifted in a half-smile. "The smell reminds me of him."

I put Søren back in his place, crouched to check out the bottom shelf.

She said, "You going to answer my question?"

A lump throbbed in my throat. I swallowed hard. "What was the question again?"

"Do you think I'm beautiful?"

"Pitt must have thought so. He married you, didn't he?" A copy of *Crime and Punishment* lay sideways on top of the bottom shelf. I pulled it out.

"Then can you tell me—why did he prefer to sleep in here, alone?"

The sound of swishing silk, a judge's robes as he enters the courtroom. I stood in time to catch the final ounce of *niqab* sliding to her feet. Janine stood naked in a pile of silk.

She was beautiful. Too beautiful. Breasts to melt the resolve of the mightiest sinner, hips that twitched, waiting for hands to command them. A long full head of soft brown hair curved at her throat, tickled her collarbone. Four kids didn't show.

The cigarette burned my lips. I spat it out and crushed it with my shoe. "Thought you said you didn't want to cheat."

"The spirit is willing, but the flesh..."

I swallowed. "The flesh."

"The flesh," she agreed, eyeing my crotch.

I tried not to look at her body. "You could always pray for strength," I suggested at last.

She shook her head, a triumphant smile on her lips. "I pray. But no help ever comes. Why do you think that is?"

"Maybe you've stopped trying," I offered.

She nodded. "I'm just no good. I never will be. Maybe that means I'll go to hell." Her body tensed at the word, shivered. "So be it. I don't know any other way to be."

She stepped out of the silk, her thighs sliding against each other. She took the book, put it on top of the shelf. "If you're a friend of Pitt's," she said, and clasped my hand, cupped it to her breast, "if you know him as I do, you will understand that."

"I can't," I said, but didn't pull away.

"You know," she said, her face close to mine, her eyes burning a path through my skull, "he hates it when I dress this way."

"You mean naked?"

"No, silly. The *niqab*. Says that he's got nothing to be jealous of."

"Then why do you?"

Her mouth quivered. She looked like she was going to cry. "Because I love him."

She grabbed my head with both hands, pulled me down to her mouth. Her tongue slithered between my teeth. I wondered how she could stand it. When did I last brush? I couldn't remember. Yes. I could. A year ago. The day we arrived in La Paz, Kate and I, the baby in tow. Pain stabbed at the back of my brain, and I stuffed the memory down as far as it would go. I stroked an open palm down her lower back, across her hip and up between her thighs.

"Like that," she hissed, and ran her fingers through my hair.

To avoid her mouth I kissed her neck, trailed my way down to her left nipple. I sucked on her breast, tit flesh filling my mouth, rubbery against my teeth like moldy cheese, and choked on a mouthful of milk. She pulled away but I held her tight, swallowed. When she was dry, I took my mouth away. There was milk in my lungs. I stifled the cough.

"No idea where he might have gone?" I asked.

"Gone?" She ground herself down on my hand.

"Pitt."

"Something heavy," she sighed into my shoulder.

"Heavy."

"On his soul."

"You mean like guilt?"

"What else would I mean?" She pushed me away, as though trying to control herself, then clutched at my back, clawed my scalp and dropped backward onto the bed, pulling me down on top of her.

"About what?" I asked. I drove the knee of my dirty jeans between her legs, bent to kiss her other breast, avoiding the nipple this time.

"Wish I knew." The words escaped from her like air from a deflating balloon.

I caressed her cheek. Her face was wet. "What did he say?"

She stifled a sob. "He quoted Camus."

I lifted my head. "Who?"

"Camus. The French philosopher."

"Who said what?"

She was suddenly cross. "What is this, lecture time?"

"It could be important. What did he say?"

She unbuckled my belt but I stopped her.

"'The only true philosophical question is suicide.'"

"Meaning what?"

"To live or to die. It's a choice. You have to choose."

"And what was Pitt's choice?"

"He didn't say."

I nibbled her neck just under her ear. "Then how do you

know he has guilt?"

"I know what guilt looks like. I look in the mirror every day." She shoved me up onto my knees and grabbed for my pants. "Now shut up and fuck me." She had my belt undone and my cock in her hand before I could stop her.

Her feather touch clouded my brain, thickened my tongue. "Where would he go?" I asked.

"God, it's huge," she said. "You live up to your nickname, I'll say that."

"We were talking about Pitt."

She tickled me in the wrong place. I gasped.

"It matter to you, baby, where he is?"

"It does. Yes."

She bent to take me in her mouth, but I covered myself with my hand.

"Hard to get." She laughed, husky, deep in her throat. "I like that."

I wasn't, actually. Hard to get. Just not worth getting. But that wasn't the point. Even though Pitt had screwed me over, and big time, I couldn't bring myself to return the favor. I'd already fucked his mom plenty. I stuffed myself into my pants, zipped up.

She sat up on her knees and cocked her head to one side. "You're serious."

"I said I was, didn't I?" It came out more tartly than I had planned.

She trailed a finger along my shoulder, came up behind me and pressed herself against my back. She took hold of my sweater and pulled. I put my arms in the air and let her yank it off me. She reached under my armpits, began unbuttoning my shirt. Her lips brushed my neck.

"Said something about volunteering," she murmured.

"Volunteering?"

"Save the planet, all that crap."

I took hold of her wrists. "You know where?"

She struggled. I didn't let go. I leaned my head back, kissed her.

She said, "Pitt always comes home. Eventually."

"Not this time," I said.

"What makes you say that?"

"Call it a feeling."

"Is it your fault?"

I nodded. "Maybe. Maybe not."

"But you have to know for sure."

I have to know how he deals with his guilt. But I wasn't about to tell her that.

I nodded and let go of her wrists. She got up, went to the rolltop desk. She bent forward, her bottom aimed at me in silent invitation. I looked away, closed my eyes, peeked.

"He keeps the things he wants to hide in here." She lifted the pigeonholes to reveal a secret compartment, and removed several business cards. I was out of the bed and snatched the cards from her hand before she could turn.

"Finally," she said. "A man who knows what he wants."

I stuffed the business cards into my jeans pocket, draped my sweater over my shoulder. I pinned her arms to her sides and inched around her to the door.

Her mouth opened wide. "Amazing. But how?"

"What's that?" I said, one hand on the doorknob.

"You're so strong."

In her Boston twang I heard my ex-wife gloating to my face outside the courthouse door. The rage made me horny. I could have fucked an entire harem and had energy left over. But not for this woman, and not for anyone like her.

I opened the door and the singed cat twisted its way into the room, meowing. A little hand snaked through the open door, clamped down on the animal's tail, pulled it back outside. I kicked at the hand with my shoe. The cat hid under the bed.

"No," I said. "I'm not."

VOLCANIC VOLUNTEERS.

Two of the business cards were in Spanish. One was a high-class brothel downtown. Another belonged to Hak Po. The third announced itself as Volcanic Volunteers. A picture of a happy smiley sun setting over a lake in the mountains adorned the card. The address was in Miraflores, right on Avenida Larco, the heart of the tourist district.

It was an hour walk from San Isidro to Miraflores, and I didn't like exercise. I was committing suicide by cowardice, dammit, and I saw no point in slowing the process. Today, though, I needed to clear my head, so I consoled myself by breathing the city's toxic fumes and holding them deep in my lungs.

What did it mean? Pitt? Volunteering? What was he doing with a bunch of no-good do-gooders with a self-righteous attitude? *Look at me, look how good I am. I spent a week playing basketball with street kids in Lima, now let me into Harvard or Princeton, please, pretty please with sugar on top?*

That wasn't like Pitt. That wasn't like Pitt at all. Pitt was more like me. Scum of the earth, didn't care who knew it. Take what you need and fuck the rules, 'cause if you don't, somebody else will.

Why did I give him Kate's postcard? I'll bet he still had it. Her cell phone number. Everything. She had said she'd found peace volunteering. No way that was a coincidence. I pulled back my sleeve and put out my cigarette. *You asshole. You could at least have kept her number. Then you wouldn't have to traipse halfway across fucking Lima to talk to some holier-than-thou morons.*

I found the volunteering office sandwiched between an internet café full of perky blondes yabbling in Swedish and a *chifa* joint that sold Peruvian chow mein, guaranteed diarrhea. To get there I had to run the gauntlet, the Shiny Happy People Zone, tourism central: overpaid stockbrokers from New York and London drinking resealed bottles of tap water, eating "guaranteed clean" imported salads slathered in human fecal material, congratulating themselves on how clever they were. They'd seen Machu Picchu. Deepest, darkest Lima, Peru, had changed since Paddington Bear made his getaway.

I cupped my hand to the glass door. Stairs led to the second floor. I depressed the dirty yellow button on the intercom.

"*Sí?*"

"This Volcanic Volunteers?"

"*No hablo inglés.*"

"Cut the crap, bitch, I know you speak English. I want to volunteer. You going to let me up or aren't you?"

A long pause. I was about to punch the button again when the buzzer sounded. I opened the door with a click, let it swing shut. The stairs were dirty and covered in speckled linoleum, the kind that's supposed to look like marble but winds up looking more like bird shit.

I reached into my pocket for my soap dish. A glint of glass above. I kept my hand in my pocket. Security camera. Interesting. It's true you can't be too careful in Lima. But a volunteering organization with a security camera in the stairwell? This was the tourist district, after all. The hotels bribed the police to keep a watch on this part of town.

On the landing, only one door. Locked. So I knocked: shave and a haircut, fuck you. A distant shuffling approached, like an ancient, dying animal. A key rotated in the lock, the door opened a few inches. A freckled face surrounded by a dandelion head of frizzy orange hair peered at me through a pair of brown plastic glasses.

"I help you?" The accent was German, Bavarian perhaps, thick and guttural.

"You always so rude to people who come here?" I asked.

"You call every woman you meet a bitch?"

"What do you think?"

She laughed. "You are not volunteer we want. Sorry."

She closed the door but it bounced back in her face, knocking her glasses crooked. My foot blocked the doorway.

"Let me be the judge of that."

I put my weight against the door. She let go. It swung open and I stepped inside. A short corridor. Mounted on the wall, a small black-and-white monitor. I could see the stairs, the street outside. To my right, at the end, a bathroom. The door was open. It looked clean. At the other end, to my left, windows. Sunlight shone in so bright I squinted.

The ever-present *garua,* the fog, was worse than San Francisco. When had I last seen the sun?

"The hell?" I said. "You got a red phone link to God?"

A big man blocked the light, hands on his hips. He was taller than me by a head. His long black hair, pulled tight in a ponytail, shimmered blue and violet in the light, announcing his Indian ancestry. The bulbous cheeks suggested a German parent.

"Echo baby, what's going on?" he asked in Spanish.

I said, "Your parents called you Echo?"

She sighed, crossed her arms, heaved skyward her enormous, sagging tits. "Don't start."

I closed the door, stuck my hand out at the big man. "Name's Horace. But people call me Horse. As in hung like a. Heard about your volunteering program."

He flicked a switch on the wall. The sunlight died. It took a moment for my eyes to adjust. His head was too small for his body, the shrunken trophy of Polynesian cannibals. His jaw was even smaller, drawn up into his head, giving him a pronounced overbite. His gut fought with the waistband of his brown corduroy trousers and won. On his feet, open-toed action-man sandals. A blue button-down dress shirt was his halfhearted kowtow to The Man.

"Sun lamps," I said.

He shrugged, took my hand. It was big but soft, a limp bit of juicy steak. "The only way to stay sane in this horrible city," he said in Spanish.

I smiled. It felt weird. I couldn't remember the last time my cheek muscles managed that distinctive upward pull. "We agree on something, then," I said. "That's a start."

He waved a hand at a metal chair covered in rotting green leather. I sat. The springs ground into the base of my spine. I crossed my legs, pressed down on one side, enjoying the pain.

I thought of Sergio. That was fucked up. What he does? To see him in the nightclub. And now again this morning, up close, firsthand.

Until today my punishment made sense. The cigarettes. The burns. Everything. A sudden darkness squeezed my chest. Was all of this a big mistake? *Goddamn you, Pitt,* I thought. *For everything.*

The man said, "You want to volunteer?"

"Either this or the Foreign Legion." I shrugged. "Never did like sand."

I looked around the room. Aside from their laptops and sun lamps, the place was bare. No posters, no pictures, not even a jar full of paper clips or a box of pencils. In the corner lay a bunch of picket signs, upside down. Stake handles resting against the wall, the poster board clean, unbent. Unused. I bent my neck sideways to read them. Echo moved to stand in front of them, but not before I got a good look at a few.

No War For Ore.

Stop Bat Guano II.

Fuck the US.

"Subtle," I said.

"How did you find out about us, Horace?" The shrunken head smiled, his eyes narrow.

"Friend of mine," I said. "Met him in a bar. The Rat's Nest, in Barranco. You know it?"

They nodded in unison, arms folded across their chests, but said nothing.

"Tell me about the bat guano," I said. "What does that mean? Second helpings of bat shit?"

The Bavarian's frizzy orange hair exploded, as though struck by lightning. "It's about imperialist fascist pigs raping Bolivia, stealing their land. It's about—"

A thick hand cut her off in mid-sentence. The man said, "The name of your friend, Horace."

I pulled out the business card, extended it between two fingers. "Sho' 'nuff," I said. "Name was Pitt."

They looked at the card. They looked at each other. The Bavarian fiddled with her bra strap. "Pitt?"

"Have a last name?"

I let my arm fall. "Watters," I said. "Pitt Watters."

Shrunken head flicked his ponytail in one hand, eyed the gaping hole in my sweater. "Are you sure it was us he mentioned?"

"Positive. Ambassador's son is a stickler for details. Like father, like son."

The man stood. He held out his hand. "I would remember the American ambassador's son."

"Or maybe you know my ex-fiancée," I said, ignoring the hand. "Katherine? Goes by Kate? Would have volunteered about nine months ago."

They both shuffled their feet. Echo let out a fart, blushed. "There are many people with that name," she said. "It is a common name. Now if you please?"

I made a show of looking past her at the picket signs. "No War For Ore," I said. "This got something to do with Ovejo? The lithium, perhaps?"

Ovejo was the socialist president of Bolivia. Pitt had mentioned him once over beers and whores. The Bolivian government was demanding more money for the mining concession, threatening to nationalize the mine if their demands were not met.

"We are busy right now," Echo said. She massaged her belly, and I realized she wasn't fat, or at any rate not just fat: she was pregnant. "Call next time. Before you come. Maybe then we talk some more. Yes?"

I climbed out of the chair, my face wrinkling with kindness, tears coming to my eyes as the spring left contact with my spine. "We must think of the unborn," I said. "What future are we leaving for our children?"

"Of course." Still the man's hand hovered in midair, an insistent dismissal.

"You got a brochure or something?" I said. "The Legion doesn't want me I'll try again with you."

A glossy trifold brochure attacked my chest. I folded it and stuffed it down the front of my pants.

"I never caught your name," I said, and took his hand.

"No," he said. "You didn't."

He released me, but I held his hand tight.

"I never said he was American."

"Who's that?"

"The ambassador's son."

I sashayed out on the landing. The door closed behind me. I went down the stairs, letting my feet fall heavy on the steps, noting the noise each made. At the bottom, I opened the door and lit a cigarette. I took a puff, threw the cigarette into the gutter. I slipped back inside as the door clicked shut.

I didn't move. I listened. Silence. I slid out of my flip-flops. Still nothing. I picked them up in one hand, and tiptoed up the stairs, skipping the creaky ones.

Voices raised inside the office. I pressed my ear to the door, careful to stand below the peephole. They argued in Spanish.

"I tell you, he knows!" The man's voice was hysterical.

"He knows nothing."

"He tries to stop us, what we're doing—"

"Gaia will never allow it—"

"—helps those who help themselves."

My eavesdropping was interrupted by a tap on the glass below. I looked down the stairs. Some kid. Wait—*Paco?* Of all people. He waved. I put my finger to my lips, shook my head.

"What if we're wrong? What if—"

"What if, what if, what if." The woman's voice was condescending, scornful. "We do her will. Have faith. We shall join her soon. All of us."

Paco tried the locked door, rattled the handle. I slashed my arms sideways, an umpire denying the winning touchdown.

"Check the video."

Footsteps came closer to the door. "Waving at the camera. Some homeless."

The woman snorted. "Doesn't know how lucky he is."

I jammed my feet back into my flip-flops. Jumped, grabbed the video camera and ripped it from the wall. Couldn't have them knowing I had eavesdropped. Plaster showered on the landing. I spiked the camera, claimed my six points and threw myself down the stairs three at a time. I was in the street before I heard the upstairs door open.

I sprinted along the crowded sidewalk, crashing through groups of Brits in zip travel pants, the kind of tourists who thought slumming in Lima made them worldly adventurers.

Behind me, a frenzy of pocket patting and slapping, and I knew Paco's magic hands were at work, even as he ran.

We didn't stop until we got to the sea. We ran the length of Avenida Larco, dashed down the stairs into Larco Mar, the cliff-side shopping mall for tourists and Lima's pathetically *petite bourgeoisie*. I slowed to a walk, hopped the escalator downstairs to the cinema. I bought two tickets to a Hollywood blockbuster whose poster of an overpaid movie actor holding a gun promised boredom. I handed a ticket to Paco. Together we entered the darkened theater.

The movie was already halfway along. A faked explosion filled the screen. Cars squealed. I yawned. Paco pulled wallets from his various pockets, siphoned the cash and dropped the remainder on the sticky floor.

"What's going on, Paco?"

He grinned. "I could also ask you that." His teeth gleamed white in the dark theater.

"Why were you following me?"

"Shh!" A gringo tourist in a blue denim shirt turned around, finger to his lips.

Paco lowered his voice. "They pay me. That is why I want talk to you, *amigo*."

"They *are* paying you. You want *to* talk to me. Fine. Who? Why?"

"Tell them where you go. What you do. They pay in dollars. Much money."

"A *lot* of money."

He nodded, peering skyward at a pair of twenty-foot-tall, surgically crafted Hollywood breasts. "A lot."

A piece of popcorn missed my face by inches. "Hey asshole,

shut up already."

"What do they look like?" I asked.

"A gringo." Paco shifted in his seat. "You know. *Rubio.*"

"We all look alike." I sighed. *Rubio* literally meant "blond." But in practice it meant anyone with hair that wasn't Latino black. My dark brown hair was, to Paco, *rubio.*

"Since when?" I asked him.

"Last week."

"When you meeting next?"

Paco grinned. "You mean, 'when *are* you meeting next,' right, *profesor?*"

A fat blob of an American stood, blocking the screen. He slobbered down at me, his words slurred by the quantity of fat dangling from his chin. "Some of us are on vacation."

I pulled a switchblade from my pocket. I flicked open the knife one-handed, stabbed him in the nipple. "Well I'm not."

Out in the midday gloom of Lima, we hurled ourselves into a passing bus.

"Where to next, boss?"

"Home. Tag along?"

"You do not mind?"

I ruffled his hair and sighed. "I'll let you know when I do."

Volcanic Volunteers' trifold brochure contained no more information than I expected. Pictures of happy brown children frolicking next to high-altitude mud-brick houses, vistas of the Andes in the background. Promises of personal fulfillment for the foreign volunteer, all for the low, low price of just two thousand dollars per week.

A picture of a lake filled the middle inside third of the tri-fold. I stared at it. I knew that lake. Knew it too well. The island in the distance, too. I swatted the memory aside, but it bounced back, punched me in the jaw like an angry midget with a two-by-four.

I had to go there. Find the volunteers. Find them, find Kate. Find Kate, find Pitt. Find Pitt...and then? Then what? I had no idea. All I knew was I felt driven. After a year of wallowing in shit I had something to hold on to, a life pre-server, and I wasn't going to let it go. Even if it meant having to dredge up the past and face Kate again.

I needed a drink. There are some things no man was ever meant to suffer. Was never meant to bear. I fingered the soap dish in my pocket, left it there. Not here on the bus. Getting caught would mean a hefty bribe I couldn't pay, and a long flight back to the States. I shuddered just thinking about it. Better death than that.

I folded the brochure into a tight square, and shoved it deep into my pocket.

I left Paco on the steps of a crumbling *chifa* joint across the street from my apartment. He promised to watch me real good. I didn't have the heart to explain that "good" was not an adverb.

I climbed the rotting planks to my apartment. The stairs bowed and creaked underfoot, threatening to send me plum-meting ass first into the basement beneath the butcher shop, impale me on who knew what subterranean delights lay hid-den below.

The door was ajar.

No sign of damage. No scratches. No splintered or broken wood. But still, ajar.

I smiled and rubbed my crotch. Momentary distractions were always welcome. I was still hard from thinking about Janine. I put my keys in my pocket. "I told you not to come here, Lynn," I called out.

I opened the door. The room was dark. "Playing games, I see. You like it that way, don't you?"

I tripped over something on the floor and fell. I landed on an arm.

"Sorry, babe, I—"

But the arm bounced, fell back, lay still. I jumped up and flicked on the light.

It was Lynn. She lay naked on the floor. I bent down, laid a finger to her lips. Nothing. I touched her throat. No heartbeat.

"Damn you," I said. "Damn you to hell."

I pulled out my cell phone. The occasion seemed to demand it. Who would I call? The police? The American embassy? Ambo direct? Ambo, I decided. He would want to know first. He would know what to do. With any luck he might even kill me.

My fingers shook as I punched in the numbers, slid on the keys, misdialed. I cleared the screen and tried again. A flash of movement in the cracked wall mirror caught my eye. A heavy weight crashed against my temple.

Pain and blackness. Far above me I heard sobbing. Drops of hot rain splattered my cheek. Then the sweet blanket of death covered me and took me from this life.

6

A VOICE SAID, "HOPE YOU LIKE IT UP THE ASS."

Pain filled my head and I groaned. A hand slapped my face. A ring dug into my cheekbone. I struggled to focus. Where were my glasses? I reached up to rub my eyes, but my hands were cuffed behind my back. I took a deep breath and gagged. It smelled like shit. Like a latrine. Flies buzzed on my eyelids. I blinked, and one settled on my nose.

"I died and gone to hell?" I asked.

"You're going to wish you had."

A fist crashed into my nose, and I saw red. I gasped, my body quivered, an orgasm of damaged nerve and broken bone. It made me feel clean, the trembling joy of a nun bathing in holy waters. For a long, glorious moment I convulsed in ecstasy, before it leaked away, taking my happiness from me. My vision slowly cleared. A black blob stuck to the tip of my nose.

"Hey," I said. "The human flyswatter."

A face loomed over me. Its ashen pallor announced a true *limeño*. My kind of guy. His nose was flat and speckled with acne scars, the kind you get from growing up in this sea of filth. He wore a gun under his armpit and a badge on his belt.

Personal favorite joke: What's a cop?

Answer: A thug with a badge.

He held a photo close to my face. "Know this woman?"

I squinted. The official embassy portrait. "Lynn." Then I remembered. "She's dead, isn't she?"

"I know she's dead, asshole. You killed her."

I shook my head. I was still half-awake. *"Me?* What are you talking about?"

He flicked a large matte photo onto the table in front of me. Lynn reclined naked on my cockroach-strewn floor. Masking tape outlined her body.

I spat blood. "How?"

"You need to ask?"

A throat cleared. "Strangled," said a voice.

I nodded at the man in the shadows. "Who's your bum buddy, *marica?*"

The man stepped into the light. It was Major Villega. He crossed his arms and winked at me.

"Figures," I said. "Scum always floats to the surface."

Villega looked at the other man's back, held a finger to his puffy lips. "Well, *profesor,*" he said in Spanish. "I see you've been involved in some extracurricular activities."

"Nothing worse than what you do every day for a living," I said. I spat on the floor.

My interrogator clutched my balls through my jeans. "You didn't even fuck her first. That's what I don't get."

"I didn't—"

He squeezed. Hard. "What kind of man *are* you?"

I kicked him in the shin with my bare toes. Savored the crunch of bone on bone. My flip-flops bent but did not break.

He swore and let go of my sack. Stood, rubbed his leg.

"The ambassador has enemies," I said. "It could have been anyone."

The man limped around behind me, tipped my chair forward. I dug in with my feet, but he twisted my handcuffed wrists sideways. I fell. He pressed his knee into my lower vertebrae.

"They found her in your apartment."

"Where they found me too," I said. "Someone knocked me out when I got home. Or what, you think I killed the woman, then whacked myself on the side of the head?"

"Then how do you explain this?"

A length of heavy rope fell to the ground at my cheek. He held up the end: a hangman's noose dangled from his hand.

"Found this in your bathroom."

A metal bucket scraped along the floor until it stood next to my head. A swarm of flies buzzed. The stench was overpowering. The man pulled me to my knees. The bucket was full of shit. The kind of bucket they use in prisons without indoor plumbing. Looked like human shit. Brown and lumpy, a fecal pudding.

I said, "I can explain."

A snap of latex as he gloved his hands.

"Well?"

I opened my mouth. Was there anything I could say that would change his mind? I doubted it. Why bother trying? I was ready to take my punishment. I shook my head. I took a deep breath and closed my eyes. He grabbed me by the hair, shoved my head into that chocolate broth.

Amazing the sorts of things that go through your head

when it's submerged in a bucket of feces. I didn't think about the multiple varieties of hepatitis to which I was being exposed, the numerous kinds of dysentery and other noxious diseases I might get. I didn't feel anger at the detective. It wasn't anything personal. I knew that. He was just doing his job.

As I inhaled a turd through my nose, and the oxygen-depleted air in my lungs leaked through my lips, and the taste made me vomit into the vile fluid, inhaling my own bile, all I could think of was Lynn. Sure, she was a bitch. But she was my bitch, and I had loved her. I realized that now. And someone had killed her.

Who would do such a thing, and why?

I would never know the answer to that question. I was ready to die. I deserved it. I would leave this world with my questions unanswered, drowned in a bucket of poo.

Hands unbuttoned my shirt, pulled it back from my chest and down to my wrists. They pinned my forearms behind me and removed the handcuffs. Lifted my head from the bucket.

I coughed and vomited in long, heaving gasps, trying to empty my stomach and lungs at the same time. Hands pulled me to my feet, wrapped a towel around my face. They tugged the shirt free of my wrists. Where was my sweater? The things you think at times like this. The handcuffs clicked tight around my wrists again. Fingers groped at my jeans, unbuckled my belt, pulled my pants around my ankles. They were going to sodomize me before I died. I was too weak to resist.

There were two of them, perhaps three. They got my trousers off me, and I was naked. I wondered what they thought of my scars. One held the towel around my face. The other shoved me forward. My hip grazed a doorknob. The shit drained from one ear. Our footsteps echoed along a corridor. A toilet flushed. A faucet squeaked. Water pattered on a tile floor. Pooled under my toes.

With the last of my strength I struck up and back with my elbow. It landed on something hard. A jaw, maybe. An unfamiliar voice swore in Spanish. A fist slammed into my left kidney, and I buckled, groaning. A hand grabbed the handcuffs, held my arms still. The towel disappeared. Someone shoved me under a shower head.

"Close your eyes."

I kept them open. Whatever they were going to do, I wanted to see.

Strong hands massaged my scalp. Clumps of shit dripped from the sides of my face. The lump on my head throbbed. My eyes began to sting. I smelled shampoo mixed in with the shit.

"The *fuck?*"

A voice chuckled. "I told you, close your eyes."

This time I obeyed.

A sponge attacked the side of my face. "Inhale deep."

Again I obeyed. The sponge sparred with my face, my broken nose, my forehead, my eyelids, the rough stubble on my chin. It jabbed against my temple and I whimpered in pain, exhaling bubbles of shit-flavored soap.

When he finished, he pushed me under the shower and let the water run over my chest and back. I cleared my throat and hawked up a turd. The shower squeaked off. I stood up straight.

"Open your eyes."

My clothing lay folded on a nearby table. My raggedy old sweater, too. Even my glasses.

"Turn around."

I turned. They removed the handcuffs.

"Get dressed."

I got dressed.

My bather wore a nurse's white uniform. Two young policemen, probably conscripts, stood with their batons in hand and watched. One held his nose pinched between two fingers, his head tilted back.

"Follow me."

The nurse led me down a long corridor, the conscripts following close behind. He opened a door and held it for me. Unlike the last room, this one was clean, well-scrubbed, well-lit. A metal desk stood in the middle, two chairs on either side. The room smelled of disinfectant.

A pair of snakeskin boots rested on the desk. Attached to them reclined a large black man, playing cards. Solitaire. His broad shoulders cast a monstrous shadow on the floor. A white cowboy hat rested on its crown at his elbow. His shaved head glistened in the harsh yellow glare of the naked bulb. The gray in his eyebrows was the only hint of his age. He looked up as I came in.

It was Ambo.

I leaned across the desk, held out my hand.

Ambo asked me, "What are you punishing yourself for?"

Nine months earlier. I'd just met Pitt. We were in the

embassy's inner sanctum, applying ourselves to a crystal decanter of Scotch. White ties fluttered under our chins, the ambassador and Pitt in tailor-made white tailcoats, me in my black rent-a-tux that reeked of diesel fumes. Ambo scratched his nose with a thumbnail, an unfiltered Camel clamped between two knuckles. Pitt was in the bathroom doing a line, and we both knew it. I coughed on my single malt. Wiped my lips and put my glass down. I was unaccustomed to such quality liquor. It was my first drink in two days.

"My conscience would look good on a stripper, sir," I said.

Pitt was mad at me. No, at Ambo. Mad in general. He only brought me along to piss off his father. *Look, Dad! Street riffraff!* I was the awkward fuck-up of an expat guaranteed to say something offensive. I came along anyway. Free booze was free booze. An excuse to break my two-day Lent, a futile attempt to free myself from my many addictions. The grating throb of a hangover tomorrow would be a welcome distraction.

"Meet my drug dealer," was how he introduced me at the gates of the fortress.

Was it a cry for attention? He was adopted. I knew that. Everyone knew that. It was pretty obvious. Who ever heard of a black man siring a Swedish god? But even in the half an hour I had seen them together, I could tell that Ambo cared. About Pitt. More than my old man cared about me, and that scumbag was flesh and blood. There was something vicious, almost ungrateful, about the way Pitt treated his father.

"You don't sell Viagra, do you?" Ambo asked, greeting me in the garden when I arrived. Held my hand in his, then winked.

I said, "In fact, I do." And rattled an orange prescription container at the side of my head. The way I treated my body, I needed it, too.

He laughed, his six-foot-something frame booming the sound into the smoggy night. On his head, a pale Stetson, curved up at the sides. He had been a pro basketball player in his youth, back before the days of the twenty-million-dollar contract, and on his right fist a diamond-encrusted championship ring sparkled dusky and hard under the fairy lights. No wonder the unpolished wedding band on his left hand got so little attention.

Now he was intent on dissecting me.

"Guilt will kill you sooner than a gun."

He dropped the Stetson onto his desk, aimed his cigarette at me. "Pieu," he said, and laughed, the smoke tickling my nostrils with promises of temporary happiness, or at least reduced anxiety. I had been cold turkey for two days. No nicotine. No booze. No cocaine. I felt like shit. I bummed a cigarette and lit it. *Two out of three ain't bad.*

"What makes you think that I have guilt?" I asked.

"Every man is guilty of something." He looked at his cigarette and ground it out, half-finished. He propped his snakeskin boots onto the wide expanse of desk. They glimmered in the dim light. "Every man sins."

I closed my eyes and felt the nicotine wash over my brain. "And you?" I asked. "Do you sin?" Wondering if he'd admit to the DSU's crimes.

"I do what must be done, Horace." He reached behind him, fingered a gold-fringed American flag.

"I mean, what's the big deal?" I insisted, pushing the bounds of good taste, and not giving a shit. "So people disagree with you. Dissidents. Whatever the fuck you want to call them. So what?"

Ambo looked at me sadly. "One man, Horace," he said. He dropped his boots to the floor. "It only takes one man. To 'save the world.'" He made exaggerated finger quotes. "Or should I say, destroy it."

I sucked on my cigarette. "And what's so bad about saving the world?"

"It can't be saved." He threw his arms out wide and knocked over a potted fern. Ignored the wreckage. "We are imperfect creatures on an imperfect planet. America is the best thing that ever happened to humanity. These people would tear down everything we have built—and put what in its place?" He shrugged. "Socialism? Dead and buried. Didn't work. Now what? They have no idea."

"So at worst they're deluded fools. Why can't you live and let live? How are they even a threat?"

"Because it only takes one man," he said again, jamming his finger down into his desk. "One voice of dissent can send ripples around the world. People don't know what's good for them. For their own sake we must prevent them from speaking against us—even *thinking* against us. Against America."

What a bunch of bullshit. "And how do you stop people thinking?" I asked.

"Fear," he said simply. "We are the agents of fear."

"And so you sin," I concluded. "Taking a bullet for humanity, so to speak."

He either didn't catch my sarcasm or chose to ignore it. He lowered his head. "And so I sin."

The vice-regal toilet flushed. Pitt stumbled from the bathroom, stuffing his shirt into his white pants. A trickle of blood shone on his upper lip. He snorted it back into place. "Dad's got lots of sins, don't you, Dad?"

Ambo nodded. "I do."

Pitt buckled his belt, flipped up his white penguin tails and sat on Ambo's desk. On the wall hung photos of the President and Secretary of State. He picked up two jars. "See this?"

He lifted one above his head. A regular jam jar, full of what looked like molasses.

"Blackstrap?"

"Oil."

Ambo chuckled. "First wildcat strike I ever done. Nigeria, nineteen—"

"—sixty-five. Number dead? One hundred and twenty-seven."

Ambo frowned, looked at the floor. He nodded again, twitched his head from side to side. "We be patriots, son. We do what must be done."

Pitt put the jar of oil back on the desk. He held aloft another jar, this one filled with white pellets.

"Vitamin C?" I guessed.

"Lithium." He rattled the jar. "My inheritance."

"That's enough," Ambo said.

"Don't you think he ought to know? I mean, if—"

"I said, enough!"

It was the first and only time I ever saw Ambo raise his voice. Pitt got off the desk, slouched down into his chair, lit a cigarette. He smoked in silence for a long moment.

I cleared my throat. "Ought to know what?"

"Only way to the top's over a pile of corpses." He turned, looked at his father. "You really feel no guilt?"

"Helps to be a Christian, son."

"I forgot. Jesus will forgive me."

"He will. Don't you ever doubt it."

Pitt made a rude noise with his mouth.

Ambo stood. Held out a hand. "Horace. A word with my son. You don't mind?"

I put my cigarette between my lips. I stood too, took his hand. "Don't rough him up too much, sir."

He slapped me on the shoulder, walked me to the door. "You're a bad influence on my son, you know that?"

I laughed. "You think so?"

He grinned, opened the carved wooden door. The noise of the party spilled into the room. A marine guard in full dress chokers stood to attention outside.

"You're too good for this world, Horace. Go do something bad."

That was the day I found out who Lynn really was.

I elbowed my way through the crowd, the men a swarm of ghosts, my single speck of black the only blemish. Waiters slid sideways through the throng, trays of champagne balanced one-handed over their heads, their free palms brushing the buttocks of Peru's leading diplomatic ladies, dresses of colorful silk, taffeta.

Men stalked the four corners of the room like boxers waiting for the bell, white cords curling from their ears. They wore blue blazers, held their hands tight over their nuts, as though warding off a low blow. Brass cuff buttons winked at the crowd from crotch level. They watched us through sunglasses. They watched me. I was easy to spot. A stain of sin in a sea of purity.

I stumbled through the crowd, wishing I had brought my soap dish. Two days without a hit. I took a drag on my cigarette, but it didn't do me any good. I was afraid I might fall asleep standing up. Where was I going to find a dealer on a dance floor full of diplomats?

Everywhere I looked I saw tits. Tits and ass. A dozen languages cooed sweet words into the ears of a hundred married women, their plunging necklines sweeping to their navels. Maybe I could find something old and skanky.

I spotted the bar across the room. A waiter passed nearby, champagne glasses aloft, distributing his worldly delight to the surrounding throng. I shouldered my way toward him but managed only to follow in his wake, collecting conversations as I went. A German whispered to an Englishwoman his preference for hot English mustard, and its application to a variety of sausage types. A Japanese man wearing a sash grinned, spoke Spanish to a Chinese woman, deploring the rape of Nanking. An American woman propositioned a timid Dutchman in glasses, her brassy tones crashing like cymbals on those around her.

I made it to the bar. I grabbed an empty water glass, pointed to a bottle of the cheapest *pisco* on the shelf. "Don't stop till I say when."

"Hey, that's my line!"

She leaned against the bar, breasts suspended in midair by a strapless blue gown. I could tell they were fake. They also looked delicious. It was time to leave. *Run away. Any woman who'd want you is a woman you don't want to know.* My hand felt wet. I turned back to the barman.

"But, sir, you did not say 'when.'"

"Funny man. Ought to come around that bar and knock you senseless."

The barman, I realized too late, was a lesser species of goon, like those in the corners. He put the bottle down. He cracked his knuckles and smiled.

"Sir, I should like to see you try."

"Asshole."

I gulped my drink, shook the *pisco* off my hand. I turned to go.

"Wait." She touched my forearm. "He doesn't just serve booze. Be nice."

"You mean—"

"Shh." She fingered her cleavage. The corner of a small plastic bag peeked out from one side of her boob.

I looked more closely at her face. Her eyes were still pretty, a striking green. She was wrinkled, but not wrinkled enough for me. My need for a hit overwhelmed my revulsion, though, and I put my hand on her bare elbow. "You want to go somewhere we can share that?"

She chuckled. "You don't remember me, do you?"

"Should I?"

She leaned into me, her whiskey breath panting on my neck. "The Rat's Nest? That booth?"

It came back to me, a sledgehammer driving a spike into my brain. The frenzied dance floor, the shots, the coke, a furious attempt to make the time pass, keep the thoughts at bay, repulse the creeping darkness that threatened to engulf my soul, then the final hurried fumblings in the dark, ending only in sadness and an abrupt return to reality, the futility of it all.

"Oh," I said. "Hi. How's it going?"

Her hand clutched my back, drowning my senses in whiskey and perfume. "I'm old enough to be your mother," she breathed in my ear, pride in her voice, the pride of a lioness in another mother's cub.

"I'm young enough to be your lover," I said. I grabbed her drink from the bar, poured it down my throat.

"Meet me at the top of the stairs in ten minutes," she whispered again, then pulled away. She held out her hand in incongruous formality. "Name's Lynn, by the way. Pleased to meet you."

Before I could think of an appropriate comeback, like, for instance, my name, she engaged in conversation in Spanish with a Peruvian naval officer in full dress choker whites.

"*Amigo.*"

A voice at my elbow. The bartender with an attitude.

"Whaddaya want, *cabrón.*"

"You should be more careful."

"Of what?" I spat on the floor. "You?"

"No, *amigo,*" he said gently, poured me a drink. "That woman."

"What about her?"

At that moment a delegation of Japanese crowded around me, jabbering in accented Spanish, demanding more liquor. The bartender said something to me. I held my hand to my ear. He shrugged, and turned to make the drinks.

Careful of what? I studied the crowded ballroom, felt the *pisco* melting my brain. Lynn was nowhere to be seen.

It was time. I pushed through the crowd, letting silken slippery buttocks caress my knuckles as I made my way toward the stairs. I climbed halfway up, to the second landing of the curving marble staircase. The bartender below was pouring drinks. He didn't look up. I scanned the room for Lynn. I didn't see her. I turned to climb again, felt a finger on my shoulder.

"You lost, sir?"

The hand dropped again, clutched its crotch. The lips plastered to the hard jaw neither smiled nor frowned. An American flag pin soiled his left lapel. Were it not for the crisp crease in his gray slacks, you could mistake him for a garden-variety rent-a-cop.

"Just going to the bathroom."

"Bathroom's downstairs, sir."

"But I was up here just a minute ago!" I protested.

The man's face was granite.

A rustling of silk charged up the stairs.

"A friend of the ambassador's," Lynn cooed. "Do let him up."

He nodded, turned aside. We climbed together, and she slithered her hand under my arm, her elbow-length blue glove stroking the back of my hand. On the top landing she led me down a familiar corridor. We passed a marine guard at attention beside a carved wooden door. I heard voices raised in argument, Pitt's voice, Ambo's voice, shouting, a crash as something broke.

"Quickly," she said, her finger to her lips.

I followed her around a corner, to the end of the hallway. She opened a door. An enormous bathroom gaped white and spotless. She pushed me inside. She looked back over her shoulder, then darted in, closing and locking the door. She fumbled for the light switch, found it. I blinked. The incandescent bulb's harsh rays shattered against the sharp reflecting surfaces.

"Well," she said. Her cleavage rose and fell.

I nodded. "Let's see it."

She reached behind her back. A zipper hummed.

"No, no," I said. "This."

I plucked the bag of cocaine from her cleavage without bothering to touch her breast.

She smiled. "First things first." She retrieved a small mirror and a razor blade from the top of the medicine cabinet. I held the bag to the light, flicked it with my fingertip. Looked to be about a gram. I opened the bag, poured the entire pouch onto the mirror.

"Wow," she said. "You're hard core."

I ignored her. I snorted more than half of the white powder, a stream of cocaine bliss. I sat on the toilet.

She said, "You needed that."

I nodded. My eyes rolled up inside my head. *Numb. So numb. The pain ebbs. There is nothing. No past. No future. Only now.*

Lynn daintily cut the rest into a fine powder. She unfurled a crisp Benjamin from her other breast, snorted a thin line. She leaned back against the sink, her hands on the lip of the basin.

"Now," she said. "Where were we."

A door slammed outside. I leaned in to kiss her neck. My fingers groped for her zipper. Footsteps came our way. A heavy hand grabbed the bathroom doorknob, yanked it, rattled it, fought with it.

Lynn pitched her voice high, spoke over my shoulder. "That you, Jeremiah?"

"Oh." Pitt's voice, muffled. "Sorry, Mom. Use the one downstairs."

We held our breath, waited for the footsteps to retreat. I pulled her zipper all the way down, stepped back. A hand fumbled below my waist. Her deft fingers released my fly. She knelt on the shimmering white tiles.

"Mom?" I said.

She giggled, her mouth full.

7

AMBO SAID, "PITT IS NOT YOUR FRIEND."

He shuffled the cards. Bridged the deck, fluttered the two halves together. He dealt a new game of solitaire.

Watch out for Dad when the cards come out, dude. It means he's pissed. Real pissed. One of those self-control tricks? When he's torturing dissidents, sometimes it's the only thing between them and a bullet in the brain.

I said, "I realize that."

We were in the warden's office. Ambo sat at the man's creaking metal desk. A Peruvian flag, red and white, drooped in one corner. Behind him, on either side of the far door—a separate entrance?—two American marines in crisp khaki shirtsleeves and blue trousers stood to attention. They wore pistols in white holsters on their hips, carried black riot sticks in their hands.

"You think he cares for you? He gives a shit?" Ambo hawked up a loogie and spat on the floor. "He used you. For a job. I told him to. And now he's using you again."

"What for this time?" I asked.

Ambo's rumpled tuxedo hung limp from his shoulders, the starch overwhelmed by his body heat. A bow tie dangled loose at his neck. Emeralds glittered at his cuffs. I thought of snakes. Where had I seen that shade before?

He looked at me over the rim of his reading glasses. "Don't pretend that you don't know," he said. "Why are you protecting him?"

I rested my elbows on my knees. The Peruvian cops breathed loudly behind me. I wiped a trickle of shit-smelling snot from my upper lip.

"Look," I said. "I was enjoying my facial scrub. Salon next door? Bucket *à la merde?* Why don't you just tell me what you want. So I can get back to it."

Ambo licked a finger, lifted a card from his draw pile. He held it out, looked down his long beak of a nose at it, discarded it. He flipped over a new card, a king. His hand trembled.

I snapped my fingers in his face. "You hear what I just said?"

Without looking up, he said softly, voice barely audible, "How old am I?"

He planted the king. A new foundation. A flick of his wrist, and an emerald winked at me. I gasped. It was Lynn, her million-carat eyes an inch from mine, the glassy sadness of an aging whore.

"How old are you," I said. "The fuck is going on here?"

Ambo drew another card. Discarded it. His tuxedo soaked up the light from the overhead lamp, a bespoke black hole, and disappeared. His black head floated above the stabbing isosceles triangle of his white shirtfront.

He said, "Answer the question." His voice was quiet, controlled. As though suppressing bottled hysteria.

"This is about Lynn, isn't it," I said. "Some sort of weird

fucked-up revenge. You're pissed that I was sleeping with her. Is that it?"

He froze for an instant, before slowly playing another card. His fist clutched the deck tight, his knuckles white.

I scooted my chair closer to the desk. Stood. Rested my knuckles on the flaking leather blotter. The mouth breathers behind me took a step forward, but did not interfere. I put my palm flat on top of his card game.

I said, "Ambo? Lynn is dead. And I am sorry." I leaned over the desk as far as I could go, trying to catch his eye, but he avoided my gaze. "But it wasn't me."

Ambo looked at my hand, as though unsure what to do with an unexpected joker. "Randy?" he said.

Before I could say, No, not really, one of the marines came to attention.

"Sir!"

He strode to Ambo's side. Peered down at the cards. His peaked cap brushed my forehead. I didn't move my hand. He pointed with an outstretched index finger, clad in white. "Black knave on red queen, sir."

Ambo nodded. He pried the jack from under my middle finger, moved it to the right. "Knave on queen. Thank you, Randy."

"Sir."

The room was cold but sweat beaded on Ambo's forehead. A drop grew in the furrow above his eyebrows, ran along his nose until it hung from the tip, a future stalactite. He looked up at me. Again, he asked, "How old am I?"

I slashed sideways at the cards, wiped them from the surface of the desk with my forearm. "Didn't you hear me?" I said. "I told you it wasn't me."

"I know it wasn't. It was Pitt." His brown eyes jumped up at me from deep inside his motionless skull. His gaze whipped my head back. I crumpled, caught myself against the back of the chair. I coughed, tasted bile.

"Pitt killed his own mother?"

"Answer the question."

"Why he would do such a thing? I have no idea, Ambo," I said. "I really don't."

His voice rose in crescendo, rage and panic blending together. "My age, Horace."

"The fuck it matter?" I stood, knocked over my chair with the backs of my calves. Brown hands gripped my shoulders, picked up the chair and slammed me down.

Ambo folded his large hands, as though in prayer. Linked together they were the size of a small melon. "How old am I?" he asked.

"Old enough to know better, but not old enough to care."

He did not so much as grin. "How old is that?"

I sat silent.

"Horace." His voice was a growl, a bear prepared to rip your throat out.

"Seventy-five."

He dropped his feet to the floor. Took off his glasses, laid them aside. Rubbed the bridge of his nose between a giant thumb and forefinger.

"Seventy-five years old." He drummed his hand on the metal desk, a sound like rain pattering on rooftops. "And this is *not*," —and here his fist smacked the hollow metal surface, the remaining cards twitching, the warden's name plaque bouncing— "*not* how I am going to die."

I looked at my own puny white hands, then at Ambo's muscular pile driver of a fist. His fingers were thick as carrots, the tips calloused and hard.

"What makes you think you're going to die?" I asked.

His fist rose up, the warhammer of the gods. Crashed down on the desk, denting it this time. He flung the remaining cards into the air, Lynn's emerald eye twinkling amidst the blue paisley rain of dots and cartoon heads. With a primeval roar he overturned the desk.

I leaped backward. Footfalls shuffled behind me, as though drawn by the disorder, some atavistic urge to corral the chaos. Stopped. The marines on either side of Ambo had not flinched.

"What makes you think you're not?" he demanded.

He glowered at me from under those monstrous eyebrows. I had the sudden vision of horns curving from his temples, a red tail twitching back and forth as he offered Faust a bargain.

I said, "So go ahead and kill me. What's the problem?"

Ambo took out a pack of Camels. Put the pack to his mouth, kissed it, came away with a cigarette between his lips. From a side pocket, a box of wooden matches. He rattled it, removed a match. Scratched the red tip against the box, the smell of sulfur floating across at me. He held the flame to the tip of the white paper.

"Let me ask you something, Horace," he said, exhaling smoke. "Do you just say that? Or do you really mean it? Are you prepared to die?"

"Prepared to—" My tongue refused to finish the thought.

I had almost died in that bucket of shit. And I realized I was not prepared. That I didn't want to die.

"Because I'm not," he continued. "At least not yet."

He puffed deep, holding the smoke in his lungs. Settled into the swivel chair. The frame creaked under his weight. The tip of the cigarette glowed orange in the dim light. He held it at arm's length.

"No," he said. "This is not how I want to die." He looked at me again, and I struggled to endure his battering gaze. "But I can see why it appeals to you."

God. I began to wish I hadn't told him. I looked at the floor. "I don't know what you mean."

Ambo sat forward, his great bulk now resting on his elbows. He blew smoke through his nose. His broad shoulders hunched over, head dangling loose, a buzzard drawn to carrion.

"You know," he said, "I understand you better than you think."

"You understand," I said, and sneered. "What do you think you understand? You sound like Lynn now."

He ignored the reference to my affair with his wife. "It wasn't the money," he went on. "You aren't the type who can be bought."

"Yeah, OK, we know that."

"And you're not a patriot."

I shrugged. "Land of the slaves and the home of the fearful."

"So I'm guessing," he said, and he cocked his head, fist at his ear, the cigarette smoldering orange at his temple, my vision of devil's horns returning in a rush that made me gasp,

"I'm guessing it's for love."

"Love?" I said. I laughed. "The fuck you talking about?"

"Was there a woman there? Is that it?"

"What woman? Where?"

"Guangzhou Higher Polytechnic."

"For fuck's sake. That was how many years ago?"

"We read your email, you know."

I'd spent a year teaching English in China. This was ten years ago, before my ex-wife, before South America, before Peru, before Kate, before La Paz. Back in the days when life was good, the world was simple and I was happy. I'd dated one of my students for a while. Ping Ping. Still sent me naked pictures by email, hoping I would return.

"So?"

"So..." He crossed his arms. "You got a big drug habit. Where's the money come from, pay for that?"

"Let me get this straight," I said. "You think I'm working for the Chinese? What are you, crazy?"

"Let's skip the denials," he said. "I don't have time. I need to know where Pitt is and how to stop him."

I held my hands out wide, gaped at the ceiling. "Fuck if I know."

"Are they blackmailing you? Is that it?"

"What blackmail? What are you talking about?"

"Maybe they tell the Peruvians you're here. An illegal immigrant. Get you deported back to the States." He spoke around his cigarette. "Is that it? So you can work pumping gas to pay back child support for the rest of your life?"

A rare moment of calm settled on my soul. I had pondered on many late drug-addled nights how to respond to such a threat, should it happen again. I was ready. I blew my nose in my palm and wiped it on my pants.

"I have a rule," I said. "A no-suicide rule. It's the only rule I have. No. Let me finish." I spoke slower now, to make sure he heard ever word. "I'm allowed to self-destruct in any way I want to. I deserve to suffer in this life. But I'm not allowed to die." I held up an index finger. "There is one exception to this rule." I moved close to his face and whispered, "Anyone tries to put me on a plane back to the States? I will be dead before it lands."

I grinned and slouched in my chair. "So go ahead and make my day, Jack." I drew my finger across my neck in a slitting motion. "You can only play that card once. It won't work a second time."

Ambo stared at me for a long moment, unmoving. The smoke from his cigarette snaked in circles around his head. He jabbed the leg of the upturned desk with a monstrous digit. The ancient metal bent under the pressure.

"Pitt is betraying his country. I know you don't care about that. But he does. And I do. Can you at least tell me why? Why would he do such a thing?"

"Why would he kill Lynn? Why is the moon a rotting hunk of Flemish blue cheese? Fuck if I know."

Ambo ignored this. "He doesn't need the money. I'm a rich man. When I die, all I have is his. He knows that. He's my son. He doesn't need to take money from the goddamn chinks. So what, then? What is going on inside his head?"

"Maybe he got sick of killing people for a living," I said.

Ambo sighed. Smoke leaked from his nose. He said, "Horace. I need your help. No one else knows him like you do."

"What makes you think I'd tell you, even if I knew?"

He ground out his cigarette against the bottom of his shoe, twisting the butt against the heel long after it was extinguished. "Human decency," he said. "You're not an evil person. You feel things. I know you do."

"You know what? You missed your true calling. You should have been a shrink."

He said, "I know your hurt."

"Don't you fucking dare—"

His hands were out, palms open. "We don't have to go there. I'm just saying. It's more than you and me. It's everyone. The entire human race."

I rolled my eyes. "Melodramatic bullshit."

"Melodramatic?" He rubbed the inside of his lower lip with a calloused finger. His eyebrows lowered, casting shadow across his eyes. "Why would you say that?" he said softly. "You think I'm exaggerating?"

He was convinced I knew something. I decided to bluff. Maybe then I'd have some clue what was going on. I said, "Pitt sent me a letter. Told me everything. The whole plan."

The whites of his eyes glowed in the darkness, floating across the upturned desk at me, enormous sockets sucking up the light. "Do you really hate the world so much?"

I shrugged. "Can't say that I'm a fan."

He nodded. His lips puckered in a frown. "No?"

"The world is a vile place and humanity a stinking infection on the face of the earth," I said, suddenly furious. "If you gave me a button and said, press it and the world goes boom? I would do so without a second thought."

Ambo's face drained of color. His eyes took on a

thousand-yard stare. "Would you really? Is that the world you know? Then I feel sorry for you, Horse."

"I don't need your fake pity," I said. "I'm not a fan of you, either. You and your bullshit, trying to steal land from the Bolivians. Not a fan of your double-crossing spy tricks for the good of corporate America. Not a fan of lying and deceit—"

But Ambo was laughing now, a wheezing asthmatic hack, his thin lips pressed tight in a bitter smile. "Here I was, all worried," he said, clutching his sides.

"I know all about it," I said. "Start a war, steal the *altiplano*. Monopolize the lithium. A replay of bat guano. Bat guano two."

He raised an eyebrow. His smirk was insufferable.

"That's it." I banged my petite white fist down on a desk leg. "I know your kind. The smug schoolyard bully. It's about time someone stood up to people like you."

Ambo heaved himself from his chair, and with a flick of his fingers straightened his tuxedo. Fished his Stetson from under the desk, popped it onto his wrinkled scalp. "Get comfortable," he said. "When this is all over we'll get you out of here."

He turned to leave. Randy the marine opened the door.

I called out, "He can't be stopped. You know that, right?"

Ambo poked his bony beak over his shoulder, observed me silently.

"You know Pitt," I said.

His head rose and fell, the steady beating of a funeral drum. "Then God help us all."

I'M PADDLING IN THE SURF BY MYSELF.

The swarm of rats arrive, swimming around me in the ocean, crowding onto the board, climbing up my chest. I look down and a newborn is in my arms, trying to touch my face. I grab a rat by the tail, flick it into the water, but for every one I knock off, three more take its place. I slap at them, punch them, but their claws dig into my flesh, climbing my biceps onto my shoulders. I look down again and the baby is screaming. It's missing its eyes, its nose, its cheeks and then a rat bites down on its neck and the screaming stops.

I bolted upright and crashed my head against something hard. I covered my forehead with my hands, struggled to focus. Major Villega sat beside me on the edge of the wooden bed. *Oh thank God.* I was in jail. That was all. I took a deep breath and let it out slowly. A monstrous pain throbbed in my skull. I must have fallen asleep. It was hard sometimes for me to separate the waking from the nightmares. I could still smell the shit in my lungs.

Villega groaned, stifled an intake of breath and rubbed his forehead. Reached down with his other hand, picked up his officer's cap. Massaged a dirty finger across the copious gold braid.

I swung my legs over the side of the bed, the wooden slats hard on my pelvis. There was no mattress. In the corner, a dark movement. I opened my mouth to scream, but Villega's hand clamped down before the sound came out.

A rat.

He put a finger to his lips. His breath reeked of liquor. I nodded, and he let go of my head. He stepped out into the corridor. He stood in the open cell door, looked both ways. He crooked a finger.

I shook my head. I was happy where I was. I deserved to be in prison. If not for this crime, then for another, one far worse.

"You leave now." He spoke in English. I supposed so that the other prisoners couldn't understand.

I shook my head again.

"You think I want you talk?"

When you've got a cocaine habit like mine, and the pathetic salary of an English teacher that I do, questions of supply dominate your lucid moments. To finance my habit, I had entered the wholesale market, buying by the kilo, selling in backpacker bars to idiot foreigners who were delighted by my cocaine-flavored baking soda.

Villega, like most cops in this town, made more money keeping drug dealers out of prison than he ever would enforcing the law. He offered protection. You worked his turf, no one bothered you. I played dumb. "I don't know what you mean."

"Look," he said. His face was close to mine, the pores on his cheeks erupting like some mutant grapefruit, his breath the stench of liquor and rotting death. "They can shoot me. For this. You understand?"

I folded my arms. "And why should I trust you?"

"It is obvious, no? I don't want you here. Talking. To any-one. About anything."

"Maybe you prefer me dead."

He pursed his lips. A corner of his mouth twitched. "Maybe yes."

I put my head in my hands, closed my eyes. I tried to for-get my dream, but there it was all over again: the blood, the cry, the rats. I couldn't stand it. I had to get out of here. Even if it meant Villega's pistol to the back of my head. *Forgive me, Lili,* I thought. *I am too weak to take my punishment as I deserve.*

"OK," I said. "Let's go."

I stepped out of the cell. Villega grunted, pointed down the corridor. I walked toward freedom. A long row of cells stretched ahead of us, twenty men crowded into each barred room, a symphony of snores echoing along the concrete cell block. I had gotten the special gringo cell. For that, I suppose, I should have been grateful.

A prisoner in the cell next to mine looked up as I passed. A smile tugged at my lips, always a unique sensation, when the world disappeared. I clutched at my face, at the rough wool that covered it—a hood, I realized, trying to pull it off, but Villega yanked me off balance.

"Has to look real," he whispered. "We pretend."

"Pretend?" I said, panting, my breath hot inside the hood. "Or for real?"

His breath came fast and short, his nose at my ear. "Easy

pretend if you think real. Hands behind."

"Villega..."

"Hands behind," he insisted.

I put my hands behind my back. Handcuffs clicked around my wrists.

Villega pushed me and I stumbled along the corridor. A brush of air fanned my face as the heavy metal door swung silently open. He must have greased the hinges; they were rusty and grated noisily when they brought me back from my fecal shampoo beauty treatment.

We turned in an unknown direction, Villega's leather shoes clacking against the tile floors. Fluorescent lights glowed through the hood from overhead. Otherwise I could see nothing.

Another door opened. The smell of vomit and diarrhea filled my nostrils. The kitchen. I had eaten nothing all day. I imagined the prison employed professional vomiters and crappers instead of chefs to produce the slop they served, guaranteed to have a domino effect on their customers.

Villega drove me deeper into the smelly haze. My thigh brushed against a metal countertop. Something furry with toenails grazed my hands. A dog? It was cold to the touch.

An outside door opened, and the cool gazpacho smog of Lima soaked through the hood, caressing my cheek. For the first time ever I was grateful for its foulness. There are varying degrees of hell, I was discovering, and leaving the prison kitchen was a step up in the underworld.

I hoped.

The hood vanished, a magician's trick, and *voilà!* The world again, ready to be loathed anew. I blinked. We stood in an alleyway. Dumpsters overflowing with garbage crowded the narrow passageway. A hiss and a high-pitched yelp. A cat bit down on a rat's neck. Despite not having eaten since yesterday, a sour taste filled my mouth. I choked down the urge to puke.

"Now what?" I asked.

Villega unlocked the handcuffs. "Now," he said, "you go away."

"What will you tell them?"

"Why you no here?"

"No. Why your momma's such a whore. What do you think?"

His face puckered, an angry grapefruit, ruby red. His pores pulsed; a zit oozed pus. A thin sliver of air escaped his lungs. "People disappear," he said quietly. "In this prison. They go away. No one ever knows. What happens. Sometimes we," and he laughed, a bitter chuckle, "we drop them in the ocean. Far out." His laughter died. "Far out."

"Far out is right," I said. "Why not? I don't even know how to swim."

He laughed. "Because you are the Horse! I cannot kill my favorite Horsie."

I frowned. "Why the fuck not?"

He shrugged, a Latin shrug, fingertips backward and skyward. "I am not a bad man, Horse," he said.

My eyes narrowed. Villega? On a charity kick?

"Anyway," he added, as though embarrassed by this admission, "you are innocent. At least of this. You couldn't hurt a fly."

"Depends on the fly," I said. I thought suddenly of the

inmate in my neighboring cell. "But someone saw us. Won't he tell?"

Villega grinned, a great slash through the pores in his orange face. "He say nothing. Or maybe he go disappear. Also."

I looked both ways down the alley. To my right, a dead end. To the left, the street. A car hummed in profile, the ambient city light coating it in a halo of fuzz.

I jerked my thumb at the car. "Friend of yours?"

Villega waddled down the alley toward the car. The cat yowled. Villega's heel had squashed the rat's internal organs.

"He take you to bus station."

I didn't move.

He said, "You don't trust me."

"Should I?"

He opened the back door of the car. "You have choice?"

I got in. All the passenger seats were missing. I sat on a low wooden stool. There was no door handle. What wasn't missing had been replaced with ill-fitting spare parts. I could trace the car's lineage to Detroit in the seventies, but the car was so Frankenstein further identification was impossible.

The driver lifted his head, examined me in the rear-view mirror, resumed his vigil of the empty street. A black woolen hat hugged his scalp, covering his ears. Sunglasses shielded his eyes. His face, though clean-shaven, was unmoving, the muscles in permanent neutral. The engine hummed, rattling the car, interrupted by the occasional clank.

A dirty fist thrust money in my face. The fist connected to a green sleeve, the sleeve to a green shoulder, the shoulder to a neck, and Villega's face.

"Take," he said.

I looked at the money. "What's the catch?" I asked.

"No catch."

"There's always a catch."

"I want you to go away." He shook the money. "Now take."

I took. In the dark the bills felt worn. Probably small-denomination Peruvian play money. I shoved them into the front pocket of my jeans.

"I guess—" I said, but my voice caught. I cleared my throat. "I guess I owe you thanks then, Major."

He leaned into the car, the crown of his head bumping against the roof, a giant jack-o'-lantern hovering in the dark. "You disappear. You get?"

"I get."

"Stay disappear. For you."

I patted his leathery cheek. "For me?"

He withdrew his head from the car. "For me too."

A thump on the roof with his palm, and the car took off, throwing me back against the rusty frame. It was black as night can get in Lima. By accident or design all the streetlights were out. The driver used neither headlights, taillights, fog lights or any other kind of light, inside or outside. He ground through the gears in time to fly through a stop sign.

I held on to the driver's seat and braced myself for impact. "Where are we going?" I shouted over the noise of the wind.

The driver said nothing.

"Bus station, that right?"

Still, nothing.

"Which bus station?"

Lima has half a dozen bus stations. Depends on where you're going, what company you're taking. I tapped him on the shoulder. He overtook a taxi, cut him off, then veered right down a narrow side street.

"First bus out of town," he said in Spanish, his voice an effeminate whisper, as though he were afraid to allow himself more forceful expression.

"Going where?"

He said nothing.

I tapped him on the shoulder again. This time he grabbed my hand, twisted my fingers in a direction they were not designed to go.

"Cuzco."

I folded my arm, then my body in the direction he held my fingers. I could not break his grip. "Anywhere but Cuzco," I said. "I'll give you anything you want. What about Ecuador? Guayaquil's nice this time of year."

Lili's grave was in Cuzco. Where we'd buried the bones. Tombstone and everything. I'd covered the slab in flowers. Didn't do any good.

Cuzco was soaked in memories for me, like a discarded rag stuffed into a Molotov cocktail. I'd left for a reason. I'd sworn I'd never go back.

The man said, "Boss say you go to Cuzco. You go to Cuzco."

"If I don't want to go? If I refuse?"

The driver looked at me again in the rear-view mirror. He smiled. Half his teeth were missing, the others black and rotting. He said, "Break your legs and check you in as luggage."

He released me. I sat back and shook my hand, flexing my

fingers. "Please," I said. "Have pity. Not there. Anywhere but there."

An early morning garbage truck loomed ahead of us, entering an intersection. We ran the red light, horn blaring, missing the front fender of the truck by inches.

The driver said, "Tell it to the major."

I climbed aboard the double-decker bus. It was raining, a rare drizzle in this seaside desert city, just enough to moisten the dust on the windshield and coat exposed skin with a thin glaze of liquid smog.

Villega's money had been enough for the bus ticket and not much more. I'd be lucky to buy a meal or two with the change left over. But for the major, that was generous, and his altruism had me on high alert. Why would he let me go? If he wanted to silence me, he could have just had me killed, like he said. Unless...

Unless they let me go on purpose. Unless they wanted to see where I'd lead them. Was Ambo that desperate? Was I his only clue to where Pitt might be? Yet another reason not to go to Cuzco.

The bottom level of the bus was full. I looked at each face. Dawn broke over the horizon, casting a jellylike orange glow over the brown Indian faces snoozing in their ponchos. I climbed the staircase to the upper deck. More Indians. There were no empty seats.

I was about to get off, proclaim the utter absence of available seating to my inimitable chauffeur below, when a hairy white finger pointed toward the front of the bus. The TV overhead blared the usual Hollywood action drek, dubbed in Spanish, blasting at high volume. Underneath was one open seat.

I grunted. *"Gracias."*

"No problem," the man said in English. He wore a Cincinnati Reds baseball cap. A backpack snuggled between his knees. Yellow earplugs bulged from the side of his head.

I trudged to the front, slid past an old woman who smelled like cheese. I collapsed into my seat. The noise from the television gave me an instant headache. I lifted myself up, looked back. The man in the red cap stared in my direction, unblinking. The engine roared. The bus lurched. I lifted a hand, waved over the top of my seat. His expression did not change.

I FOUGHT TO STAY AWAKE. IT'S A TWENTY-HOUR bus ride from Lima to Cuzco. Sea level to 3400m. I had no cocaine. No cigarettes. No booze. And no way of getting any, either. The only thing I had in my favor was the nonstop racket from the television and the headache it gave me. Thank God for Mexican voiceover actors, who made everything sound like a ridiculous *telenovela*.

Bleary-eyed, burnt-out, waking became dreaming, the nightmares returned, my eyes wide open, the road ahead an endless stream of dust and sorrow, and the day that Pitt betrayed me shoehorned its way into my brain.

It had started as a weekend getaway at their rustic cabin on the coast, but took a number of unexpected turns along the way. Mode of transportation for one.

"Get yourself to the airport, and the rest is on us," Pitt had said. Easier said than done, considering the bastard taxi drivers' union kept the airport fare artificially high. Four hours of local buses later, I finally arrived at the airport with a crowd of janitors and security guards. I made my way to the private departures terminal, where Pitt escorted me onto the tarmac.

"Ain't she a beauty?" Ambo shouted when he saw me.

He threw one arm around me and another at his Piper Mirage four-seater. Leaning against the fuselage, munching a carrot, reclined Lynn, sunglasses covering half her face. Despite the cold and gray, she wore a green bikini, a transparent yellow sarong draped around her waist. The bikini top covered her nipples, but not much else.

She pushed off from the plane, crunched her carrot. "His very own salad shooter."

"It slices, it dices, it purees!" Ambo clapped me on the back. "What do you think?"

"You know how to fly this thing?" I studied the propellers, ignoring the busty ghost in my peripheral vision.

He laughed. "Is oil from Texas?"

We were aloft then, the four of us, a chitty-chitty-bang-bang of the skies, Ambo at the wheel, Pitt his copilot, Lynn and I in the backseat, avoiding knee contact.

"So you're Pitt's mother," I said, turning to her.

"Birthed from these very loins." Her broad lips, thick with red, twisted in a cartoon squiggle. She looked out the window at the long strand of beach below.

"Name's Horace." I held out my hand. "I don't believe we've had the pleasure?"

"I don't believe we have."

Ambo shouted over the roar of the motor, "She's my trophy wife."

"Trophy wife?" I shouted.

"First prize, oil drilling. Picked her out of the catalog. On special, too. Ain't that right, dear?"

She laughed. Her hand squeezed my crotch, and I set my face to frozen. "And me so lonely in that li'l ol' catalog, too."

I tapped Pitt on the shoulder. The hand on my crotch held me tight. "Dude. You never told me your mom's a babe."

"For good reason. Daddy here's the jealous type!"

Pilot and copilot high-fived, and the plane dipped sideways, sending my guts skyward. Ambo put his hands back on the wheel. I swallowed hard. Shifted sideways, sat as far from Lynn as I could, but with her Valkyrie wingspan she clutched my nuts tight in her hand.

The plane landed with a series of bumps in Chiclayo, the biggest city near the surfing mecca of Huanchaco, in northern Peru. A shooting pain stabbed my scrotum. Lynn had shoved a crumpled piece of paper into my jeans. I opened my mouth, let my chin bob with the movement. With my palm, I pushed down on my pants, crushed the paper. I looked out the window, fascinated by a passing windsock.

A security detail waited for us. We caravaned to Huanchaco in three black SUVs. Bulletproof, Pitt boasted.

"Great," I said. "Someone's taking shots at us?"

A shrug. "Doing what we do, we don't make a lot of friends."

The "rustic cabin" turned out to be a beachside mansion. Four enormous Greek columns supported the entryway. My flip-flops echoed on the polished marble floors. A butler in a red Hawaiian shirt and white polyester slacks showed me upstairs to my room.

"Tomorrow's surfing," Pitt said, shoulder against the door frame of my room, watching me unpack the dirty canvas sack I used as luggage. Extra pair of jeans I found in a dumpster. Check. Long-sleeved shirt I hadn't washed in six months. Check. Three soap dishes of cocaine. Check.

He threw a wetsuit on the bed and said, "Eat light, easy on the booze, up at dawn."

"What's this for?" I asked, fingering the neoprene.

"Water's cold out there, man. You're going need it."

I opened the window. The thin white curtain fluttered into the room on the evening breeze. The ocean rolled and crashed against the beach a hundred meters away.

"It have to be so early?" I asked.

The sharp edges of the crumpled note still stabbed at my left nut. I enjoyed the pain. I had left it there. All throughout dinner I had wondered. What did she want? She hadn't looked at me, lifting forkfuls of *seule meunière* to her lips, licking away the creamy sauce with a darting tongue.

Pitt was yammering on about surfing. Could he tell? Did he know? Did he suspect? *Act natural.* I put my right foot on the bed frame, rested my elbow on my knee. What would he think if he found out? He couldn't find out. It had to end. That was the only solution.

"What's that in your pocket? Let me see."

"See what?"

His hand grabs my crotch, pushes me back against the wall. He's got his hand on the bulge now. I'm fighting him off but he's about to pull the paper from my pants, so I knee up between his legs. He bends over. I knee up again, into his face. His nose explodes. He sits back on the bed, and I connect with a left hook to his eye.

"Blame the moon," Pitt said, and grinned, his undamaged, perfect face beaming chaste friendship at me.

I blink. Shake my head. The vision dissipates. Schoolyard nightmares. The peculiar charisma of the schoolyard bully: push me, beat me, rob me: give me more.

"The moon?"

"Tide waits for no man," he said, and punched me in the shoulder. He left the room with an Indian war cry, chopping an imaginary tomahawk over his head.

I went into the bathroom and shut the door. I fished the jagged paper from under my testicles. It was an electricity bill, still in its envelope. On the back, printed in her precise, feminine hand:

the dunes 2 a.m.

I tore it into pieces, again and again, until they were practically dust. *Open lid. Flush. Again. Again. Again.* The toilet was empty, but still I flushed.

I lay in bed staring at the ceiling. It had to end. The choice was simple: her or her son. She was a decent lay, or at least as decent as I deserved. But Pitt...he was a worse human being than I was. Just being around him made me feel better. Which was more important? Sex you can pay for. Listening to Pitt's atrocities was priceless.

No. It had to end.

I stared at the alarm clock. Hypnotized by the glowing red numbers. Every half an hour I got up to renew my dose: snort of coke in each nostril, swig of *pisco* to wash it down.

Two fifteen. I sighed. I got out of bed, went to the window.

The full moon shone on the beach, its weakened spotlight hiding the earth's blemishes. The sand sparkled silver. Palm trees swayed and rustled in the night breeze. A woman walked the dunes, her figure draped in a flowing cotton robe. She moved in slow motion, doing T'ai Chi.

I crept down the stairs barefoot, my flip-flops in hand. I slid my feet into the sandals, stepped out onto the cool sand. She stood on top of a dune, between two tall palms, her feet apart, knees bent, arms out, holding an imaginary ball.

She had shown me some T'ai Chi one drunken afternoon in a filthy motel in Callao. "Let's play with the imaginary ball," she'd crooned from the bed, and leaped naked onto the floor, crunching a cockroach underfoot. It was her way of relaxing when nothing else worked, she had explained, after her screaming subsided and she'd washed off her foot. When drugs and alcohol didn't work, she had purred into my ear, and there's no eligible male nearby, T'ai Chi is all you've got left.

That. Or a bullet in the brain.

I climbed the dune. Put my hands in my pockets, affected nonchalance. I stopped next to her and looked out at the sea. "It's over," I said. "You know that."

Her eyes remained closed. She breathed slowly, lips unmoving. "Security's watching us."

I looked back at the house. A dark shape clung to the roof. Cigarette smoke curled from the window of an SUV parked by the side of the house.

"Good night, then." I put a foot into empty space, launched myself down the dune.

"He's going to take you." The sea murmured on the sand.

The tide was coming in. I could taste the salt spray on my lips. "Like he took me."

I looked up the dune at her. I had the sudden urge to crouch low, stand up inside her imaginary ball. Instead, I scooped up a handful of sand, letting it stream through my fingers.

"Take me," I said. "What does that mean?"

"What he wants, he takes. He wants you."

"Who does? Pitt?"

"Ambo. Look what happened to my husband."

She stood motionless. I squinted at her face. White powder circled her nostrils.

I sighed. "Easy on the dope, alright, Lynn? Ambo is your husband. I'm going back to bed."

Her voice cracked. "I mean Pitt's father."

That stopped me. "What about him?"

"Industrial accident." She pronounced each consonant, her lips hissing, groaning the syllables. "Oil rig."

"What happened?"

Her fingers shook. The imaginary ball was in danger of bouncing free. "Ambo wanted me. So he took me."

"You mean—"

"Yes."

"He murdered your husband."

"Yes."

"And then you *married* him?"

Her breathing came in gasps, no longer the steady meditative breaths of T'ai Chi. "He can be very persuasive," she said. "He decides he wants you, he will take you too."

"What could he possibly want from me?" I laughed. "What am I, Lynn? You tell me, huh?" She didn't move.

"Or you want me to tell you?" I climbed back up the dune, stood in front of her, an unspoken challenge to open her eyes and meet my gaze. "I am a worthless piece of shit. I am scum. I am a drug addict who teaches English to criminals so they can rob tourists. I will most likely die of a drug overdose or a knife between the ribs. And you know what?" I smacked at her fingers with my open hand, but she refused to look at me. "You know what?" I said, growled the words at her. "I don't really give a shit."

Her face quivered. She punched her lips together. Tears dropped from the corners of her eyes.

"Ah shit, Lynn."

I scratched at the back of my head with my nails, wishing I could rip the flesh from my body, my face from my skull, peel back the layers of skin and be faceless, nameless, without body: some spirit. I turned to the sea, as though begging for guidance, but heard only the soft roar of the infinite deep.

"What do you care anyway?" I said. "This is just—"

"Just what?"

I held my hands to the stars, pleading with the Milky Way for answers, but the mute universe cursed me with its silence.

She said, "Who do I have left to love?" A long thread of snot trailed from one nostril. She snorted it back up and swallowed. Tears dripped from her chin.

Love. That word. I bit my cheek, twisted my foot into the sand. "What is that, that I'm supposed to—"

"My husband doesn't love me."

"So what if he doesn't? You think that makes you special?"

"He can't love me. Won't love me." She fought to hold on to that goddamn imaginary ball, eyes squeezed shut, hands shaking wildly, but her head fell to her chest, her face cast in shadow. "He stole Pitt's father from me. He took Pitt. Now he's taking you. Who else is there? What do I have left?"

"Shit and piss," I said. "That's what you got. Just like me. Same as every other goddamn person in this whole fucked-up world."

My flip-flops broke as I tramped back to the house, pounding my feet into the sand to get away from her, away from the thoughts that filled my head. I left the sandals where they fell, more garbage to coat the world, fill the belly of some unlucky whale.

I didn't look back until I had tracked sand all the way up the stairs and into my room. From my perch in the lightless window I looked down at her. She lay on the ground in a heap. The waves crashed loud on the shore, the tide getting higher, higher.

She stood, her bathrobe trailing from her naked limbs. Her hairless body emerged as though from a cocoon. She ran along the sand into the breakers, jumping as each wave hit, the bare cleft between her legs grinding down on the foamy waters. A bigger wave heaved itself over her naked body, and she fell. She did not get up. I waited. Still she did not get up. The water was cold. The current was strong. She would be washed out to sea. She was going to die. I opened my mouth to shout for the security detail, but as my lips parted she crawled onto the sand. She lay there, soaking up the darkness. The waves washed away the sand around her, digging her a hole in which to hide.

I dragged myself into bed. Huddled deep inside my blanket, eyes wide open, wishing myself deep in the bowels of the earth. I snorted a continuous stream of cocaine to ward off sleep. Blood and snot mingled on my pillow. I shivered the night away.

The next morning I was in the bathroom when the door banged open. A purple dawn filtered in past the dark figure blocking the doorway.

Pitt's voice said, "Hey man, ready to hit some killer waves?" Followed by a gasp.

I stood on tiptoe, reached up to undo the noose. A knife flashed in the dark, sawed through the rope that hung from the ceiling. I coughed, struggled to pull up my pants. Failed. Wiped the K-Y off on my shirt. I clawed at the rope around my neck with my clean hand.

"The *fuck*, dude," I said. "Don't you ever knock?"

10

WE SHOWERED AND WERE ENJOYING A COLD
morning beer when the maid announced lunch.

She was a plump little number, firm flesh bulging in all the
right places. Don't fuck with her, Pitt had warned me. She's
security. The tip of her fingernail dug into Ambo's shoulder
as he sat down at the table. He frowned at his empty plate.
Lynn sat beside him, her menthol cigarette trailing smoke
from between her fingers. Did she see the gesture? Sunglasses
hid her face.

Pitt and I had waded into the surf that morning strangers,
and waded out again as friends. He'd made no mention of
my autoerotic habit. I'd tried to raise the subject but he spoke
over me, banishing the theme to the heap of unmentionables.

Meanwhile, every time I looked at Lynn I saw her naked
in the waves the night before. I closed my eyes, but there
she was, twitching in the surf, groping at the sand. I shook
my head, trying to free myself from this vision. I drank deep
from my glass of *Cusqueña*.

"Nothing like a cold beer before noon," I said.

"Except perhaps a second." Pitt grinned. He was topless
again, in jeans and flip-flops. The sun filtered through the

latticed wooden canopy onto our table on the beachside patio. He laughed and slapped his ribs.

I rubbed my damaged side through my crusty brown sweater. I was sweating in the noonday heat, but I didn't want them to see my scars. The injured rib was down low, on the right. I hissed at the pain.

"You hurt yourself?" Lynn leaned over her martini. Her triangular bikini—pink this time—did nothing to hide her rubbery pectoral missiles.

"That's why surfers have flat chests." Pitt's lips were tight, his eyes on Lynn. Perhaps he remembered the smaller glands he'd suckled as a child.

"Well," she said, and sipped from her cocktail, "remind me not to take up surfing."

Pitt put his glass down. "Let's have a look at you."

"What for?" My scars itched under my shirt. Lynn knew about them. Obviously. Pitt saw them this morning when he barged into the bathroom. All the same I didn't want to be their freak show entertainment for the weekend.

Pitt said, "My guess is, it's cracked. Could be broken. We should check."

I shrugged. "If it's broken, it'll mend."

Pitt grabbed the bottom of my sweater and T-shirt, yanked them up to my nipples. My scars cringed in the open air. My ribs bulged like some starved Ethiopian orphan. Maybe I could get UNESCO to send me emergency rations, couple metric tons of cocaine, I thought. I pulled my sweater down to cover myself.

Ambo tipped the omnipresent Stetson farther back on his head and whistled. "Christ, son. Don't you never eat?"

"I'm sorry?" I had been expecting a question about the scars. Had my car crash story all ready to go. The Burn Unit. Intensive Care. Sadistic hospital nurses with fangs and forked tails. You know. The usual.

Ambo patted his belly. "You look half-starved, boy."

Pitt felt my rib cage. His finger traced the injured rib.

"Eating's not really my thing," I said. Did Ambo really not notice? Or maybe he was just being nice. A thumb dug into the bump where the bone had split. I made a noise.

Pitt sat back in his chair. "I got just the thing for that."

"Pitt." Lynn. The voice a warning.

"Herbal remedy, Mother. Purely medicinal."

"Not here. Not now. We have a guest?" She gestured at me with her cigarette.

Pitt shrugged, smacked my rib cage. I opened my mouth but held on to the pain, not wanting to share it.

He said, "You'll live."

I took a deep breath. "Not serious, then?"

"Standard case of surfer's chest."

The maid came out with a pitcher of ice water. Conversation stopped while she filled our glasses.

"*Que tenemos hoy?*" Lynn asked.

"*Ceviche, señora.*" The maid put the pitcher down, studied her fingernails. She twisted her hands behind her back and marched off unbidden.

"Funny how I'm never consulted on the menu, don't you think?" Lynn said in the direction of the ocean.

Ambo put his elbows on the table. Asked me, "You like *ceviche?*"

Pitt came to my rescue. He lifted his glass of beer. "Who

doesn't like a bit of raw fish?"

Ambo laughed, pounded the table with his fist. The crockery trembled.

The maid returned carrying a large platter. Dropped it in the center of the table. *Bang.* She slopped mounds of raw fish on our plates. Could have been a prison matron feeding convicts roach-flecked oatmeal. A bottle of white wine rested in an ice bucket. A flick of her wrist, a deft twist of a corkscrew, and she drowned our glasses in *vino,* until they overflowed onto the table and dripped between the slats onto our toes.

I took a bite of the marinated seafood, a mixture of fish, conch and crab. Ambo shoveled large spoonfuls into his mouth until his cheeks bulged. Pitt poked at his with a fork. Lynn nibbled, a Scandinavian parakeet. I put my fork down, sat back, drank beer.

Ambo swallowed a gargantuan mouthful and belched. He wiped his lips with the back of his knuckles. "Not a fan?"

"Like I said, I don't really eat."

"You must eat something."

I drained my beer and waved it at the maid, who snatched the empty from my hand and sulked off back to the kitchen.

Ambo laced his fingers together, lowered his eyebrows. "You do eat, don't you?"

"Mostly junk food," I said. Eating healthy used to be an obsession. These days, the quantity of cocaine I consumed pretty much numbed all desire to eat. When I did, it was hamburgers, potato chips, Inca Kola. All of which made me feel like shit. Which was the point.

The maid brought me another beer. She slammed it down next to my plate so hard that foam shot from the neck of the bottle, pegged her in the eye. She went rigid, wiped the suds from her eyelid. No one dared laugh.

"Let's get this boy some real food," Ambo said, staring at the maid's firm thighs. He aimed an open palm at her muscular bicep. "Bring out the dips."

Pitt swallowed a mouthful of fish, put a hand in his pocket and drew out a plastic bag and some rolling papers.

Lynn looked at Ambo, at Pitt. "You aren't going to let him toke. Right here. In front of me." She waved her wrist in my direction. "In front of us."

Ambo shrugged, lit a cigarette. "You toke too. Don't be such a hypocrite."

She stood, glared at us. "So now I'm a hypocrite, is that it?"

She finished her martini, and replaced the glass on the table. It shattered with a sharp crack. She studied the broken stem, as though unsure of her own strength, then lay the empty glass down sideways.

Pitt said, "But, Mom, you'll miss the dips."

"I've lost my appetite."

He held up a half-rolled joint. "Got the cure for that right here."

Lynn nearly ran into the maid, who held a large glass punch bowl in each hand, bags of corn chips under each arm. The two women swayed back and forth, a wordless contest to see who would triumph, until Lynn seized the maid by the waist, shoved her to one side and left the patio.

Pitt called after her, "Come on, Mom. Relax. Take a toke already!"

In reply, the sound of slamming doors echoed from the house. Pitt chuckled, shook his head, licked the seam of the joint. There was a momentary quiet.

An earthquake shook the table. The maid had deposited the two punch bowls in front of us. "Guacamole." She stabbed a manicured fingernail at each in turn. "Salsa." She hurled the corn chips between the bowls, as though determined to reduce them to dust.

I liked guacamole. I had told Pitt that once. It was one of the few things I enjoyed eating. That was why I usually avoided eating it.

"You're trying to fatten me up," I said. I scooped a glob of guacamole the size of an apple onto a shard of a chip, shoved it in my mouth.

"Can't have you starve to death, now can we?" Ambo said.

"Worse ways to die," I mumbled around the crashing of the chip disintegrating against my molars.

Pitt put the joint to his lips, lit it, and took a long drag. He held it out to me.

I shook my head. "Not my style."

He exhaled a thin stream of smoke. "Uppers are good. But you're on vacation. You need to relax."

Then why did we bring a kilo of coke? I was tempted to ask.

He nodded again, as though drumming the bass backbeat to an unheard song. He held the burning tip under my chin, the smoke tickling my nose. I took it.

It had been a while since I last toked. Better days, better times. The joint dangled between my fingertips. I could feel the heat. The wet seam hissed where Pitt had sealed it with his tongue. I put the joint to my lips, inhaled.

Burning marijuana filled my lungs. I held it in, feeling the particulate matter stick to my insides. The drug hit me, melting me, a puddle of contentment and hunger. I closed my eyes. I took another hit, and the puddle deepened, and I reclined in the mud bath of artificial happiness.

Opening my eyes, I stepped into the past. A black-and-white past. There I was in the back room of a frying pan factory, a shiny Chinese face bending over me as I rubbed cocaine on my gums. Thick bundles of black hair spewed sideways from his ears. A blue Cubs cap shaded the man's priest-like smile. In my shirt pocket, a thick wad of money. I blinked. A glossy past, not matte. White edges surrounded the vision. My plate glistened in the sun around it.

I picked up the photo. Ambo sat forward in his chair, elbows on the table, a cigarette horn burning at his right temple. His eyelids drooped low, watching me. I turned to Pitt. He sat with his legs crossed, fingering his shark-tooth necklace. He looked at his lap.

"The fuck is this?" I asked.

"Hak Po."

"I know who it is. What's he doing on my plate?"

Ambo didn't answer.

"Pitt?"

He shrugged. He didn't look at me. "It wasn't my idea. I swear."

I flipped the photo across the table. It landed on top of Ambo's *ceviche,* splattering fish juice on his lime-green polo shirt. I dropped the joint in my wineglass. It hissed and went out, a paper fish drowning in Chardonnay.

"We need your help," Ambo said.

"You never thought to just ask?"

His eyelids didn't flicker. "You'd say no."

Pitt sighed. "Dad. Give him a chance."

"A chance to what?" I asked.

Ambo lifted a basketball from under his chair, held it upside down with one large hand. "Help your country. Stay out of jail. Maybe make some money on the side."

"Are you threatening me?" I said. I stood. "Fuck you, alright?"

Ambo raised his voice. "What about your country, Horace?"

"My country?" I said. "Do it for the red, white and blue, star-spangled banner and apple pie *à la mode* watching drones kill innocent women and children, the NSA spying on people, the concentration camp at Gitmo, and you assholes torturing and killing dissidents?" I panted for breath. Pitt's mouth hung open. Ambo didn't move. "Fuck my country," I said. "I've got no country."

Pitt touched my forearm. "Come on, bro. Just listen to him. What he's got to say."

"You part of this bullshit?"

"Honest to God, man. I swear."

"Then what the fuck?"

"Just listen, OK?"

I sat down again. "So talk."

Ambo held the basketball skyward. "Hak Po."

"What about him."

"You buy your coke from him."

"Sure."

Ambo turned suddenly, raised his eyebrows. "Nothing else?"

"Don't need another frying pan."

"Trust him with your life?"

I snorted. "Wouldn't trust him with a glass of milk."

Ambo stood and stretched, his wingspan a reminder of the pro basketball player he once was. He palmed a second ball, held them both out at his sides, a bald black statue, bright orange buoys to left and right.

"Tell him, son."

Pitt swallowed a mouthful of guacamole. He looked at his plate. He cleared his throat.

"Hak Po. Born Lima, 1970. Parents fled Cultural Revolution in China. Moved to La Paz, Bolivia, as a child. Parents owned a corner store. Attended university, La Paz. This is when, we believe, he was recruited by the Chinese Secret Service. On their way to his graduation, his parents died when their bus went off a cliff." He shrugged, not looking at me. "Happens a lot in Bolivia."

The munchies hit me, a pile driver in my gut. Weeks and months of unsatisfied hunger had been unleashed by the unexpected marijuana hit. I pulled the guacamole bowl closer, began eating with both hands.

"So," I said, spitting flecks of food as I spoke, "Hak Po's a spy. So what?"

"He's running agents in Peru," Pitt said.

"I should give a shit, exactly why?" I shoved a mutant double corn chip in my mouth, loaded with pureed avocado.

"Horse, come on." Pitt punched me in the shoulder. "Someone at the mine is selling secrets. Hak Po is the middle man. Production info, important stuff."

"Fucking gooks." Ambo dribbled a ball, let the second bounce free. He faked a jump shot at a nonexistent basket.

His snakeskin boots scuffled against the brick patio deck.

Pitt said, "We need to find out who his contact is."

"You got security at the mine, don't you?"

"Of course." Pitt sat back, scratched his hairless chest.

A bottle of single malt cozied up to Ambo's plate. I cracked the seal and drank from the bottle. "So search all your employees when they leave. That's what they do in diamonds, right?"

"That's—"

"—classified." Ambo crushed the ball between his hands. The ball echoed, a mournful ping.

Pitt grinned. "It has to be one of two people. Australian or Brazilian. Engineering exchange techs."

"Fine," I said. "But what's that got to do with me?"

Pitt scooped a handful of ice from the wine bucket, crammed an empty highball glass full, put it in front of my plate. "Backwash, dude."

"Sorry." I poured liquor into the glass, put the bottle back on the table.

"Suffice it to say," Ambo said, hustling around the empty half of the patio, the basketball in one hand, a cigarette dangling from his lips, "we did not make the same offer to the Chinese."

"These exchange techs. Sort of legal spies, as it were," I said.

Pitt filled another glass with ice. He covered the ice with Scotch. He didn't look at me.

Ambo sat down again, breathing hard, puffing smoke. He rested the ball on his thigh, thick forearm dangling on top. "One of these guys is wearing out his welcome."

I drained my glass. "I know the feeling," I said. "So why don't you just interrogate them both?"

"Because one of them is innocent, Horse," Ambo explained patiently. "It would cause a diplomatic incident."

"So what am I supposed to do about it?"

Pitt pulled a white envelope from the back pocket of his jeans. He opened it, extracted a small white button. He put it down on the table with a soft click.

"Sew this onto your shirt. One with long sleeves. Loose, so it hangs by a thread. Next time you visit Hak Po, let the button fall to the ground, against the wall or under a desk, somewhere dark and dusty. Fisheye lens. Sees everything. Doesn't matter where you drop it."

I picked it up. "Looks like an ordinary button to me."

Pitt grinned. "That's the idea."

I put the button down. "And once you find the guy...this spy...he's going to have an...accident, is that it?" I glanced at Pitt.

He fiddled with his drink. "Something like that, yeah."

I considered this. Listening to Pitt's murders was one thing. Participating was something else entirely. Was I really prepared to go there?

"So that's it?" I said. "That's all you want?"

Ambo scooped up a handful of chips. "That's it, kiddo."

I stood, picked the black-and-white photo out of his *ceviche*. "This picture."

They looked at each other. "What about it?" Ambo said.

"This was taken in Hak Po's office."

Pitt frowned at his single malt.

"You've already got a bug in there," I said. "What do you

need me for?"

Ambo cleared his throat. Pitt held out a warning hand.

"Hak Po's a clever guy," Pitt said.

"That's true." I remembered the first time I'd bought coke from him. My first kilo ever. He'd overcharged me three hundred percent. The next time I harangued him for an hour, until he lowered the price for his "new special customer."

Pitt pursed his lips. "He found the bug. The last one."

"The camera that took this photo."

"Yes."

I narrowed my eyes, looked down at Pitt. He tapped a fingernail against his glass. Again he refused to meet my gaze.

"What happened to the guy who put it there?" I asked.

Pitt drained his Scotch, reached for the bottle. Ambo knocked his hand away.

Ambo said, "We need someone he knows. Who he trusts. Someone he would never suspect."

I lifted the bottle of Scotch. Ambo took away his hand. I filled Pitt's glass until it overflowed, then put the bottle to my lips and drank until it was half-empty, long gulps cascading down my throat. I came up for air, liquid fire churning inside me.

"You haven't answered my question," I said.

"What's that?"

"Why should I help you? Why should I care?"

Ambo fondled the basketball. He bounced it against his chin. "I got to spell it out for you?"

"I was never very good at spelling."

"Alright." Ambo tapped the photo in my hand. "I'm sure you wouldn't want Hak Po to see this picture. Might think you were one of us."

I shrugged. "So tell him." I pushed my chair back from the table. It fell over. "That's all you got, you better think again."

Pitt touched my forearm, almost a caress. "I don't think you understand."

I jerked my arm away. "What's to understand?"

"Hak Po and his people, they will hurt you. They will kill you."

"Great," I said. "Sounds like a plan. You got a phone here I can borrow?"

Ambo frowned. "What for?"

"Find me an undertaker."

Pitt sat forward now, his face contorted in concern. Real or faked? It was impossible to tell. "You know what they did to the guy who planted that camera?"

"Pitt—"

"Shut up, Dad. They broke his kneecaps, is what."

"Why didn't they just kill him?"

"No," Ambo said. "They don't kill you. At least not right away. They understand suffering. They understand pain. Death is too easy. Too simple. They prefer to hurt you in ways you'll never forget."

Pitt took a big gulp of his Scotch. "They don't like being double-crossed."

I looked at him, searching for a sign, some confirmation of sincerity. "Neither do I."

Pitt's lips quivered. His eyes dropped to his lap. "Please, Horse." Were those tears in his eyes? The big bad CIA assassin himself? "I don't want to see you hurt."

"You forgot one thing," I said.

Ambo dropped the basketball in his lap. He bridged his fingertips. "Oh? What's that?"

"A man without his legs can always crawl." I tore the photo in half and dropped it into the salsa. "Closer to the ground where he belongs."

The two of them exchanged glances. Pitt stared at the ground.

"You know, Horse," Ambo said casually, "you're an illegal immigrant to Peru."

Panic stabbed me in the gut. "You wouldn't dare."

"Your ex-wife is badgering the State Department to get you home. Seems you owe back child support."

Red spots filled my vision. "For a kid who isn't even mine!"

He shrugged. "Whoever said life was fair?"

I tipped the table over. Wineglasses, half-eaten plates of *ceviche,* and two enormous bowls of guacamole and salsa smashed to the bricks. Ambo jumped out of the way. I staggered toward the house.

Pitt grabbed my elbow. "It's not what you think."

I threw my elbow back, hoping to connect with his face, but managed only to break his grip. "Then what the fuck is it? This your idea? Pretend to be my friend, then stab me in the back?"

I lurched drunkenly to the door. The maid blocked my path.

"Move your ass, bitch," I said in Spanish.

She put her feet at shoulder width, her arms loose at her sides.

"Three-time Peruvian judo champion," Ambo called out. "I wouldn't fuck with her."

"I told you not to do it this way."

Ambo sighed. "Maybe you were right."

"No fucking maybe, Dad."

"Hey," he said. "Watch the mouth."

"For fuck's sake."

Ambo's finger wagged enormous, the size of a carrot. "I mean it."

"Let me out of here," I said. "I'll take the bus. You and your CIA bullshit can go screw."

I looked around. Swaying. Drunk. Only way out was by the beach. I stumbled toward the brick steps that led to the water.

Something heavy hit me in the back, fell to the ground. "Think fast," Ambo called out.

A manila envelope lay at my feet. I picked it up. "What's this?"

They didn't say anything. I opened it. Wads of US currency. Used bills.

"Benjamins, my friend," Pitt said. "Big BFs."

"How much is in here?"

Ambo leaned sideways on the overturned table. He looked bored. "Twenty thousand. Another twenty after."

I took out the bundle of money. I unbound the packet of bills. It felt like a brick in my hand. I ran toward the edge of the patio, hurled the stack of bills into the air. They travelled a few feet before exploding in a shower of green and black. The sea breeze caught them, carried them fluttering across the beach.

"You think you can buy me?" I said. "Think you can threaten me? Fuck with my head? Send your son, tell him to be my friend? What kind of bullshit is that, man?"

I stumbled onto the beach, looked up at them on the patio. I shouted, "What kind of people are you?"

Time passed. I walked along the beach for ages, but it couldn't have been that long, because when I sat down there were wet hundred-dollar bills on the sand. I picked one up. It was covered in vomit. Who would vomit on all that money? My mouth tasted sour. Furry. The sun blared down judgment from its noontime perch. The waves rolled out to sea, retreating from the earth. I clutched my shins with my hands, rested my chin on my knees.

Sand dusted my toes. I took a deep breath, let it out. I lifted my head, blinked in the sunlight. Pitt sat next to me, legs reclined, resting on an elbow. He twiddled his toes in the sand.

"It isn't what you think," he said.

"No," I said. "It's worse."

"I actually like you, you know. I do."

"So you admit it."

He lifted a handful of sand, let it trickle through his fingers. "At first it was just business." He shrugged. "But then I got to know you."

"For fuck's sake."

"Believe what you want." He sat up. "I told him not to do it. Not this way."

"Why did you go to all this trouble?" I asked. "Why not just blackmail me and be done with it?"

"Would that have worked?"

"Well... No."

"You see? I told him." His hands beseeched the heavens for understanding. "Not the kind of person that you are."

"Quit your ass-kissing and fuck off," I said.

"I'm not kissing your ass."

"Whatever." Another thought. "There must be dozens of people with access to Hak Po's office. Why does it have to be me?"

Pitt scratched an ear. "I've asked myself that too."

"What? I mean, you don't know?"

"I do what the boss tells me. It's not my job to question orders."

"Well you can tell the boss I'm not going to help you."

His head dropped to his chest. A wave crashed into shore. He said, "Alright."

I swallowed. My throat was dry. "Alright, then."

He touched my shoulder with his open palm. "You're an alien species to me, you know that?"

"That's me," I said. "Little green man from Lima."

"I've never met anyone who was so hard on himself."

"How am I hard on myself?" I said.

"You see? You don't even realize. You hold yourself to an impossibly high standard. You hate yourself for a terrible thing that happened to you—"

"Goddammit, don't you dare—"

"—happened *to* you, that was not your fault!"

I rolled onto my knees, climbed to my feet. I walked toward the ocean, Benjamin Franklin's face sticking to my plantar warts.

"You need to move on with your life," he said. His feet slapped behind me. "You hear me?" he shouted.

I broke into a drunken run. He ran after me onto the wet sand. Breakers trickled through my toes. Something sharp bit into the bottom of my foot, a shell perhaps, and I fell to my knees in the thin waves. My hands plowed into the soft sand. The smell of the ocean forced its way into my sinuses, filled my lungs with a purity unknown in Lima.

Pitt dropped to the ground in front of me. "I won't lie to you," he said. "You were a job for me. I admit it. But you've made me rethink what I do and why I do it. You have that affect on people."

"Really," I said. You could spread my sarcasm on toast.

"You had that affect on me." He laughed. "The last dozen dissidents I killed, it took all my self-control to pluck their eyeballs out and chop off their fingers. To let them suffer for days. I didn't even enjoy raping the women. I wanted to put them out of their misery, but those weren't the orders."

"Ambo's orders."

"Yes," he said simply.

The sun was hot on my neck and I felt dizzy. I vomited into the surf. Long choking heaves. I recognized the guacamole, the corn chips, the *ceviche*. The back of my throat burned with stomach acid. I didn't understand what he was talking about. What effect could I possibly have had on Pitt? I scooped up chunks of my vomit, pressed them together to make a mound in the sand.

Pitt slumped down next to me. He rested his elbows on his knees, stretched out his arms to the sea. "Will you do this for me?"

"Do what?" I mumbled, scooping up more vomit for my sand castle. Or was it a vomit castle?

"This one thing."

I jerked my head at the house. A wave broke over my

hands, dissolved my sculpture. More food for the crabs. I said, "What Ambo wants."

He ran a sandy finger across his sunburned lower lip. "Never ask you for another favor."

I hung my head. He was waiting for an answer. What was I supposed to do? What was I supposed to say? My stomach cramped in sour knots. I squinted at the sun.

He lowered his voice. "We can get you a new passport," he whispered. "Even pay your child support for you."

My head jerked sideways. "You'd do that for me?"

"Sure," he said. "What are friends for?"

I nodded drunkenly. "Friends." Is that what we were? I was no longer sure.

Pitt was talking again. "All we need is this one little favor." He held out his fist. It was covered in bits of dry sand, and tanned to a deep brown. It seemed different, harder, sharper than it had that morning in the surf.

He said, "Do it for a bro?"

My head hurt. "For a bro."

"Yes," he said, fist unwavering. "For a friend."

I dug my hands deeper into the sand at my sides. In the year since Lili died, he was the only friend I'd made. And a pretty lousy friend, too. I did not like being threatened or bullied. But if he really could get me a new passport, get me off the hook with my ex-wife, I'd be able to travel again... I had to take that chance. Even if it meant being complicit in the murder of an unknown spy. I said, "You ask this of me, it's the last thing we ever do."

The fist quivered in the air in front of me. "You don't mean that."

I looked at the water as it rushed in to shore, imagined the millions of organisms in a single drop, simple creatures unworried by questions of betrayal, guilt.

I said, "I do."

"Don't be like that."

I shook my head. The fist twitched and fell, limp in the ocean. Pitt looked at the blue sky above us, the departing clouds, the sun burning down on our heads. Back at the house, a thin stream of smoke rose from the patio.

"I need this favor, Horse. Please."

I lay on the sand as Lynn had done the night before. The waves curled around me, digging me deeper into a sandy grave. I closed my eyes, let the sun burn my white skin.

I said, "So be it."

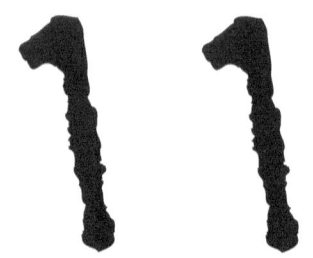

11

FUCK IT, I THOUGHT, AND SLAMMED MY WAY through the front door to Hak Po's factory. *Either I would win my freedom, as Pitt had promised, or I could look forward to the agony of torture and a slow death at the hands of an enraged Chinese spy.* A win-win.

So why was I so nervous?

The bell jangled against the glass door. There was no one behind the counter. Piles of cast-iron skillets lay stacked around the shop, covered in dust. Hak Po manufactured three sizes of skillet. I picked up a small one, the size to fry an egg with, and hefted it in my hand. If things went wrong, it could serve as a weapon.

Voices from the back. They came closer, talking in Spanish. Hak Po's accent, thick and juicy. I put the frying pan down, kept my hands behind my back. I fingered the button attached to my right cuff. Tried to look bored.

"Always a pleasure," boomed a familiar voice, and when Major Villega entered the front of the shop, I knew Pitt had advised me well.

Get there early, he'd said. *Catch Villega in the act. Get yourself out from under his thumb. Get him under yours. Hah!*

"Hak Po!" I bowed my head.

"It is Horse!" The Chinaman shuffled out from behind Villega.

His ear hair had grown since I'd last seen him, inches of curly black luxury, thicker than the hair on his scalp. I had thought him sixty or seventy until Pitt showed me his birth certificate.

Forty-two years old. Too much of the sniff-snort, you know?

Only ten more years and I'd look the same. I could hardly wait.

Hak Po floated across the room in his black slippers. "So please see you!"

"So please see you too," I said.

He took my hand, squinted at me. "We both please see us."

I looked over his shoulder at Villega. "I see you've met my favorite student."

An open yellow mouth, a contorted *O.* "You two know each other?"

Villega cleared his throat. "Horse teaches English. Very good teacher."

Still I held Hak Po's now-limp hand in mine. "You should take my classes too, Hak. Then you can butcher two languages instead of just one."

Hak Po looked back at Villega, then at me. "Friends hard find this town. You two good each other, no?"

I slapped Hak Po on his slight shoulders. "We very good each other. No you worry."

Villega walked to the door. I stepped in front of him, put a palm on his chest. I said, "See you in class tomorrow, old friend?"

I patted his left breast with my right hand, flicked the corner of the manila envelope that protruded from his uniform.

Villega's face narrowed in a leathery orange crease. A cloud of liquor fumes engulfed me. "Of course. Old friend. Tomorrow. So good to see you."

"Don't forget your homework!" I called after him, but the door tinkled, and he was gone.

Hak Po bustled past me, shut and locked the door. He flipped the sign to *Cerrado.* I looked at my watch. Five-thirty.

"You know cop?" he asked.

I shrugged. "He keeps me out of jail."

"Me too. Nice cop."

"Yes," I said. "Very nice cop."

Hak Po glided back behind the counter and the little-used cash register. I followed. He led me along the back corridor into the factory. The workers had gone home, leaving the great cauldrons of liquid iron, stamping presses to cool in the chill Lima air.

He led me toward his office. The spittle-coated floor would be perfect for losing the button without him realizing, I thought.

This time, though, he walked past his office, continued down the narrow hallway to another door.

"Where're we going?" I asked.

"Special place I show," he said, fitting a key in the door. "Where I cook."

I raised my eyebrows. "You cook?"

He held the door open for me. The smells of half a dozen recipes lingered in the air. Cast-iron skillets full of food cooled on the countertops. Cornbread peeked over the edge of a black skillet. A blackberry crumble overflowed from another. A stack of pancakes towered next to the stove. There were omelettes, fried steaks and sausages, even a skilletful of stir-fried broccoli.

"Gotta tell you, Hak. Don't know where you put it all."

Hak Po locked the door. "I like taste. Little bit everything. You hungry?" He fanned his mouth with his fingers, the Latino gesture for "eat." I looked again at the skillets, the piles of food. Each had a small scoop missing from one side.

"No," I said, as he picked up a plate. "You bring Villega here, too?"

He frowned, stabbed a sausage with a long fork, nudged it onto a plate with a dirty finger. "He pig. No feed pig."

Black cabinets lined the walls. The room had no windows, and the only way out was the way we came in. Hak Po had put the keys in his front-left trouser pocket. I adjusted myself in my pants. I could overpower him, take the keys, but if this were a trap, there would be others waiting outside.

"What's wrong with your office?" I asked.

"Insect trouble."

"Insects?" My throat felt raw.

"Bugs." He slapped a scoop of blackberry crumble next to the sausage. "You too skinny. Need eat."

"No hungry." I squeezed his elbow. "I didn't come here to eat, or talk about your cockroach problem."

"Food first. Business later."

I yanked the plate away from him. "Business *now*."

He scooped broccoli onto my plate, clattered a fork on top of everything. "You eat. Understand?"

Hak Po had a reputation. Quiet as a mouse, treat you

right. Pleasant businessman. Ferocious haggler, but nothing personal. Business is business. Just don't cross him. I had never seen him angry before. Now his eyes narrowed, his breathing increased in speed. He was not in a good mood.

But then again, neither was I.

I flung the plate on the floor. It shattered. "I don't want your food, Hak," I said. "You know what I'm here for, so quit your fucking games!"

Hak Po glared at me for a moment. Then he turned back to the kitchen counter. *Round one to the Horse.* He plucked a meat cleaver from a wooden cutting board, unwound intestines from a nearby pot. He chopped the tripe into thin rings.

"How your friend, Horse?" he asked.

I looked at the tripe on the chopping board, trying to identify the animal. I hoped it was cow.

"What friend? Villega?"

"No. Gringo. One came with before."

"Pitt?" I snorted. "He's not my friend. Not anymore."

"This Pitt," he said quietly. "Now him I remember. Think long. Hard. Tell me, what he do you no like?"

Alarm bells rang. How much did he know? How much did he suspect? I found refuge in the truth.

"He's an asshole," I said. "Let's put it that way. And what do you care, anyway? You're a seller. I'm a buyer. We do business. We do good business. What is going on?"

"Why should something be going on?" He raised his voice, as though talking to an unseen audience.

I sighed. "Hak. Dude. You got the coke or not?"

"Oh, coke," he said loudly. "Sure, I get you coke." He skated in his slippers across the tile floor, and took a glass bottle from the fridge. He popped the top off, held it out to me.

A Coca-Cola.

I took the bottle. Looked at it. Smelled it. Took a swig. It was soda, nothing more. I held it out at arm's length and let it drop. It smashed open in a spray of secret formula.

Hak Po shook his head and tsk-tsk'ed. "Terrible insect problem." The meat cleaver dripped intestinal juices onto the floor, mingled with the soda suds. "Lots of bugs."

Round two to the Horse.

"Well then." I put my hand on the doorknob. If he wanted to play games, so could I. "I better go. Let me out of here, will you?"

"Before you go, perhaps you like some sugar in your tea?"

"My tea?"

"I know how much you like your tea."

"Yes," I said. "Of...course. My tea."

Hak Po buried the meat cleaver deep in the grain of the chopping board. He wiped his hands on his apron, reached up to a top shelf. He brought down a large plastic bag. He held it out, presenting it to his unseen viewers. The label declared it to be *ORO DE LAS INCAS AZÚCAR*.

"Perhaps you like try first," he said. "See how sweet?"

I grinned. "Little bit of sugar makes the world go around."

He gave me the bag. "Hold by corner."

"Why?" I said, but complied, pinching the bag between thumb and forefinger. Hak Po fetched the meat cleaver. Before I could protest, he slashed the meat cleaver sideways, severing a plastic corner of the bag, taking part of one of my fingernails with him.

I fumbled to hold on to the bag. He grabbed my belt and

unzipped my fly. I backed away by instinct, but stopped when I felt my horsie resting along the edge of a very cold and very sharp meat cleaver.

Round three to the Chinaman.

"I ask you question now, Horse," he said, looking me in the eye. "You answer true."

I swallowed. "I answer true."

"Friend Pitt spy. America spy. You know this?"

I nodded.

"So why you come here today?"

I opened my mouth. The knife twitched.

"Think careful before you say."

I was risking my cock—for what? "To buy cocaine. Careful!"

A drop of blood ran down into my pants.

"That all?" he asked.

I returned his gaze. "That's all."

"You no lie Hak Po?" he asked quietly. "You no want me make you nice sausage?" Another nick.

I stiffened. "Swear on my dead daughter's grave."

His eyes widened. "A terrible swear." He let go of me and stepped back. "You have dead daughter? What happen?"

I collapsed against the countertop, stuffed myself back into my pants. *Sorry, Lili,* I thought. *A false oath damns a man how many times?*

"I'd rather not say."

He shaved the back of a knuckle with the meat cleaver.

"Say." He frowned. *"Say."*

"It happened in La Paz," I mumbled. "She died." I put the cocaine on the counter and covered my face with my hands.

"It was my fault."

Hak Po listened to me sob. He patted my shoulder. "I believe. Here."

He presented me the bag of sugar. Yay. Enthusiasm. Not. I dug my finger into the bag and shoved it up my nose. What remained of my septum went numb. So did the memory.

I sighed and licked my finger. "That's better. Thanks, Hak."

He bobbed his head, meat cleaver twitching at his side. "Price go up."

"Since when?"

"Exterminators expensive. Cost of business more."

"How much more?"

He smiled. "How much you got?"

I wiped my nose with my forearm. Now was not the time to negotiate. I stuck my hand down the back of my pants, dragged out a bundle of used American twenty-dollar bills. Pitt had given me the money that morning.

"Make sure you kill them all," I said.

"Not just kill." The meat cleaver hung low in his fist. "Exterminate."

He took the money, planted the meat cleaver back in the chopping board, started counting the wad of dirty bills.

I still held the bag in my hand. "Got something I can carry it in?"

"Do some shopping."

He twitched his head toward the opposite kitchen counter. Mountains of food threatened avalanche: kilo bags of white rice, boxes of black tea, powdered milk, canned tomatoes. A roll of plastic grocery bags sat to one side.

Hak Po flicked through the cash. I filled a shopping bag with the assorted goods on the counter.

I held up the bag of coke. "You got tape?"

"By your head," he said, still counting.

Attached to an upper cabinet at eye level was a clear plastic tape dispenser. I ripped off some tape and sealed the bag, nestled it next to the rice.

I fingered my shirt cuff. Hak was counting the money a second time. Was it worth the risk?

Come home without planting the bug, dude, and you're on the next plane back to the States. Drop a button, win a prize! Pitt laughed at that. *Carrot and stick, dude. I know it sucks. Don't blame me. This is Ambo talking.*

"Been a while I see you," he said. "Where you get money?"

The kitchen floor was clean. It gleamed with a recent coat of wax. The button was white, the floor black. There was nowhere to hide it.

"Rich uncle I know. Name of Samuel."

He cocked his head to one side. "Samuel. That funny name."

I pinched the button and stray thread, yanked.

"Isn't it, though?"

I coughed, dropped the button to the floor.

Hak Po deposited the money into a hidden pocket of his apron. He looked at the floor, up at me.

"You drop something."

"What I drop?"

He walked over, poked the button with his shoe. "You drop button."

Think fast. I checked my shirt. "Isn't mine."

"No?"

He ran his fingertips along my shirtfront, touched the collar, lifted my wrists, turning them to show the buttons. He grunted.

"Paranoia, dude," I said.

"Paranoia good for business."

Hak Po knelt and scraped the floor with the meat cleaver. He lifted the button to eye level, the edge of the cleaver an inch from my nose.

"Better you take button with."

He held the cleaver there, the thin line of the knife dividing his eyes from the rest of his face. He held my gaze, his eyes unwavering, studying mine. Tripe juice dripped on my shoes.

I laughed. "Don't know what your game is, dude, but I ain't taking what ain't mine."

The blade touched the tip of my nose. He frowned. "Really not you?"

I shook my head. "Really not me."

Hak Po stood straight, lowered the cleaver. The frown, however, stayed intact. "Someone else, then."

My head bobbed of its own volition. "Someone else."

We looked at the button resting on the side of the meat cleaver.

"Better throw away," he said.

He walked over to the sink and turned on the faucet, flicked the switch for the garbage disposal. The room filled with the growl of that insatiable mechanical demon.

"Wait." I crossed the room, caught the button as it slid from the cleaver, my hand over the gaping maw of the garbage disposal. "Don't you want to know who put it there?"

Hak Po shut off the disposal, turned off the water. "What you mean?"

"Maybe it's a test. See if you'd notice."

"I notice. You see I notice."

I shrugged. "Maybe another customer. If you didn't notice, then they'd plant a real bug."

His eyes bulged from his head, his jaw clenched. "Find them."

"Yes."

"Who did it."

"Yes."

He went back to the wooden chopping board, seized the tripe and in great strokes slashed at the intestines, cleaver high overhead, thunking down onto the wood.

"Find them. Hurt them. Teach them."

"Teach them, yes."

"Not to—" *Thwack!* "—fuck with—" *Thwack!* "—Hak—" *Thwack!* "—Po!"

I pulled a piece of tape from the dispenser, pressed the button to the sticky side. I held up the tape for him to see.

"What you do is this."

I pressed the tape to a cupboard at eye level, just over the stove. The white button stood out as a blemish against the surface of the black cupboard.

"Yes," Hak Po said, slammed the cleaver into the wood. He slapped me on the back. "We teach them lesson."

"Wait for the guilty face."

"The guilty one, yes." His arm was tight around my shoulder.

"See guilty face," I said. "Hurt guilty face."

I winked at the button. Hak Po saw the movement.

"You OK? Want some drops? I got drops. Drops right here."

"It's alright. Just something in my eye." I rubbed it with my finger. "It'll be fine. I should get going."

He pointed at the mess of food and soda on the floor. "But you eat nothing, Horse!"

I rubbed my stomach. "Not so hungry."

Hak Po shrugged his shoulders. "Insult chef. See I care."

"You know how it is."

"Too much snort-snort. Not good for you."

I scratched my nostril. "Never said it was."

Hak Po escorted me through the factory, past the presses and the cauldrons glowing orange, back to the dusty shop. He unlocked the front door. Held out a hand.

"Always pleasure do business with honest man."

I shook his hand. It was dry and leathery, as though the entire covering of skin was about to peel. I tried to smile, but the muscles refused to obey.

"What would I do without you, Hak?"

He inclined his head, and I stepped into the street. The evening darkness accumulated on street corners, and against the graffiti-stained walls. The damp smog cloaked me in welcome pollution as I walked down the street. A black-haired woman emerged from the sooty mist. A well-dressed *limeña*. Must have been a beauty once. Now prematurely aged. My stomach revolted, and I bent over, vomited on her shoes, remnants of yesterday's junk-food binge coating her elegant patent-leather flats.

The woman gripped her purse tight. "Think I'd fall for

that?" She stepped around me, marched off down the street, heels retreating. I sat there on my hands and knees for a long moment, the grocery bag at my side. The heels came clacking back. An explosion of pain made me double over. She kicked me in the stomach a second time, this time connecting with my still-broken rib.

"Asshole," she hissed.

Evening commuters stepped over me where I lay, another Lima bum. When rush hour was over, I got to my feet, clutching the grocery bag at my side. At the corner I hailed a passing mini-bus. I jumped the turnstile, thrust a few stained notes in the driver's direction. He cursed me for a gringo dog; I told him his mother was of dubious moral virtue. I squeezed down the narrow aisle and sat on the wheel hump. I ignored the grim faces of the other passengers, each intent on his own losing struggle with life.

From time to time I looked out the back window. When the bus ground to a halt in the middle of downtown traffic, I hopped off. Outside a hotel I spotted a cab rank. A well-fed American with a double chin stood holding a door open. He wore a plaid check suit and a large Panama hat.

"I don't care if you're fucking the bellboy, honey, got to hurry now, or we'll miss our flight!"

I ducked under his arm into the back of the cab, fished a fifty-dollar bill from my rotting jeans, held the money over the seat to the driver. He grinned.

"Where to?"

"Miraflores. No rush."

The cab rolled forward, pulled free of the man's hand. He shouted after us, ran a few steps, arms gesticulating like some kind of a puppet. The last I saw of him, he was resting his palms on his knees, panting for breath. The driver looked at me in the rear-view mirror.

"You in hurry."

"Just drive."

When we started the slow crawl down Avenida Larco, I checked over my shoulder. No tail that I could see.

I draped an arm over the front seat. "Parque Municipal, Barranco."

The driver held up the note I'd given him. "Don't expect no change, then."

"From you? It'd be counterfeit."

The cab dropped me off at the park.

"Fuck you and your mother," he called after me.

I slapped the roof of the cab. "Please forget to use a condom."

He peeled off, the muffler belching a cloud of dark gas in my face. I took a deep breath, held it, let it out in a long thin stream. Almost as good as a joint.

I strolled along the disco strip, past the whores and the pussy-collecting gringo tourists, until I came to the Rat's Nest. In the basement bar I ordered a *Cusqueña Dark*. I paid the bartender, surveyed the room. I had met Lynn here. The beer was cold and sweet. In a corner, a gringo slouched in a chair facing the television. A bullfight flickered on screen. The gringo wore a black baseball cap pulled low over his eyes. I walked over, sat down opposite.

"Didn't know you were a Pirates fan," I said. "They teach you that in spy school? Wear a baseball cap, no one's going to notice?"

Pitt sucked on his beer, wiped his lips with the back of his hand. "So how'd it go?"

"You play this stupid game. Hurting people. Risking lives. Killing, raping, torturing. For what? The Lincoln Memorial and 'God Bless America'?"

He lifted his eyes to the bullfight. The *banderilleros* had done their job well. The bull bled from the hump, its head lowered. The matador reentered the ring, sword in hand.

"You never think that what you do is wrong?" I asked. "Oh wait. I forgot. You don't have a conscience. How convenient."

In the dark of the barroom, I almost thought I saw him blush. His eyes did not flinch from the screen.

"It went OK, then?" His voice was calm, resolute.

I finished my beer. I lifted my hand, snapped my fingers at the bartender. "Another one?"

"You're still alive. Guess Hak Po didn't catch you, huh?"

I held up two fingers, pointed at Pitt. The bartender nodded. He put two beers on the bar, cracked the lids with a bottle opener, brought them over. He stood at our table, looking down at us, an ominous presence, judgment day come early.

"Your turn, dude," I said.

Pitt frowned. He arched his pelvis, pulled a wallet from his front jeans pocket.

"No," I said. "I mean my fucking passport. And the bank account you promised?" Enough to pay for sixteen years of child support.

Pitt fished out some play money, paid the bartender. "We need to talk about that."

My grip on the beer bottle tightened. The bartender glowered at us, as though charging us with centuries of crimes against his people. Finally he left.

"What's there to talk about?" I hissed. "You promised!" Panic bubbled inside of me like lava.

The matador lifted himself on tiptoe, sighting down the blade, the sword hilt held high, point low.

"First things first," he said. "Did you have any trouble?"

"I planted the fucking button, if that's what you mean." I took a long swig of my beer. "He knows you're a spy, by the way. Almost cut my dick off with a meat cleaver."

Pitt dipped his finger in the condensation on the table, doodled. "Yeah," he said. "I know." He added, "Sorry about that." Almost shyly.

"How do you know that?"

He held up a PDA he'd been watching under the table. It showed a button's-eye view of Hak Po, cleaver in hand, singing to himself in Chinese, obliterating what remained of the tripe.

"You watched the whole thing?"

"You were awesome. 'Find guilty face.'" Pitt smiled, sipped his beer. "I nearly pissed myself."

I aimed the bottom of my beer bottle at the ceiling, emptied it down my throat. I picked up my grocery bag, pushed back my chair.

I said, "I'll take what's owed me now."

He plucked at his lower lip. "Ambo wants to use you again, for another op."

"Is that how it is?"

A shrug. "Blackmail starts, it never ends."

"It ends with me." I pulled out a kilo bag of rice and flung it at his chest. White grains exploded across the table and the floor. "Fuck you and Ambo both."

"C'mon, man. Don't be like that." His voice crooned, the insistent softness the best salesmen possess, the vocal tremolo that coaxes the wallet from your pocket and the panties off your girlfriend.

The bullfighter and bull came together in a sudden desperate act of lust: the sword penetrated through the hump, deep into the beast's body, into its heart, two primal creatures united for a fleeting instant in an act of ferocious love.

I shook my head. "I told you on the beach. We're done. Goodbye."

The bull stumbled. It spun in a half circle, looked at the crowd in astonishment, and collapsed, hooves twitching. The matador held up his open palms in triumph. I pounded my way to the door, my flip-flops slapping against the wooden floor. Footsteps behind me. A hand on my elbow. I bent at the knees, turned and slammed my fist upward into his stomach.

Pitt doubled over. He opened his mouth. He took a breath.

"I deserved that," he said.

The bartender stood watching us, a tea towel in one hand, a half-dried beer mug in the other.

"Yes," I said. "You did."

12

I WOKE SCREAMING FROM MY NIGHTMARE. THE old lady next to me on the bus smacked me in the face with her handbag. It smelled like moldy cheese.

"*Gracias,*" I said. "I needed that."

Withdrawal raged inside me, an empty hole demanding to be filled. I stared out the window at the gorges below, tried to remain calm. The bus crept its way along the side of the cliff. The television blared crash-bash-smash directly over head. In the window's reflection I could see the man, the beak of his red cap lifted in challenge.

This whole thing pissed me off. Bastards let me go, why? Just so they could follow me? They think I knew where Pitt was? Was that it? *Let Horse run. But keep him on a leash, see where he takes you.*

I looked over my shoulder. There he was, the red cap perched on his head, flecks of hair sticking out over his ears. He stared back at me, unflinching. The man sitting next to him got up, went downstairs to the lavatory. I lurched from my chair, stepped across the old woman. The cheese smell lingered in my clothing. I walked three rows back and dropped into the empty seat.

"So you're a spook," I said.

"Sorry, what's that?" He removed an earplug.

"I said, you're CIA."

He looked puzzled. "You mean like a spy or something?"

I pointed ahead at my seat. "Following me. Watching me. Looking at me all the time."

He laughed. "You got the wrong man."

"I don't think so."

"Sounds to me like you're paranoid."

He reached up to put the earplug back in, but I knocked his wrist away.

"Then what are you—" I shouted, lowered my voice as heads turned. "What the fuck are you doing staring at me?"

A long arm pointed in the direction of my seat.

"Exactly," I said.

The arm didn't waver, finger extended. He pointed at the television over my seat. Some kind of shootout was in progress. Its relevance to the plot was tenuous.

I let go of his arm. "Then what are you going to Cuzco for?"

"What do you think?"

"I'm asking you."

"Take the train to Machu Picchu. Hello?"

"Disculpe, amigo. Está en mi puesto," said a voice from the aisle. A *campesino* in a green poncho tapped me on the shoulder.

I cleared my throat. Stood up. "Sorry," I said. "Don't know what to say."

Red Cap tapped the side of his nose, winked. "Go easy on the white stuff, eh?"

***

The road wound in hairpin turns through the mountains. The movement helped keep me awake. I maintained my vigil all day long and into the night, the curtains propped open with my foot, staring at the barren, ugly scenery of Peru, unchanging for hours on end. The front wheel of the bus crunched against the gravel verge, sending rocks tumbling over the cliff. If I was going to die here, the bus jumping off the highway into a brief pause before death came, I wanted to be awake to experience that momentless twitch of eternity.

Just when I thought I couldn't keep my eyes open any longer, the bus pulled off the road at a small restaurant in the middle of nowhere. Chickens clucked and scattered in the headlights as the bus came to a halt. My ears popped. The driver stood and announced a meal break. A concrete hovel squatted under the glare of a solitary streetlight. The old woman beside me got up, joined the stampede down the stairs and out the door into the dirt at the side of the road.

I waited. Now was my chance. Villega put me on the bus, but he sure as hell couldn't keep me on it. I patted the volunteering office's brochure in my pocket. The police had confiscated my switchblade and fake passport. Somehow I had to get to Puno and Lake Titicaca. Cross the border into Bolivia. It was the logical next step in my search for Pitt. But there was no reason I had to go through Cuzco to get there.

I stood. Red Cap was heading down the stairs. He took an earplug from his ear. He said in a voice louder than necessary, "Come grab a bite?"

"Do so at your own risk," I said.

"It's OK," he said, and laughed. "I got my dehydration salts with me." For diarrhea.

"Well that's a comfort," I said.

I followed him off the bus. The driver was waiting for me. He locked the door, pulled me aside.

"Don't go wandering off, friend," he said. "They asked me to keep an eye on you."

"Who did?" I said. "Who's they?"

He shrugged. "Who knows? Who cares? For that kind of money I'd fuck my own mother. Now eat something. It's another twelve hours to Cuzco."

"Twelve hours?" I said. "We've already been on the road for fourteen."

"You don't like it, complain to the bus company," he said, and walked off, chuckling under his breath.

I meandered into the small restaurant, past walls of dusty bags of potato chips. Cigarettes filled plastic display cases. I could kill for a smoke, but I only had fifteen *soles* left. The smell of charcoal meat filled the room from a grill just outside. There were no windows, just holes in the walls. It was cold at this altitude. Skewers of meat sizzled over the coals. *Anticucho.* Grilled beef heart. Tough as shoe leather, and less tasty. I dropped my last coins into the vendor's hand and he proudly held out two sticks of half-burnt, half-raw meat.

The passengers milled around outside the restaurant, smoking, drinking beer, masticating their *anticucho.* The bus would be here for half an hour, at least. I wandered through the crowd, making a point of being seen, the sticks of *anticucho* in one hand, my jaws grinding away at the big ball of meat in my cheek. I could hear the people gossip about the shabbily dressed gringo who smelled bad.

When I was sure the bus driver had seen me, I clutched my stomach and rushed off to the side of the road, just beyond the glow of the light from the restaurant. I spat out the meat and stuck my fingers down my throat. Gagged loudly. Sounds of disgust. Another gringo with a delicate stomach.

I crept farther from the light. No one followed. I jogged off for a few hundred meters, fell back to a walk. Talk about not being in shape. Thought I'd have a heart attack. I rounded the bend in the highway until I was out of sight of the diner. A pair of headlights approached from where I'd just come. A car. Perfect. I stuck out my thumb. Maybe I'd get lucky.

The car got closer. White with stripes. Lights flashed on the roof. *Shit.* I dropped my thumb. The car rolled to a halt beside me. The cop shone a flashlight in my face, blinding me. He said, "Get in."

"What for?"

"Get in the fucking car, jackass."

I walked around. Got in the front passenger seat. Just to piss him off. Something big and shiny flashed in the cop's hand. My eyes were still adjusting from the brightness of the flashlight, and I heard him cock the revolver before I realized that's what it was. He pointed it at my head. Pressed the cold metal opening against my temple.

"Here's the deal, cockroach," he said. "You get back on the bus. You stay on bus. Is that clear?"

The man stank. Worse than I did. Moonlight slashed the windshield. He was Indian. Quechua, Aymara, who knew. Not that it mattered. Under the Incan Empire he would have been an enforcer for the king, strangling dissidents with his bare hands—someone like Pitt—or cutting throats in blood-thirsty rituals to the sun god. Now he was a little man who wished he lived in Miami and got to shoot people for a living, like he saw on TV.

"Why are you people so goddamn obsessed with me going to Cuzco?" I asked.

"I do what I'm told, gringo," he said. "So should you."

He returned the gun to its holster. Swung the car around and drove back to the restaurant. He parked behind the cin-der-block hovel. That's why I hadn't seen him. *Note to self: check behind hovels for cops during bus trip meal breaks.*

"Can I ask you something?" I said.

He kept a hand on his gun. "That depends."

"Are you with the CIA?"

The man stared at me. "Do not make fun of me, grin-go," he said. He poked my broken nose with his index finger, cocked his thumb.

I flinched. "Then how did you know?"

"Ah," he said. "I see. I know a friend of yours."

My chest tightened. A friend of mine? No way he meant Pitt. I said, "Who would that be?"

He pulled out a toothpick, flecked orange chunks from between his teeth against the inside of the windshield. *"La policía.* In Lima. I do him a favor, now he owes me." He turned to me in the half light and I gasped. His nose was missing. Syphilis? Wild dog? Who knew. He saw my reaction.

"Now get the fuck out of here."

Back on the bus, Red Cap said, "Have some trouble with the cops?"

"Yeah," I said. "Wanted to know what you were up to."

He grinned. "You tell them?"

"Sure," I said, and shrugged. "But they didn't believe me."

The bus crept toward Cuzco in low gear, grinding up the unforgiving mountain roads. I peered over the safety bar at the driver's speedometer. It rarely exceeded forty kilometers per hour. Part of me wanted to get there already. Another part wanted the trip to never end, to never have to set foot in Cuzco again.

For a brief moment, I had been happy there: a new life, my dream come true.

Then a single act of recklessness destroyed it all.

The day I met Kate she was bitching about her ex-husband. How much she loathed American men.

It was hate at first sight.

"Bunch of effeminate wusses. I want a man, not a fucking mouse. Hello. What's your name?"

I lurked at her side, a beer in my hand. We were at an expat barbecue in Cuzco. I liked the town. Liked the vibe. Wanted to open a hostel, have some fun. All those horny Eurotrash backpacker girls? New pussy every week. It was great.

"Squeak squeak," I said. "Squeak squeak."

"Oh I'm sorry," she said, and crossed her arms. "Did I offend you?"

"You couldn't offend me if you tried." I put my arm around her waist, whispered in her ear. "Name's Horace. But people call me Horse. As in hung like a."

She glanced at my waist. "Are you really?"

"Wouldn't touch you with it, though, bitch. Fucking American cunts."

I laughed, and the other men at the party chuckled uncomfortably.

That got her attention. "Why do you hate American women so much?"

I drank my beer. It tasted good. "Why do you hate American men so much?"

We were in bed together before the sun went down, and stayed there until well past noon the next day. She cancelled her plane ticket home. We opened the hostel together a month later. Talked about getting married. I even quit sleeping around.

She teased me about it. "All the girls are jealous," she said. "They want your horsie. Don't they try to seduce you?"

"Sure they do," I said. "But we're together, you and me. That would be wrong."

"Even if you knew I'd never find out?"

I nodded gravely. "Even then."

She never went on the pill. Don't know why. Never really talked about it much. Problem is, condoms don't fit me too well. Even the extra large is a bit on the small side. One day a condom broke.

"I could get pregnant," she said.

"That's OK," I said quickly.

She seemed surprised. "You sure?"

I had spent two years loving a child that wasn't mine. It was hard letting go. I wanted back what I had lost: a new wife, a new home, a new family.

I stroked her back. "Sure," I said. "I don't mind at all."

Business boomed. We had to hire staff. Kate missed her period. Then another. Then another. And one day a baby popped out, and it was the most glorious day of my life. The gods who I had so long thought malevolent were smiling on me once again. I felt like I should sacrifice a small animal—a guinea pig, or maybe a chicken—by way of thanks.

Maybe I should have.

Lili's grave called to me through time and space, an accusation hurled across four dimensions like a thunderbolt of Zeus himself. I longed for a lit cigarette, a lighter, a razor, something to alleviate the pain. I was reduced to giving myself paper cuts with my bus ticket. And failing.

Dawn came again, a brilliant smear across the windshield. Made me squint. Two hours later we rolled into Cuzco. At the station, the Indians and backpackers scrambled to get off. Twenty-six hours locked in a double-decker bus with one overflowing toilet? Six hours more than scheduled. By then I wanted to get off, too. I stepped down the stairs into the early morning sunshine. It was cold, but warming fast. I put my hands in my pockets by instinct to ward off pickpockets, but realized I had nothing to steal. Or spend, for that matter.

Despite the cold I was sweating. Colored spots swam across my vision. My brain felt like it was melting. My limbs trembled under my sweater. I needed money, cocaine and *pisco,* in that order. And fast.

I looked around me. Things hadn't changed much since Kate and I were here. That had been, what? A year ago? I sighed, plastered my don't-fuck-with-me frown across my face. An essential accoutrement for the Cuzco experience. I hoped I wouldn't meet her here. Those were happier times.

The other passengers were engaged in a scrum for their luggage, then a mad dash for a taxi. I didn't have any money, so I decided to walk into town. A block or two along Avenida del Sol, Cuzco's main thoroughfare, a voice called after me.

"Hey, wait up!"

Red Cap chugged up behind me, full backpack swaying from side to side. I walked faster. He panted, trying to catch up, the air thin at this altitude.

"Where you going?" he called out.

"Where you think?"

"I come with?"

I about-faced. He jumped on tiptoe to avoid crashing into me. "No."

He hooked his thumbs under the pack straps, struggling to get his breath. Before he could say anything, I crossed the street. A taxi blared its horn, just missing me. Red Cap shrugged, held out a hand in salute. Another taxi stopped, and he got in.

At the Plaza de Armas I turned left on Calle San Juan de Dios, ducked right on Calle Meloq, and walked up a steep hill. I panted to a halt in front of an ancient stone building. The sign over the door proclaimed it the Hostel Thor. A car door slammed shut behind me. Red Cap got out and puffed up the hill. He entered a cheap hotel farther down. I dove into the hostel. It was early afternoon. A dozen backpacks sat by the door, waiting for their outbound owners. The lobby was quiet.

"Buenas tardes. En que puedo servirle?"

A German girl talked Spanish at me. She had dimples in her cheeks and blue ribbons tied in bows around her braided hair, a prize pig at the county fair. Her breasts hung heavy, braless. I ignored her. I lifted the countertop, went behind the desk.

"What are you doing?" she asked in English.

I took the cash box from under the counter. I spun the key and opened it.

"*Scheiss,* what the fuck?"

I lifted the false bottom of the box.

"Alex!" she shouted. "Al-*EX!*"

"Yeah!" came the distant male reply.

"Call the police!" She stood in the far corner, clutching a pen like a dagger.

"Shut up, bitch," I said. I flicked through the money, a mixture of US dollars and Peruvian play money. I rolled the money into a tight cylinder, shoved it deep in my jeans pocket. I put the tray back in the cash box, closed the countertop behind me.

"You can't do that!" she screamed.

"I just did."

Footsteps ran along the corridor, slapping against the stone floors. A red face and crew cut appeared.

"That is him!" the German girl yelled. "Right there!"

He was six foot tall. Six foot two and a half in socks, to be precise. He ran at me, his broad chest aimed at my face. I braced for impact. He grabbed me in a hug, squeezed me to his chest, thumped me on the back. I beat my fists against his ribs until he let go.

"The fuck, man?" he said. "It's been how long?"

The German girl stared, her heavy Teutonic tits sagging. "You know this guy, Alex?"

Alex slapped me on the back. He put his arm around my shoulder. "Berta, baby, this guy owns a third part of the hostel."

"Guess that makes me your boss," I said.

"What's up, man? You need a place to crash?"

"Crash is right."

Alex went to the girl, caressed her bare arm. He kissed her cheek. "It's cool, baby. Clear the honeymooners out of the presidential."

"Please don't do that," I said.

"You deserve it, dude. You built this place from scratch, remember?" He jerked his head toward the hallway. "Come into my lair." He laughed. "I mean, your lair."

The hostel was a three-hundred-year-old stone mansion. It had seen its share of Latin-chanting monks and sword-wielding Spaniards, plus the usual assortment of Indian slaves, North American vagabonds and cocaine addicts. Kate and I had bought the place from a company that wanted to demolish it.

The building was structurally sound but otherwise a pigsty. Literally. We'd sold the swine and shoveled out their slop, laid new wooden floors in the rooms, built the kitchen, transformed it from nothing to something in a month flat. Alex was our first hire, and the only one who showed any real interest in the business. When things went bad between me and Kate, we sold him a third share in the business, let him manage the place.

Alex sat down behind my old desk, pulled open a drawer.

He took out two water glasses and a bottle of *pisco,* filled the glasses half-full. He held out a glass. I took it.

He said, "Kate's the same, you know."

"How's that?"

"Doesn't want me to send her money." He shook his head. "Your share is yours. I ain't gonna touch it. Every month it goes into the bank."

I drank the glass of *pisco* and coughed. "Keep it," I said, and wiped my lips with the back of my hand.

Alex put his drink down untouched. "You mind I ask?"

"Of course I mind."

"You're in trouble."

"You fucking think?"

Alex whistled. "You are wound up tight."

I poured myself a second glass, full this time. "Year in Lima does that to you."

He put his hand on top of my glass. "Easy, bro. It's not your fault."

"Why does everyone keep telling me that?" I drank from the bottle. "Of course it's my fault. Everything's my fault. The whole fucking world."

"What happened to you could have happened to anyone."

"But it didn't, did it? It happened to me. And I am dealing with it. And right now," I said, and took his hand by the wrist, removed it from my glass, "right now I need a favor."

Alex rocked in his chair. It creaked. "Shoot."

"Need a train ticket. Machu Picchu. For tomorrow."

He blinked. "In high season?"

"Know where I can scalp one?"

Alex sipped his *pisco,* grimaced. "Machu Picchu's not your

thing. Never was."

"It's not a tourist visit."

He nodded. "How much you willing to pay?"

"How much I got?"

"From petty cash?" He gnawed his lower lip. "Around five hundred US. Enough."

I put my glass down empty. "You make it happen?"

"Sure, man. Whatever. I'm always here, you need me."

Why had Alex and I never become friends? We had worked together. Liked each other. He was a good guy. He could have been the friend I needed. Maybe it was Kate. She was jealous of everyone, male and female. Oh well. Too late now.

I stood. "I got a little thing I got to do."

"Sure," he said. "What's going on?"

"Nothing." I avoided his gaze. "Just a thing. I got to do." I stopped, bit my lip. "That is—"

"Of course." His open hand: say no more. "Remember how to get there?"

I halted, my hand on the doorknob. "How could I forget?"

My flip-flops smack-smacked against the worn bottoms of the hallway's ancient flagstones, deep bowls of sorrow and longing, puddles of lost youth: long-dead adventurers now dust. The dark corridor vomited me forth into the modern computerized lobby. I waved to the Saxon princess, shot out into the bright mountain air.

I humped my way down the hill, past the Plaza de Armas, past the touristy restaurants and the street vendors selling crap. I walked out of the center into the slums that surround Cuzco, corrugated tin hovels sheltering small brown faces embedded with impossibly bright eyes. The hovels got smaller and filthier the farther I got from the center.

Then I was there.

A rotting wooden fence like a corral served as the cemetery boundary. I found what I was looking for in the corner. Someone had dumped a pile of garbage on the grave: decomposing banana peels, eggshells, bits of broken glass, decayed chunks of llama offal.

I scraped it aside with my foot. The gravestone lay flush with the earth. I knelt. Cleaned the crude stone with the palm of my hand. Bits of glass cut my skin. I relished the pain. The stone read:

Liliana Mann
Daughter of
Horace Mann & Katherine Bittre
Forgive Us If You Can

I waited. Nothing happened. I had feared this moment for so long. Avoided it at all costs. I hadn't been here since the funeral, and I don't remember that day, I was so drunk, so high...

What did I expect? Her ghost to rise up in a translucent cloud of ectoplasm, and curse me in the incoherent babble of a six-month-old? Or do dead infants develop the capacity for speech in the underworld?

The smell of garbage rose thick in my nostrils. A light breeze ruffled my hair. Still nothing. *Was this all there was?* A rectangle of fake granite and tiny limbs decomposing six feet beneath me? Or maybe that was it. Nothing more. *A bit of sky and sunshine is all we have,* I thought, *and when we disappear underground it is forever.* I wished I was with her. I'd be joining her soon enough. I took the picture from my pocket, put it away again. I wanted to cry. I had tried to cry so many times these last twelve months. And now? Here I was and I couldn't even shed a drop. *What kind of scumbag are you?* I wanted to shout.

I looked around. A pack of street dogs swarmed a yellow-backed bitch, yelping and nipping each other to see who would be next. A wrinkled Indian woman across the street swept her front porch. A flash of red caught my eye. Behind a tombstone? Or was it my imagination? I picked a final bit of dog shit from Lili's gravestone, and stood up.

Pitt, I thought. *Where are you? What do you know? What do you mean by end the guilt?* It hung heavy from my shoulders now, heavier than ever before. Maybe he'd found some secret key that lifted the burden, freed you to live again. I doubted it. Or maybe he had, but it was some religious bullshit. Like Ambo and his Bible-thumping hypocrisy. I had to take the chance.

I walked back to town, one hand in my pocket, clutching the cash, the other beating away the clamoring young thieves whose inexpert hands darted in and out of my empty pockets. I climbed the hill once more to the hostel. Berta was there. The flaxen-haired Visigoth.

"You known Alex long?" I said.

Her cheeks flushed pink. "Just a few weeks. Here's your key."

"Alex goes through women like I go through socks." I shrugged and took the key. "Guess you know what you're doing, though."

The room was just how I designed it. Simple, durable furniture. Bed that didn't squeak. Floor-to-ceiling windows that let in the evening lights of Cuzco. Big bathroom with a tub. A hideaway for lovers, a hotel room in a hostel. It had been our love nest, Kate and I.

I sat on the bed. She had given birth here. Liliana had taken her first lungful of air in this room. This was where it all began. What I had been avoiding for so long. Now I was here and I felt like a stranger in my own home. I closed my eyes, rubbed the bridge of my nose.

I stank. For the first time in a year I was aware of my own smell. Maybe it was the altitude. And after the time in jail, the bus ride... I was putrid. I took my clothes off and sniffed them. Not worth saving. I showered, resisting the temptation to soak in the bath. Too many memories lingered in that tub. I got out of the shower, put a towel around my waist and walked out into the hallway. Berta was arguing with Alex.

"So what am I, just another weeklong fling?"

I looked over the banister into the lobby. Alex put his hands on her hips. She pushed him away. The room next to mine was Alex's. I tried the knob. Unlocked. I went in, rummaged around in the closet. I stole a couple of T-shirts, a clean white dress shirt, a pair of jeans, a sweater, a leather jacket. I closed the door behind me. From a broom closet I pinched a length of rope. Then I went back to my room, got dressed. The clothes were all three sizes too big. I had to roll the jeans halfway to my knees. The rope I chucked under the bed.

Alex had left a courtesy gram of cocaine for me on

the pillow, plus an unopened bottle of *pisco* and a pack of Hamiltons. *What a guy,* I thought. *Damn. I should really be nicer to him.* I shoveled a pinch of cocaine up my nose and took a big swig from the bottle to wash it down. I began to feel human again. That is to say, another piece of shit floating in a sea of filth.

I jumped down the stairs three at a time, turned toward the lobby just in time to see Berta slap Alex across the face.

"Got those tickets, Alex?" I shouted.

"Working on it. Hey—" I kept walking. I was almost to the door. "I need to talk to you," he said.

"Sorry, gotta run."

The evening chill had fallen on Cuzco, a faint orange glow in the western sky. I pimp-rolled down the sidewalk stairs, looking into every open window, checking over my shoulder. On Calle San Blas I joined the promenading gringo throng. I pretended to read restaurant menus, studied the reflection of the crowd behind me.

There he was. A change of clothes, but the red cap remained. Did he want me to spot him? What an idiot. He lingered in front of a café on the other side of the street. I strolled along to the next restaurant, looked in the reflection again. He matched my pace.

A Peruvian tout clung to my arm, tried to drag me inside his establishment. I shook myself free, cursed his mother, threatened physical violence to his testicles, if he had any, the existence of which I declared in a loud voice I doubted, then went into the British-owned restaurant next door. I perched in the window on a high stool. Red Cap stood across the street, peering into the opposite eatery, his back toward me.

The waitress offered me a menu. I had no real appetite but I needed to eat something, keep my strength up. Digesting fatty foods at altitude was hard, especially if you've just come up from Lima. So I skipped the steak and fries and asked for a big bowl of rice and beans. Healthier than my normal fare, but junk food would probably have me puking all night long. I declined the offer of a beer. I had *pisco* enough back in my room. When I finished ordering, Red Cap had gone. The food tasted good, better than I expected, and for the first time since La Paz I treated myself to a cappuccino for dessert.

I paid the bill. The sky was black. The slender tropical twilight had come and gone. The Southern Cross and the Big Dipper fought for supremacy at opposite ends of the sky. I walked down the hill to Plaza San Blas. I circled the square, looking over my shoulder. Red Cap trailed along. I gnawed my lip, headed back to the hostel.

Berta wasn't there. A new girl had taken her place, a redhead with a thick Irish accent. She wore a V-neck wool sweater that clung to her body.

I leaned across the counter. "Got something for me?"

She wiggled her eyebrows. "Better believe it, baby."

I laughed, but the muscles were so unused to the activity that it came out a long, hacking cough. My rib cage spasmed in pain. It had been months, but the broken bone still throbbed.

She slid an envelope across the counter, room key on top. Inside I found the train ticket, and a note from Alex.

> *Dude,*
> *This one's insatiable. Wanna spit roast?*
>
> —*A*

I put the ticket and note back in the envelope, shoved it into my pocket. I picked up the key. "This isn't mine."

"No," she said, and bent forward. I had a view down her shirt. "It's not."

I slid the key back across the counter. "Just my room key, please."

She grinned, sank her chin into her palm. "You sure?"

"I'm sure."

She straightened up, took a key from the wall. She dangled it in the air between us. "Your loss."

"It always is."

I spent the night huddled in bed against the cold, nipping at the cocaine and *pisco* to stay awake. My scars itched. I kicked the down comforter off me, lifted my shirt. I lit a fresh cigarette and burned a peace sign into my abs. The closest to peace I was ever going to get.

Why did Alex have to give me this room? He couldn't have picked another room, maybe one of the singles on the ground floor, or the rowdy dormitory next to reception? A room without memories.

I stared out the window at the twinkling lights of Cuzco. Five hundred years ago it had been the capital of the savage, continent-spanning Incan Empire. Now these feudal overlords were reduced to groveling to gringos for tourist dollars. *What goes around comes around.* I wondered if there was a lesson in there for me somewhere.

Against my will I took out Lili's picture, smoothed the corners where they had bent. A blast of the cocaine roared up my nose in a futile quest to silence the memories.

Taste of metal on my tongue. On my lips. *Shit. Not again.* I tilted my head back. Too late. Blood splattered on the photo in my hand. *Shit shit shit.* I stumbled across the darkened room, nose in the air, banged my knee against a chair. Fucking power company. Incompetent Peruvian bastards. I fumbled for the tissues on the desk, stuffed one into each nostril. Stepped to the window, held the photo to catch the moonlight. Wiped away the drops of blood.

There she was. My baby. Six months old. Never get any older. Never go to school. Wear a pretty dress. Drive me crazy dating the wrong boys. Never let me walk her down the aisle. She was dead. Because of me.

I pulled the chair closer to the window. Slumped down into it. The photo glowed in the moonlight. I couldn't look away. What time was it? Three, four in the morning? How long had it been since I slept? The days and nights blurred together in one long filthy smear. My eyes felt raw and itchy. Without thinking, I rubbed them with my fingers. Saw stars.

I open my eyes. Look down. A crying baby in my arms. Red-faced and small. My Lili. But how—? A miracle. Those eyes that look like mine. Fingers so tiny. *I don't understand,* I whisper. *I thought you were dead.* Sunshine streams in the window. Katherine sits up in bed. Kate? Sweat plasters her hair to her forehead. She holds her arms out for the baby. This is our room. Our hostel in Cuzco. The midwife beams at us. How is this possible?

My stomach lurches. We're on a bus. Steep drop outside

the window. A hairpin turn. Rear wheel spins in space. Kate comforts the baby, who's frightened by the noise and the movement. We crest a hill. La Paz spreads out before us. Greg and Luisa meet us at the terminal, sweep us back to their hostel, the Merry Mariner. A shark in a sailor's cap greets us above the door.

They are old friends of ours, eager to catch up. We send them guests, they send us theirs. They toast us with frosty mugs of Bolivian *weiss* beer. Kate looks at me, eyes wide. I smile. Why not? She went sober when she found out she was pregnant. To make things easier on her, I quit too. After she gave birth, we were too tired to go out. Six months of midnight breastfeeding and poopy diapers. Can't say I blame her for wanting a break.

She puts Lili to bed, and for the first time in more than a year savors a glass of Argentinian Malbec. Her favorite. I say nothing. She's earned it. I sip my beer and laugh at Greg's hearty Australian jokes. After so long without a drink, the beer goes straight to my head.

"Let's go out!" someone is shouting.

Laughter. "Go where?"

"Come on, you bloody pikers," Greg roars from the front door. He's got one arm in the wrong sleeve of his jacket.

"But what about," a hesitation, and Kate speaks for both of us, "what about the baby?"

"What about her?" Greg wants to know, chasing his other sleeve.

"We can't just leave her."

"I'm sure we could find you a babysitter," Luisa says.

The night guard volunteers his sister. "You can count on

Carlos," Greg booms, slaps me on the shoulder. "Works the graveyard shift. Trust him with my life, mate."

Kate looks like a cornered animal defending her young. "But I'll worry."

I bend down and nibble her neck. "Just because we're parents doesn't mean we can't have fun. That what you want? A no fun life?"

I sat up in my chair and screamed. Until my chest squeezed tight and my eyeballs bulged. Then I screamed again, fists clenched at my side, as loud and as hard as I could. I yanked open the window and screamed through the iron bars at the lightless city. A passing taxi swerved, honked. A man on the sidewalk crouched over a prone figure, grasping the other's pockets. A bloody knife glinted in his hand. He didn't look up.

Cocaine. I needed more cocaine. I unplugged my nostrils, blasted three huge pinches of coke up my nose, capped them again with fresh tissues. Thank God the stuff was cheap down here. Unscrewed the bottle of *pisco*. Took a long swig to wash down the blood and phlegm. I coughed on the harsh liquor. So much for being fresh tomorrow. Half a pack of cigarettes on the table. I set them all on fire, puffed them hot and held the burning tips to the inside of my elbow. *Yes. That's it. Good.* The cigarettes went out. I put them back in my mouth, lit them again. Over the stink of the memories and the vile cigarettes, I could smell my own flesh burning.

I deserved it. All of it. More. No one else was going to punish me. The cops refused to do so. Carlos bribed his "sister" out of jail. Not that I blamed her for what happened. It was my fault. I should never have trusted her in the first place. And now everyone thought it was over. Last year's news, right? Except for me. Except for Kate. Wherever she was.

My eyelids felt like concrete slabs. Coffin slabs. The kind they used to cover Liliana's grave. I had to get out of here. Might sleep again. I dragged on the last of my cigarettes. Let them burn out with a hiss against my knuckles.

My hands were empty. Sudden panic. I patted my ribs. Where was it? The photo. Where was the photo?

On the floor I groped in the dust. Cockroaches scuttled across my fingers, probing the fresh, gooey burns. Would have to have a talk with Alex. Why were the maids neglecting to clean under the bed? Cursed myself. *How can you even think about such trivia at a time like this?* Found the photo. Wiped off the dust and the roach shit. Pressed her against my heart, deep inside my shirt pocket.

In the bathroom I tied a noose with the rope I'd stolen earlier. I hung it from the shower rail and stuck my head in the loop.

When I was done, I ran the cold water in the sink, the mountain water freezing my fingers. I splashed my face until the skin was numb, and dry shaved against the grain. I'd pinched a razor from Alex's stash when I raided his closet. By some miracle I didn't cut myself. Although the red welts it left on my face made me look like a pimply teenager with a raging case of acne.

The brochure I'd picked up from Volcanic Volunteers lay on the desk where I'd left it. I studied the photo. Lake Titicaca. Isla del Sol, home of the Incan gods. I tore the brochure into tiny pieces, flushed it down the toilet. In case the CIA caught me I didn't want them to know where I was headed.

I counted the money I had left. About four hundred bucks. I rolled up two hundred in small bills, stuffed it into a plastic bag and hid it where the sun don't shine. The train ticket and the remainder of the cash went in a more accessible location. I wore both the sweater and the jacket. It was cold in the unheated room—I'd switched off the heating before going to bed—and it would be even colder on the *altiplano*. The brisk air nipped at my toes, stiffened my flip-flops. I might get frostbite and lose a few toes. They'd turn black and eventually fall off. That would be cool. No need to bother with boots.

I went down to reception. Reached over the desk, yanked the telephone from the curvy night clerk's hands. Unlike Berta and the Irish lass, this one was dark-haired, Peruvian. She protested in a violent chirping of rapid-fire Spanish.

I put my hand over the receiver. "He loves you, bitch, but I gotta use the phone."

"Horse, that you?" Alex's voice growled in my ear.

"Who else?"

"You off?"

"See you later." I cleared my throat. "Maybe never."

"Dude, listen, when you get back—"

I hung up, dialed a taxi company. When I finished, I handed the phone to the night clerk. She glared at me, put the phone back in its cradle.

"What is love?" I asked her.

She said, "Not that."

There are two train stations in Cuzco. One for the trains to Machu Picchu, another for the trains to Puno on the

Bolivian border. Arriving at the Machu Picchu station, I paid the driver the precise amount owed, ignoring his protestations that "all foreigner give tip." The terminal overflowed with Americans and Europeans dressed in water-resistant, zip-off trousers: an army of khaki and forest green, the AARP militia armed with cameras instead of guns.

We boarded the train. I found myself sitting across from a Dallas oil tycoon.

"I call myself that," he said humbly. "Just another Texas ty-coon."

Within five minutes I knew his life story: the wives; the daughters; the daughters' wives; the cancer; this was his first trip overseas. Maybe his last. The pretty young Peruvian girl at his side stared at my crotch.

The train whistle blew. We lurched, began to move. I stepped into the aisle. A pair of fingers pinched my ass. The Peruvian girl winked.

I elbowed my way down the aisle, past the conductor, jumped onto the concrete platform. I ran through the terminal, hopped into the fourth taxi in the line, held out a big piece of play money and told him to take me to the Puno train station as fast as possible.

We raced through Cuzco, cutting through the shantytowns, splashing piles of steaming donkey dung, until we jerked to a stop in front of the smaller, less elegant train station that would take me to Puno, the border, and Lake Titicaca.

The train was leaving. I lowered my shoulders and charged a Peruvian cop. Had always wanted to do that. Probably wasn't necessary, but it sure was fun. I knocked him over, dropped a twenty-dollar bill on the ground as I did so. I ran onto the platform. The train picked up speed. I caught up to the train, grabbed hold of the vertical steel bar at the end of the final car and heaved myself aboard.

"Ticket, sir?" The conductor swayed backward, eyes wide.

Sprinting at 3400m above sea level is harder than it sounds. I fought to catch my breath. "I'm sorry?"

"If your grace wishes to ride the train, he must first pay."

I fished a hundred-dollar bill from my pocket and shoved it in his hand. "A private room. First or second class, doesn't matter. Keep the change."

His eyes widened. He held it to the light, creased it, rubbed it between thumb and forefinger. Satisfied, he slid it into his shoe, and escorted me through the train to the second-class carriage. He opened the door to an empty compartment.

"No first class?" I said.

"So sorry, sir. It is all full. Your grace knows how it is."

I nodded. "Very well."

The conductor held out his hand, expecting a tip. After a hundred-dollar bill? What an asshole. I ignored it. I shut the door, slouched back into the seat and looked up into the barrel of a gun.

WITH HIS FREE HAND, THE MAN LIFTED HIS
red cap and scratched his bald spot. "Right on time, Horse.
Glad you could make it."

The gun was small. Big enough, though. An automatic of
some kind. He pointed it at my chest. His hand did not waver.
I folded my hands on my stomach, settled myself into the
worn fabric of the seat.

"Always happy to oblige," I said.

He grinned. He pulled the cap low over his eyes. I glanced
out the window. The train was passing through the outer
reaches of Cuzco's shantytowns. The snow-topped Andes
surrounded us on all sides.

He said, "Open the window."

"Why?"

"Do it."

I stood. He nodded. I went to the window. I unclicked the
latch at the top, slid it down. The stench of the passing slums
filled the compartment.

"Now take your clothes off."

I crossed my arms. "Go fuck yourself."

Red Cap rested the gun on his knee. His eyes narrowed.

"Take them off or I will shoot you."

Infallible logic, that. I took off my jacket, the sweater. I reached up to my shirt, but he stopped me with a jerk of the gun.

"All of the buttons, if you please?"

"So you *are* CIA, then," I said, but got no reply.

I unbuttoned the shirt, took it off, dropped it on the seat. I unsnapped my jeans, stepped out of them. I was left wearing an oversize T-shirt I'd stolen from Alex that read "World's Greatest Lover," my old rug-burned tightie-whities—I couldn't bring myself to steal Alex's underwear—and flip-flops.

"All of it."

The remainder went on the floor. I stood there naked. I wondered what he thought of my body scar.

He didn't even blink. "Now pick everything up. Flip-flops, too."

I hugged my clothes to my chest.

"Now throw everything out the window."

"Then what am I going to wear?"

He aimed the gun at my crotch.

"Do it."

I took Lili's picture from my shirt pocket, and shoved the wad of clothing out the window. The wind snatched it from my hands, flung it into the brush. We had entered the *altiplano* desert outside of Cuzco. Perhaps some wandering llama herder would find Alex's T-shirt and get lucky.

"Now the glasses."

"But I can't see without my glasses."

"You can't see without a head, either."

My glasses joined the rest.

"The piece of paper, too."

"It's a photo of my daughter," I said.

He cocked the gun. "I said, throw it out."

"Go ahead and kill me then," I said. "This photo is all I have left of her."

Red Cap considered that for a moment. "Let's see it."

I showed it to him.

He grunted. "Alright," he said at last. He aimed the gun at my ankles. "Now take it out."

I covered myself with my free hand. "It already is out, asshole."

He sighed. "Under your seat."

I crouched down. A small backpack nestled there. I looked back at him.

"Put them on."

The bag contained a clean pair of jeans my size, plus hiking boots, woolen socks, long underwear, a flannel shirt, a heavy sweater, a jacket, woolen hat, even mittens.

The wind blew through the open window, chilling the compartment. I got dressed. Everything fit. I wondered how he knew my size. When I finished, I sat back in the seat. For the first time since I had been knocked out in my apartment in Lima, I felt warm again.

He held out a small plastic case.

"What's this?" I asked.

"Contacts. Put them in."

I slid the plastic lenses against my eyeballs. Blinked. "How did you know my prescription?"

"Little birdie told me."

I studied Red Cap. He was middle forties. Wore shiny new hiking boots, an expensive blue Gore-Tex jacket, zip-up travel pants and a purple scarf. No flab lingered on his muscular frame.

"So where do they teach you to kill?" I asked. "Langley? The CIA parking lot?"

"I'm not CIA."

"Really. Then what are you?"

A grin tugged at his cheek. "All will be explained. But not here. Not now."

I sat forward. The gun tracked the movement. "Doesn't have anything to do with lithium, does it? A land grab? Steal the *altiplano* from the Bolivians?" I waved a hand: earth to dude. His face was a stone. "Hello? This ringing any bells?"

But he said nothing.

We stared at each other. I made clown faces, stretching my face in obscene contortions. But the stone, as the Zen masters might say, just was.

Hours passed. The train trundled across the high plateau, gaining altitude. The highest pass was five thousand meters. It got colder in the compartment, the bitter freeze of the equatorial mountains.

"Mind I shut the window?"

He shook his head. "Put your coat on."

"But it's cold."

"Hurts, doesn't it?" He grinned. "That's the whole point."

"That's the craziest thing I've ever heard." *Not believing a word I said.*

"Comfort makes you stupid. Pain keeps you sharp. Know what I mean?"

My body scar itched. "Yes," I admitted. "I do."

He crossed his legs and sat back in his seat. "We're going to get along just fine."

Even with the coat I shivered. I was feeling plenty sharp. A little bit of comfort would not have hurt in the least. The sun burned high in the sky, its warmth unfelt. A nice hot bath would be nice. *Wrong way! Go back!* I covered my face with my hands.

Giving Lili her bath was my favorite part of the day. Singing her to sleep in my arms, telling her that she was safe, telling her that I would always be there for her.

Lies, all of it.

I blew my nose on my sleeve. The train began to descend. Red Cap kept the gun in his lap, pointed at me. He had not moved since I entered the compartment. I had had enough of this shit. I stood and stretched, yawning. Gestured to the door.

"Gotta use the bathroom, you don't mind if I—"

"Sit down."

I hesitated.

"Now."

"You want me to piss all over the floor?"

"If you have to."

I sat down again. My bladder filled, for real this time. The altitude's a diuretic. The train descended toward the Bolivian border.

A knock at the door made us both sit up straight. Red Cap put the gun in his pocket, but kept it aimed at me. He jerked his head toward the window. I slid over, away from the door.

"Who is it?"

"*Comida, bebida,* snacks!"

Red Cap stood and unlocked the door with his free hand. He sat back, the gun hand still in his pocket.

A greasy Asian face, bubbling with pimples, poked its broad slash of a smile through the doorway. A wooden tray hung from his shoulders. Glass bottles of yellow Inca Kola, bags of potato chips and cigarettes protruded outward from his belly.

"What can I get ya?" His accent was crude Lima slang. Another escaped inmate from the city's million-strong Chinatown.

Red Cap held up two fingers. "Water."

"Fuck you," I said. By now I had to piss, and bad.

"Don't want some crunchy, tasty *plátano?* I got it *frito?*" The slitted eyes narrowed, the smile pushing the boundaries of good taste.

"Just the water."

"Long train voyage, sir." He lifted himself up on his toes. "Nothing else I get ya?"

Red Cap craned his neck to look at the man. He blinked. "That's all, thanks."

"Pack of Hamiltons," I added.

"And the smokes."

The man took two bottles of water from his tray, held them out to Red Cap. He tossed the pack of cigarettes to me. Red Cap caught them in midair.

"Keep the change."

Mister Pimples took the rumpled piece of play money. "Very kind, sir. Oh so kind." He put the money in his pocket. "Let me help you with that window, sir. So very cold in here, no?"

He folded the wooden tray up against his chest. Straps held his wares in place. He sidestepped through the narrow doorway. A small side table protruded from the outside wall. He leaned over the table, reached for the window. His jacket rode up on my side, revealing a snub-nosed revolver tucked into his pants. My eyes widened. I jumped up, made for the door. An enormous firecracker went off next to my ear.

The Chinaman made a sound, a sort of chuckle-groan, and tipped sideways. In one hand he held the revolver. He fell against the table. The impact tore it from the wall. One side of the man's head was missing. Potato chips, bottles of Inca Kola scattered across the floor. Mister Pimples had burst.

Red Cap turned his gun to me. "Now we move."

Screams came from adjacent compartments. Doors opened, voices raised in argument. Red Cap flipped the dead man's gun out the window, then prodded me into the hallway. He locked the door from the inside, slid it shut. He pointed the gun at my back.

"This man just killed the Chinese vendor," he shouted in Spanish, then in English at the faces peering out of their doors. "He is under arrest. Please stay in your rooms until the investigation is complete."

"It's a lie," I shouted. "He's the—"

The side of my head burst in a flower of pain. Red Cap shoved me in the back. I stumbled ahead, eyes closed, one hand on my scalp, the other held out in front of me.

We came to the back of the car, crossed over into the next. I looked down between the cars. We were going at least eighty clicks an hour. Could I jump? Would I survive? A sharp poke in the kidney jolted me into action. I swung open the door into the third-class carriage. The gun disappeared into his jacket pocket.

Rows of seats faced each other across tables piled high with guidebooks, maps and snacks. We went from carriage to carriage, past platoons of flirting backpackers in travel gear, digital cameras recording every mundane detail of their trip.

As we moved through the train, the descent became more pronounced. Outside the windows, llamas grazed. Brown-faced women grimaced at the train as it passed.

At the end of the final passenger carriage, we came to the locomotive. We could go no farther. Backpackers murmured, pointed at us. Outside, new shantytowns appeared, collections of rusty lean-tos, children playing in the desert dust. The train slowed.

"That's them!" someone shouted.

The conductor strode down the aisle toward us. It was the same prick who'd shown me my seat. Two train guards followed him. They drew their guns. A *campesino* in a green poncho trailed behind. The man from the bus.

Whoa. So the *campesino* was the spy? Then who the hell was this dude in the baseball cap?

"Between the cars," he ordered.

"But I—"

"Do it, Gaia damn it!"

I tugged open the door between the carriage and the locomotive. I stepped across the gap, clung to the chains that led to the locked engineer's compartment. Red Cap stepped after me. The small town grew in size as we neared the center. Juliaca. Not three meters from me, street vendors lined the dusty roadside. Hanging from every beam, orange-brown leathery things that looked like roadkill. Llama fetuses. I remembered the time Kate and I had eaten one together. Revolting. An aphrodisiac, or so claimed the local witch doctors.

"When I say jump, you jump!"

I swallowed. The train slowed further. We were going maybe twenty clicks an hour now.

"Aye aye, cap'n!" I shouted, and touched my forelock.

The train guards stood on the other side of the glass door. One of them aimed his gun upward at an angle, fired. The glass shattered. A warning shot. The next one wouldn't miss.

Red Cap shouted, "Now!"

I leaped as far from the train as I could. Landed in something soft and wet. Red Cap landed a few feet to one side. I found myself wrist-deep in llama dung. I shook the shit off my hands. The train squealed, slowed to a stop. I turned to Red Cap, pulled back my fist, but swarms of hands grabbed me from behind. Red Cap lifted his chin and smiled.

"Just as we planned," a male voice said.

Hands held me tight. They hustled me through a gap in the fence that divided the train tracks from the town. The men behind me broke into a jog, forcing me along in front of them. A white van stood next to a nearby stall; llama fetuses hung from wooden beams. The back doors of the van popped open. One hand forced my head down, the others shoved me inside, through a tumble of wild-eyed llama abortions.

"I gotta take a piss," I said, but they ignored me.

It was dark in the van. My eyes adjusted. Six Buddhist monks surrounded me. They sat in lotus position, ankles on knees. Their shaved heads glowed dimly in the darkness. Two wore glasses. All wore the orange-and-scarlet gown of Tibet. Around the back of the van hung more llama fetuses, like Christmas decorations. Black fabric taped to the windows let in a thin sheen of light.

The van rocked as someone yanked open the driver-side door. Red Cap got in behind the wheel. The van roared and shot forward, throwing me back on my hands. There was gunfire in the distance, a great hubbub, shouting. The van picked up speed. All I could hear was the high-pitched whine of the underpowered motor.

Glass shattered onto the floor. A limp hand fell across my face. I looked up into an eyeless socket. The monk next to me was toast. I pushed the body off me. It tottered and fell into the lap of an adjacent monk. Blood poured from the dead man's ear. Something pricked my palm. I picked a blade of glass from my hand. Sunlight poked in through a small hole in the cloth that covered the rear window.

An older monk, darker than the others, said something in a language I didn't understand or recognize. The monk at his side produced a large black handgun from the inner folds of his robe. He swung the barrel of the gun against the glass. The window shattered. The glass caved out and fell into the road. He peeled away the black cloth, scraped the gun barrel along the edge of the window. Small shards fell into the vehicle.

He peered out the window, searching for pursuers, but found none. He sat back, resumed his lotus position, closed his eyes. I considered grabbing for the weapon, going berserk, but there were five of them left, and one of me. I rested my shoulder against the side of the van and tried to relax. Tried to ignore the rapidly cooling body next to me.

Potholes made this impossible. The van bucked and pitched along the cratered road for hours, nudging my new dead friend against me every time we hit a bump in the road. Blood soaked into my underwear. Chunks of brain quivered like jelly against my boots. My bladder felt like it was going to explode. I thought about letting go a stream right there. Outside, seagulls cawed. Seagulls? The ocean? No. The lake.

The van ended its violent pounding against my skull. Red Cap got out and opened the rear doors. Two monks helped me to my feet.

We stood on the shores of Lake Titicaca. The view was the same as the photo in Volcanic Volunteers' brochure. The same photo as Kate's postcard. The sun peered over the tops of the western mountains. Isla del Sol hulked in the middle of the lake. I fought to catch my breath. I had been too long in the smoggy wasteland below. At four thousand meters the air is for saints, not sinners like me.

The monk in the passenger seat shifted over behind the wheel. Red Cap leaned back in through the window.

"Ditch the van," he said. "No one finds it. Not a trace. Not now. We're too close."

He slapped the side of the vehicle and the driver spun the wheels in reverse, did a three-point turn, and was gone.

We walked down to the water. A monk in a boat held an empty palm to the sky. The others returned the gesture, waded in to their knees and climbed into the boat.

"The water's cold," I said. "Can't you get it any closer?"

In answer, the monks manhandled me into the lake, and

marched me through frigid water up to our thighs. I seized the opportunity and emptied my bladder into my pants. The long stream of hot piss kept the brass monkeys at bay.

Four wooden benches had been laid across the width of the boat. Two outboard motors pointed their blades in the air. A monk on shore untied the rope that held the craft to a small jetty, then ran into the water, robes flying, and clambered in to join us.

Oars appeared. Two monks pulled us into deeper water. The outboard motors splashed astern. A pull of the chains, and they growled and hissed, darted forward, nearly knocking us off our seats. I held on to the wooden plank with both hands. We headed toward Isla del Sol. After a few minutes, though, we veered to the left, back to the Peruvian shore.

"Where are we going?" I shouted. The cold lake water sprayed up on both sides. No one answered me.

The sun began to set. Shadow advanced toward us across the lake. In the east, still wrapped in sunlight, a tour group disembarked from the reed islands, near the Bolivian shore. Our boat hopped and skipped across the light waves. We sped west into shadow, into the darkness, back toward Peru.

Several dozen wooden houses lined the strand. Lights shone in every window. Children ran and shouted. Small boats lay beached on the sand. On the rocks higher up, green fishing nets dried in the cool air. To either side the beach petered out into a solid rock wall. A mountain loomed snowy above us. Our boat slowed. The pilot cut the motor. A monk vaulted over the side, trailing the rope. His robes floated in the freezing water. The others jumped after him, and together they heaved the boat onto the beach. Red Cap strode ahead and alone into the village. He disappeared around a corner.

I got out of the boat. The others ignored me. There was nowhere to run. Plus, I was soaked from the waist down. My testicles were tight balls of brass. I had no more piss left to warm them with. My feet squelched freezing water in my boots. A sliver of sun remained above the mountaintops. If I tried to escape I'd freeze to death in the night.

The path Red Cap took was a mixture of sand and gravel. I followed it. On either side, new wooden houses. Solar panels glinted on their roofs. A trickle of smoke emerged from each house's chimney. One building was marked *Escuela*. The schoolhouse. Another, painted with a red cross, Hospital.

Children swarmed the gravel path, chasing each other, shouting in Quechua. One boy crashed into my thigh. He dug his fingers into my leg. I knelt. He looked like he was about to cry. I smiled, brushed the sand out of his black hair. He observed me with enormous brown eyes.

"Pitt?" I said in Spanish. "Do you know Pitt?"

"Pitt!" the boy said, and giggled, his torso twisting. "Pitt Pitt Pitt!"

He tore free and ran off, gyrating in circles before disappearing into a house farther along the row. I followed. I peered in through the glass windows of the houses as I passed. Well-dressed locals sat around tables spread with food. White teeth gleamed under electric lights. Dentures, most likely.

I came to the house the child had entered. He sat at a table, fidgeting. He caught me looking in at him, and waved. The family turned to see who it was. The squat Indian woman in her fake braids ducked her head. Her husband lifted his chin, a curt masculine gesture that said: welcome, and beware. Six more children sat at the table. Their plates were full. No sign of a six-foot-tall blond gringo. I waved back and continued my sightseeing.

Next to the house was a small mud-brick hut. A toothless old man sat in the doorway, darning an ancient fishing net. He looked at me and laughed. He cackled, a bitter sound, then hacked and finally gargled up a blob of red, which he spat in the dust at my feet.

His was the only hut of its kind in the village, the lone holdout, it seemed, against modernity. I walked quickly now, as the sun set, past another half a dozen houses.

The path ended in the mouth of a cave. Two monks sat cross-legged on either side, their hands in their laps. I ignored them, walked toward the entrance of the cave. The monks simultaneously lifted pump-action shotguns, chambered a shell each and pointed their weapons at my abdomen. I stopped, held out my empty palms.

"The welcome wagon plum forgot to teach you manners," I said.

"Hello, Horse."

A woman stood inside the cave. The early evening shadow obscured her face, but I would recognize that voice anywhere.

"I didn't come here to see you," I said.

"I know."

"I'm looking for Pitt. Friend of mine. Is he here?"

The woman stepped from the shadow, and the face of Katherine, my Kate, my once-wife, my ex-wife, my never-wife, emerged into the brightening moonlight.

"He is, and you shall see him."

SHE SAID, "MOTHER EARTH'S IN DANGER."

"Why?" I asked. "Has Papa Earth been a bad boy?"

We walked in growing shadow. I took off my wet boots and socks, felt the frigid sand between my toes. The sun had set behind the mountains, but there was still daylight on the lake. A cold evening breeze numbed my ears. We strolled along the shore, past a row of half-completed wooden houses. A dozen men and women labored on the empty shells, hammers banging, saws grinding.

"Yes," she said. "He has."

Kate put her arm through mine. Unlike the other monks, who wore orange and scarlet, her robes were black. The feel of her wrist in the inner softness of my elbow, even through four layers of clothing, broke open the dam of my memories. It also broke open half a dozen fresh burns. She looked up at me. How many times had she done that, wanting to be kissed? But those days were dust and ashes.

"Now we must atone," she said.

"For what?"

"For hurting her."

I swallowed. "Hurting who?"

"Gaia."

"Oh."

She led me along the beach. I studied the workers, looking for Pitt. They wore jeans and Incan beanies with woolen ear flaps. They were gringos, all of them, and ranged from late twenties to early eighties, including a pair of grandparents who later tried to put me to sleep with photos of their off-spring. None of them was Pitt.

"Don't tell me you've gone New Age."

Kate grinned and closed her eyes. She nodded her head. "Gaia is the world, Horse. She is the mother spirit who inhabits every living thing." She stopped walking. "And yes, she is in danger."

"You tried calling 9-1-1?"

She laughed, her face tilted up at the moon. "Never lose your cynicism, Horse," she said, and lay a cold knuckle against my cheek. "Gaia is everywhere, even in you."

Her touch hit me like a downed power line. All the memories, the longing and the loss, crackled between her skin and mine.

I nuzzled her hand, feeling the coldness. "Why am I here, Kate?" I asked. "Did you plan this?"

She pulled away. "Plan what?"

"You kidnapped me, didn't you?" I threw out my arms. "Well here I am. You wanted me that bad, why didn't you just say so?"

She drummed her fingertips against her face. "Horse," she said, and looked at the ground. "Horse, I—"

"Blessed Katherine, please tell us, when will be the leave-taking?" The voice came from the last of the construction sites. A fat man in blue overalls three sizes too small for him climbed out from under a wooden porch. His voice was effeminate.

Kate pulled away. "Soon," she called out, on tiptoe, as though willing him not to come near.

"We are all of us so impatient to go." The man waddled toward us. His face held the cherubic innocence of a child. He waved a chubby hand at the houses. "This building activity. It grows tiresome."

"You're paying what, two grand a week to be here, and you're in a hurry to leave?" I asked.

He smiled the smile of an idiot. Or was it a saint? "What does money matter at a time like this?" He clutched his chest with both hands, inclined his double chins to the heavens. "So close are we to bliss!"

"Patience, Blessed Jonathan." Kate squeezed his upper arm. I gritted my teeth. Was this her new lover? Not really her type. If I sucker-punched him, could I take him? And what was up with this "blessed" crap, anyway?

"What says the Blessed Victor?" he asked, bending over at the waist. "Have we earned our robes?"

Kate lowered her voice. "He is almost ready. You may tell the others."

The man bounced on tiptoe and clapped his hands together. "Yippee!"

"Will Pitt be leaving with you too?" I asked.

The man beamed. "I should certainly hope so!"

"You know Pitt?"

"Sure." His lips parted. Yellow teeth gleamed dully inside his shiny face. "The Blessed Pitt came to us about a month ago. Didn't know a thing at first. But he soon learned."

"What did he learn?" That was the rub.

A chuckle. "What all of us must learn."

I made a show of looking around. "Where is he now?"

"He has gone."

"Gone where?"

"Where all of us will soon be going." The man addressed Kate. "This one," he said, and jerked his head at me, "he is a new recruit then?"

"Yes." She answered for me. "I have much to explain to him."

"Such happiness! Such joy!" He embraced me. "Oh welcome, welcome, welcome!"

I pulled away. He stank of incense and patchouli oil.

Kate tugged at my elbow. "Dinnertime soon. Why don't you take some sacred sustenance?"

His tongue wagged like a puppy dog. "I shall savor every bite."

I stared at his retreating figure. "'Sacred sustenance'? 'The Blessed Katherine'?"

She lowered her eyes. "It is our form of address."

"Kate, what the fuck is going on here?"

"I don't know what you mean," she said quietly.

"Who are these people? What is with all of the guns? What are you doing here? And where is Pitt?"

She didn't look at me. "Maybe I should let the Blessed Victor explain."

"And who the fuck is Victor?"

"Victor," she said, and paused, a thin smile on her lips, eyes lifted once again to the moonlit sky. "Victor is a man."

"I see," I said. "At least we know he's not a god."

Kate pulled again on my elbow. "He wants to meet you."

I pitched my voice high in a sci-fi monotone. "Take me to your leader."

She laughed, leaned into me. "You'll see."

We walked along, her arm through mine, huddled close against the chill. That old familiar happiness crept in. I piled high the barbed wire, mounted the machine guns, but like a chlorine gas attack it swept across the trenches and descended into my lungs, poisoning my soul with delirium.

I turned to face her. "Kate?"

"Yes?"

"Do you believe in better late than never?"

She smoothed the hair out of my eyes. "With all my heart."

"Because I have to say," and I gestured at the barren beach, the badly built houses, the lake placid and freezing, "I don't see what this is doing for you."

She laid a hand on my chest. "Let the Blessed Victor explain. It will all make sense."

I put my arm around her waist. She left it there.

"Alright," I said.

We came to the cave again. At its mouth, to one side, a small generator hummed and throbbed, burping diesel fumes. The monks didn't move, shotguns in their laps. We walked between them, ducked our heads and stepped inside the cave. A thick orange extension cord ran from the generator into the darkness. We shuffled ahead, bent at the waist.

Ten meters into the cave the tunnel widened, and we stood up straight. At regular intervals the extension cord linked to another and branched off, and a caged construction lamp dangled from a hook on the wall. The cave was the size of a cathedral. Stalactites like organ pipes hung from the roof. To one side, monks in orange and scarlet sat cross-legged in a semi-circle, their focus a stack of wooden crates. A monk in an elaborate scarlet headdress stalked the shadows, a small whip in the crook of his arm.

"The fuck is this place, Kate?" I said. "You gone and joined a cult?"

She laughed. "They will call us that, I'm sure. But when they see what we've accomplished, it won't matter what they think."

"What have you accomplished?"

But she refused to say. One more time she slid her arm through mine. The orange extension cord continued to the center of the cave. It ended at a small wooden desk, where a man in blue jeans and a worn tweed jacket sat typing on a laptop.

Construction lamps on wooden posts cast light on the man's face. He was early fifties. A gray combover draped itself like a dead squirrel from one ear to the other. His head was enormous, out of all proportion to his body. Despite the cold in the cave, he wore no hat. Perhaps they didn't make hats that size.

"Two percent," he muttered to himself in a childish sing-song falsetto. He bit a thumbnail. "Two percent, two percent."

"Two percent of what?" I asked. "You a dairy farmer?" My voice echoed in the cave.

"Chance of failure." He sat back in his chair and looked up. He was slight of build. Looked underfed. "Kate, my dear.

Please." His accent was Russian. "New recruits go over there."

He jerked his thumb over his shoulder, resumed his frantic typing.

Red Cap knelt on the floor near the wall. He clutched an armful of orange and scarlet to his chest. His cap lay up-turned on the floor. A monk shaved what remained of his hair with a straight-edge razor.

"In the next life. What will you be?" intoned a second monk.

"A plant, maybe," Red Cap said excitedly. "Krill."

"Victor," Kate said.

She draped an arm around the Russian combover dude's shoulder, a casual act of intimacy that made me gasp for air.

He frowned at his computer screen. "What is it?"

"This is Horace."

"And who might Horace be?"

I slapped the laptop shut on his fingers. "Horse. The friend of Pitt's? Kate's husband?" I laid emphasis on the final word.

Victor pushed back his chair with a screech, bounded to his feet, hair bobbing on his balloon-like head, hands swaying as he breathed, a high-altitude, cave-dwelling jack-in-the-box.

"Horse! Of course!" He turned to Kate. "Why did you not say so?" To me. "We have much to thank you for!"

His hand was fatty despite his leanness, the handshake like squeezing a sponge.

"For what?"

"For *what?*" He clapped his other hand on mine, sandwiching my knuckles between two soggy palms. "For sending Pitt our way!"

I pulled my hand free, wiped it on my trousers. "The hell is that supposed to mean?"

"What do I *mean?*" He waved his hands out wide, a marionette on a string. "Without him, none of this could be!"

Kate pulled a folded, dirty postcard from inside her robes. "My postcard. The one I sent you?"

I took the card. On the front, a picture of a sunset from Isla del Sol, the sun setting behind the Peruvian Andes. I flipped it over. The sight of her neat block capitals made me sit on the edge of Victor's desk. It was dated nine months ago. Couple months after what happened in La Paz. The ink was stained with drops of blood and warped by beer, but I could still read what she had written to me then:

My Horace-Horse,

I found a job. Volunteer work. Yeah, I know. But it keeps me busy. The mind busy. Tire out the body, exhaust the mind, the memories aren't so bad. It's a kind of drug, I guess. Don't know how long I'll need it for. Maybe forever.

You and me...we're self-destructives. There can be no forgiveness, what we did. Nothing we can do will change the facts. But every day I find redemption in my sweat. A way to end the guilt. Working for a better world. A world that I deserve. A world that we deserve.

You and me both.

Please come.

Yours (if you want me)
Kate

She'd scribbled a cell phone number below her name.

How many months I'd kept that postcard in my pocket, taking it out in dimly lit bars, struggling to read a message I'd already memorized, laying it down in puddles of beer, never quite able to abandon it, never quite able to call her, a living reminder of my sin.

Yours. If you want me.

And then Pitt had plucked it from my hands in a BDSM strip club slash brothel.

"Redemption?" he asked me later in the cab. "What the hell is that?"

I slouched back into the cum-stained interior. "If you don't know, I can't explain it to you."

"'A world that we deserve,'" he read. "What do you think she means by that?"

I shook my head drunkenly. "No idea."

He flicked the postcard with a fingernail. Pointed to the phone number. "You gonna call her or what?"

"Or what. Turn here, driver." I knew a cheaper brothel two streets over. The whores were uglier there.

"Last chance, man," he'd said. "Sure you don't want to

keep this?"

"No," I said. "I don't." I meant it.

I looked up from the postcard. Kate and Victor watched me in silence. The straight-edge blade rasped against Red Cap's skull. The meditating monks released a simultaneous mantra, an *om* that lingered in the cavernous space, reflecting off the many-colored walls, until it splintered against the rocks overhead and no sound remained but white noise.

"Pitt called you," I said.

"Yes." She bit her lip.

"He came here."

"Yes."

"And he believes in all this Gaia crap?"

Victor beamed. "Absolutely! That's why he had you kidnapped!"

"Whoa," I said, and put the postcard down. "Pitt had me kidnapped? Explain."

"He heard that you were in danger. Thought you'd want to be here, share the joy that he has found in Gaia."

That meant—*no.* I covered my face with my hands. But what else could it mean? Pitt would never fall for this Gaia bullshit. He was fucking with me. Fucking with them. This was payback from Ambo for refusing to do that second op. I was a fool to think I could just walk away.

Send me on this insane search for Pitt, torture me by forcing me to go to Cuzco, and now...now the DSU was going to kill all these volunteers, and probably me as well. Maybe there was still time to save them. Although I doubted it.

"The fuck are you talking about? What joy?" I grabbed Kate by the arms. "Don't you understand? Pitt kills people like you for a living. This volunteering bullshit, protesting a war... All it's going to do is get you dead."

She didn't look at me. "We know all about Pitt's past."

I raised my eyebrows. "All of it?"

Victor crossed his arms. "Pitt has resigned from the Dissent Suppression Unit. He feels guilty for his many crimes in service of the American imperialist tyrants. We help him cope."

"Pitt with guilt," I snorted. "That I got to see with my own eyes."

"Believe it," Kate said. "It's true."

I farted. Loudly. "Something smells fishy here, you know that? And it's not just me, either. I mean since when do Buddhist monks carry guns and go around kidnapping people?"

"We want only to be left alone," Victor said. "To meditate. To be at peace with Gaia. One with Mother Earth."

"Bullshit. The only thing Pitt would ever do with Mother Earth is rape and kill her."

"Also, we offer our services. As volunteers. We construct homes for the local people."

"That's it?"

"What else could there be?" Victor shoved his palms into the back pockets of his jeans, thrust his hips at me.

I felt relieved. There was no hope. Never had been. Never would be. World without end. Amen.

"Well, have fun then, boys. This is one wild-goose chase that is over." I picked up Kate and threw her over my shoulder. She squawked. "Come on, girl, let's go back to Cuzco."

She beat her fists against my back. "Horse, put me down!"

I struggled to stay on my feet. "You've put on weight." Either that or I had lost muscle mass.

"I have not!" she said.

I raised my voice. "Come on, Pitt! I'll save you from these goody two-shoes! Come out, come out, wherever you are!"

My voice boomed in the cavern. The monks went silent and stared at me. A sudden commotion made us turn.

A long, stuttering plume of abuse trailed into the cave. The pounding pistons of the woman's stubby legs churned out oath after guttural German oath. She waddled toward us, great with child, swatting away the bevy of monks who tried to help her. Her frizzy hair sprung wild about her head, a fluffy orange dandelion waiting only for a breath to strip her naked.

Kate tickled me in the one spot no one knew but her. I let her go and she slid to the ground.

"Always lovely to see you, dove," Victor called out as the volunteering coordinator drew near. "What fortuitous happenstance brings our favorite Echo for a visit?"

"Fortuitous happenstance, bah." She planted her feet in front of him, stabbed his chest with her finger. "They betray us, is what."

He held his head to one side. "Has something happened, dear?"

"*Dumkopf.* The Americans raid the office."

Victor raised his eyebrows. "And they let you go?"

"I am here, aren't I?"

He shook his head. "You shouldn't have come."

"Where else you suggest I go?"

I cleared my throat. "They say hell is nice this time of year."

She took one look at me, and from the way she inhaled, I would have been afraid to be a little piggy. The exhalation came, made me wince. I leaned backward, away from the blow.

"This is the one." Her outstretched fingertip quivered. "He comes, asks questions. Where is Pitt? Then *they* come, take away my man."

Kate put an arm around Echo. "He's with us. It's OK." She drew the woman's contorted face down to her own shoulder. "Just tell us what happened."

Echo pushed her away. "What are you doing?" She wiped at her eyes. "Don't you understand? They have taken Umlaut."

"Wait a sec," I said. "Umlaut. Is that your boyfriend?"

"Ja, of course."

"With the shrunken head?"

I thought she was going to punch me. "His head is normal size."

Kate waved at me to shut up. Victor's face was grim. He said, "Tell me what happened."

"We went to the embassy," she sniffled. "Like we planned. Protesting. A few of us. It was good." A smile. "Then we went home. But the road was blocked off. Police everywhere. Men talking in English. American English. Umlaut go crazy. Bite the grass."

"Bite the grass," I said. "You mean, bite the dust?"

"Bite the dust, whatever!" she said. "Now is not the time."

Victor licked his lips. "What did Umlaut do?"

"*Scheisskopf.* Picked up a stone. A cobble. How do you say? Part of the road. Attacked them. Killed a little boy. A spy. We saw him on the surveillance camera."

"Whoa," I said. "You killed Paco?"

"You *see?*" That accusing finger again. The others glared at me.

"He was an English student of mine," I said. "A pickpocket. He didn't deserve to die."

"He was working for the American imperialist tyrants."

"But he was just a little kid!"

Kate put her arm on my elbow. I sighed. What was I getting so upset for? "None of my business what my clients do with their newly acquired language abilities."

Victor squeezed Echo's shoulder. "And then what happened?"

"Two Americans tried to stop him. He killed them both with the stone. The local cops finally got him. Beat him so bad..." Her hands pressed together in prayer, her eyes red and swollen. "So bad, so bad, so bad."

Paco. Dead. The hell was going on? "I still don't understand why he killed the kid," I said.

They ignored me. Victor kissed the woman's temple, caressed her hair. "He was always so impatient, Umlaut."

"Another week or two," she bawled. "That's all. But no. He could not wait."

"Be at peace," Kate said. "Pitt is almost ready."

"Oh thank Gaia," Echo said. "A gift from Mother Earth to save us all."

I snorted. "'A gift from Mother Earth'? Who, Pitt? Are you people for fucking real?"

Again they ignored me. Victor nodded. "Our preparations are well under way."

"Preparations for what?" I asked.

The three of them huddled together in silence. Echo's shoulders shuddered and heaved, went slack. Victor crooked a finger at a nearby monk.

"Take care of this one," he said to the man. "She has suffered much for Gaia."

I snapped my fingers in his face. "Hello? Earth to cult leader? Pitt or no Pitt?"

The monk nodded, draped Echo's arm around his neck, and led her away.

Victor sat on the edge of his desk, stared at me with a grin. "You ask where Pitt is. He is here. With us."

I looked around the cavern. "Can I talk to him?"

Victor crossed one arm over the other, perched his head on a long forefinger. "He's with us here in spirit."

"Fuck this spirit crap," I said. "Where's the flesh?"

He hid a grin with his hand. "Pitt said you'd never believe me."

My God. Was it possible? "What have you done to him?"

"I promise you will see him soon." Victor put the flat of his palm on Kate's navel. She sat on his thigh. "Why don't you get some dinner in him, babe? He looks hungry."

"And where do you get off calling her 'babe'?"

He nuzzled her neck. "Did you not tell him?"

"Tell me what?"

Kate pulled away. "Victor, please—"

Victor patted her butt. "She's my wife."

"Your what?"

"We've been married now six months and more."

I turned to her.

"You didn't come." She shrugged, a tiny, frightened bird, fluttering its wings.

"You and him?"

"Why not?" Her face sagged, gray with sadness. She put her arms around his neck, pressed her face against his chest. "He's a good man. We're happy together."

In that moment, what little hope for love or life I had left was extinguished, replaced with a burning hatred of the world and all things in it. I ground my teeth. I clenched my fists. My breath came fast and hard.

I said, "You kidnap me. You brainwash Pitt. And now you steal my wife?"

My left hook connected with Victor's elegantly upturned nose. There was a gooey sound of cartilage snapping. He fell onto the desk. Kate jumped sideways, her mouth open, but no sound came out. I grabbed Victor by his tweedy lapels, threw him onto the floor. I fell to my knees and punched his face, alternating fists. I cut my knuckle on a jagged tooth. I broke at least one finger. He didn't fight back. The pain drove me on. Wanting more. Kate screamed, pounded my shoulders with the flats of her palms.

A sea of orange and scarlet filled my peripheral vision. Hands dragged me to my feet. I kicked at the air, connected with a gun barrel. Automatic gunfire roared in the cave, plumes of flame spouting over my head. My ears rang. Stalactites crashed to the floor. I stood still. Metal clacked on empty palms. A ring of monks aimed AK-47s at my chest. The wooden crates were now empty, the lids discarded.

"What kind of fool you think I am?" I shouted. "Bunch of idiotic activists. Think that you can stop a war."

Monks lifted Victor to his feet. He held a white handkerchief to his nose. He tipped his head back, pinched his nostrils. His eyes were bruised. He'd look like a raccoon for some time to come.

"Seems I erred," he said.

"You fucking erred, alright." I twisted my arms, trying to break free. "You fuck with Pitt, you fuck with me!"

"Horse, please." Kate stroked my face with her fingertips, and I stiffened at her touch. "Just listen to what Victor has to say. Then you will see why Pitt is here. And you will want to join us, too."

VICTOR'S VOICE WAS MUFFLED THROUGH THE
bloody handkerchief. He asked, "What do you know about
bat guano?"

"Hang on a second," I said. "Since when do Buddhist
monks have crates, plural, full of AK-47s?" Strong arms held
my wrists between my shoulder blades. I arched my back to
ease the pain, nose in the air, head horizontal.

"I'm explaining it to you," he said.

"Because of bat guano?" The words soared to the cavern's
ceiling, only to shatter into tiny echoes.

Victor jerked his head. The monks let go of my arms, but
kept a grip on my shoulders. I shook my hands to restore the
circulation.

"Humor me, Horace."

"What do I know about bat guano?"

"Yes."

"Enough to know it's not a breakfast cereal."

"Anything else?"

"What is this, seventh-grade science class?"

"Alright." Victor pressed the handkerchief tighter to his
nose. He turned to Kate. "Bring us some chai, will you, my

dear? We'll be in the alcove."

Kate's face had gone white. She did not look at me. Come to think of it, she had never seen me violent before. She nodded her head, a nervous twitch. About-faced, and strode off into the shadows.

The monks let go of me. Victor said, "Come," and minced across the cavern to a nook about five feet high. I followed. A lantern lit the alcove.

On the floor, a low table surrounded by bean bags. A chessboard sat ready for battle. Blood dribbled from Victor's broken nose. He beckoned a nearby monk. "A pair of pliers. And some medical tape. Fetch."

The monk's shaved head bowed, disappeared.

I eased myself into a bean bag. "So," I said. "Bat guano."

"You play chess, Horace?" Victor moved his king pawn forward two spaces.

"No," I said. "Can't say I do. And what does bat guano have to do with—"

"The key," he said, "is to know your opponent better than he knows himself."

"Like, duh," I said. Not that I ever bothered to think that far ahead, mind you.

He reached over the board, responded with my queen knight. "To know what he's going to do before he does it. Anticipate everything. Plan for everything." He looked at me. "Then it doesn't matter what happens. Every which way you win."

I said, "I suppose you know what I'm going to do now."

He wagged a finger at me. "You're a wild card, Horace. But that also makes you predictable."

"Oh yeah? Did you predict this?" I swept my arm across the board, sending the pieces flying.

He laughed. "Indeed I did. You are predictable in your wildness."

I frowned. "Maybe I am, maybe I'm not. How do you know that about me?"

"Pitt speaks highly of you, Horace. And now you are impatient for me to elaborate on the theme of bat guano. Am I not correct?"

"I still don't see what bat guano has to do with Pitt becoming a born-again whatever-you-are. But go ahead." I sat back in my bean bag. "Talk."

A grin peeked around Victor's hand, his voice nasal. "You are aware," he said, "of how Bolivia lost its coastline?"

"Sure," I said. "There was a war. Back in the 1880s. Over the bat guano. But what's that got to do with me and Pitt?"

"Thousands of years of bat droppings accumulated in the Atacama Desert. The Europeans and Americans paid big money for the stuff. So Chile declared war on Bolivia and took away her coastline. Some of Peru's, too."

My applause echoed loud in the cavern. "Wonderful history lesson. Get to the point?"

We paused as Kate approached, teapot balanced on a platter. She knelt, put three cups down in front us, poured tea in two. It smelled of cardamom and cloves. I tasted it. Brewed in milk. But it was missing the secret ingredient.

"What," I said. "No *pisco?*"

She shook her head. Bit her lip.

"We do not permit alcohol here," Victor said.

"Whoa," I said. Touched her elbow. "How do you survive?"

She stood without looking at me. "There are other ways of coping, Horse."

Victor smiled at her. "Thank you, my dear."

Kate marched back into the darkness of the cave.

"No *pisco*," I said. "That's what I call doing it harsh."

"That is a matter of perspective." Victor sipped his chai. "For instance, losing your coastline is harsh. Becoming a landlocked nation is harsh. How would you feel?"

I shrugged. "Must have pissed them off."

"It still does," said Victor. "Know what tomorrow is?"

"Two days after yesterday?"

"Maritime Day. In La Paz. At 4000m above sea level. You believe it? There will be marches, parades, speeches. President Ovejo will fire his pistol in the air, demand Chile return their land. Bolivians will wave their flags, stomp their feet and go home unhappy."

"They want their bat guano back."

Victor chuckled, blew on his tea. "Bat guano is worthless these days. What they want is a road to the sea."

"Hence the Bolivian navy on Lake Titicaca."

"If you can call it a navy."

I sipped my chai. Without liquor it was undrinkable. I hurled the cup at the wall. The impact splattered Victor with hot tea. I stood, stooping under the alcove's low ceiling. "It's been lovely. Really it has. But either you tell me where Pitt is, and what the hell is going on, or I'm walking out of here right now."

"I'm afraid I can't let you do that, Horace."

A bald head descended into the light, a pair of pliers glinting in an outstretched palm. Beside it, a roll of green medical tape. Victor flicked the tape at me.

"What's this for?"

"Broke a finger, didn't you?"

The pinkie on my left hand was mashed. I had forgotten about it. "Oh. Thanks." I unrolled a piece of tape, tore it off with my teeth. The thudding pain of broken bone made delightful background noise to this uninvited conference with Victor. I bound the injured digit to its neighbor.

Victor weighed the pliers in his palm. He said, "Pitt is on Isla del Sol. You'll see him tomorrow. Now sit down."

"What's he doing on Isla del Sol? Hanging out with a bunch of tourists?" I finished the job on my finger.

He shoved the pliers in his mouth. "No, actually. He's negotiating with the CIA. To try to stop the war. Now sit."

The lantern light illuminated half of Victor's face, leaving the other side in darkness. He twisted the pliers. I could hear the roots of the tooth shred as it separated from his flesh. His head jerked back. Clamped between the pliers was a broken tooth. He asked, "What do they produce at that mine?"

"Where Pitt works?"

He waved a hand. "The Anglo-Dutch mine. Yes."

I took off my woolen hat and ran my fingers through my hair. "Lithium."

"Foreigners wanted bat guano, so Bolivia lost its coastline." He spat blood, put the pliers back in his mouth. "Now the foreigners want the lithium."

I shrugged. "So they're going to take it."

"Precisely." He spoke around the pliers. Another jerk, another tooth. "Ovejo's a socialist. Ninety percent of the world's lithium comes from the *altiplano*. The salt flats." Victor mopped his lips with the crusty handkerchief, fished around in his mouth with an index finger. "The Chilean mine just across the border produces most of the world's lithium at present. There are also small deposits in Tibet, Afghanistan and Australia, but the world's biggest reserves are in Bolivia itself."

I sat down again. "So what?" I said. "Has the entire world gone manic-depressive? Is the demand really that high?"

Victor paused, his cup halfway to his lips. Blood leaked onto his chin. "Do you not read the papers?"

"I've got enough misery in my own life without reading about the rest of the world."

"The oil is running out. You know this." It was not a question.

"Sure."

"What happens then?"

"We all die. And good riddance."

A raised index finger. "Lithium is used to make batteries for electric cars."

I asked, "Why can't the Americans just buy the lithium? Wouldn't that be cheaper?"

"At Ovejo's extortionate prices? Think OPEC, only ten times worse."

I considered that. "What's the pretext? For war, I mean."

Victor shifted sideways in his bean bag until he sat next to me. He lowered his voice. His hairy knuckles caressed my forearm. "A bomb, Horace. They are going to blow up the Bolivian mine. The CIA. Make it look like the Chileans did it."

"Are people going to believe that?"

"The domestic situation in La Paz is tricky. Ovejo will have to respond. Support for his policies is fading. He is a maniac for power. He will have to invade Chile just to save face."

"Then what?"

Victor settled back in his bean bag. "Peru and Bolivia have a secret alliance. Peru will break the alliance. Bolivia invades Chile, Peru invades Bolivia, together the two countries divide the *altiplano.*"

"And once again Bolivia gets screwed."

He poured himself another cup of chai. Every movement in the cave echoed, a chattering of shuffled feet and subdued voices.

"How do you know all this?" I said at last, dreading the answer.

"You know my source already."

I choked on my own saliva. "Pitt."

"Who else?"

Victor held the teapot over the empty third cup. I nodded. It was better than nothing, I supposed. He poured.

I said, "So Pitt finds out about this plot. He comes here? To you? Why?"

"Pitt is a man of conscience."

I made a rude noise.

"If you think that," Victor said, "then you do not know your friend as well as I had hoped. He came here to atone. For his sins."

"Was he successful?"

"Yes. And you can be too."

I looked around me. Water dripped from stalactites. "By chanting mantras in a freezing cave?"

"He saw what we have here. What we do. That a war would destroy all this."

"All what?"

He shrugged. "Our work. Volunteering. Meditation. Our search for peace."

The hot chai burned my lips. I drank anyway. "How," I said, "do you propose to stop this war?"

"We've got a plan." He held up a hand. "Forgive me if I do not tell you all my secrets on first acquaintance. But if you're willing, we'd like you to do the honors."

"I'm sorry?"

Victor leaned into the light, his raccoon eyes puffing many shades of purple. He snuffled on blood, swallowed.

"Pitt had you kidnapped," he said, "because he thought you'd want to be here."

"You keep saying that, but all I see are a bunch of self-righteous volunteers in orange-and-red sheets."

"Here you can find the redemption that you seek."

I lifted one side of the chess table. The teapot and chessboard crashed to the floor. "No redemption here," I said. "Hello-o?" I hollered. "Redemption? Woof-woof? Doggy treat, big boy?"

"Stop the American evil." Victor's voice was sharp now. "Send it back where it belongs. Turn the tide on the forces of imperialism, be part of something great. The greatest thing to ever happen to mankind."

I frowned. "That's not a war you can win. That's why I left the States in the first place."

"You cannot escape them," he said quietly. "Their monstrous reach extends to every corner of the globe."

"Tempting," I said. "Find brick wall. Apply forehead. Tally ho!"

He took a picture from his pocket and held it out to me. A pretty blonde woman, mid-thirties, and a girl, obviously her daughter, aged twelve or so.

"See this?"

"Your favorite whores?"

I didn't see the hand coming. My cheek burned. I blinked a couple of times. I thought about slugging him back, but decided I deserved the slap. "Not prostitutes then," I said.

"They are my family, Horace," Victor said. His face was intense. "The Americans killed them."

"Bullet, blade or bomb?" I asked.

His hand shook. He put the picture back into his shirt pocket. He said, "Blade. A not very sharp one, either."

"Oh," I said. It leaked out against my will. "I'm sorry."

"First the CIA tortured them. With a rusty steak knife. In front of me. These very eyes, Horace." He chewed his lip. A trickle of blood ran down his chin. "Then the Americans raped them. And when I still refused to talk, they hung them from the ceiling by their toes and set them both on fire." He rubbed an eye. "The screams...they made me watch."

A bubble of silence surrounded us. I spoke first.

"Why would they do something like that? Are you a dissident?"

His fingers threaded together and apart. "I made a great discovery, Horace." He lifted his chin. "I am a geologist. I found a way to harness the Earth's energy. For peaceful purposes. But they wanted me to make a terrible weapon. That uses the Earth's own power for destruction. I refused."

"So how come you're still alive?"

He tapped his temple. "Because of what's in here. They kill me, they will never know the secret."

"What's the weapon?"

He shook his head sadly. "That will go with me to the grave."

"And now you want your revenge, is that it?"

He sat back, examined his fingernails. "I have passed beyond the revenge chakra, my friend. Gaia shall exact true justice on our oppressors. I seek only peace in what little time remains to me."

I chuckled. "With a little help from a brigade of activist monks armed to the teeth, is that it?"

"You like what you see here?" Victor asked.

"You mean living in a cave?" I said. "Not really, no."

"Horace." His eyebrows narrowed. "We do, actually. We ask only to be left alone. And a war would destroy this. All of it."

"But we're on the Peruvian side of the lake," I objected.

"You think that's going to make a difference when the shooting war starts?"

"Look," I said. I drank my tea. It burned its way into my belly. "Everybody's got to die. Nothing I can do about it."

"Just one man, Horace." Victor sat back, his face now in darkness. "One man can save the world. One man can destroy it. Which man are you?"

"Funny. Ambo told me the same thing. Although according to him the world can't be saved."

"He was half-right," Victor said with a smile. "It only takes one man. You're more powerful than you realize."

"You're both wrong," I said. "Hell, I can't even save myself. How am I supposed to save the world?"

"It is by saving the world that you save yourself. The work is the cure."

I sneezed. "Bullshit."

Victor's head bowed, the crown of his head in the light. "I'm sorry you feel that way."

Guilt tugged at my soul, buried itself like a frightened chipmunk in my astral carry-on baggage. *What's an extra gram,* I thought, *when you're carrying multiple metric tons.*

"It's none of my concern." I drained my chai, let the empty cup crash to the floor at my feet. "They want to kill each other? I say, let them."

16

THE DINNER HOUR.

Cauldrons bubbled over wood fires on the smooth pebbles high on the beach. Victor brought me here, put a bowl in my hands, then excused himself. I stood in line, a single file of silent monks. A cold wind blew. I shivered. The monks were dressed in less than I was, but either did not feel the cold, or pretended not to.

I shuffled forward, my boots hissing against the small stones. My body was in agony from lack of my usual medications. Food might help me think more clearly. I had agreed to wait until tomorrow to see if Pitt would show up. Not that I had much choice in the matter. Where was I going to go?

I tapped the monk ahead of me in line. Asked, "You guys been here long?"

He looked over his shoulder, wagged his finger at me, put it to his lips.

"What, no talkie-talkie? Moron."

My turn came at the canteen. A fat monk spooned rice into my bowl. His face shone with sweat. It trickled down his chin, dripped into the pot beneath him. He scooped some broth over my rice. I looked up, expecting more.

"That all?"

But his frantic waving told me to move along, that he too could or would say nothing.

The monks scattered across the beach. They sat along the shore, watching the moon hover over Isla del Sol.

"Hey! Everyone!" I shouted. I waved my arms to get their attention. Thirty or so shaved heads regarded me in silence. "I'm looking for my friend Pitt! Any of you seen him? No? No one? Anyone?"

They shook their heads in unison, brought their fingers to their lips. "Goddamn deluded idiots," I said, and plopped myself down in the sand.

No chopsticks, no spoon. As I puzzled over the best way to eat my meager meal, a monk sat in the sand a few feet away. Blue denim peeked out at his ankles. So that was how they kept warm.

The broth scalded my tongue. I scooped up a wad of rice, burning my fingertips, juggled it against my molars, relishing the pain. The monk at my side stopped eating. He watched the food travel from bowl to mouth.

"Have *you* seen Pitt?" I asked, breathing steam.

Pitt? He mouthed the word, then said it out loud. "Pitt?"

"You talk?"

"Shh!" He pointed. I followed his gaze. A fire burned at the far end of the beach. Victor and Kate knelt, studying what appeared to be a map. The master monk sat near them, his elaborate headdress adding an extra two feet to his height. The whip curled over his shoulder.

"So what's the deal?" I said. "No one wants to talk to me."

"I'm just a volunteer," he said, voice barely audible. He

looked out over the water, bowl under his chin, lips barely moving.

"Volunteer. Is that the word." I opened my mouth wide, letting the cold air soothe my burnt palate. "Bunch of morons, you ask me."

"They haven't brainwashed you then." He picked at his food.

"I'm sorry?" I said, and studied him, but his face was low over his bowl. I looked back. The master monk walked along the beach toward us, arms crossed over his chest.

The monk passed. I turned again to my dinner companion.

"Can't say I see the appeal, no." I lowered my voice. "You don't sound like the others. What happened? The brainwashers missed a spot?"

He kept his eyes on the ground, moved his lips imperceptibly. "Let's just say I'm beginning to have my doubts."

I swallowed a mouthful of rice. "You really think Victor can stop the war?"

The guy choked on his soup. The monk with the whip looked sharply at us for a long moment. I waved. He looked away.

"Is *that* what he told you," the guy muttered.

"What," I said, "you mean, there's more?"

He leaned his head toward the fire, toward Victor and Kate. "Get a hold of that map. See if you can—"

"Michael!"

My eating buddy swallowed, an audible gulp of unchewed food.

"Bowl down. On feet." The accent was thick, strange, Asian. The same I'd heard in the van.

Michael stood. He covered his ass with his hands.

"Vow silence, Michael. When you learn?" The master monk stood between us. The whip dangled from his hand. It resembled Sergio's cat-o'-nine-tails. Four feet long, a dozen strips of leather ending in twists of barbed wire. He said, "Ten strokes."

Michael reached under his robes, unsnapped his jeans. He pushed them down to his ankles. He lifted his robes, exposing his bare cheeks. He took the whip, hefted it in one hand.

"One," he said. He whipped the instrument over his shoulder. It dug into the skin. He yanked it free, and bits of gore flecked onto the sand.

"Two."

In slow strokes he slashed at his exposed flesh. Blood poured from deep gashes. He counted to ten, numbering each stroke, but otherwise made no sound.

The robes slipped to the ground. He bowed toward the master monk, returned the whip.

The monk bowed back. "Flesh weak. Mortal. Must teach it, obey. Then, mind free."

Michael closed his eyes, nodded. He stepped out of his jeans, draped them over his shoulder. He bent down for his bowl of food, but the master monk kicked it away, spilling the broth in the sand.

The beach. Later. The man in the moon hid behind the gathering clouds, ashamed to look at us. Kate sat on the sand at my side. It was cold. We hugged our knees with our arms. The night was a long, bitter silence between us. I spoke first.

I knew the answer before I opened my mouth, but said it anyway.

"We could try again. Have another child."

"No!"

There was fury in her voice, the untouchable righteous anger that had once drawn me to her. Smite all injustice, tear down the corrupt, rebuild the world anew. Her impossible idealism had been the perfect counterpoint to my cynicism.

Until La Paz.

"We are but a speck of dirt on Gaia. We are cockroaches," she exploded, in answer to my unspoken question.

"Yeah," I said. "I'd agree with that."

"No," she said. Her finger out, instructive. "An infection. A disease. We are leeches sucking the life force from this planet." She put her lips an inch from my ear. "A liver fluke. A brain parasite."

I did not turn. I stared at Isla del Sol. One by one the lights on the island went out. I wondered if Pitt really was over there. If he was looking back at us right now. If he felt the same way.

"Parasites," I said, and imagined myself as groin lice on an ugly whore.

She followed my gaze. "Yes. Parasites. We deserve to die."

"I suppose we do."

"All of us."

"Absolutely."

The memories flooded in. I could no longer hold back the images, the torn, shredded cries that lingered in my soul.

"This ends here." She stabbed my knee with her finger. "With me. I will not spread the infection any further."

"Is that why you're with him? With—" I forced the

word out, like a tough turd. "With Victor? Playing activist? Stopping a war?"

She rested her chin on her knees. "Wars are petty things. They do not interest me. I think only in the end of days, and the care of my soul."

"End of days. Care of your soul." I stared at her in profile, her forehead hard and white in the moonlight. "It's just a stupid fucking war. What is this talk of apocalypse? You expecting a pale horse?"

"No," she said, looking dreamily at the stars. "The apocalypse will be man-made. It will be an enormous, global orgy of self-destruction, a long asphyxiation on exhaust pipe fumes, and coal plant dust, and heavy metal poisoning. In our greed and ambition we will achieve only death."

I found myself in the unexpected role of devil's advocate to a cynic. "Is there no hope? Treaties, and all that. Stop global warming?"

"No," she said. "There is no hope. Man is an evil, base creature who deserves to die. Deep down we all know that. Understand that. We deserve to be punished. Can't you see?"

She turned to face me now, lips close enough to feel her hot breath on my cheek.

"And Gaia will punish us," I suggested, with a laugh that withered on my lips.

"She will." Kate looked at the stars again, nodded her head. "Oh, she will. All equally. And all just as fatally."

I remember holding Lili in my arms for the first time. How she howled! The sweetest sound I ever heard. Everything was new. Everything was different. We were pioneers in a world of delight. Diapers? What a wonderful surprise! Weeks without sleep? No problem! The world was young and we were in it and we were happy.

After a couple of months, we got restless. Twelve-hour days running the hostel followed by twelve-hour nights with the baby exhausted us both. And diapers soon lost their luster.

"Take a week off," Alex had shouted across a throng of backpackers. "Hell, take a month off. You've earned it."

So we did. We came to Lake Titicaca. Stayed a week on Isla del Sol. Warm days, cold nights. Kate nursed. Slept. I hiked the island, admiring the never-ending views. One could live here, I thought, peaceful till the end of days.

It had been Kate's idea to visit the island. She had studied anthropology, and was fascinated by the Incan death cults. When she was strong enough, she'd traipse around the island in the afternoons, visiting archaeological sites and practicing her Quechua on the local llama herders.

The Incas, she told me breathlessly one night as we struggled toward orgasm, had a deluge story, like in the Bible.

"You mean like Noah."

"Like that," she groaned. "Yes, like that. One day the volcanoes will erupt."

"Which volcanoes?"

"All of them. At the same time. Yes. Like that." She quivered, gasped, lay back on her pillow. "And it will herald the end of the world."

"Sounds deep," I said.

She giggled. Stretched her arms over her head. "Lake Titicaca will evaporate, and the island will become a mountain in a dropless sea."

"What a seriously downer take on life," I said.

"Isn't it, though?"

***

That was when we got the email. From Greg and Luisa.

Cross the border. Let's party!

Some party.

***

The hostel in La Paz. Lili asleep in the borrowed crib. I stroke her forehead. Turn back to Kate. "Just for a few hours. You need a break. She'll be fine."

"But are you sure?" She frowns at me, forehead crinkled.

Greg drains his beer and belches. "You lucked out, mate. Didn't even know he had a sister."

"If you say so," she says, and buries her nose in my neck.

"Couple hours," I say. "Back at ten." I put my arms around her waist. "What could go wrong?"

Chicken curry sparkles on my tongue, the best I've had in ages. Candle wax curls in swirls of multicolored bliss down the sides of a Chianti bottle. Kate lifts her glass in a toast to the world: to motherhood, Liliana, me.

"May you have many more!" Greg yells, already shitfaced.

"Maybe we should have one, darling," Luisa says, fingers plucking at the back of Greg's thinning hair.

While they smooch, I lead Kate to the tiny dance floor. I'm not a fan of amplified pan pipe music, but right now I'm so happy I don't care. Her hand in mine, my palm cupping the curve of her spine, her lips at my throat, we sway to the music, the rhythm pulsing through us, making us one with the universe.

Back at the table, Greg and Luisa argue. He's drunk. No he's not.

"Don' wan' no water," he mumbles at the top of his lungs.

"I'm not cleaning up your puke tonight." Luisa pushes a glass of water toward him.

He huffs and frowns, head lolling on his shoulders. He reaches for the water glass, knocks it over. Kate shrieks as the cold water lands in her lap. We jump up, mopping the spill with a fistful of paper napkins.

"Sorry," Greg mutters, eyes glazed. "Sorry, sorry, I—"

"It's fine. Don't worry about it." Kate is unfazed. Nothing can ruin her night out. She is happy. "What's the time?"

Greg studies his watch, cogitation slowing to a crawl. "It is," he announces, lips parting carefully, readying the words, "almost two o'clock."

Later than we thought.

A rusty taxi with holes in the floor grinds up the cobblestone hill to the hostel. The night guard doesn't answer the bell. We shiver in the bitter air. What could have happened? What's going on?

"Relax," I say, as much to myself as to her.

Kate's grip tightens on my arm. Carlos comes to the gate, buckling his belt. Runs a fat finger under his nose, wipes away a ring of white powder, pops it in his mouth. From an upper window a woman peers out, clutching a blanket to her chest.

Kate has been holding her breath. "Oh thank goodness."

"*Disculpeme,* Don Gregorio," Carlos says, and scratches his crotch. "I sleep poorly. The baby."

Kate tenses at my side. "The baby? Whose baby. Our baby?"

"What a set of lungs, that kid. Finally shut his yap so I can sleep."

Kate surges up the stairs. Greg vomits in the toilet. Luisa lays a finger on my arm. "We had fun," she says. "We're glad you came."

"We're glad we came too," I say. A tired smile dimples my cheeks. "It was a good night."

A feral shriek above stiffens my spine. I scramble after Kate, taking the stairs two at a time, tripping, drunken, cracking my shins against the bare boards. Kate screams again.

"I'm coming!" I shout.

"What's the matter?" Luisa behind me.

I gasp for breath, stumble along the hallway, my hand on the wall. I lean into our room, shoulder on the door frame. Kate is bending over the crib.

"Baby, what's going on?" I ask.

A rat runs across my foot. Two more follow. They stagger down the hallway, skin stretched tight across their bloated bellies.

"What the hell?" Luisa says.

Kate takes another breath, exhales a screech so sharp it hurts my ears.

"You'll wake the other guests," Greg grumbles drunkenly in the doorway, wiping vomit from his lips. "What are you—"

But I stand next to Kate now, looking down at the crib.

Looking down at Liliana.

Or what is left of her.

We sat cross-legged on the sand. Kate stared across the lake, a blanket wrapped around her shoulders. I wondered if she was thinking about that night, too.

It was freezing but she wasn't wearing gloves. I pulled off a mitten with my teeth, took her hand in mine. Squeezed. Her frozen claw crushed my fingers, as though unsure what to do with the sudden warmth. A drop of water splashed the back of my hand. Was it mine? No. Was it hers? Her dry cheeks reflected the merciless moonlight.

I opened my mouth, but the cold, thin air rasped in my throat. No words could do her sorrow justice. I pried my hand from hers. Put my arm around her and drew her down to my shoulder. Unable to cry. Unable to sob. Unable to grieve. She pressed herself into my chest. We two impotent monsters clung together in the cold and the dark, and waited for the light.

17

ACROSS THE LAKE ON THE ISLAND, A FLAME appeared, bulged bright in the midnight blackness. It paused, as though catching its breath in the thin mountain air, belched skyward at the stars.

Kate's cold nose dented my neck. She gasped, pulled away. The rumbling bass of the explosion reached us, a growling thumping of deep white noise. Another explosion ripped free of its earthly moorings, then a third. We tensed, waiting for the rest of the symphony to bounce across the waveless waters.

They've killed him.

"I hope not," Kate said, and I realized I'd spoken out loud.

I pushed myself up from the cold beach, my feet wallowing in the soft dry granules. I brushed my butt clean. "Better get over there."

"I wouldn't," she said. And pulled me close.

"If they've killed Pitt—"

"Then he's dead. There's nothing you can do."

"But if we can catch the DSU, whoever did it—"

"They will likely kill you too."

I unhooked her fingers from my pants. "That's the point,"

I said.

"I'm sorry, what?" Her voice, wounded.

I sighed. "Look. I can't go back to Lima. The Americans want to deport me. This stupid wild-goose chase trying to find Pitt, and all I get is a bunch of ashram do-gooder mumbo-jumbo. 'End the guilt,' my ass. And you." I turned away. "It was stupid," I said. "I know. You moved on. Of course you did."

"Horse," she said. "I—"

"Now let me have one of those AK-47s. Couple extra clips of ammunition, and I'll go over there, see how many of the fuckers I can take with me." I forced a grin. "Least I can do."

The sand spurted under my heels. I clumped in hulking strides to the safety of the driftwood and the high water line. Her light feet danced behind me.

She said, "Horse." She said, "Please."

I called over my shoulder, "If I died right now, who would miss me?"

She staggered in the sand, a ship in a squall. I held out my arm and she grabbed it. "I would miss you, Horse."

I avoided her gaze. "Nice of you to say," I said as roughly as I could. "Now why don't you go chant a mantra or something."

"I'm not just saying it, Horse." She hugged her arms to her chest.

I held her close to me. "Come with me if you want."

"Horse..."

"We deserve to die. Your words." I stood back, held out my hand to her. "Now's your chance."

She tucked her chin into her chest. The tears poured freely

now. "I just don't want them to hurt you."

I kissed her cheek. I whispered, "Goodbye, my love."

Down along the curve of the cove sat half a dozen fishing boats, outboard motors in the air. I had no idea how to use one, but a couple quick tugs on the engine cord ought to be enough. A pyramid of stacked AK-47s stood conveniently close to the boats. There was even an open crate full of ammunition. A monk with a rifle patrolled the far end of the beach.

A hand trickled across my vision. Cold fingers brushed my broken nose, my cheeks. My lips. *Sausages,* I thought. The fleshy butt of her palm pressed against my stubble. I bit it. Tasted blood.

"That's new," she said, nursing her wounded hand. "You learned that from someone else." Her eyes like dinner plates, a feast for the hungry soul.

"Don't toy with me," I said. I aimed for softness but it came out a sneering curse.

Her eyes flickered across my face. Then her lips were on mine, her bleeding palm behind my neck, her tongue like liquid fire past my teeth, past my defenses, into my holy of holies, and I cried out my sorrow, pouring it down her throat, pumping a year's worth of agony and soul-blackening disease into this old receptacle, newly provided for my salvation. We clung to each other, two heavily dressed lovers fumbling for maximum access and minimum exposure on a cold dark beach.

Purple streaks of light on my eyelids. Then orange and pink. A sudden whiteness. Fluttering fingers caressed my face. One word:

"Goodbye."

I opened my eyes, squinted at the fierce sun on the horizon. A dozen of the worst hangovers of my life partied simultaneously between my ears. Going cold turkey on a diet like mine was no fun. Then I remembered.

I groped the sand next to me. A cold indentation stretched out parallel, a snow angel of the beach, a sand angel, the footprint of heaven.

An angel gone missing.

So. I had my answer. But not the one I had expected. And not the one I had hoped for.

"Hold on to me till morning and I'm yours," she breathed *in my ear.*

"And if I fall asleep?"

"Then this will be goodbye. Forever."

Another piece in the puzzle of the Incompetent Asshole Horace. I pulled my woolen hat lower over my ears. Each breath drained vital vapor from my lungs. I was thirsty. A thin denouement of smoke rose from Isla del Sol. I got to my feet, joints aching from the cold. In the sand, she had written, *Liliana.* Like I needed a reminder. I scrubbed it out with my boot, and ambled back toward the cave.

I had no hope left. But that was OK. I felt an amazing sense of freedom. I had nothing left to lose but my life—and what was that worth? Cockroach shit. I would go out in a blaze of glory. Give me something to gossip about with the other inmates of hell, anyway.

Monks jogged to and fro between the cave and the boats, racing through the tiny village pushing wheelbarrows.

Others patrolled the shore, automatic rifles over their shoulders, hands shading their eyes, as though expecting unwanted visitors.

The volunteers in street clothes sat on the ground, backpacks and suitcases at their sides, singing "Kumbaya," praising Gaia. Each fondled an orange-and-scarlet robe. A monk with a sledgehammer stood at the mouth of the cave, smashing the generator. Another chopped electrical cable into pieces with an axe. A third stood by with a pitchfork, filling a nearby wheelbarrow with rubbish before racing off through the village. In the distance an outboard motor roared. The boat darted a few hundred meters into the lake, dumped its load, then buzzed back to shore.

I barged my way past the monks into the mouth of the cave. I bent double, stumbling ahead in the dark, before crashing my skull into something hard.

The something hard swore.

"Seen Victor?" I asked.

"Inside. Take this."

He pressed a flashlight against my chest. I switched it on, continued into the cave.

Headlamps on foreheads flickered around the cavern. Victor sat at his laptop in the center of the overarching dome. I strode across the smooth floor.

"Victor," I shouted. My voice echoed in the chamber. The taste of his wife resounded in my nose.

"No need to shout," he murmured, finger to his lips, studying the laptop display.

I dropped my palms on the desk, the flashlight skewing upward at my face, illuminating me in goblin shadow. "The fuck is going on? And where is Kate?"

He looked up. "We're evacuating. What does it look like?"

"And Kate?" I insisted.

He looked back at the display. "Kate has gone to a safe place."

Did he know about her and me, last night? She had said she suffered from insomnia. That they rarely slept together. Could he guess? I didn't think so.

I snorted. "There are no safe places if the Americans want you dead."

"Safer than here, anyway, Horace. Come with us if you like."

"And then what?"

"What do you mean?"

"You're here to stop a war, right? What's your next play?"

He shrugged. "Pitt was our last 'play,' as you put it. He was our secret weapon. We tried to negotiate. To keep what we have built here. We lost. Now there is only to retreat."

"That's it?" I said. "Are you serious? Fuck that. Give me a gun and a boat. I'll be your one-man fucking army."

He laughed. "A big change from last night, Horace. Are you sure you don't prefer to just 'let them kill each other,' as you so eloquently put it?"

"There are worse ways to die than going out guns blazing. Any CIA left on that island, I'll find them."

He laughed again. "Which will be none. I know little about assassins, but I imagine they do not stick around for a long time after killing people."

"So what, I should go hide in a hole somewhere with you?" I said. "So they can hunt me down and kill me?" A new thought occurred to me. A glimmer of—

"Besides," I said, "how can you be sure Pitt's dead?"

"Pitt has gone to Gaia. We shall mourn him later. Right now we have to get out of here, or they will kill us all." He slapped the laptop shut, stowed it in a black vinyl case at his side.

"But how can you be sure? Maybe he was in the bathroom or something when the bomb went off. Maybe he's wounded, and needs medical attention."

"That's noble of you, Horace. But Pitt has resources, as you know. If he's still alive, and they haven't captured him, he will make his presence known."

The truth bubbled up, unbidden. "To see the body, then. Make sure he's really dead."

"Is that what this is all about?" Victor asked. He put his hand on my arm. "You don't have to see the body to know he's dead."

"But how can you be sure?"

"You saw the size of that bomb, Horace," he said. "There might not even be anything left of him to identify."

He strode to the exit. I trotted after him. His headlamp darted from side to side, as though he expected the floor to be booby-trapped.

He was right, of course. But I couldn't accept it. It drove me crazy. I had come all this way for nothing? Kate had said goodbye for good. What did that leave? I needed to tie off this loose end. What's that word overeducated up-their-own-asses yuppie American women in SUVs use? Closure. I needed to find "closure."

I rubbed my face with my fingers. They smelled like pussy

juice. "I'll just have to take that chance," I said. "I have to know."

Victor sidestepped around me and stooped to enter the tunnel. "And what are you going to do then? You find his body, assuming there's anything to find, then what?"

I stooped over and followed him. "Hunt down the ones who did it. Take revenge."

Victor spun on his heels, and I danced on tiptoe to avoid crashing into him. "Gaia is a jealous goddess, Horace. It is not for you to kill. Revenge is hers alone."

He strode toward the sunlight at the end of the tunnel. I grabbed his elbow. We glared at each other from under our eyebrows.

"I have to see the body. Know that he is dead. Know that there is really no more hope."

He put a hand on my shoulder. His face was swollen from yesterday. "There is always hope, Horace. Although what you hope for and what you need are sometimes different things."

We surged out into the morning sun. I turned off my flashlight and gave it to him.

"I'm going," I said. "With or without your permission."

I broke into a run, passing wheelbarrow after wheelbarrow of frayed orange electrical cable. A spare fishing boat lay beached at the end of the sand. A green fishing net stretched across it. I yanked the net from the boat, dug my toes into the sand and heaved. The boat slid into the lake, the freezing water soaking my boots for a second time. I helped myself to a spare AK-47, a box of ammunition, and jumped into the boat.

"Hey!" a monk carrying a rifle shouted at me.

I yanked the engine cable. Not as easy as it looked. The motor spluttered, but did not respond to my caresses.

The monk pointed his rifle at me. I yanked again, and a third time. The motor finally roared to life. I gripped the tiller. The boat shot ahead, nearly tumbling me into the lake. A burst of gunfire shredded the stillness. Splashes of water astern. I looked back. Victor stood next to the monk, one hand jamming the offending weapon skyward, the other hand held high, an unmoving salute. The monk shouldered the rifle, watched me for a long while.

Halfway to the island I beat my head against my palm. She had said so many things last night. So many things I had wanted to tell her—everything—but the hinges were rusty, the lock was broken, a crowbar was needed to reopen my heart.

"Ever think that we could try again?" I asked her. The truth was better than burning myself with cigarettes. More painful, and left a deeper scar.

"You can't undo the past."

I kissed her, drew her closer to me. "The hostel's still there. We can have the life we dreamed of. You. Me. A family."

She pushed me away. "I told you already. No."

I sat up on my elbow. "Then what is Victor?"

"Victor?"

"Yes."

She stretched out flat on the sand. "Victor is Victor. That's all."

"What does that mean?"

She was suddenly furious, beating her fists against me. "You could have come. You didn't come. Why didn't you come?" She beat against my forearms, but then I let them drop and her fists pounded my chest, my face, my shoulders. Her cold nose dripped snot and tears onto my neck. She fell, her face on my chest.

"So it's my fault then," I said.

"It's not that." She wiped her nose with her robe. "Victor is useful."

"Well that's a recommendation."

"You don't understand."

"I think I do."

She sat up and traced the lines of my face with frozen fingers.

"No," she said at last. "You don't. But that's alright. I don't want you to." She bowed her head. "Not yet, anyway."

I pulled her down to me. She lay her head on my shoulder.

"But you've found peace."

"Yes," she said, the tears dripping from her chin. "I've found peace."

"You chant *om* and wear funny clothes and that helps, does it?"

She laughed. She never used to have such massive mood swings. "There are few things in this world I'll miss, Horse. You're one of them."

I sat up next to her. "That's a funny thing to say. You planning to exit stage left?"

"We go when Gaia is ready," she said simply. "Not before."

I frowned. "Kate. Is there something you're not telling me?"

"Like what?"

I thought of Michael the monk's words. "Like what's on the map you and Victor were looking at."

"Escape routes," she said quickly. "In case the CIA attacks. Why do you ask?"

I looked at her sideways. "What's really going on here?" She said nothing. I groped for my pants. "I really ought to get over to the island."

She held me tight. "What do you think's going on, silly?"

I was on top of her and in her before she could cry out. "Ditch Victor," I said, my face in her hair. "We can be happy together again."

She lifted my head and looked me in the eyes. "Hold on to me till morning," she said. "Then I am yours."

"And if I fall asleep?"

She pulled me down into her. "Then this will be goodbye. Forever."

Two Bolivian gunships. Cannon pointed at me.

I rounded the corner of the island and there they were, gray behemoths armed by sailors with saltwater envy. They were anchored just offshore, blocking my path to the south beach, the main landing area for the island. I nudged the rifle under a pile of life preservers with my foot.

A narrow space between the two ships. I slowed the engine, aimed the launch toward the gap.

"*Quite el motor!*" a megaphone trumpeted.

I cut the engine, let the momentum carry me alongside. A potbellied dwarf looked down at me. He wore a blue uniform and his cap, weighed down by mountains of gold braid, tilted low over his nose. Two grunts in camouflage and helmets dangled their rifles over the side, loosely pointed at my vital organs.

So this was the mighty Bolivian navy. The guns were real though. I smiled and put my hands in the air.

"*Sí, señor,*" I said. "*Que está pasando?* I want to visit the island."

"No one gets on or off the island today."

I winced. Two meters above me, the dwarf leaned over the gunwale, shouted straight down at the crown of my head through his megaphone.

I said, "Friend of mine is on the island. Want to know if he's OK."

"*No go, gringo,*" growled one of the grunts cheerfully.

"*No soy gringo!*" I thrust my fist in the air. "*Viva la revolución!* Death to the American imperialist tyrants!"

The two marines ducked their heads, chuckling. A yellow hand touched the braided dwarf on the shoulder. The dwarf turned. From the way his shoulders twitched, he was arguing with someone. He turned back to me, megaphone still glued to his lips.

"Proceed to the island. Land at the eastern end of the beach. Report to the federal police." An unamplified expletive. "That is all."

The marines withdrew their weapons. "*Viva la revolución,*" one said to the other. The dwarf smacked the back of the marine's helmet, then hopped about, shaking his palm.

I performed CPR on the motor, puttered at low throttle between the ships. I looked back. An Asian man next to the dwarf turned away as I did so, a blue baseball cap pulled low over his eyes.

A Cubs cap.

18

I LANDED ON THE BEACH AS INSTRUCTED. Puttered in on low power. Cut the engine. Paddled the boat into shore, then jumped out, pulled the launch onto the sand.

The beach was swarming with backpackers. Happy-go-lucky souls who seemed to think the world was a beautiful place. Foreigners untouched by the world's true misery. They strutted like peacocks on the sand, colorful backpacks and expensive waterproof, quick-dry, zip-off pants. Prestidigitation made easy: look, Ma, now they're shorts!

The beach was not long. A few hundred meters. A backpacker per square meter, or thereabouts. How many spoiled middle-class brats was that? I suppressed what remained of my math cortex for once, lest the answer result in nausea.

A group of tall, blond, dreadlocked Swedes surrounded a pair of midget policemen in oversize peaked caps. All the Swedes' worldly possessions lay at their feet. They spoke Spanish with an Argentinian accent.

"Terrorists try to blow us up, here on the island, and you won't let us off?" one said.

The police officers simultaneously opened their arms wide in sympathy, a Bolivian sister act in camouflage drag. "But we feel the same way, *señor.* No one gets on or off the island. This is all we know."

I edged my way through the crowd, avoiding the cops. A huddle of girls spoke low in English, a thick British drawl.

"What's going on?" I asked.

"Like you don't know," said one with sunburned cleavage and Liverpudlian twang.

I hooked my thumb over my shoulder. "I just landed. Got my own boat."

The girls sat upright, a festival of perky mammaries. Soft Liverpudlian fingertips caressed the back of my hand. "Can you get us off?"

"Sure," I said, rolling my jaw. I tried not to look down their shirtfronts, failed. "As many times as you like," I added.

They groaned. Fists went to mouths, covered sudden smirks. One was not amused, however. "You got a boat or don't you?"

I smiled at their discomfort. "Of course." I pointed. "Right over there. What's with all the cops and stuff?"

A redhead with freckles scratched her cleavage, pulled down on her shirt so I could get a better view of her green bikini top. "You didn't see it last night?"

"See what?"

"The bloody fireball, mate. The explosion."

"Hotel Finski went fucking boom," said another, a blonde with a smoker's throaty voice and a T-shirt that showed stick figures engaged in various improbable sexual acts. "Must've killed a dozen people."

You can live in fear or you can live, Pitt had said. *Your choice, bucko.*

"Holy crap."

"Bucket brigade's been running up and down that bloody hill since before dawn." The redhead nodded over her shoulder. Stone and gravel steps led to the top of the island, four hundred meters above, where most of the hostels and hotels perched.

"Looking for a friend of mine," I said. "Name of Pitt. Any chance you seen him?"

"Pitt," puttered the Liverpudlian. "Pitt Pitt Pitt."

What was it about the man that left women and children stammering his name?

"American," I said. "Long blond hair, surfy looking? Shark-tooth necklace?"

"Pitt!" squealed the redhead.

"Everybody saw him." A roll of the eyes. Toss of blonde hair.

"Why? What happened?"

"Disgraceful." Her intonation and vocabulary verged on Valley Girl. "Total scene. Two girls got in a total clawing match over him."

I grinned. "That's Pitt, alright. What'd he do?"

The redhead held out a hand to silence her companion. "Told them both to fuck off."

"Let him drink his beer in peace."

"Too right."

The Liverpudlian and the redhead looked at each other, then at the sand. I got the feeling they were the two girls in question.

I raised my eyebrows. "Seen him since, by any chance?" My voice trailed off into the upper octaves.

"Not since yesterday."

"Oh. My. God." Naked palms caressed bare cleavage. "You don't think—"

"I don't," I said. "I just want to know." I craned my neck up at the hill. "They taken the bodies out yet?"

"No," said another, a silent scornful brunette with a tattoo of a penis on the side of her neck. "Still up there. Bloody Bolivians. You know how they are."

I turned and made for the stairs.

"Hey!" the redhead yelled after me, her green bikini-clad boobs falling out of her shirt at this point. "You gonna get us off or not?"

"Count on it," I said, and to my dismay they whipped their heads in mosh pit giggles. I heaved myself through the crowd to escape from the sound.

The *Escalera de las Incas,* as they are known, are steep. At four thousand meters, even without luggage, the climb was strenuous. I panted to a stop halfway up. An eruption of yellow hair quivered on a stair, the body beneath it curled into a fetal ball.

I gasped for air. "You're blocking the path."

A sob shook her. I squatted on my heels, pushed the hair out of her face. "Hey," I said. I patted her cheek. No response. I patted harder. I shook her shoulder roughly.

"You filthy pig!" she shouted, her accent Swedish, and swung a bare-knuckled punch at my face. I ducked. Her fist crashed against the back of my skull.

I grabbed her wrists. "Girl. Chill."

She clung to me, her head on my shoulder. "Why won't they let me see him?"

"See who?"

Her tears trickled down my neck. "Go away," she growled into my shoulder. "Let me die."

"Happy to," I said. "Do unto others and all that. First tell me what's the matter."

She clung to me tighter. "It's Sven."

"Who's Sven, baby?"

She sat back, dug her wrists into her eye sockets. "Sven is Sven." She tried to smile but failed. "Burnt and crispy. Toasty, even." She lowered her head into her hands.

"Where? How do you know?" I shook her. "Tell me."

"The fucking Finski. Boom." Her fingertips traced an explosion in midair.

"What happened?"

"We had a fight. Told him I was sick of traveling. He said I could go back to the hostel if I was tired."

"Did you?"

She nodded, lips pressed together, a trumpeter preparing a high note. "He went to have a beer. Finski's got a bar."

"I know." I'd gotten drunk there many times myself. "And?"

Her lower lip cavorted like a whirling dervish. "The last I saw him alive."

"And the bodies?"

This triggered the garden sprinklers for a second time.

I shook her. "The bodies. Where are they?"

"The fuck you care?" she wailed, chest heaving with sobs. "He's dead. Don't you see?"

"Hey," I said. She was yabbling away to herself in Swedish. I raised my voice. "Hey," I said. "I know how you feel. But I need your help."

She beat her forearms against my head, a toddler's tantrum. She screamed, "You don't know shit how I feel!"

I slapped her. Hard. She went still. Back straight, mouth open. I said, "You think you're the only one who's ever lost someone?"

She stared at me in wonder. A little voice came out of her face. "Have you lost someone too?"

I sat on the stair next to her. "Look. Just tell me where the bodies are. I'll leave you alone then. Promise."

"Who're you—you—" she stammered, and swallowed some snot. "Who're you looking for? Who did you lose?"

Below, black dots milled about on the beach. The warships stood offshore. I tried to block the memory. Failed. I said, "Who I lost is none of your business. I'm looking for a friend of mine. Name of Pitt. Blond hair, shark-tooth necklace?"

She shook her head. Pursed her lips to catch a sob. Her hair stuck to her face.

I said, "I have to go see if his body is there."

"They won't let you."

"Who?"

"You'll see." She raised her voice, claws extended, and screeched at the gorgeous blue sky. "Fucking animals!"

"Hang on," I said. "How do you even know Sven's dead? If you haven't seen his body, I mean."

"I stood here and watched," she said. "Everyone's down on the beach. The police insisted. Sven didn't pass by."

"So how can you be sure?"

"I saw... I saw, I saw..." She hyperventilated, and I slapped her again. She sat back on the stairs. She took a deep breath. "I saw his shoes. Sticking out. From under the blanket. Handmade shoes. I made for him. A gift. For this trip."

We sat there a long moment. The cold mountain wind blew through us. I put my hand on her shoulder. "I'm sorry," I said at last.

"Everybody's fucking sorry," she said. Shook her shoulder free. "That doesn't bring my Sven back."

I stood. Nodded. I'd been there. There was nothing I could say or do to help her. I left her sitting on the gravel-packed staircase, screaming Swedish curses at the empty heavens. I ran the next few stairs, eager to get away from her. She made me uneasy. I couldn't quite put my finger on why. But my progress was soon reduced to a slow, painful slog, pushing my protesting knees beyond their natural limit, the sound of her voice nagging at me like my overactive conscience.

I panted up the steep incline. At each step I passed fond memories, recollections I did not deserve, did not want to remember. Times of happiness and joy. The hotel where Kate and I once stayed. The restaurant where we ate breakfast, the view of the lake prominent from the garden terrace. The bush where we had made love, despite the thorns. The stretch of grass where we had lain, Liliana on my stomach, until she pooped and it trickled from her diaper onto my shirt.

The stairs evened out. I pushed myself forward along the now gentle incline. The haze of smoke in the sky grew nearer. I rounded a bend between two houses and there it stood:

the charred remains of the Hotel Finski: "Fun" Finski owner and sole proprietor, best backpacker hostel and bar on the island, and home to the only chef in Bolivia who knew how to prepare an authentic Malaysian satay.

The stench of burnt flesh filled the air. A crowd of soldiers loitered near the blackened shell of the building, smoking cigarettes. Empty buckets lay on the grass. A grunt with a machete hacked at low-level shrubs near a neighboring building. The remaining embers of the fire hissed and smoked.

Scattered about on the grass lay a dozen blankets covering body-length lumps. I started to run, my oxygen-starved muscles complaining, my lungs hungry for air. I fell to the ground next to the nearest corpse. Lifted the blanket. The skeletal face of an old woman grinned at me, bits of flesh attached to the jaw. Gray threads of silken hair twisted from the scalp. I slipped on the wet grass and pitched onto the body, the blanket slipping, the smell of burnt meat and hair enveloping me.

A shout behind me grew into a chorus. I humped the corpse, trying to get up, but fell again. The soldiers dragged me to my feet and held me tight.

"Looking for a friend," I said in Spanish.

A soldier in army fatigues with two chevrons on his sleeve swaggered over. A cigarette stuck to his lower lip. He looked me up and down. A rifle hung from his shoulder.

He said, "What kind of friend?"

"A friend. I told you. I think he might be here." I nodded at the bodies.

"The kind of friend who bombs hotels? Suicide bomber, maybe?"

"*Hijo de puta,*" I swore. "I saw the fire on the island. My friend was staying here. Let me find the body."

A soldier fished through my pockets, looking for my ID.

"*Pasaporte,*" the corporal said crisply.

"*No tengo.*"

"No passport?" He plucked the cigarette from his lips, blew smoke in my face and grinned, gold teeth glittering in the early morning light. "Then you are an illegal immigrant to Bolivia."

"I crossed the lake this morning. In a boat." I pleaded with the platoon of thin conscripts. "I just got here." I gestured to the corpses on the ground. "I saw the explosion. I was so worried, I must have left my passport at the hotel."

"And where is your hotel?"

"In Puno," I lied. "In Peru."

The corporal sucked on the stub of his cigarette, dropped it to the ground. The cinder flickered in the cold breeze. Smoke trickled upward toward my nose, died.

"My brother went to your country. He was an illegal. They put him in jail. They raped him in the ass. Your black people. Then they deported him. Now he has AIDS." He spat. "Why should we not do the same to you?"

I clenched my buttocks, wondering how to avoid an unwanted party in my pants.

"I have committed a grave crime against the Republic of Bolivia," I said. "While there is nothing I can do to make this right, perhaps as the smallest token of my sorrow, you will accept the two hundred US dollars in my left front trouser pocket as an on-the-spot fine."

The soldier holding my arms relaxed his grip, but did

not let go. The corporal pushed his pockmarked face close to mine, the tobacco stench masking the reek of death surrounding us. I thought about asking him for a cigarette, but decided against it.

"You try to bribe me, gringo? In my country, bribery is illegal."

I avoided his eyes. "In mine too, corporal. I would never think of something so base as to offer a bribe to an upright, outstanding exemplar of Bolivian *machismo* such as yourself." I angled my head toward the sky off my left shoulder, spoke to the soldiers behind me. "I mean no offense to the great people of Bolivia. I merely wish to ascertain if my friend be alive or dead. If what little I have can atone for my breaking of your sacred law, then I hope such a pitiful sum be sufficient that you forgive my atrocity."

The man behind me snickered. "He talks funny."

The corporal held my gaze. Then he clapped me on the shoulder and laughed. "We don't want your money, gringo." He jerked his chin at the man behind me. "Let him go."

I took a deep breath and rubbed my wrists. "Thank you, sir," I said, looking around at the blankets stretched out on the ground, wondering which, if any, of the lumps was Pitt. "If I can just—"

The corporal blocked my path again. He grinned. "Private Gonzalez here needs to see a dentist." The private in question smiled broadly, offering his black teeth into evidence. "The army does not pay privates much money. Perhaps you could help him out?"

"Of course," I said. I took the money from my pocket. It was all I had left from raiding the hostel's cash box. While crossing the lake in the boat, I had transferred my stash from its hiding place to my pocket, thinking I might need some money when I got to the island. I hadn't realized I would need it so soon. "How much does that cost?"

The corporal took the money from my hand. "I think forty dollars ought to be about right, don't you?"

I nodded vehemently, my chin banging against my collarbone. "That seems fair."

His boots crunched on burnt grass as he indicated another conscript. "Huevito here is nineteen years old and has five kids. They all need shoes. Ten dollars a pair, no?"

Private Huevo and I nodded enthusiastically at each other. "Absolutely," I said.

"Ten dollars each for these other gentlemen, who have been of such great assistance to your grace this day," —the money was duly handed out— "and a little something for my wife back in La Paz."

He handed me a five-dollar bill. "Your contrition has been noted and accepted. You have twenty-four hours to leave the country."

The men grinned at me. I cleared my throat. I said, "Permit me to inspect the bodies?"

The corporal scowled. "Make it quick."

One by one I peeled back the blankets, the fabric sticking to charred faces. In addition to the old woman, I saw the skinless skulls of two blond-haired guys, neither of them Pitt, a Bolivian child, five broad-shouldered Argentinians wearing rugby jerseys, and two overweight white women in their fifties.

Only one body was left.

I knelt, took hold of the edge of the blanket. I held my face to the sky, felt the sun warm on my cheek. I breathed in deep, held it, fighting the nausea, and yanked back the wool covering.

A blackened, eyeless face stared up at me. Clumps of blond hair clung to the top of the skull. Burned deep into the flesh below the neck, a shark-tooth necklace.

THE GRAVEL CRUNCHED UNDERFOOT. I dropped myself from one step to another, not paying attention to where I was going, so long as it was down.

Now what?

Pitt was dead. I had my soccer-mom closure. Motherfucking bullshit. Nothing was closed. Only a million unanswered questions that no longer mattered. *I came all this way to find you, Pitt, and you had to go and die on me before I could hear it from your lips. Maybe then I might have believed in this touchy-feely ashram bullshit.*

But Pitt was dead and his secret along with him. Ambo had tricked him into showing up—*You want to talk? Sure, let's talk!*—and killed him. Plus a bunch of other innocent people. I wondered what excuse he'd give the press. Bolivian Terrorists Attack Tourist Watering Hole? Some bullshit. Did Bolivia even have terrorists? Whatever. In a week or two it would all be forgotten.

What was Pitt's secret? It made me crazy. What did he want me to know? Or maybe this was it: death heals all wounds. There was no peace on earth and never would be. But I hoped that whatever was left of him, his consciousness—his soul, if he had one—had reached a cease-fire with existence.

But my war was just beginning. Vengeance is mine, say-
eth the Horse. Fuck Gaia. I owed Pitt a debt. A life for
a life. For a brief moment in time I had believed that redemption was possible. Taunting me with that momentary
glimpse of Eden... I imagined my hands around Ambo's
throat, squeezing the air out of him. Watching him suffer.
Watching him die.

Gentlemen of the jury, the facts are simple: Ambo ordered
the execution of his own son, Pitt. Had his own wife murdered. Of course he did. Why would Pitt kill his own mother?
Ambo framed me for that crime.

What's more, Ambo let me out of jail to help find Pitt.
And they'd found him, although without my aid. What were
Ambo's plans for me now? The only logical answer: he would
kill me. Or try to.

But what about Kate? I could go to her. Woo her. Try to
build a life again.

Right...now who was kidding who? She'd said goodbye. I
was pretty sure she meant it.

What if she didn't? What if there was a chance? She still
had some feelings for me, that was clear. Or why had she
seduced me on the beach?

I was unsure of myself, for the first time in a long while.
Even if I could persuade her to leave Victor and come back
to me—by no means a likely outcome—she was a reminder
of my sin. Our shared sin. I couldn't look at her without seeing our dead child's face. I didn't deserve to be happy. But if
she had found peace, maybe she could teach me how. Maybe
we could build on that. Make some kind of life together.

We could run. Go to Brazil. Learn some Portuguese. I frowned. But too much happiness was possible in Brazil. The beach? Not for me. Sun, sand and threesomes with the golden girls of Rio? Not my style. To be so close to happiness might give me a heart attack.

More to the point, if Ambo was trying to kill me, it didn't matter where we went. He would find us. He would kill us both. I didn't care too much what happened to me. But I didn't want anything to happen to Kate.

No. It was time to go back to Lima. Confront Ambo. Demand the truth. Then kill him. Kill or be killed. The law of the jungle. The law of Lima. It had come to that. I took a deep breath, exhaled slowly. I entered my verdict: the defendant is guilty on all charges, Your Honor.

First step was the ashram. Victor and Echo and the rest. If I could catch them before they left. They were my logical allies. Play along with their plan to stop the war—as if that was going to make any difference. I would need their help to get back down to Lima. I flexed my fingers. They itched. I got a hard-on just thinking about Ambo's throat. No Viagra necessary.

I squeezed the air in front of me, wishing his neck was between my hands. I could almost smell his dying breath. I was so absorbed in this daydream I nearly stepped on her. My blonde bundle of joy. She looked at me, as though expecting a greeting. Her eyes were red but the tears had stopped. She'd braided her hair, two long cords of yellow down each side.

She asked, "You find your friend?"

I grunted. Stepped around her. Clomped my way down

the stairs.

A timid voice said to my back, "I ask, you find your friend?"

"The fuck you care," I said, not bothering to stop.

I heard her stand up. "Where you going?"

"Get off this island."

"They won't let you."

"Got a boat," I called over my shoulder.

"Can I come?" she asked.

I didn't turn. "No."

Booted feet danced on the gravel beside me. "I'm serious," she said. "Take me with you."

"So am I."

She panted for breath, trying to keep up. "My name's Aurora. I'm coming whether you want me to or not."

I turned to confront her. She crunched to a halt on the stair above me. I said, "Fuck off already, will you?"

She slapped me across the face. Hit hard for a girl. Her thumb grazed my broken nose. I saw white. Ground my teeth together, clenched my fists. Opened my eyes. She stared at me, her face wide with fear. But she did not flinch. Did not back down. I tensed my arm to strike.

She said, "You're not the only one who's lost someone. Remember?"

She held up her open palms to block my blow. Maybe she was right. Damn, she *was* right. There was plenty of grief to go around. I lowered my fists.

"I'm sorry," I said. "But you can't come with. What I've got to do is dangerous."

"And what's that?"

I lifted my shoulders, let them drop. "Find the bastards

who did this. Make them hurt. Kill them if I can."

She pulled at her braids. Blood seeped from the roots. "You mean you know who did this?"

"Assassins for the CIA," I said. "Call themselves the Dissent Suppression Unit." I nodded up the hill. "They did it to keep my friend from talking." I added, "They're probably out there somewhere, waiting for me. To kill me. Which is why you can't come along."

She grabbed my arm. "I'm not asking."

"If you come, the Americans will kill you too," I said. "I've got enough dead people on my conscience already. I don't need any more."

"Sven and I were going to get married. Have babies. You understand? We've known each other since kindergarten. If I hadn't picked a fight he'd still be alive. It's my fault he's dead."

"Isn't that a bit harsh?" I asked. "I mean, how could you have known?"

"That's not the point!" she screamed at me. Her face turned purple. "You are such an asshole, you know that?"

I nodded. Vigorously. "Yes. I do."

She ducked her head, frowned at her boots. Her lips puckered. "I can't stay here. I've got to get off this island. And if that means I get killed, I don't care. But I've got to do something. And you're the only something I see happening around here."

Every general needs cannon fodder, I thought. I didn't much like the idea. I didn't want her along. But if I said no she'd cause a major scene, and getting off the island was going to be a lot harder than getting onto it. Plus, if she stopped a bullet somewhere between here and my hands around Ambo's throat, I wouldn't complain. She could be my Swedish body armor. Then maybe I'd survive long enough to see Kate again.

I said, "You get killed, it's not my fault. Got it?"

She tugged on her braids, spoke to the ground. Spat the words like bullets. "Let's go kill the fuckers."

When we got back to the beach, the police did not want to let us off the island. No surprise there. Neither, for that matter, did the English girls. Two conscripts with AK-47s stood guarding the boat.

"Who's the tart?" the Liverpudlian asked.

"My fiancée," I growled. "Wanna make something of it?"

The girl stroked Aurora's cheek. "She's cute. Wanna party?"

I had to pry Aurora's fingers from the girl's hair.

Darting away from the amused if sluggish police contingent, we humped back up the hill, in search of a boat. We descended to the Hotel Pelicano, on the water's edge, and, I am ashamed to say, stole their boat. Given the ruckus on the island, I was amazed there was no one guarding it. Unlike my little aluminum dinghy, this was a proper speedboat, with twin 110-horsepower engines and a computerized navigational system, which seemed like complete overkill on a land-locked lake at four thousand meters. That is, until they started shooting at us.

Gunshots splashed the water off our bow. A puff of smoke hissed upward from a gun turret; a whistling sound; and a shell exploded in the water not ten meters away, soaking us with spray, nearly swamping us.

"Grab the gun!" I shouted.

"What gun?"

"Shit!" I'd left it in the other boat.

I crouched low, opened the throttle, and we shot across the lake, bouncing off the low waves. More shells splashed around us, but the speedboat outpaced them, until the destroyer receded to a dot on the horizon.

But they wouldn't be far behind us.

"You did this," Victor said. He pointed the gun at my head.

Fresh bruises littered his face. Wet strands of combover hung at his shoulder. His sweater was torn down the front. The gun twitched and bobbed in his hand. He looked like a homicidal raccoon with a bad case of the DTs.

This was the man Kate preferred to me? I was no great catch. I knew that. But this was the competition? I put my hands in the air and considered my options.

Hmm. There weren't any. I wondered what I'd say to Pitt if there really was an afterlife. What I'd say to Lili.

"I'm sorry," I said. "I should have flushed."

Aurora trudged through the sand, around Victor, up the gravel rise to the main street of the tiny village. Victor's gun wavered between my nose and her buttocks. "Come back here!" he shouted. "I'll shoot!"

"Go ahead, for all I care," Aurora said.

"Hey," I said, "that's my line."

She rounded the corner and stopped. She swayed on her feet. Fell to her knees. "Oh my God," she said. She covered her face with her hands. "This is real. This is happening."

"What is?" I asked.

But all she said was, "Who could do such a thing?"

"Do what?"

"As if you have to ask," Victor sneered. He put both hands on the gun, as though willing himself to shoot, but unable to do so.

"Before you kill me," I said, "let me find out what I did?"

He jerked the gun, motioning me toward Aurora. I climbed the gravel embankment and joined her in a front-row seat to an oozing pile of dead bodies.

A realtor would have said the houses were ready for new occupants, as long as you didn't mind the bullet holes in the exterior wood paneling, or the shattered glass. And hey, blood comes out with just a little elbow grease, right? But really, sorry, hey, the corpses of the previous tenants have to go. Maggoty cadavers lower property values for everyone, not just you.

Whoever had done it had not been satisfied with merely massacring everyone in sight. No. They had to stack the bodies in a pile taller than me. Blood and piss formed puddles on the hard-packed earth. Orange-and-scarlet robes mixed with denim. A toothless mouth gaped at me upside down, and I knew the old fisherman's net would never be fully mended. The little boy, the one who'd crashed into me, he was there too, eyes missing from their sockets, Bolivia's hopes for the World Cup now dashed. Echo's pregnant belly sagged amidst the carnage, one less angry volunteer for the Lima office. I picked up a red baseball cap, and half an eyeball plopped onto my shoe. I dropped the cap on the ground. I wondered if Kate was buried somewhere in the mess.

"It was you," Victor said. His breath came in snorts and gulps, his nostrils vibrating. "You. And him. Michael." He kicked a corpse on the ground, separating it from the main pile. He flipped it over with his toe. It was the talkative monk/volunteer/freakazoid from the night before. The auto-flagellating weirdo. The back of his head was missing.

"Why would he do such a thing?" I asked.

"Don't pretend you don't know."

"You know the dead guy?" Aurora asked me.

"I ate dinner with him last night. He said all of a dozen words before whipping himself with barbed wire."

"He was CIA!" Victor raged. "Had to be. Or why did he do all this?"

"So what happened?" Aurora asked. "All of a sudden he just started shooting?"

"Pretty much." He wiped the sweat from his palms against his sweater, one at a time, but kept the gun pointed at my chest. He said, "We were loading the boats. Preparing to flee. We expected American aggression." He spat. "Michael had a gun." He looked at the weapon in his hand. "This gun. Just started killing people. Clip after clip after clip. Men. Women. Children."

I swallowed. "Kate?"

"How convenient," he sneered. "I told you. Kate got away. A boatload left this morning, before you got up. Crossed the lake, took a jeep into the mountains."

"And you think I had something to do with this."

"I know you fucking did!" he shouted, his wet combover slapping against his right shoulder, his scalp pink in the late-morning sun.

"I know you did," he said again. His lips curled inward in a face-puckering howl. His shoulders shook. The gun rattled in his hands. "And now you'll get your fucking war."

"Wait a second. What war?" Aurora held her palm in front of the gun barrel. "And how do you know it was this guy?" She jerked a thumb in my direction. "What was your name again?"

"Horace," I said. "But people call me Horse. As in hung like a."

She giggled. "Really? Like cloppity-clippity-clop, ride off into the sunset?"

"More like pulling heavy loads until you lie down at the side of the road and they shoot you. But close," I said.

Victor stepped between us, pointed the gun at her, then at me, back and forth, as though confused who to kill. "You murder dozens of innocent people, and you stand here talking about ponies?"

Aurora held up her hands again. "We had nothing to do with this. And Horse has been on the island all morning."

"Of course he was," Victor said. "All he did was lead them here so they could kill us all."

"But you just said the dead guy, Michael was it? Was CIA. How long has he been here for?" she asked.

Victor's combover trembled. "Months. Three months. Three and a half."

"So they already knew you were here. Since ages ago. So what exactly is Horse guilty of?"

The gun trembled in his hand. "That doesn't mean he didn't do it. Both of you. You're part of it too. I can tell." He pointed the gun at her, then at me. Aimed at my head. His eyes narrowed, like he was about to pull the trigger.

My body moved on autopilot. I smacked my fist down on the gun with one hand, slapped Victor across the face with the other. He let go of the gun. I picked it off the ground.

"I feel the same," I said. He continued to convulse. I slapped him again. "It will not do you any good. You understand?"

He cringed on the ground, covered his face with his forearms, hands flat on his scalp. "Do it quick and get it over with."

"For fuck's sake," I said. "We're not going to kill you. Will you snap out of it?"

"He's in shock," Aurora said. "Give him some time."

"We haven't got time," I said. I flicked the gun into the lake. It splashed in the water and disappeared.

"Happy now?" I asked.

He peeked between his wrists. "You're not? Going to kill me, I mean?"

"Why would I want to kill you?" I asked him. I held out my hand. "Come on. Get up. Be a man."

He took my hand and I heaved him to his feet. He gaped at me. Glanced over his shoulders, as though expecting an assault.

"Are there others?" I asked him. "The ones who did this?"

"No," he said. "Just Michael."

I looked at Aurora. She shrugged. "Other survivors, maybe?" I asked.

Victor shook his head. "No one," he stuttered. "No one left. No one."

"How did you survive?"

He went limp. He flopped back on the ground, arms

slapping against the sand. "I was taking a shit," he wailed. He looked up. "Too much coffee," he added, pleading for understanding.

"I thought you drank tea," I said.

He held out his open palms. His face contorted in sorrow. "Fifty people just got murdered and you're worried about what I drink with breakfast?"

"So you heard gunfire," Aurora suggested.

He twisted his limp arms in circles, a woebegone duck.

"Why didn't the monks fight back?" I squatted next to him. "They all had guns. AK-47s, it looked like. Shotguns, too."

"They tried." He raked his combover back onto his scalp. It lay in thick clumps across his naked pate. "They are not warriors. They are not soldiers. Most don't even know how to use a rifle. Never even pulled the trigger. The bullets we gave them were blanks."

"Then what'd you give them guns for, for heaven's sake?" Aurora said.

"The lake pirates." He waved a limp wrist at the water. "Prey on the villagers. It was for show, don't you see? Not to actually be used, not against..." He shrugged, left the thought unfinished.

I stood, kicked the bottom of Michael's boot. "It was just him, then. No one else. He did all this."

A miserable nod. "Yes."

Aurora asked, "Any idea why he started shooting?"

Victor snorted a long strand of bloody mucus back up his nose. "The Americans destroy dissent. So much as a peep and the Dissent Suppression Unit will kill you. The things Pitt told me..." He lowered his chin. "Pitt's dead, isn't he."

I nodded. "Saw the body myself." The smell of his burnt flesh even now lingered deep in my sinuses.

"See?" Victor said. "The Americans will have their war." The hectoring professor slashed the air from his muddy lectern. "Cover up the inconvenient truth. What's a few dead volunteers in exchange for some cheap lithium?" He laughed, a bitter bark. "Hell, if I hadn't been taking a crap, he'd have got away with it. Saunter out of here on a boat, report back to headquarters. Get a medal for it, I expect."

"What war is he talking about?" Aurora asked me.

I said, "The US is trying to steal the lithium fields in the *altiplano* from Bolivia."

"Is that why Sven died?"

"Yes."

Victor and I looked away. We stood in silence for a long moment. We watched the bodies, hoping for signs of movement, knowing there would be none. Buzzards circled overhead. Flies drifted in waves from the corpses, sampled our faces, rejected us for being insufficiently dead.

Aurora strode off toward the boat.

"Where you going?" I called after her.

"We got a war to stop, don't we?"

20

AURORA SAID, "I THINK WE GOT A PROBLEM."

I heaved a cardboard box of canned spinach into the boat, pushed it snug against a twenty-gallon bottle of water. It was all we could salvage from the cave. What a great meal that was going to make.

"What's that?"

A high-pitched whistling noise split the air. She held up her index finger: Exhibit A, Your Honor. Across the water, two Bolivian warships chugged toward us. Half a dozen more approached on the horizon. I felt like a deer crossing a highway at rush hour, doomed to watch death approach, unable to look away.

The explosion roared in my ears. The sand beneath my feet shifted sideways and I fell to my knees. Pebbles rained on our heads. A crater gaped just outside the cave.

"Where's Victor?" I shouted.

"Gone back for his laptop!"

Another whistling noise overhead. *This is no time to sit around waiting to die,* I told myself. *Revenge waits for no man.*

"Get down!"

We threw ourselves face first on the beach. The explosion

was louder this time. The sand trembled against my body. A boulder the size of a basketball landed next to my head. My ears rang. I got up on my hands and knees, peered over the top of the beach. The cave had collapsed.

Aurora took hold of the gunwale. "Get the boat in the water!"

Our legs churned sand until the icy water covered our knees. I looked back. The houses nearest the cave were in ruins. "The fuck is Victor?"

"There he is!" She pointed.

He ran toward us, his combover flopping at his shoulder, laptop under his arm. A third explosion destroyed half the village, blew him flat on his stomach, next to the pile of bodies. The laptop flew from his grip, smashed against the wall of a surviving house. He picked himself up, clawed at the innards of the computer.

"Come on!" I shouted.

Victor held up the hard drive, stumbled down the beach, through the water and dove into the boat. I tugged on the motor until it woke, and we roared away from shore. More shells whistled toward the mountain. Houses the volunteers had labored for months to build now disappeared in puffs of splinters. The medical clinic vanished. The pile of bodies evaporated. Cadaverous parts rained around us, plopping in the water beside us, flecking us with bits of toasted gore. I lowered my head against the wind, aimed the boat for the southern shore of the lake.

"They're shelling Peru, for chrissakes. They start the war without us? Did the bomb at the mine go off early?"

"They're not attacking Peru," Victor said. "They're

attacking us."

"What for? Why do they want to kill us?" Aurora asked.

"Same reason they killed Pitt. Same reason they killed your boyfriend." Victor hurled the hard drive into the lake, and slumped into the bottom of the boat. "Michael failed in his mission. Now they have to make sure no one gets out alive." The spray soaked his combover. He lifted the wad of hair and plastered it to his scalp, thick strands of clotted gray, like rotting coils of intestines.

"Hang on," I said, one hand on the tiller. "Those are Bolivian ships. What are you saying, the Bolivians are working for the CIA?"

"Precisely!"

"But I thought the CIA was trying to steal the *altiplano* from the Bolivians!"

Victor shrugged, eyes half-closed. "Don't underestimate the CIA. Probably told the Bolivians we're terrorists or something, get them to do their dirty work." He slumped lower into the freezing water at the bottom of the boat.

"Figure it out later," Aurora said. "Right now, where are we going?"

I kicked Victor's foot. "Good question!"

He shook his head, as though waking from a nightmare. All those dead bodies. I hoped the shock would wear off soon.

"Puno!" he said finally. Puno was the Peruvian border town, just opposite Copacabana on the Bolivian side.

"But there's police in Puno," Aurora said.

"Peruvian police," I said.

"Peru, Bolivia, doesn't matter. They're all against us." Victor pushed himself up against the bucking gunwale. "Just outside Puno." He pointed. "There. See those trees?"

A tight copse of scrubby pines clustered next to a red barn. A giant green peace sign adorned the side of the building. I adjusted our course. We crashed across the waves, propelled by two hundred and ten horses. More shells obliterated all trace of human habitation at the ashram. Machine-gun fire cackled and flashed in the distance, aimed at us, but the trace rounds fell into the lake hundreds of meters away.

"What's there?"

"Transportation," he shouted. Then added, "You know, you're lucky you got off the island alive. If you'd stayed, they'd have killed you for sure!"

The ships were closing the distance rapidly. I aimed the boat for the beach at full throttle. At the last moment I cut the engine. "Hold on!"

The boat threw itself onto the beach. Holding on was useless. I hurtled through the air, shoulder-planted myself into the beach, got a mouthful of sand for my trouble.

"Everyone alright?" Aurora asked.

"Tasty," I said, tonguing the grit that lodged itself between my teeth.

Victor trudged up the sand to the building. "This way."

He slid open the main door of the barn. The smell of manure was overpowering. Light filtered in through slats in the walls, reflecting off the dust motes. Half-dried llama abortions hung from the rafters. The unlucky llama mothers spat at us from their stalls. Aurora shuffled toward one the color of dirty coal, stroked its mangy fur.

"You look hungry," she cooed. "Yes you do. Who feeds you, huh? Who feeds you?"

My eyes adjusted. Parked in the back corner stood a van covered in burlap tarp. I put my hand overhead and smacked the roof of the vehicle with my open palm. It rang hollow. I said, "Thought you said you had a jeep?"

Victor stuck his hands into a pile of llama manure, massaged it with his fingers. "Katherine has it," he said.

"I thought you said she left. And what are you doing?" I asked.

He straightened up, a set of car keys dangling in his shit-covered hands. Strode across the sawdust-scattered floor. Held the keys in my face. "She did. Is there a problem?"

Aurora waved a hand between our faces. "Yo. Guys. Who's Katherine?"

Victor and I glared at each other. I spoke first.

"Ex-wife."

"Wife."

She bit her lip. "I see…"

Victor yanked the tarp off the van. A miasma of llama dander fogged the air. I coughed and sneezed. Put a finger to each nostril and emptied it onto the floor. Wiped my nose with the back of my sleeve. One of the van's rear windows was missing. The others were covered with black cloth. Llama fetuses festooned the interior. It was the same van, I realized. The van they'd kidnapped me in. Victor hefted a bale of hay from behind the back wheels.

"So where's she gone?" I asked.

"Katherine?"

"No, the teddy bear I lost when I was twelve."

Victor panted for breath. At four thousand meters, every movement was an exertion. He said, "We've got another place. Where we can hide. We were worried something like this might happen."

"Which is...where?" I asked.

He wiped his hands on the dirty tarp. "Forgive me if I do not tell you all my secrets on first acquaintance."

"You said that at the cave," I pointed out. "We're no longer first acquaintances. More like second acquaintances. Now spill."

"Alas," he said, "nor on second acquaintance either."

"Let's just go," Aurora said.

"Can't." Victor got in the van, started the motor. "It's in the mountains. Need a jeep to get there."

"Fine," I said. "You two go. Just drop me off at the bus station on the way."

"The bus station?" he said. "What do you want to go there for?"

I raised my eyebrows. "Take a bus?" I said. "You go wherever you want. I'm heading back to Lima."

"You can't do that," he said.

"Why not?"

"Because they'll kill you."

"Fine with me," I said. "As long as I kill one man first."

An explosion outside rattled the building. Bats in the rafters squealed, thundered out of the barn in a cloud of flapping wings, splattering us with guano.

"They're shelling us," Victor shouted. "Come on!"

Aurora got in and straddled the gear stick. "So where are we going then?" she asked.

I hopped in beside her and slammed the door. "As long as it's near a bus stop, I don't care."

Victor reached between her thighs, reversed out of the barn. "I know a guy. In La Paz. Get us a jeep."

"But how are we going to cross the border?" Aurora shouted over the roar of the engine. "Won't they be looking for us?"

Victor ground the gears, his fist in her crotch. He flung the van around, facing the lake. "You never crossed this border before?"

"Crossed it last week. Why?"

"You weren't paying much attention, then."

An explosion shattered the remaining rear window. Splinters of wood and bits of llama, both fresh and dried, hailed down on the windshield. I looked back. The barn no longer existed. Victor spun the wheels, surged onto the gravel road that ran along the edge of the lake.

Aurora said, "They're not joking, are they? They really want to kill us."

"It's not a 'they,'" I shouted. "It's a him. One man."

"Yeah? Who's that?"

"Ambo."

"Who's Ambo?"

Victor braked hard, throwing us against our seatbelts, ending conversation. Aurora braced her hands against the dash. Victor hunched over the steering wheel. He counted to ten out loud, then lurched forward. An explosion shook the van, made us fishtail on the pitted gravel road.

The bombardment continued. Victor braked at random intervals, accelerated for a few seconds, slowed, advanced. Explosions ripped craters behind us, ahead of us, around us. Each time Victor edged around a crater, I closed my

eyes, convinced the gunners would finally get it right, con-
soling myself that I would disappear in a puff of painless
mitochondria.

An explosion tipped the van sideways onto two wheels,
and Victor fought to bring it back to earth. Another shattered the side window, splashing my lap with shards of glass.
I picked fragments from my cheek. *Don't let me die yet,* I
begged the earth. *I've got one thing left to do.*

"Who's Ambo?" Aurora asked again.

"The man I intend to kill."

Aurora said, "So you guys in or aren't you?"

We sat in line at the border, a long string of trucks ahead
of us. The lakeside gravel road had finally curved inland and
mounted a paved highway. We had joined a caravan of trucks
and buses heading for the Bolivian border. With any luck I
should be able to grab a westbound bus at the border post.

"In?" I asked.

"Well," she said, "we have a choice." She turned to Victor.
"Don't we."

Victor rested his hands on the steering wheel, his chin on
his knuckles. "I'm for it."

"For what?" I asked.

"Stop the war."

I clucked my tongue. "How do you suggest we do that?"

"Call the papers," she said. "Expose this to the world."

"What planet do you live on?" I said. "You think the
scum at the *New York Times* aren't working for the CIA?
Or any other newspaper for that matter. It's big business,

baby. Money is all that matters to them. The truth?" I farted, and the stink of my rotting carcass filled the van. "Plus, even then, assuming you found an editor who didn't have the CIA blackmailing him, you'd need proof. How you going to prove there's a plot?"

"So we put it online, like Wikileaks," she insisted. "The net is still free."

"For now," Victor said.

"That might work," I admitted. "But you would still need proof. Hard evidence. Where you going to get that?"

She curled her knuckles tight, pressed them between her thighs. Bowed her head. "There's got to be something we can do," she said. "And I don't care what. Those fuckers killed Sven." A tear trickled down her cheek.

She looked so forlorn. I felt sorry for her. I rolled down a window, and cold mountain air swept away my scent. I put my arm around her and pulled her head to my shoulder. "It was nothing personal," I said. "It was Pitt they were after. Sven was just collateral damage."

She pulled away. "And that's supposed to what, make me feel better?"

Victor held up a hand. "I like the idea," he said abruptly. "It's a long shot, though."

"What's that?" Aurora asked, wiping her cheeks with her fingertips.

"We can go to the second refuge, where Kate and the others are. Or," and he lowered his voice, "we can go into the Salar de Uyuni. We can go to the mine."

"And do what?" I asked. "Get killed in the crossfire?"

He held up a cell phone. "Satellite roaming," he explained.

"If we can get video evidence of the bombing, I can send it via satphone. Get it out to the world."

"But what does a video of a mine blowing up prove?" I demanded. "How is that evidence of CIA involvement? And how are the Americans planning to frame the Chileans, anyway?"

"These are all good questions, Horace," Victor said, and fingered the bruise under his left eye. "I don't know the answers. All I'm saying is, let's go and improvise. Document what we can. They aren't expecting visitors. The mine's in the middle of nowhere. There must be some kind of evidence we can find once we're there on the ground."

"And even if we do find some evidence," I said, "what good does it do? By the time the bombing takes place, it's too late."

"Too late to save the mine. True. But if I can get the video to the Bolivians, plus whatever evidence we find, it might be enough to prevent them from invading Chile. We still got," he said, and shook his wrist, consulted his watch, "two days before the bomb goes off."

"Two days?" Aurora said.

"Well, a bit less, actually. Day after tomorrow at 11:37 in the morning, what Pitt said."

"But the CIA knows you know," she said. "Knows that Pitt told you that. Wouldn't they push forward the timer and blow the mine immediately?"

Victor shook his head. "They are arrogant Americans. They think they can do what they want and get away with it. Why should they change their plans just because of some annoying activists who live in a cave?"

"We couldn't just, you know, like, pick up the fucking

phone?" My voice rose in a crescendo. "Look under the bed, boys, there's a fucking bomb there?"

The truck ahead of us spewed a thick stream of diesel exhaust, ground ahead a few meters, stopped. Victor followed, the van gliding ahead in neutral.

"It's not as simple as that," he said, his voice so quiet we had to strain to hear him. "The Anglo-Dutch management is working with the CIA. They're afraid of Ovejo. Nationalization. All their work up in smoke, you know? The company wants this war. They'd rather let the CIA sabotage their mine than lose the entire concession. Best case, you call them, they ignore you. Worst case..." He left the thought unfinished.

"I've got a better idea," I said.

"What's that?"

"Go back to Lima. Find Ambo. Stick some jumper cables on his balls. Make the fucker squeal."

"Who is this Ambo?" Aurora asked.

"I told you. The guy I intend to kill."

"And who is that?" she insisted.

"Jeremiah Freeman Watters. The *Amm Basderr a tha Yoo Ni Stase a Mareka*. Pitt's father."

Aurora gasped. "Assassinate the American ambassador?"

"Stop him, you stop the whole thing. He's the key."

I didn't believe a word I was saying, of course. It would make no difference in the grand scheme of things if I killed him or not, although it would sure as hell scratch my itch. But I had no money, no documents and no vehicle. I could use their help.

"And how," Victor asked, "do you plan to do that?"

"Confront him," I said. "Demand the truth. Bring a gun. Maybe a car battery."

Victor looked straight ahead. His eyes were pale, translucent half-orbs in the afternoon light. He said, "You think that, you're a fool."

He could see it too. "Am I?"

"Pitt's father is a replaceable pawn, just like everybody else," he said. "The machinery grinds ahead. All parts can be replaced. Or are you," and he laughed, that barking sound again, "are you planning to fly to Washington, start shooting people at the CIA?"

I toyed with the idea. It would be fun. Multiple murder-suicide. But all I'd kill would be a bunch of underpaid rent-a-cops. It wouldn't make any difference. The creeping American evil would continue to spread across the globe like a plague.

"You want revenge," Victor said. It wasn't a question.

"The only thing I want."

"Stop the war, you destroy his career. Everything Ambo has built. Then you can go kill him. If killing is really what you want."

Destroy his career.

I hated to admit it, but Victor had a point. *Hurt Ambo where it counts. His pride. Stop the war. Destroy his life. Then you kill him.* So much more satisfying that way.

"Now you're talking," I said. "I'm in."

"And the worst case?" Aurora asked.

"Worst case what," I said.

"Worst case if you make that phone call. To the mine."

Victor sighed. "Worst case, they trace your call and send a missile in to take us out." He uncurled his fingers from the steering wheel and blew air through his teeth, mimicking an explosion.

The three of us looked at each other. Aurora cleared her throat. "Maybe we should take a bus."

"Good point," Victor said. "Now that you mention it. Do. Let's."

Two trucks ahead of us in line was a bus. Victor pulled the van to the side of the road. He left the keys in the ignition, the doors unlocked. We hopped out and jogged to the bus. We were still a good half a kilometer from the border crossing.

The hydraulic doors opened with a shriek and a hiss. A squat, potbellied Indian in a blue poncho looked down at us from his throne. Amplified Andean pan pipe music blasted from the bus's speakers, rattling the windows. Purple-and-green fringe dangled from the top of the bus window. On the dashboard a candle burned in a large shrine to the Virgin Mary, a cherubic Jesus held out in her arms.

"*Sí?*" the man shouted over the music.

"*Para La Paz?*"

"*Subanse.*"

We got on.

Fifty unwashed Indians reclined in their rotting chairs. A Bolivian woman in traditional hoop skirt squatted on the floor, a puddle of urine spreading with each movement of the bus. We sat across the aisle from her, opened a window and did our best to hold our noses.

"How far is it to La Paz?" Aurora asked.

"Eight hours."

"Oh God." She stood, stuck her head out the window and breathed the cold, dusty mountain air.

***

Bolivian immigration is a joke. Hell, after closing time you can just walk across. It's your job to get the stamp you need. Once, Kate and I arrived just as they closed up shop, and they waved us right through. "Come back tomorrow," they said. "We're going home."

The question was, would they be on the lookout for us? They saw us land on the Peruvian shore. Bombarded us as we drove east toward Copacabana. You didn't have to be a North American imperialist running dog to guess where we were headed.

"See anything?" I asked Aurora.

She gulped diesel fumes, squinted ahead of us. Her ass wiggled in my face. "What am I looking for?" she asked.

"I don't know. Sharpshooters on the rooftops? Tanks and barricades? Squads of black-clad commandos with night-vision goggles?"

"It's daytime."

"Whatever."

Victor said, "They won't bother with any of that."

"How can you be sure?" I asked.

"I can't be," he said. "Not entirely." He fingered his lip. "All the same, our best bet is to walk across like we're tourists."

"With no luggage?" Aurora asked, pulling her head in the window. "No backpacks?"

He shrugged in his seat. "You got a better idea?"

I stood, stepped between Aurora's legs and stuck my head out the window. We were close to the Peruvian immigration post. I'd crossed here dozens of times, and it looked the same as always. Street vendors selling diarrhea on a stick. Money changers with their counterfeit play money and "fixed" calculators. It all looked normal.

Maybe Victor was right. Could we really just walk across? Unless there was a commando team hiding in the bushes ready to jump out and say "boo," in which case we were fucked. But no. Better to be aggressive. Time was on our side. If we waited until nightfall, it only gave them more time to get ready for us. Plus, we would be a lot more conspicuous after dark. Foot traffic slowed after sundown.

I sat back in my chair. "Alright," I said. "Let's do it."

The bus squealed to a halt outside the Peruvian immigration post. We shuffled off with the other inmates, joined the crowded lineup. I looked around casually, just another gringo tourist gawping at the locals. Still nothing. The bus drove off, and I had a momentary panic before realizing the driver was only moving the bus toward the Bolivian post a few hundred meters down the road. The handful of police didn't give us a second glance. I frowned. It was almost too normal. Did they want us to get through?

One by one we slipped off to change money, without returning to the scrum for an immigration stamp. No one seemed to notice. No one seemed to care. I was about to change my lonely five-dollar bill into *bolivianos* when an explosion shook the air. Behind us, a plume of black smoke unfurled skyward.

Van? I mouthed the word.

Victor nodded. "They know we're here."

"Bastards," Aurora said.

"Against the bus. Now," Victor ordered under his breath.

We scuttled the rest of the way up the line of parked traffic, pressed our backs against the bus.

"What is it?" I asked.

"Spotter." He scanned the sky. "Five o'clock. Motorcycle helmet."

I found the man. He sat low, head down, over a high-powered Honda. Kept his helmet on, shade closed. His black leathers looked new.

"They wouldn't," I said.

"Not with so many people around."

"How can you be sure?" I asked. "They blew up the Finski, didn't they? All those dead tourists, just to get Pitt."

"You got a better idea?"

"Spotter," Aurora said. "What does this word mean?"

"Laser-guided missiles need a ground spotter," Victor explained. "Shine a laser on our foreheads, ram a missile down our throats."

"What the hell," I said. "They know we're here. Why don't they arrest us?"

Victor crossed his arms, chewed his lip. "Maybe it's easier to kill us. Or maybe they know about the other jeep, and they want to drive us forward, find out where Kate and the rest are so they can kill us all. Make the cover-up complete."

Aurora patted her clavicle, as though she had something stuck in her throat. "I see," she said.

I put my hand on her shoulder. "You don't have to come with us if you don't want to."

"Too late now," Victor said. "They've seen you. You try going solo, the CIA'll grab you and interrogate you." He looked away. "I'd hate to think what they'd do to a pretty girl like you."

"Fuck the CIA," she said. "You couldn't pay me enough to stop me from going with you."

A stream of passengers returned to the bus. The driver unlocked the door. We resumed the journey to La Paz. Aurora pinched her nose, held her breath.

"It's only eight hours," I said. "We should be there by midnight. Maybe we can sleep."

She stuck her head out the window again, like a dog addicted to the wind. "I don't think I'll ever sleep again."

"Tell me about it," I said.

21

THE CITY OF RATS.

I looked down at La Paz from the lookout point where the bus had stopped. A city of gnawing, chewing, eat-any-thing, eat-everything rats. Indestructible, high-altitude varmints that cannot be shot, beaten, trapped, poisoned or killed. Cockroaches with teeth and tails.

The bus ride had taken longer than eight hours. More like fourteen. Why couldn't we go faster? Victor kept wondering. The clock was ticking. When we stopped for gas in the middle of the night, I peered back down the highway. The helmeted motorcyclist got off his bike for a piss.

"Still with us," I said, returning to my seat.

"Else is new," Victor said, his socks draped across his face in a vain attempt to repel the odor.

At dawn the bus began to crawl its way uphill, up the switchbacks, up the outside of the crater in which La Paz sits. The city lay below us now, the worst-named city in the world. La Paz. Peace. Lights extinguished themselves as night gave way to day. Along the rim opposite us crowded the slums of El Alto. In the midst of the slums, an airplane took off from the world's highest airport, bound for better climes, or at least lower altitudes. At the bottom of the crater squatted the city center.

A grunt of pleasure at my feet. A Bolivian woman sat on her haunches by the side of the road. She wore a black bowler hat three sizes too small. Long fake braids dangled to her waist. Her blue hoop skirt piled up around her, and a trickle of diarrhea formed a puddle between her ankles. She grinned at me. I spat in the dust.

Victor put his hands in his pockets, shivered in the cold. "Can you handle this?" he asked.

"Why shouldn't I?"

"I know what happened." He put his hand on my shoulder. "She told me."

"You know nothing." I jerked my shoulder away. I spat again. "We need that jeep. Let's get this over with."

I stepped up into the bus, turned back to Victor. A red pen light danced on his jacket.

"Watch out!"

He glanced down at the laser beam aimed at his heart. He chuckled. "They're not going to kill us. Not here. They could've taken out the whole bus on the highway. But they didn't, did they? They want us alive. So they can follow us." He gestured an open palm at the motorcyclist, and shrugged. He climbed aboard the bus.

"All the same, this is getting tiresome," I said.

"Agreed."

We descended into the madness, inched through traffic, edged our automotive might past the horse-drawn coca leaf vendors, the garbage scavengers, and the rest of the flotsam and jetsam of this remote Andean outpost.

"How long's the drive to the mine?" Aurora asked.

"Half a day or so."

"We'll need supplies." I thought of the canned spinach and containers of water we'd left in the boat by the beach, abandoned when the barn blew up.

Victor nodded. "Gasoline, too."

My nose itched. "Should get some coke as well," I said, looking out the windows at carts piled high with bright green coca leaves. Without my regular dose of cocaine it had been impossible to stay awake on the bus. My withdrawal left a dull ache in my soul. "Something for the altitude, no?"

On the bus the night before, I woke to screams. For a change they weren't mine. Heavy peasant boots kicked the back of my seat, accompanied by a muttered oath in Spanish to shut the fuck up. Aurora quivered against me.

"What's the matter?" I asked.

She pressed herself tighter into me, like she wanted to disappear. Squeezed me for hours. I held her. Stroked her face. Wiped away her silent tears. Told her that everything would be all right, that no one was going to hurt her. Dawn fluttered orange-and-purple streaks across her face before she spoke.

"Nightmare," she mumbled.

"You want to talk about it?"

She exhaled a shuddering breath. "Pile of bodies," she said. "But all of them look like Sven. I hold out my hands in horror. And I have a gun. Like Victor's gun. It was me that killed him. Killed them all."

"That's terrible," I said. The sound of the road under the

wheels of the bus lowered in pitch. We lurched up a steep incline.

"It was awful." Her fingernails dug into my side. A yellow braid attacked my chin.

"It was just a dream," I said. I stroked her face once more, cupped her cheek in my hand. I said, "I have dreams too."

She lifted her head. "Do you?"

I nodded.

She buried her face in my sweater. "Thank you."

"Don't worry about it."

The bus vibrated, shook us in our seats.

"Can I ask you something?" she said.

"What's that?"

She loosened her fingernails, rested an open palm against my chest. "Who was your loss?"

I sat up. She pulled away. Her eyelids hung crooked, trying to stay awake. I was suddenly cold. Huddled together, we had warmed each other.

"Why do you want to know?" I asked.

She fumbled with her hands, trying to get the words right. "On the island. The stairs. You said I weren't—wasn't—the only one who ever lost somebody."

Sleep still fogged my brain. Holding her had soothed me. Not just brute animal friction, with a whore, or with Lynn. Not hurried, desperate, grief-infused sex on the beach. Aurora needed my help. I could no longer say the same for Kate, I realized.

"I'm sorry," I said. "I was harsh with you, wasn't I?"

"That's OK," she said quickly. "It's just I...I'd like to...to know what happened."

"Would you?" I peeked at her sideways.

She lay a cold hand against my cheek. "It would make me feel better."

I stared at the stained seat in front of me. And hesitated. Unlike the others, I wanted her to like me. Then I told her anyway. Everything. The hostel. Kate. The baby. La Paz. My swan dive into the open sewer that was Lima. When I finished, she sat silent for a long while. She would hate me now. She would judge me. Like everyone else.

"Well?" I said, as roughly as I dared.

She took my hand. Tears dripped down the outside of her nose. She said, "That's the saddest story I ever heard," and kissed me on the forehead.

The bus weaved its way through traffic in La Paz, heading for the terminal. I leaned out the window, haggling with a coca vendor. My five dollars wasn't going to be enough.

"Won't revenge taste sweeter with a clear head?" Victor asked.

Aurora spoke first. "It isn't revenge I want."

"Hang on," I said. "I thought that was the point."

"Sven is gone and isn't coming back. Neither," and she clutched my wrist and held it, her fingers taking my pulse, "neither is your friend Pitt."

I shook my head, chased away the memory of last night. "What changed?" I asked. "What happened to 'kill the fuckers'?"

She said, "Remember my nightmare?"

"What nightmare?" Victor asked.

I nodded. "The one she had last night."

"How many people do we have to kill to equal that body count?" she said. "We're talking about mass murder. How many is enough? When do we stop?"

"As many as it takes," I said.

"But what does that make us? Make me? I don't want to be that person. I couldn't live with myself."

"Then why are we doing this?" I asked.

Aurora shut her eyes. "Because stopping the war is the right thing to do."

I ruminated on that. Revenge was the only thing that gave me hope. A reason to live. Pitt's own father had killed him. Justice demanded a life for a life. I sat sideways, gazed at Aurora's silent features. *Suppose you manage to find him and kill him,* I asked myself. *What then?*

What then?

"What is the right thing to do?" I whispered at last. But no one answered.

The cab driver swerved around a mule-drawn cart piled high with dirty cardboard, swore in Quechua at the muleteer. He splashed the tiny taxi through a puddle of llama dung, and turned the corner onto Calle Villacabamba, the city's main avenue.

"Guys." Aurora tugged at my sleeve.

"Was it jealousy?" I asked Victor. "Or just business?"

"What's that?" he said.

"The Americans killed Pitt. Right?"

"Correct."

"So Ambo had his own son killed."

"Guys!" Aurora tugged again at my sleeve. I waved her away.

Victor said, "Adopted son."

"Still. The man ordered the execution of both his wife—"

"—who you admit you were screwing—"

"—and his own son. The mind boggles. I just can't get my head around it."

Victor reclined in the backseat of the taxi. He ran his fingers through his combover, trying to separate the dreadlocked chunks into more presentable waves. Shrugged. "Ruthless men for ruthless times. What do you expect?"

"Guys!" Aurora clawed my knee with her fingernails.

"What already?"

She jerked her thumb over her shoulder. Several cars behind us, the black motorcycle idled in heavy traffic. Despite ample space between the lanes to pass, as other scooters were doing, he seemed content to hang back. Like he wanted us to know he was following us.

"Still there," I said.

Victor rubbed his hands together, a smile forming on his lips. "Not for long."

"What do you have in mind?"

"You'll see." He tapped the driver on the shoulder. *"Chofer."*

"Si?"

"Turn here, please."

The cab ducked down a steep alleyway and emerged into a narrow lane. Metal shanties surrounded us on both sides. Dried herbs hung from their eaves. Under cover hung the main course: llama fetuses dangling from wooden beams.

Aurora clapped her hands. "Calle de los Brujos!"

"The Witches' Market," I said. "You know it?"

"Sven and I, we—" but she stopped, and sat back, and put a finger to her lips.

Ahead of us, a horse-drawn cart slowed traffic. Behind us, three taxis and a tour bus downshifted to a crawl. The motorcyclist had followed us into the alley, and now puttered along two taxis back. Halfway down the lane, Victor told the driver to stop.

He said to us, "Wait thirty seconds and follow me."

"But what are you—"

"Just do it."

The taxis behind us honked their horns. Victor got out, walked over to a vendor's stall. He held up his open palms to the blockaded taxis, begging forgiveness in advance. He entered the dark shop.

"Ready?" I asked.

"Not thirty seconds yet," she said.

"You always do what people tell you?"

I got out of the cab. She followed. The taxis' horns blared. The driver shouted abuse in Spanish, Quechua and bad English. I smiled and waved, nodded. *Just another dumb gringo tourist who doesn't speak Spanish. Just got off the Inca Trail. Smile some more.* I pointed at my watch, held up two fingers.

Victor was talking to a gargantuan hoop-skirted Indian. Her typical highland finery was regulation issue, except her clip-on braids, which were orange instead of black. The color looked real. I wondered what the Scottish lass who'd sold her hair would think of its new owner.

He shouted at the woman in Spanish, turning sideways so the other customers could hear. "Pay me what you owe me, or I take back my merchandise!" He gestured at the meat hooks from which hung the llama fetuses.

The hoop skirt rustled in retreat, returned with a man from inside the shop. He was short and dark, his face splattered with flecks of blackened gore. He carried a meat cleaver in one hand. His blood-encrusted apron hung stiffly from his neck.

"I come for what I'm owed," Victor said.

The butcher planted the cleaver deep into a nearby beam. "Don't have it for you. Come back tomorrow."

Aurora's hands crept to her jacket pocket. Pulled out a digital camera. She was staring at the orange-braided woman. She seemed fascinated by the deep creases in the woman's face, the single tooth jutting from her lower lip, the black bowler hat perched precariously on the side of her head.

"Don't," I whispered out of the side of my mouth.

"Not her, numb nut," she whispered. "Motorcycle guy."

Victor continued to argue loudly with the butcher. I went and stood next to the butcher's wife. Raised my eyebrows, pointed at Aurora's camera.

"Photo?" I asked.

"Five dollah," she said.

My wildly gesticulating limbs pantomimed shock. "Too much," I said.

"Give it to her," Aurora growled.

I took the last of my money and put it in the woman's palm, trying to avoid touching her. She grinned broadly, confirming the lonely tooth was a solitaire, and threw an arm around my shoulder. She stank of shit and piss and sex and rotting teeth.

Aurora looked at the camera's screen. She muttered something about "bad light." Gestured us sideways, farther, farther, until our backs faced the street. Our taxi driver honked his horn, yelled at us to hurry. The motorcycle rider was behind me now. I imagined him resting his feet on the ground, chin on one fist, wondering when and how to murder us all.

"Say 'whiskey!'"

"Wee-skee!" my newfound lover said, hugging me to her chest.

The camera flashed. Aurora checked the photo, gave me a thumbs up.

"What are you doing?" Victor asked. He eyed the commotion in the street. "Come inside."

The butcher wrenched the meat cleaver from the beam. We followed him into the shop. In the middle of the room stood a concave butcher's chopping block, worn smooth from years of scrubbing. A rotting llama carcass hung from a hook in the corner, a wriggling mass of maggots. The butcher picked up the cleaver, slashed the animal from tail to neck. Maggots writhed, spilled to the ground. A heavy plastic bag thumped at the butcher's feet. He picked it up.

Victor took the bag and fished out a gun. He put it on the chopping block. It was an ancient six-shooter.

"Colt .45 Peacemaker," he said. "Weapon of cowboys everywhere."

He laid a box of ammunition beside the weapon and discarded the bag at his feet, where it slithered and hissed on the tide of maggots. He loaded the gun, one bullet at a time.

The butcher said something in Quechua. Victor's one-word

answer did not please him, and he slashed the meat cleaver, filthy with maggot juice, down into the cutting block an inch from Victor's fingers.

Victor laughed. He threw his arms wide, chest forward, neck back, as if to say: only kidding. He pulled out a wad of US dollars, rolled together with a rubber band, and slapped the green cylinder onto the chopping block. The butcher picked it up, flicked away the rubber band. Thumbed through the bills. Nodded, hid the money in his apron pocket.

A voice at the door interrupted us. Our taxi driver swaggered his thin frame through the open door. *"Hijo de puta!"* he swore. "Pay me so I can go!"

His eyes fell to the gun in Victor's hand. Too late. Victor shut the revolver, pointed it at the taxi driver and pulled the trigger. My ears rang. A fountain of red exploded from the side of the man's neck. He clutched his throat. The blow spun him around. Victor shot him again, this time below the left shoulder blade. The man pitched against the wall, streaked a crimson path across the cinder blocks. He careened through the doorway and fell to the ground. Outside, someone screamed.

"The fuck was that?" I said.

The blood drained from Aurora's face. I patted her cheek. She didn't react.

"Don't faint on me now, girl," I said.

Victor jammed more bullets into the gun, tucked it into his pants at the small of his back. Dropped the box of bullets into his jacket pocket. He smiled. "Knight takes pawn." The butcher shouted, gestured toward a rear door with his meat cleaver.

"Come on!" Victor shouted.

He banged through the door. I pushed Aurora in front of me. Her legs began to move. We stumbled through the living quarters the butcher and his wife shared with a small army of rats, and out another door into an alleyway. We zigzagged to the left, ran toward the light. Emerged, panting for breath, on a major thoroughfare.

We dashed across the road, traffic honking at us. Victor threw up his hand at a passing bus marked El Alto. The bus was full. Passengers stood in the stairwells. We elbowed our way aboard. Victor pressed coins into the driver's hand, enough for the three of us, and the bus roared uphill, aimed at the lip of the crater.

It was only then I realized Aurora was crying. I touched her cheek.

"Why did you do that?" she said. "Why did you have to kill that guy?"

Victor took a deep breath. Exhaled slowly. "The driver was CIA."

"How do you know that?" she asked, pushing her face into my neck.

"Yeah," I said. "He have a tattoo on his forehead that said, 'I'm a spy, shoot me'?"

"Look." Victor lowered his voice. Our fellow passengers jostled against us, a sea of sweaty armpits. "These people are trying to kill us. They almost killed me. They will kill you if you let them. Cut me some slack, OK?"

"So was it worth it, then?" I asked. "Have we lost them?"

"For now."

The bus ground its way up the mountain, panting in first

gear. It slowed every hundred meters or so to pick up or drop off passengers. My ears popped. Twice. Finally we crested the lip of the city's giant crater. The bus meandered its way through that giant high-altitude slum.

"*Aqui, por favor!*" Victor called out. We descended to the broken pavement, shivering and gasping for breath.

"Now what?" I asked.

"We find Fritz."

"Who is who?"

"A man with a jeep."

The shanties grew smaller and more rustic the higher we climbed, punctuated here and there by an eye-popping new medical clinic or brand-new school.

"This is where Ovejo buys his votes," Victor said.

"I thought you were on the Bolivian side."

"I am. I don't want to see the US bully anyone. That doesn't mean I have to like the local politics."

We turned down a side street. There was a conspicuous absence of motor vehicle traffic. We walked on the sunny side of the street, straining to soak up as much warmth as possible. Children played soccer in the street, but stopped when they saw us. One picked up the ball. Another hid behind his playmate's back, his finger in his nose. From an open widow, a wrinkled old woman spat a stream of tobacco juice in the dust at my feet, then slammed the shutters closed in our faces. A teenage boy took a butterfly switchblade from his pocket. He flicked the knife open, threw it at the wooden door of his house. He stepped to the door, removed the blade, looked at us, then returned to his target practice.

"I don't think we're welcome here," Aurora said.

Victor waved a hand. "They won't bother us."

"They haven't seen too many gringos, I would think," I said. "We do not belong here."

"You don't."

The muffled voice came from a man with a scarf wrapped around his face. Only his eyes and dark forehead were visible. A heavy green-and-purple poncho hung from his shoulders. He pointed a shotgun at my balls. A second barrel pointed at my face.

FIVE BOLIVIANS. THEY ALL WORE HEAVY *RUANAS,*
the woolen Andean poncho, and scarves hid their faces. Their
weapons were antiques inlaid with silver, glimmering in the
weak midday light. We put our hands in the air.

"Gringos far from home," one said.

"Nah," I said. "Home is where the heart is," and got a gun
butt in the kidney for my trouble.

A sharp word in German. The booted foot stepped away
from where I lay on the ground.

"Sprechen zie Deutsch?" Victor asked.

"What is that to you?"

I looked up in time to catch Victor's smile. "You must be
the grandsons. He's told me so much about you."

The man shifted his weight. "I don't know what you're
talking about."

"Fritz is a good friend of mine. He tells me everything."
Victor's smile widened. "Everything."

I rubbed my lower back with my hand. "Some friends," I
said.

Victor spoke to them in German, at first haltingly, then at
greater length. He gestured to us, then turned around, hands

in the air. Their leader removed the gun from Victor's belt, tucked it under his poncho.

A hand from the heavens descended to my level. I looked at it, still rubbing my kidney. "Come," a voice said from above. "Take my hand. We go inside now."

I accepted the hand and pulled myself to my feet. They led us down a nearby alleyway. It twisted to the right, then left, then out onto a parallel street and into a mechanic's garage. A battered hatchback with multicolored panels and no fender sat high in the air. Two men consulted its organs from below. We passed through the clank and the stink of automotive repair, through a narrow door, and time-warped from the Bolivian Andes to the Swiss Alps.

A cuckoo clock hung from the wall. A walnut entry table drowned in white lace. Framed in gold and covered in glass, a pair of green lederhosen monitored our progress down the hall, the nostalgic reminder of some mountain farer's distant youth.

We entered a living room. In the middle of yet more walnut and lace, a crystal bowl overflowed with *lulos, pitayas,* cashew fruit and other tropical wonders I couldn't identify.

Light fixtures designed to resemble gas lamps lit the room. A bundle of green-and-yellow wool emitted a wheezing cough from a leather armchair. A thin arm pushed its way through the blanket. An old man struggled to his feet, gripping a gnarled wooden cane. Long white mustaches drooped from either side of his upper lip. Thick eyebrows hooded his sockets. He grasped a heavy pewter crucifix at his chest, a gruesome depiction of Christ's suffering.

A young woman stood at his side. She wore a blue kerchief

in her hair, and a brown dress that might have been in fashion in Zürich fifty years ago. The blanket slipped to the floor, and she stooped to pick it up. She wrapped it around the old man's shoulders, but he shrugged it off.

He barked at her in German, and she retreated from the room. "My niece," he grunted in Spanish.

"You are Fritz?" I asked.

The man looked me up and down, as though judging me worthy of a reply. "I am," he said finally. He addressed Victor. "You have met my grandsons, I see."

The five men removed their scarves. They arranged themselves around the room, sitting on the edges of the furniture, leaning against the walls, shotguns draped across their thighs. The leader unwrapped a chunk of pink chewing gum, laid it gently on his tongue.

"Fine young men," Victor said.

"I had not expected to see you so soon," Fritz said.

Aurora plopped onto the empty sofa. "That's because everyone's dead."

Fritz's eyebrows rose, a squirrel's tail, ready to pounce. "Everyone?"

"Her boyfriend," I said. "And a friend of mine. Name of Pitt."

"He knows Pitt?" Fritz asked, with a sudden intake of breath.

"Indeed I do." I marveled at the odd creatures a CIA assassin collects in the line of duty.

Victor's voice was low and even. "His closest confidant."

I dropped onto the sofa next to Aurora, draped my arm around her shoulder. She didn't pull away. "Plus about, hell,

I don't know, a couple dozen innocent Peruvian fishermen, an ashram full of wannabe Buddhist monks and a handful of weirdo volunteers."

Fritz shuffled to where Victor stood. He looked up at the younger man, laid a hand on his forearm. "These people. You trust them?"

"They are friends."

"Not," he said, and twisted his neck to look at us, "not enemies?"

Aurora stood, her fists on her hips, an indignant five-year-old. Assaulted him in a sudden torrent of German.

Fritz nodded. "I see."

"What was that?" I asked.

"I told him we're against the war too."

"Great," I said. "Am I the only one here who doesn't speak German?"

She squeezed my shoulder. "It's not your fault you were born American."

The niece bustled in with an ornate silver tray. On it she carried a full bottle of Ribena, empty glasses, a pitcher of water and a plate of cookies. She poured a finger of Ribena into each glass, and topped the glasses with water. We stopped talking, and there was a prolonged silence.

She looked up, realized we were all watching her. Her face went red. She clutched her skirt and ran from the room. Fritz grunted, shook a liver-spotted fist at the table.

"Goddamn diabetes," he grumbled to no one in particular.

The cookies were ginger snaps, crunchy and buttery, pungent with spice. When was the last time I'd eaten? A couple days without coke and my appetite returned. I stuffed another in my mouth.

"You know about the war then, do you?" Fritz boomed, driving the tip of his cane into the paisley swirls of the Turkish carpet.

Victor bowed his head. "They know all about Pitt's CIA connection. The American plot."

"Well I'm sorry they had to know the truth."

Aurora was crying. She held a half-empty glass of Ribena in her hand.

"What's wrong?" I asked, squeezed her bicep.

"It tastes like home," she whispered. She looked at me, lips parted, stained red. "It tastes like Sven."

I took her glass and put it on the table. I drew her head to my shoulder.

Fritz returned to his chair with the air of King Solomon deciding the fate of the world. "You must leave," he said. "At once. Go to Paraguay, my advice. We can smuggle you there if you like."

"What?" Aurora's head jerked up.

"Paraguay?" I said. "What the hell's in Paraguay?"

Fritz stroked his long white whiskers. "The war cannot be stopped. The CIA wants you dead. What would you have me do? Send you to your deaths?"

"Well," I said. "If the CIA wants us dead, they can kill us just as easy in Paraguay as they can here in Bolivia."

Fritz rested his chin on the handle of his cane. "Young man, do you have the faintest idea what you're up against?"

"What's the worst they can do?" I said. I put down my empty glass and stuffed another handful of ginger snaps in my mouth. "Kill me? Go ahead. Let them. But not," —and here I slashed the air with a half-eaten ginger cookie— "not before I take some of the bastards with me first."

The old man cackled, the delight of a witch discovering a particularly rare form of newt. The cackle disintegrated into another long, wheezing cough. "You've got an immovable object here, Victor."

Aurora nuzzled my throat, her hot breath panting against my skin. "Can't we just stop the war?" she mumbled into my shirt collar. "I really don't want to kill anybody."

"Maybe I don't want to either," I whispered. And realized that I meant it.

Victor sat next to Fritz. "It could work."

Fritz grunted. "Suicide mission."

"Maybe. Maybe not."

"Are they the ones to do it, though?"

"Who else is there?"

"Enough talk," I said. "We want a jeep. Victor says you've got one. *Vamonos ya.*"

Fritz coughed again, a long, hacking bark that went on and on, as though he were struggling to expel something lodged deep within his lungs. He drew a handkerchief from his pocket, wiped his lips. Blood stained the fabric. When the fit subsided he sat back in his chair, his face whiter than before. He lifted a bony hand and pointed at the wall.

"Where are my sons now?" he challenged me, a teacher interrogating a precocious student.

The wall was covered in black-and-white photographs. Bearded men wearing lederhosen held skis, posed in front of a simple wooden chalet. Jagged mountains punctured the sky between them. A ski lift rose high above the mountain mist. A more recent color photo showed Fritz with his arm around two younger men. Both had European features, but the brown skin of Bolivia.

I looked around the room. The five members of our welcoming committee looked away. The resemblance was unmistakable.

"Well, Fritz," I said. "I don't know what happened to your sons. I gather something bad."

"Something bad, bullshit," he said. "They died, that's what."

He put an inhaler to his lips, took a sharp breath, pumped the medicine into his lungs.

Victor lifted his eyes meaningfully at the ceiling. "World's highest ski lift."

"Highest ski *resort*," Fritz retorted. He thumped his cane on the floor. "And a bloody good resort it was, too."

"OK," I said, stuffing more cookies in my mouth. "I'll bite. What happened?"

"Global warming happened." The leader of the grandsons spoke. He blew a gum bubble, popped it with a crack of his teeth.

"How's that?"

"Why you think we're here and not there?"

I shrugged. "Not the season for snow?"

"It is always the season for snow at five thousand meters, young man." Fritz was agitated now, grinding and pounding his cane into the rug. "Unless the fucking glacier melts, that is."

"Which it did," I offered.

"Little by little." His great eyebrows bowed low. "Then

one day, *woompf!*"

"Avalanche," said the bubble-gum-popping grandson.

"What do you expect?" Fritz continued. "We must all suffer so fat Americans can drive SUVs."

I swallowed my ginger snaps. I felt vaguely ill. "Speaking of SUVs," I said.

Fritz nodded. Snot dribbled down his long mustache onto the handle of his cane. He said to Victor, "What say you, old friend?"

Victor crossed his arms, tucked his chin to his chest. "Likely to be a useless errand. But under the circumstances, I don't see how it can hurt."

"We can pay you," I said. "Victor has money. Right, Vic?" I clapped him on the back. Victor looked at me sideways, horrified at the familiarity.

"No, no money." Fritz squinted at his offspring. "Manuel?"

"*Abuelo?*" The leader of the grandsons stood. He cracked his gum. It formed a bulge in his right cheek.

"Show them where the jeep is. Make sure the water and gas containers are full."

Manuel held his shotgun loosely in his hand. "*Abuelo.* Please." His voice held in check the frustration of the parents of a two-year-old.

"Not in front of the guests," Fritz said.

"Is that what they are?" Manuel looked at us, our dirty clothes, our unwashed faces, Victor's swollen eyes. My broken nose. "We give away the jeep, what are we going to use?"

"To what, hump your girlfriends in the back?" Fritz said. "Get a fucking room, kid."

"For these religious crazies?" Manuel stood over Victor,

towering above the much shorter man. "This is the second jeep in two days."

"Who took the first jeep?" I asked.

"Kate and the monks who escaped," Victor said.

"Kate was *here?*" I asked. I looked around me. "In this very room?"

Manuel looked about to explode. "Who is this man, anyway?"

"I told you," Fritz said, and there was a pause while he coughed again. "Met him at the ashram."

"The ashram." Manuel nodded. He went to his grandfather, put a hand on his shoulder. "*Abuelo,* you are a Catholic. We are all Catholics here. Not Buddhists."

Fritz straightened, or tried to. He glared at Manuel. "You are young. Prepare for life. Let me prepare for death."

"And what is all this talk of wars?" Manuel insisted. "The CIA," he sneered. He gestured at us. "Crazy people. Crazy talk."

"Enough!" Fritz lifted the cane and struck his grandson on the upper arm. "I am not asking you. I am telling you. Give them the jeep."

Manuel sighed. He bowed his head. "Alright, *abuelo.* It will be as you say." He tucked the shotgun under his poncho, went out into the chill afternoon.

Fritz said to us, "I apologize for my grandson's rudeness. You will need supplies as well, no?"

I drained my third glass of Ribena. I blinked, alarmed at the heights of my sugar rush. I was going to crash, and soon. My addictions were forgotten. My body craved nutrition. "Could use some real food," I said. "Haven't eaten since dinner, day before yesterday."

"Well why didn't you say so?" Fritz said. "Helena!"

The cute half-breed niece poked a nose around the door, one eye visible. "*Sí, tío?*"

"Dinner for our friends. Empty the larder."

I checked my watch. "Can you chuck it in a basket for us? We can eat in the jeep."

Victor pinched his lower lip. "Why don't we eat here, with friends? An hour rest will do us good. We can still get there in plenty of time."

"You're assuming the CIA haven't changed their schedule," I said.

"In which case they've already blown it up," Victor said. "Besides, we don't want to get there too early. Otherwise they might catch us before we can record the event."

The door banged shut behind the niece, the hem of her skirt swirling against the door frame.

Fritz held a finger high. "Let no one say I don't know how to welcome guests."

Fritz's hospitality was duly confirmed. The table was piled high. We ate like the hungry revolutionaries we were. Soup, roast beef, fried plantain, rice, German bread, a heroic attempt at a green salad, homemade pickled cucumbers, ice cream and a three-layer Bavarian raspberry-chocolate torte that just happened to be in the refrigerator.

It was late in the afternoon when we finished. The sun crept in sideways through the windows. Manuel returned with the jeep. He laid the keys next to my empty plate. I

checked my watch. It was later than I thought. I pushed myself from the table, finally sated. Picked up the keys, twirled
them on my finger.

"Shall we?"

"Nonsense," Fritz said, still meditating over the same let-
tuce leaf he'd shredded on his plate when he first sat down.
"Dusk is come. We have beds here you may use."

"Yes," Manuel said, stooping in a mock bow. "Do stay the
night."

"Hello," I said. "How much time we got left? Less than
twenty-four hours. So let's hit the road. Ready, toots?" I wiggled my eyebrows at Aurora, and for the first time I heard
her laugh, a satisfied, contented giggle that ended abruptly.

"It's a fourteen-hour journey," Victor said. "And there are
dangers traveling the salt flats at night. We could nap for an
hour or two. Better to be well-rested, don't you think?"

"Be my guest," I said. "Or rather, be Fritz's guest." I stood.
"Remind me, when does the bomb go off?"

Victor looked at his watch. "11:37 tomorrow morning."

At that moment, all the clocks in the room struck six. I
held out my hands, let them drop. "That's cutting things way
too close. I say we go now."

"Let me take a shower first, if I may," Victor said, and
looked at Fritz, who lowered his regal head with the finality
of judgment.

"Sho' 'nuff," I said. "But save your wanking till later,
get me?"

Despite their open hostility, the grandsons grinned at each
other. Helena blushed and looked down at her half-eaten
cake.

"Can I, too?" Aurora asked.

"What, wank?"

"No, shower. Nong."

"For crying out loud."

"I'll be quick," Victor said, and went off in search of a clean towel.

"We're on a deadline to stop a war and you want to take a shower?" I said. "This is important."

Aurora sniffed my neck loudly. "So is being clean." She turned to go.

"Yeah, well." I slapped her on the ass. She delayed her public outrage long enough to show me she didn't mind.

"I stink," I said. "No amount of soap can change that fact."

We were loading the jeep when Manuel caught me by the elbow, drew me aside. "You know what you're getting yourself into?"

"Not a fucking clue," I said.

He jabbed a gun into my ribs. The thin equatorial twilight cut his face into dark shards. His whisper was hot on my cheek.

"Grandfather has Alzheimer's," he said.

I shook my arm free. "Is that all?"

He grabbed my ear and lifted. "No," he said. "You bring me back this jeep. Not a scratch. Or I come looking for you. Hear?"

He pressed the gun into my hands. The barrel was enormous. It was a flare gun. He pulled harder on my ear, and I lifted myself on tiptoe.

"I said, 'hear?'"

"I hear you," I said. "Message clear. Understood. Absolutely crystal. Fuck! Goddammit. Thank you."

23

THE JEEP CRUNCHED ACROSS THE SALT FLATS.
We drove without headlights. The full moon reflected off the
crystallized former lake bed. Isla de los Pescadores rose on
the horizon, a deformity on the otherwise flat surface.

It had been a long night of driving. We'd left La Paz after
dinner and made it to Oruro before midnight. Around four
in the morning we sped through the outpost of Uyuni, heading our way southwest into the heart of the Salar. We were
ahead of schedule. At this rate, we could expect to reach the
mine just after dawn. Plenty of time to poke around, see what
there was to see. Record the bombing when it happened.

We stopped every few hours to take a leak, our urine rising hot on the night-frozen salt. It was cold in the jeep, and I
had no gloves. Victor and I took turns driving, and each time
we stopped to swap seats, I had to pry my fingers from the
steering wheel.

Staring at the night sky, at the dome of the heavens ancient and haunting, I was reminded of my smallness, the
pointlessness of all existence. And as the urine dribbled from
my body, my dick in my cold fingers, I thought of Pitt. Those
empty eye sockets, the skin crumpling and flaking under my

fingers, his flesh cooked to a soggy medium rare.

Pitt is dead. It sinks in now. He's gone. He isn't coming back. Aurora understood that, I realized. *Nothing I can do, no revenge, will bring him back to life.*

"No woman will ever understand you the way another man will," Pitt said.

We were sitting on the beach, watching the sun set, beers in hand, a chaste distance between us. In Huanchaco, the night before the blackmail. Before the rope. Before everything between us changed.

"To friendship," I said, holding out my can of *Cusqueña*.

We clinked our beers and drained them. Sighed at the same time, and exchanged glances of shared happiness. Together we leaned back in the sand. Across the waters of the Pacific Ocean, a ball of fire ninety-three million miles away said goodnight. Or was it goodbye?

And he was right. I've had many lovers, but only one friend. He didn't understand me. Not really. But he didn't judge me, either. In his eyes I had done nothing wrong. Whenever I was with him, I could lay down my burden. I felt the loss more sharply than any failed infatuation.

But he betrayed you.

Was it betrayal later that night, when I sobbed on his shoulder, called out for my missing girl, my dead child, mourning to the heavens, cursing all existence and the fates who gave me life?

"It's not your fault," he said. His hand on my ear guided my tearless eyes to his shoulder.

"You must think I'm a wuss to go on like this." I tried to free myself, but he held me tight.

"We have all sinned." He talked over my head at the waves. "We are all human. We are all guilty." He stroked my hair. "Sometimes I wonder how I'll ever cope."

I pulled away. "Since when do you have guilt?"

He didn't look at me. "Since always. It's just taken a while for me to know that's what it was."

"What's the worst thing you've ever done?" I asked.

He drank his beer. "I once poisoned a river. Killed thirty thousand people." He held out his open palms and laughed. Or tried to. "In the jungle, no one cares."

I sat up. He let me. I slapped at the tear stains on his shirt. They weren't mine. I said, "Sorry, man."

He blew his nose on his shirt. "It'll wash out."

"So," I said, "what happened to mister sociopath, I don't have a conscience, I make 'smores out of dissidents' testicles? Since when did you go all gooey?"

"Gooey," he said. "Is that what I am?" He looked at the full moon. He reached for another beer. Cracked it open, poured the entire can down his throat. Dropped his head to his chest.

When he looked up, he held a clove of garlic between thumb and forefinger. He rubbed it in one eye and grinned. "Just fucking with you, man."

I turned away. "Christ, you're an asshole."

He laughed. "Dude... Don't take it so seriously."

In spite of myself, I found myself grinning too. "That's the Pitt I know and love."

***

"What was that?" Aurora gasped from the backseat. She huddled in a blanket against the severe cold.

"What was what?" I said.

"That sound. Listen."

A clunking noise from the engine. A grinding sound. The engine sputtered and went silent. Victor coasted to a halt. He reached over and removed a flashlight from the glove box. Gave it to me. He said, "Come on."

We stepped out onto the salt. Victor hefted a metal tool-box from under the seat. Lifted the hood and propped it open, immersed himself in the innards of the jeep.

I looked down at the engine. I was lost. I'm one of those overeducated morons American universities churn out every year, men without any discernible ability or skill, except perhaps for drinking beer, doing drugs and licking pussy.

"Well?" I said at last.

Victor pointed. I looked. I shook my head. "So?"

"So?" he said. "Somebody sabotaged the engine. And I have a pretty good idea who it was, too."

"Manuel."

"Who do you think?" He threw a heavy wrench on the ground.

The moon hung high in the sky, taunting us with its glimmer of reflected warmth. I pulled my woolen hat down over my ears, crossed my arms and hugged myself.

"Now what do we do?" I asked.

"We wait."

I peered at my watch. It was many hours before dawn. The danger of freezing to death was real. Insulated by the jeep, and warmed by the heater, we had passed the night without too much discomfort. Until now.

I got into the backseat and closed the door. "Share that blanket with me?" I asked Aurora.

"Sure."

She snuggled close. She laid her head on my chest. I pulled the blanket up to cover us both. She shivered.

"We could both die here," I said.

"I'll be seeing Sven soon, then."

I stroked her hair, pulling it away from her face. I lifted the flap of her woolen Andean hat to expose an earlobe.

"And if we live?"

She nuzzled closer. "We'll cross that bridge when we come to it."

She got back into the jeep after taking a piss. I could hear her urine splashing against the hard-packed salt. The rustle of her pants. The zipper of her jacket. She closed the door, cuddled next to me under the blanket. Somehow she looked different. Then I realized what it was.

"Is that lipstick?" I asked.

"What? No."

I rubbed my thumb against her lower lip, and she flinched. I held my hand up to the window. The moonlight showed a darkened smudge.

"OK, so it is," she said. "What about it?"

"I just think it's strange, that's all," I said. "Why would you wear lipstick out here in the *altiplano?*"

I knew exactly why. She wanted to play, we could play. But by my rules, not hers.

She shrugged. "No reason."

"Where did you get it?" I asked her. "You travel with lipstick in your pocket?"

"No. Of course not."

"Then who gave it to you?"

"What is this, an interrogation?"

"I'm just asking," I said.

"Fine," she said. "Helena did. The Swiss-German girl. She gave me one of hers."

I shook my head. "I don't understand," I said. "Why would you want to wear lipstick in a place like this?"

She frowned. "Well, why not?"

"Lip balm, maybe," I said. "Against exposure. But lipstick?" I looked at my thumb again. "Much less red lipstick?"

"Goddammit!" she said, and sat up straight. "Because I wanted you to kiss me, alright?"

"Try to keep it down back there, will you?" Victor said from the front seat, where he'd curled up in his jacket to try to keep warm. Fritz had given him a new sweater, some hefty mittens and a down parka.

"You wanted me to what?" I asked, feigning astonishment.

She sat back against her seat. "Well I *did*, anyway."

"No, no, no," I said. "That's...fine. It's just, that's...the last thing I was expecting, is all."

"Forget about it," she said. She tucked her chin to her chest. "Never mind."

I took her chin in my hand. She looked up at me. Sorrowful green eyes of another human being. Someone other than me. *Other people exist,* I thought. *Not just me. What an amazing thing.*

"I didn't say no," I said, and kissed her cold lips.

She didn't respond. I pulled away. She kissed me back. Wrapped her arms around my neck and licked my teeth. All of a sudden, she jerked back, as though stung.

"Was that alright?" I asked.

She hugged her arms to her chest. "We shouldn't be doing this."

"OK..." *Talk about hot and cold.* "Well," I said, "we don't have to if you don't want to."

She pursed her lips. "Sven's been dead for less than two days. And here I am snogging you."

"But Sven's not coming back," I said. "Not any more than my Liliana is ever coming back. When is enough, enough?"

She said, "But you still mourn."

I slumped back in my seat. "Touché."

"But when is it enough?" she asked. She sat on her knees and faced me. "It's like you said. We could freeze to death. Weeks from now the native salt traders with their llamas will come across this jeep with three human popsicles inside. Right now could be all we have."

"You're right," I said. "So what do we do about it?"

She straddled me, her crotch warm against my thigh. Put her arms around me. Touched her cold nose to mine. "Maybe death is a reminder for us to live."

She inhaled my tongue. She was the best kisser I had ever met. My cock throbbed in my pants. Guilt twisted my guts. I pushed her away.

"What is it?" she asked.

"What about Kate?"

She ground herself against my leg. "What about her?"

Victor could hear everything. If we survived, he would tell Kate about it. But did it matter? Kate had made her position clear. Carrying a torch for a woman, much less an American woman, was a fool's errand. And if we froze to death here in the Salar, it wouldn't make any difference anyway.

"Nothing," I said, and pulled her down on the seat next to me.

Afterward, neither of us could sleep. Aurora took out her camera and showed me pictures.

Sven and me in Buenos Aires. Sven and me in Rio de Janeiro. Sven and me in Bogotá. Sven and me in bed. Oops. She grinned and bit a fingernail. Fast-forwarded through a few shots.

He was a tall, blond Swede. In each successive photo his hair grew longer. Didn't want to cut his hair, she explained.

"What's this?" I asked.

The motorcyclist filled the frame.

"I'd forgotten," she said. "Motorcycle dude. Yeah."

I took the camera from her hands. Zoomed in. The man sat astride the bike, face hidden beneath the smoked visor. Yellow hair trickled from underneath the helmet. At the throat, partly obscured by the leather jacket, the point of a shark tooth stabbed upward.

"Crap," I said.

"What?" She pressed her breasts against my shoulder.

"I didn't know better, I'd say this was Pitt."

***

Dawn crept over the mountains. My fingers and toes tingled with the cold. Victor got out of the car and started doing jumping jacks. Frozen air blasted us through the open door. I shook Aurora awake.

"Sven honey, not yet, I'm so tired."

"Just me, I'm afraid."

She sat up, looked around her. Kissed me on the lips. She put her arms around my neck and squeezed me tight. Trembled. Her breath was hot on my neck. She smacked her lips, licking away tears.

"Pawn to Queen Six," Victor muttered outside. "Right on schedule."

"What's that?" I asked.

His mutter grew into a shout. "Ahoy! Over here!"

Aurora and I pushed each other away, jumped out of opposite sides of the vehicle. Another jeep moved on the distant horizon, heading north, back to La Paz. We joined Victor in his desperate calisthenics, throwing our hands and feet in the air. Victor climbed on top of our jeep and waved his handkerchief.

"We're off the tourist track," I said. "They'll never see us."

"Victor!" Aurora said. "What about your gun?"

"Shit," he said, "you're right." He fumbled under his jacket, drew his six-shooter. Pointed it at the heavens. *Bang.* Nothing. Emptied the cylinder, *bang-bang-bang-bang-bang.* The jeep continued to move across the horizon, not getting any bigger. He took the box of ammunition from his jacket pocket. He slid new bullets into the weapon. His fingers were obviously stiff.

"What about the flare gun?" I said.

They both said, "What flare gun?"

"This flare gun," I said. I drew the heavy-caliber pistol from my jacket, put my finger in my ear and pulled the trigger.

A flare hissed skyward and exploded. Flashing bits of metal cascaded down in a haze of red smoke. The jeep slowed, turned in profile. Was it coming toward us, or going away?

I reloaded the two spares, fired them both, until the sky lit up like a battle zone. Our jumping jacks became hysterical, raw recruits on speed.

Panting, I rested my hands on my knees to catch my breath, the cold, thin air stabbing my lungs. The jeep was bigger than before. I sat on the fender, rubbed my ungloved hands together.

"Manuel gave you flares," Victor said. He climbed down off the roof. "Good one."

"Looks like he sabotaged the jeep, but didn't want us to die," I said.

Victor frowned. "Interesting move."

We waited for the jeep to arrive. Victor put the gun away. We were out of breath, but warmed by the exercise. The horizon on the Salar is as far away as it is at sea. It took time for the jeep to reach us. As it got closer, I could tell from the expensive foreign-made backpacks strapped to the roof it was a tourist jeep. It slowed to a stop, tires crunching on the salt.

The driver lowered the window. "You alright there, mate?" he called in a New Zealand accent.

Aurora whooped. "We are very glad to see you!"

"Broke down last night," I said. "Any idea how to fix an engine?"

He grunted and swung open his door. "Let's have us a look-see, now, eh?"

The eight tourists in the back stared at us. Fear? Or boredom? Maybe they were just cold. They got out and walked around, stretching, beating their arms with their mittened hands. Four young backpackers chattering in Dutch amused themselves by taking humorous photos. A white-haired couple got carefully from the jeep, clucking at each other in French, as though afraid any sudden move might break a hip. Two overweight Japanese men clambered from the back, lit cigarettes.

The tour guide bent over the engine block. "The bloody hell happened to your face, mate?" he demanded of Victor.

"Fell down some stairs."

"Stairs?" The guide straightened, looked around us at the vast emptiness of the Salar. He winked. "Missus, eh? Say no more."

The verdict was soon in coming. "You've had some bloody gremlins at work here, mate. Mucked up the works big time."

Victor picked up the wrench, looked over the man's shoulder. He pointed the tool at the engine. "It looks as though someone deliberately damaged the—the thing here. How you say in English?"

The guide said, "Who rented you this piece of shit, anyway?"

Those were his last words. Victor smashed the wrench across the back of the man's head. The guide fell to his knees, slid across the grill of the jeep and landed face down on the salt.

A bellowing bull sounded her charge. The white-haired Frenchwoman pounded her chest with her fists, expelling a primal growl of surprise and anger.

I knelt down to where the man lay. Put my fingers to his neck. "He's dead." I looked at Victor. "You killed him."

"I know. Queen takes pawn."

"Have you lost your mind?" I said. "This isn't a game, man. This is real life."

He shrugged. "We need the jeep."

"You're going to tell me he was CIA, too?"

Aurora beat her fists against Victor's back. "You couldn't have just asked him for it?"

The tourists approached us in a herd, a stampede of Gore-Tex and Lycra. The two Japanese men broke off and headed for their jeep.

Victor's face was grim. "You didn't see the pile of bodies at the ashram?"

"So this is what, revenge?" she said. "Murdering other innocent people evens the score?"

The Japanese flicked their half-finished cigarettes onto the salt. The tourists shuffled toward us, eyeing the wrench still in Victor's hand. They were drawn to him by some savage impulse that overwhelmed their fear.

"You keel zees man?" The French bull's mate squeaked.

The Japanese succeeded in starting the jeep. They slammed the doors, fastened their seatbelts.

"We need your jeep," Victor said. "Matter of national security."

"Well maybe if you hadn't killed their fucking guide!" Aurora shouted.

The emergency handbrake shrieked. The other jeep rolled forward, pointing away from us. It accelerated. I ran after it, shouting the only Japanese I knew: *"Konichi wa! Konichi wa!"*

The jeep did not slow. It turned in a wide circle, then aimed itself at us. I stood in its path. It did not swerve. I jumped out of the way. The Japanese driver rammed it into the side of our jeep, smashing the windows, grinding the front wheels over the still-warm corpse of the Kiwi guide. The driver reversed.

I ran to his window, jogged along beside him. "You have to help us. Please!"

His companion in the passenger seat leaned across the steering wheel. "You kill friend. Why?"

Before I could reply, a shot rang out. Aurora held Victor's six-shooter in her hand. She pointed it at Victor's chest.

The Japanese driver braked to a stop. "Ah, so."

Aurora slammed the hood shut, climbed on top of our now smashed-up jeep. She kept the gun aimed at Victor. "I want you all to hear this," she shouted in Spanish. "Three days ago, my boyfriend was murdered. This guy's best friend—" a finger pointed at me, "—was murdered too." She pointed at Victor. "Almost fifty people he lived with at a Buddhist ashram were massacred. On the shores of Lake Titicaca. And you want to know who did it?"

The tourists shivered in the cold. A few shook their heads.

"The CIA! And you know why?"

"No idea," one of the Dutch backpackers said.

"They want to start a war. Between Bolivia and Chile and Peru. And if we don't make it to the Anglo-Dutch lithium mine today, before noon, it will be too late. More innocent people will die."

A backpacker in a woolen hat with ear flaps emblazoned

with llamas cupped his hands to his mouth. "Why did your friend kill our guide?"

Aurora's shoulders sagged. She shook her head. "I don't know. Maybe he's tired. Maybe he's stressed. Maybe he thought you were following us."

"We've been here on the Salar freezing our ass off for the last five nights!" objected a Dutch girl with freckles the size of maple leaves.

"And what an ass it is, too," her boyfriend cooed in her ear. She elbowed him in the stomach.

Victor held out his hands, empty. He bowed his head. Tears trickled down his cheeks. "I am so sorry," he said. He fell to his knees.

Aurora shouted, "We need to stop the war. But we need your help. Are you with us?" She punched the air with her fist. "Will you let us have your jeep?"

The herd crossed its arms and lowered its collective head. They huddled, shoulders shifting from side to side. Finally the French bull-woman pranced forward.

"Only if we come with you," she announced in halting Spanish.

The others frowned their approval. Heads nodded. Aurora lowered her voice, asked me, "Can we all fit in one jeep?"

"Sure," said the Dutchman in the ear flaps. "It'll be a squeeze, but we've managed OK so far. Another day or two isn't going to kill us."

We felt like circus clowns piling into a Volkswagen bug. Concerns like seatbelts and who was pinching whose ass were quickly forgotten. We strapped the Kiwi guide's body to the roof. After a few kilometers we realized we were attracting the local bird life, and we covered the corpse with a blue tarp. At one point, Victor asked for his revolver back. Aurora kept it in her lap, her finger on the trigger.

"Reckon I'll hold on to it for now," she said.

The sun had crept over the mountaintops when we saw them.

"Hey, cool!" someone cried out, rolling down a window. "Tanks!"

The others fumbled with their cameras. Everyone turned in their seats, trying to get a clear shot.

I was driving. I glanced out the window. Resisted the urge to say, "You're welcome." The tanks were headed south-west, toward the border with Chile. Same as we were. They stretched in a line on the horizon, spaced at intervals, kilometers of hard green metal squeaking and clanking and grinding their way toward the mine.

Grinding their way toward us.

"We're too late," Victor said.

The Dutchman draped his arms over the front seat, woolen hat bouncing against the roof. "You mean the war has already started?"

"Without us?" cried his girlfriend.

I hunched over the steering wheel. "Nowhere else to go but forward."

The tanks got bigger. A whistling noise overhead. An explosion splattered the windshield with salt. I swerved to avoid the crater.

"Not funny," a Japanese guy said. In the rear-view mirror I saw him wave his hand in front of his face, point to his companion's crotch. The smell of shit filled the enclosed space. The others rolled down their windows.

I pressed the pedal to the floor. The humming of the tires on the even salt flat filled the jeep with a loud high-pitched whine. The tanks changed course, converging on our position.

"What's the top speed on one of those things?" I asked.

"No idea!" the Dutchman shouted.

Aurora peered at the bouncing speedometer. "We're doing one fifty," she said. "No way they're going to catch us."

One fifty... I translated in my head. Ninety miles an hour or so. Fast enough.

"You make false assumption!" squeaked the male appendage of the French bull-woman.

"What is that?"

"That they want us alive!"

We were silent after that. I gripped the steering wheel tight. Tank shells blasted salt into the air all around us. For the second time in two days, bullets the size of my wrist were trying to kill me. I thought about Victor's ploy, random unpredictable speeds. Fuck that. I held the pedal to the floor.

The line of tanks curved, gun turrets pointed at us, metal treads patiently crunching their salty path toward the border. Salt splashed the windshield again. I swerved violently, throwing my passengers to one side.

"How we doing?" I shouted.

Victor tapped me on the knee. "Stop looking so worried," he said.

"How's that?" I said.

"They're Bolivian socialists," he said. "They're incompetent. They couldn't hit the side of a barn."

"They hit a fucking barn yesterday, dude!"

Victor shrugged, sat back in his seat.

His nonchalance proved well-founded. We drew away from our pursuers. The tanks were soon specks again on the horizon, and the explosions ended.

"How much farther?" I shouted over the noise of the freezing wind blowing in the window.

"Not far," Victor said. "Another hundred clicks or so."

I struggled to keep the steering wheel straight. "What time is it now?"

He pushed back his sleeve. "Eleven o'clock."

"Shit."

We weren't going to make it.

The sun was high in the sky when we spotted the mine in the distance. My watch read twelve noon exactly. We were late—but there was no smoke, no sign of bomb damage. My spirits lifted.

"Get your cell phone out," I called to Victor. "And... action!"

He nodded grimly and began recording, then swore.

"What is it?" I asked.

"They're jamming the signal. I won't be able to upload the video from here."

"Then we'll just have to hand-deliver it, won't we?"

We stopped the jeep for a herd piss. The Frenchies loaned

me their bird-watching binoculars.

The sign at the gate read: Anglo-Dutch Mining, Ltd., Authorized Personnel Only. Beyond the gate, the mine itself covered several hectares. It was all just as Pitt had once described it. Pumping station, to suck the lithium brine from the aquifers beneath the Salar. Drying pools, the only economical way of concentrating the lithium salt. Refining equipment, to filter the impurities. Storage tanks, to hold the unstable finished product.

Aurora stood on tiptoe, rested her chin on my shoulder. "We made it."

"I don't understand," I said.

"Understand what?" She laughed. "How we made it this far?"

"No," I said. "How come the mine is still intact."

"What do you mean?"

I held my wrist to my chin so she could read my watch. "We're late. It's still here."

"But that's great news," she said. "Let's poke around, like Victor said. Maybe we can find some proof of American involvement. Now give to me, please."

I unlooped the binoculars from my neck. At that moment, an explosion of light blinded me. I closed my eyes. It was like ten thousand suns going nova right in front of my face.

"Don't look," I shouted. "Turn around! Cover your eyes!"

The sound of the explosion reached us a moment later, the moan of metal tendons and hydraulic muscles torn free of concrete bones, the flesh of the operation returned to the dust from which it came.

The fierce light continued to splay itself against my eyelids.

Even with my back to the mine, my hands over my eyes, I could still see it. Then I understood.

Mix lithium with water. Pure boom, Pitt had laughed. *The savior of the world is an explosive device.*

There had been no bomb, no booby trap. Someone had sabotaged the pumping station. Pump water into storage tanks—

Boom.

After many minutes, the hissing sound dissipated. I opened my eyes. For a moment I thought I was blind. It was still afternoon. How come I could see nothing?

I blinked. Slowly my eyes adjusted. "Everyone OK?" I asked. "No one lose an eyeball?"

A blurry figure swayed in my vision. Victor. His arm held out. Finger extended. I squinted. What was he pointing at?

The black blob grew outlines. An SUV. Four men in camouflage pointed guns at us. Goggles hid their eyes. The dying glow of the lithium explosion flickered off their brown faces. To one side: two more jeeps, eight more men. Behind us, another pair of SUVs. Five glossy black vehicles in total, showroom new. Guns all aimed at us.

At me.

"End of the line, folks," I called out. "Thank you for riding with us. Remember to check under your seat for any personal belongings." I put my hands in the air. "Not that you'll need them, where we're going."

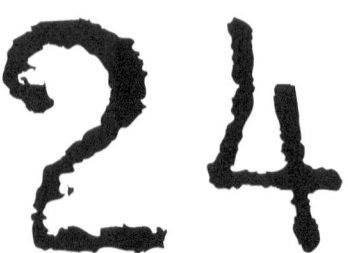

THE SUV IN FRONT OF ME ROCKED ON ITS SUS-
pension. A man slid from the passenger seat onto the ground.
Wisps of black hair straggled from his ears. A blue fitted
Cubs cap perched on his scalp.

I said, "Hak Po?"

He winked at me. The SUV rocked again, this time a
heavy dip and shudder, like a small boat in high seas. Ambo
emerged. He adjusted his Stetson, scuffed his boots in the salt.
When he saw me, his head jerked back and he grinned.

Kill.

My molars ground the word and spat it out a hiss. He had
driven me from Lima. Killed his own wife. Framed me for
her murder. Killed Pitt. Tried to kill me. Ordered the deaths
of dozens of innocent people. Now was his moment of triumph. To gloat. But not if I could help it. By habit I went for
my switchblade, forgetting the cops had taken it. Shit. Now
what was I going to do? Just let him walk all over me again?
An explosion at my right ear deafened me.

I flinched. The SUV's windshield cracked, but no bullet
hole appeared. To my right and behind me, Aurora jumped
on Victor's back. He must have taken the gun from her. He

held the pistol tight in both hands, tried to point it at Ambo.

All around us, safeties clicked off. "Hold your fire!" Ambo roared.

The Frenchwoman bellowed, pounded her fists against her breasts. I grabbed hold of Victor's wrists, tried to bring the gun down, but he squeezed off another shot. *Damn you,* I thought. *Give me the fucking gun. I want to kill him. Not you. Me. Let me do this one good thing before I die.*

Gloved hands pried Aurora off Victor's shoulder, dumped her on the ground. She let out an outraged squeak in midair. Cute. A soldier in camouflage loomed behind us. He snaked his arm around Victor's neck. Lifted him off the ground by the throat. Battered the gun with his other hand, but failed to disarm him.

"Drop the weapon," the man grunted in Spanish.

I fought with Victor, trying to pull the gun free, but he fired again.

"They've won," I said, grappling with him, my lips close to his ear. "We lost."

"We. Have. Not." He fired twice more. The bullets ricocheted off the roof of the vehicle.

I put all my strength into my thumbs, tried to break his grip. There was only one bullet left, and I wanted it. But I could not budge his fingers. Between clenched teeth, I said, "Live to fight another day, dude."

"No," he said. "Too late. To stop it." He clutched at the commando's forearm. "All. Going. To die." He put the gun barrel in his mouth, said, "Checkmate," and pulled the trigger.

Brains, blood and bits of skull exploded backward, showering the tourists in a cloud of freshly dead vulcanologist.

The commando looked like a watermelon had exploded in his face. He let go of the body, dabbed a gloved fingertip at the blue-gray goo splattered across his goggles.

My hands were covered in gore. I wiped them on my trousers. *I am such an asshole. I can't do anything right.* Why didn't I just let him shoot Ambo? Victor would have killed him. Might have, anyway. And now what? Six bullets and the bastard was still standing. *Now what the hell do I do?*

I was considering the available options when two commandos tackled me from opposite directions, crushing me between them, knocking the breath from my chest. They slammed me to the ground, cheek first into the hard-packed salt. My broken nose throbbed from the impact. A knee ground into my left kidney. The commandos bound my wrists behind my back with flexible plastic.

"That the best you can do?" I said. "Come on, make it hurt, *marica!*"

One of them rabbit-punched me in the neck. I blacked out for a moment. A voice like an echo down a long tunnel said, "That can be arranged."

Pointy green snakeskin boots scuffled to a stop inches from my nose. A drop of blood fell onto the salt. Ambo's voice, far above, said, "Stand him up."

Two soldiers yanked me to my feet. Ambo clutched his left shoulder with his right hand. Blood seeped through his down vest. It looked like something he'd bought in the seventies, and never bothered to replace.

"Cut him loose," he ordered.

A knife brushed the inside of my wrists and I was free. I rubbed my neck with my good hand.

"Well, Horse," he said, "I guess I owe you one."

"For what?" I asked, incredulous.

He nodded toward the dead body. "For trying to stop him."

"You mean Victor?" I said. "I wasn't trying to stop him."

"No?" He raised his eyebrows. "Then what were you doing?"

"I wanted to kill you myself."

Ambo made a fist, backhanded me across the face. My broken nose snapped a second time. I groaned. Tasted blood. My legs went rubbery. He caught me as I fell. Put his good arm around me and pressed me against him.

He said, "I don't know whether to shoot you or give you a medal."

"I'm not particular," I said, and spat in his face. Blood and phlegm trickled down his cheekbone. "Fielder's choice."

He pushed me away. Wiped at the gob of spit. His monster fist clutched great folds of my jacket, pulled it tight against my body, lifted me on the tips of my toes. He put his nose close to mine.

"I didn't kill Lynn."

"You found out I was fucking her."

His gaze wavered. "I am an old man, and a fool."

"We agree on something, then."

"I didn't kill Pitt, either."

"So you say." I grinned. "There's only one thing I regret."

"What's that?"

I smirked at his wounded shoulder. "It's a shame that Victor missed."

Ambo let go of me. Shook his head. "You just love that righteous anger, don't you. You got no fucking clue."

"Don't I? Mister Captain of the Dissent Suppression Unit, I kill people who threaten American corporate profits?"

"This isn't a DSU case," he said.

"What company are you working for this time?"

He gestured over my shoulder. "And your new friends? Are they deluded activists as well?"

The others lay on the ground, orange plastic one-time cuffs around their wrists. The earflaps of the Dutchman's woolen hat fell to the side, knitted llamas prancing in the salt. The Frenchwoman coughed up incoherent oaths on the commandos' boots. The Japanese men puffed on their cigarettes from where they lay on their stomachs.

"They know about the sabotage. They know about your plan to start a war. You'll have to kill us all, you realize that?" I smiled triumphantly. "'Cause we're all witnesses. To this atrocity."

"No more kill. Kill no good." Hak Po appeared soundlessly at my side. "Horse," he said. "So please see you." He stretched his lips tight across his teeth. Held out a hand.

"Hak Po," I said. I looked at Ambo for an explanation. He offered none. I shook the bony hand. "Love your new home delivery service. How much for a couple grams of your finest?"

Hak Po laughed, slapped my arm. "We not here satisfy your cocaine fantasies, my friend. Much bigger eels to boil." His hand lingered on mine. "Elephants to hunt." He leaned into me, whispered, "Big game."

"Speaking of which," Ambo asked. "Have you seen Pitt?"

"You son of a bitch," I said. I pulled my hand from Hak Po's skeletal embrace and swung my fist at Ambo's head. It landed in the padded softness of his white palm. He held my hand firm.

"You see?" he said to Hak Po.

"Maybe you right."

With my left hand I aimed an uppercut at Ambo's head. This time I connected with his jaw. A snapping noise and an explosion of pain announced a second fracture of my little finger. In the rush of adrenaline and cold, I had forgotten about it.

"Motherfucker."

The pain was intense. I rode the wave. Gasped from deep inside my chest. My eyes rolled back in my head. But a thought dampened my joy: was this an addiction too?

Ambo squeezed my right fist in his paw. "Suppose," he said, and looked shyly at the ground, "suppose I told you Pitt wasn't dead."

"Suppose I told you cocaine cured cancer, Lima was beautiful, and America was a free country." I took another swing at his head with my broken fist, looking for more pain, but Hak Po latched on to my arm with both hands.

"No time for this," he said. "Need your help. Come with us. Now!"

The mouth of a volcano.

The satellite image zoomed in. Snow encircled the peak. A man stood at the lip of the crater. The image zoomed in again, until I could see the man's face.

It was Pitt.

"When was this taken?" I asked.

"That's a live feed, son," Ambo shouted from the front seat of the SUV. "He picks his nose it's real time."

"For fuck's sake," I said. "Pitt's dead. I saw the body." I looked up from the video display on my lap. "You killed him."

Ambo sighed, rubbed his jaw. "I am beginning to wish I had."

"You *what?*"

"It's a long story, Horace, and we have little time."

"Well then you'd better be quick about it," I said. "Use easy words. I'm not too smart."

On either side of me, brown-faced Bolivian commandos in American surplus camouflage sat rigid, rifles at their sides. On a distant mountaintop, Pitt paced back and forth.

The caravan of SUVs stopped in front of a concrete bunker just outside the perimeter of the mine. The exterior was blackened and scorched. The acrid smoke from the explosion billowed around us, singeing my nose. A sign on the wall of the bunker declared: Gentleman's Rec Centre, Condoms Mandatory.

We traipsed inside. Half a dozen rooms stood open, green sheets crisp and tight. Shower stalls along one wall gleamed with a recent cleaning. The place smelled of bleach.

Hak Po opened a heavy wooden door. "Sauna," he said. "Soundproof. No bugs." He grinned at me.

"Bugs bad," I said.

The three of us stepped into the small room and closed the door. Ambo threw off his jacket, unbuttoned the collar of his green-and-black checked flannel shirt. Hak Po pressed a scratched red button on the wall, and the heating element crackled.

Ambo plucked at his lower lip. "Where should I begin."

I said, "Let me see what I can guess."

He closed his mouth and shrugged, winced at the pain. "Go ahead."

"Pitt's gone rogue. He faked his death, and he's trying to stop the war over the lithium."

Ambo nodded. "Not bad. What else?"

"You've been trying to kill me because you don't want the truth to come out. Don't interrupt me. And you will probably drop me down a mine shaft as soon as you finish this interrogation. Which," I said, "does not motivate me to tell you anything."

Ambo massaged his palm across the stubble on his head. Wisps of steam rose from the heating element. "So what's Pitt doing on top of a volcano?"

The hot air caught in my throat. "That I don't know."

Ambo said, "He wants to destroy the world."

"Spare me," I said. "It's not the end of the world just because you can't have your little war."

"War's off, Horace."

"Then what'd you blow up the mine for?"

"Who said that was us?"

"Victor. Industrial sabotage, provoke Bolivia into a war."

"We were going to have a war. I don't deny it." Ambo poked at his wound. The bullet hole in his shoulder dribbled blood with each pulse of his heart, soaked into his shirt. He peered at it curiously, as though it were some rare cosmic phenomenon, but did nothing to staunch the flow. "But then Pitt got involved," he said. "Why do you think the Bolivians are helping us?" He waved a hand toward the door.

"Maybe they're part of it. They want their land back. Maybe they're colluding with you to start the war, and plan to double-cross you later."

Hak Po shook his head. "When Ambo say 'end world,' he mean 'end world.' You listen me?"

I turned to Ambo. "And what the fuck is going on here, dude? You're sitting here with a Chinese spy."

"Well, *dude,*" he said, glaring at me, "if you shut up for a minute and listen, you might find out."

"Listen?" Hak Po asked again. "Patient?"

I sat. The sauna's warmth brought circulation back to my fingers. My left hand throbbed. I fingered the bone fragments floating around in my pinkie. Better than coffee.

"Make it quick," I said.

Hak Po cleared his throat, spat on the floor. He pressed his knees together, hands folded on his lap. He looked at the floor, admiring his loogie. "There two places in world with lithium. You know this?"

"Tibet and the Salar de Uyuni," I said, remembering Victor's lecture in the cave. "Plus Afghanistan and Australia."

"But Tibet deposits small. Other deposits very small."

"Which means Bolivia is the proud owner of most of the world's lithium. Your point?"

"Yes. Cocaine no fry brain." He smiled at his joke. I said nothing. He continued, "There faction of monks in Tibet. Hate modern world. Fight against China, what they call China's 'occupation.' Even though for centuries Tibet lawful ancient part of Chinese Empire—"

"Hak." Ambo's voice a warning.

"These monks want destroy modern life. Want destroy

lithium."

"What for?" I asked. "I mean, what does that have to do with anything?"

Hak Po shrugged, poked at his loogie with the toe of his boot. "Petroleum run out. Lithium battery new gasoline. No lithium, then when oil go away, many people die. Maybe billions. Many Chinese. World go back old ways."

"Why is that a problem?" I asked.

"Horace!" Ambo said. "Everyone would die."

"I say again, why is that a problem?"

They both started talking at once.

I held up my palms. "Sounds to me like what the human race deserves."

"Most people aren't like you, Horace," Ambo said. "Most people want to live."

"I'm not so sure about that. But what the hell," I said, before he could interrupt. "I'll play along. How, exactly, do a bunch of mystical Tibetan Buddhist monks plan on destroying a naturally occurring mineral?"

A yellow finger pierced the air. "Victor Ivanovitch Strezlecki."

"Who has super cow powers?"

Hak Po lowered his head in a quick bow. "Victor vulcanologist. Talented man, Mister Victor. World number two at chess when child."

"A master manipulator," Ambo broke in. "For all I know, this conversation is part of his end game. He should have been a spy."

Hak Po continued. "Victor twenty year study volcanoes in Andes. Peru, Bolivia, Chile. Top expert. No one else close."

Ambo ripped his shirtfront open. Buttons skittered across the wooden bench onto the damp floor. He held out his cuffs to Hak Po, who undid them. He slid out of the sleeves. The wound to his shoulder blossomed across his chest like a Rorschach ink blot. He pressed the bunched-up garment against the wound. "The man did his postdoc at Oregon State. Speaks perfect English."

"I noticed," I said. "But what does any of this have to do with Pitt being on top of a volcano?"

"He's getting there," Ambo said, and closed his eyes. He slumped back against the wall.

Hak Po continued. "We watch Victor long time. Wife, daughter die in car crash. Here Bolivia."

I snorted. "Who the fuck told you that, Hak?" I jerked my head at Ambo. "The land of the slaves and the home of the oppressors here tortured, raped and murdered Victor's wife and daughter. True or false?"

Ambo chewed his lip. "Sure we did. I'd do it again, too. What if a rogue state got a hold of his weapon?"

"You mean a rogue state like America?" I shouted.

"Boys! Boys!" Hak Po held up a hand between us. "Save for later. Point: After family die, Victor go Tibet. Five year ago. Meditate. Last year, big explosion at lithium mine. Very bad. No production. Victor suspect. But, no volcano in Tibet. So no do more damage."

"Why? Is he going to blow up a volcano?" I joked.

Hak Po nodded. "You understand lithium in water. Under Salar."

"Duh. Yeah."

"Very costly mine. Pump out water. Dry for one year,

longer. Concentrate solution. Very low percent solution. Not like gold or diamonds, dig out of ground. What he do, try do, Mister Victor, is blow up volcano. Here Bolivia. The Salar. Vaporize salt water. Then, no more lithium."

I frowned. "Let's assume for the moment you aren't talking completely out of your ass. Is that even possible? Making a volcano erupt on command?" Then the penny dropped. "You mean that's Victor's weapon?"

Hak Po smiled. "Good boy. Smart."

Ambo didn't join the smilefest. "Why do you think we tortured his family, Horace? For kicks?"

"With you?" I said. "Hard to say."

"We show data to scientists," Hak Po said. "They say, Victor that good. If Victor say, dynamite right spot, they believe he make volcano blow up."

"OK," I said. "But he'd have to do that for every volcano in the region."

"Big fault line under Salar." Hak Po traced a line of spittle on the wooden floor with his boot. "Dynamite right spot set off chain reaction."

"A chain reaction," Ambo echoed, taking the reins, "that will cause the volcanoes that surround the Salar to erupt, spewing lava across the salt flats."

"Yeah, OK. But would that—"

"—do significant damage? The surface lava, no." Ambo rode over my interruption. "Although it would be a nuisance for future mines. Victor's true genius was discovering the fault line had weak spots. Trigger points, if you will. We ran his raw data through supercomputers. Simulations show his theory to be correct. The magma will well up under the fault line. There's a ninety-eight percent chance it will break the surface. Even if it doesn't, it will vaporize the salt water under the salt flats, cooking the water from the soil, and leaving the lithium trapped in the sands. It would become impossible to mine."

The cave. Snatches of conversation. "Two percent of what?" I asked. "You a dairy farmer?"

"If you believe the shit you're shoveling," I said, "why didn't you take out Victor years ago? You knew what he was trying to do."

Ambo lifted his right shoulder, let it fall. "We wanted to know his secret. How his weapon works. He wouldn't talk. So we let him go and spied on him instead."

I looked from one to the other. "But this is crazy. You think he can actually do this?"

For the first time, Hak Po looked at me. "Would Chinese government send me here, work with CIA, with Ambassador, if not believe threat real?"

Ambo's eyes rose from under his bushy eyebrows. "This transcends petty national interest. This is not about what's good for China, or what's good for the US, or even Bolivia. It's about what's good for everyone. The whole world. The human race."

"The human race?" I said. "What about all those innocent people you murdered? What about what's good for them?"

The door to the sauna opened. A soldier stepped into the room. He carried a red-and-white plastic tackle box marked Med Kit.

"Not now," Ambo barked, or tried to. Blood streamed down his chest and pooled at his toes.

"Maybe he fix you," Hak Po said.

"This is too important," Ambo said, panting for breath. "Not now."

"Sir, you need to stop the—"

"I said, not now!"

The medic's face puckered, turned red. He about-faced and left the sauna.

I rested my elbows on my knees. "You were explaining how murdering dozens of innocent civilians was good for mankind."

Ambo lit a cigarette, puffed deep. Smoke trickled between his lips. "Dozens of innocent—" He coughed. "What are you talking about?"

I rolled my eyes. "Not like you don't do it for a living."

"Yes, but which ones?"

"Isla del Sol, the ashram—"

"That wasn't us."

"Of course not," I said. "The Dissent Suppression Unit never murders dissidents. They just go dancing among the flowers, quoting poetry and smoking pot. What a crazy idea."

"Victor did that murder," Hak Po said quietly.

"At the ashram," Ambo added.

"Really," I said. "Not your undercover agent, Bill or Ted or whatever the fuck his name was?"

"*Michael* planted a recording device that caught the massacre on camera. It's been transmitting the whole time. Ever since he got there months ago. Want to watch?"

Without waiting for an answer, Ambo plunked the laptop onto the seat next to me. Pitt ceased his pacing on the lip of the volcano. Replaced by a view of the beach, Lake Titicaca.

From above the mouth of the cave.

"Fast-forward," Ambo said, and pressed a key.

Monks scurry about carrying boxes, pushing wheelbar-rows. Isla del Sol in the distance. The sun rises. Kate gets into a boat. Boxes of weapons are loaded in after her, fol-lowed by a host of monks. The boat pushes off from shore.

"Is Kate involved in this?" I asked.

Ambo held out an open palm. "Wait."

On screen, I straggle into the picture, gesture at the island, hop into a boat, zoom off.

"Here we are," Ambo said.

The image slowed to real time. Victor gestures, shouts, the words unheard. Everyone assembles, bags at their feet.

"There's no sound," I said.

"No microphone."

A cauldron of food bubbles nearby. The volunteers heft building tools over their shoulders. They are swaying side to side and singing what looks like "Kumbaya." They've put on monk robes over their street clothes. Fishermen and villag-ers hold empty food bowls in their hands. An old man hoists a little boy onto his shoulders. Everyone smiles, laughs. The fat monk waves an empty ladle. Counts heads with his fin-ger. An empty space in line, a missing monk. Who's missing? Where is he? It's Michael. He joins the others in their ranks. Food is served.

An Uzi appears in Victor's hands. He points it at the as-sembled throng. The monks and volunteers step forward in unison, heads thrown back, hands in the air. Ecstasy glistens on their faces. I recognize Mister When Is The Leave-Taking.

Fire bulges from the tip of the gun. The villagers try to

flee. Volunteers and monks grab them, hold them in place. People drop as though punched. A pause. Victor changes the clip. Michael jumps up, knife in hand. Victor blasts him at point-blank range. Blood splatters Victor's face. Michael drops. Victor empties the clip into Michael's twitching body. He changes the clip, fires again, spraying more bullets into the corpses.

Ambo reached around the display, pressed a button. The image fast-forwarded again.

Victor pulls the bodies into a pile. Runs to the water, comes back without the Uzi. He's dripping wet. He draws a handgun. Aurora and I wander onto the beach, point at the pile of bodies.

"Enough," I said.

Ambo stopped the playback. He folded his hands on his lap and looked at me.

I chewed a fingernail. "And Isla del Sol?"

Hak Po shrugged. "Pitt need disappear. Fake death. Find look-alike. Swedish national. Spike drink, swap clothes, hotel go boom. Then Pitt go way."

My voice was quiet. "What was the name of the Swedish national?"

"Does it matter?" Ambo asked.

"What was his name?"

His lips crinkled in annoyance. "Sven," he said, waved a hand. "Sven something."

Hak Po consulted a notebook. "Sven Larrsen. Why you ask?"

I jerked my thumb over my shoulder. Aurora and the others had followed us into the building, and were doing God knows what the other side of the sauna door. "Aurora's boy-friend. The girl who came along for the ride."

A thought occurred to me. "Why didn't you go into the ashram and arrest them ages ago?"

Hak Po tapped a slender finger on my knee. "Peruvian authorities no cooperate. Want proof. Say, volunteering good. Say, no crime done."

"Since when does that stop you people from doing any-thing?" I said. "Conspiracy to commit first-degree Gaia-cide. Make something up."

Ambo's face was ashen. Blood clotted in his wiry chest hair. "It was my fault."

"I do same if I you." Hak Po patted Ambo's knee. "I father too."

"Do what?" I asked. "What did you do?"

"What if Pitt got hurt during a raid?" he asked. "I could never forgive myself."

"Much better the world go boom," I agreed.

Ambo stretched his long arms wide, as though begging my forgiveness. "How could I be sure?" he asked. "Was he a part of Victor's group? Part of the conspiracy? Or was he just another lost soul doing yoga and building houses?"

"What difference does that make?" I asked.

"Without Pitt, they could do nothing. I knew this. Without his contacts and his knowledge of the mine, they could not have pulled it off."

"Pull what off?" I said. "What does the mine have to do with blowing up volcanoes?"

"It has to do with destroying the lithium. Just like he did in Tibet. Tons and tons of the stuff, a year's production."

"Plus distraction," Hak Po said.

"Exactly," Ambo said. "While we're all fighting a war, he's up on the mountain blowing the world to kingdom come."

"But why now?" I asked. "Why didn't Victor blow up the volcano months ago, years ago?"

His right side shrugged again. "He was waiting. Taking samples, surveying the Salar. Calculating how to do it. Using the ashram as cover. Then he got lucky. He met Pitt."

"And how was that your fault?"

"Maybe it wasn't exactly luck that they met," Ambo said.

"Not exactly—you mean you *sent* Pitt to him? To the ashram?"

"It was a job. Don't you see? To find out how far along Victor's plans were. Michael had failed to gain Victor's confidence. So we sent in Pitt. He managed to steal a copy of Victor's laptop hard drive. All the data, his calculations up until then. A team of scientists back in the States analyzed the data. Guess what their report said."

"You already told me, dude. That his theory was correct."

"Yes. But that Victor himself *hadn't figured out how to do it yet.*"

"So what are you saying?" I asked. "That somehow Victor got a hold of a copy of that report?"

"Not somehow. Pitt gave it to him. Stole it from us. Are you getting the picture?"

I swallowed. "Holy crap. So then what happened?"

He rested his head against the wooden wall of the sauna. "I made my second mistake. After he disappeared, I tried to talk to him."

"To Pitt?"

"I organized a meeting. He pretended to still be working for us. He's my son, don't you see?" He pleaded with me now, palms upward. "I had to give him one more chance."

"So what happened?"

Ambo gazed at me down the length of his nose, eyes half-closed. "He promised to meet me at the Hotel Finski for a beer."

My nostrils flared. "You mean he tried to kill you?"

"I got there just in time to watch the hotel explode."

"Dude..." I said. "You screwed that pooch five ways from Friday."

Ambo gasped for breath in the steamy air. Sweat trickled down his face, dripped from his nose. He closed his eyes, nodded his head in agreement.

I crossed my arms. "So then you followed me."

His shoulders twitched weakly. "We needed you to lead us to Pitt."

"You mean you thought I was part of Victor's plot?"

"Of course. I'm still not entirely convinced you're not."

"And that's why you tried to kill me."

"Kill Victor," Hak Po corrected.

"But if you had accidentally killed me in the process, that would have been an acceptable outcome."

"We weren't really trying to kill you," Ambo said. He avoided my gaze. "We asked the Bolivian gunners to aim to miss. Just scare you enough to show us where the bomb was. Where the rest of them went."

"Kate," I said. Sat up straight. "Where *did* the rest of them go? Is she with them? You follow her too?"

"Lost her and monks in La Paz," Hak Po said. "Disappeared

off map. Most impressive. Still not know how did this."

I said, "A family man named Fritz."

"Sorry?"

I pitched the keys to our abandoned SUV into the air. They fell to the wooden floor with a clatter. *Look, Manuel, here's all that's left.*

"World's highest ski resort," I said. "Assuming we're all still alive when this is over, you need to buy the former owner a new jeep." I turned to Ambo. "So you have no idea where Kate is?"

Hak Po leaned forward. "No say that."

"So you do know." My chest tightened. "Where is she? Is she safe?" I looked at both of them. "What's going on?"

Ambo bridged his fingers, rested his forehead on his thumbs. "Remember Sergio Salazar?"

"I've heard the name."

"Flew back to Lima. Had a little chat with him last night."

"A private one-on-one," I suggested.

"Something like that." Ambo grimaced. "You know, it's hard to interrogate a masochist. Torture doesn't really work."

"Yuck," I said. "What did you do?"

"Put him on a morphine drip. Finally cracked this morning. Just a couple of hours ago."

I laughed. "What did you find out?"

"Sergio has been working for Victor all along. It was his idea I send Pitt to the ashram." A bitter laugh. "Victor played me like a champ. Played you too."

"How's that?"

"Kate told Victor about you. Victor already knew about Pitt from Sergio. Victor had Sergio suggest you for the Hak

Po job. Put you and Pitt together, build a guilt complex in my son...now Victor's got access to our supercomputers and a highly trained DSU operative to run interference for him. Which, I might add, Pitt did very successfully, considering I trained him." A wry grin. "And you're the missing link. Pitt used that postcard of yours to get in touch with Victor. The one Kate sent you."

"So the whole thing's my fault," I said. "Anything else you want to blame me for?"

"Don't be like that, Horace."

"Like what?"

"Look, Victor played you both. Pitt never even realized."

"That's supposed to make me feel better?"

Ambo let out a puff of breath. "Anyway, the information Sergio gave you last week was a deliberate red herring. He wanted us running around after you instead of focusing on Pitt."

"So did he tell you where they are?" I asked.

"Sergio knows these mountains as well as anyone. He was one of the original surveyors who planned the Anglo-Dutch mine. We finally got the name out of him. Mount Testimony."

"Testimony?"

"*Cerro Testimonio* in Spanish."

I gestured at the laptop, where the image of Pitt had resumed its clockwork back and forth. "Where Pitt is now."

"Katherine too."

I studied the volcano's summit. "Where? I don't see her."

Ambo flapped his great hand at me. "They're guarding Pitt's flank. At the bottom of the mountain, watching the path that leads to the top. It's the logical thing for them to do."

"But when the volcano blows, they'll all die."

"There are worse things than death." He looked at me. "You know that as well as she does."

"So what are you going to do?" I asked.

"Why we need you, Horse." Hak Po's grin stretched rubber-band tight.

Hands out: halt: stop: red light. "Need me? For what?"

Ambo passed a hand across his forehead. "I need you to go up there and talk to him. To Pitt."

"Hello! The monks are guarding the path. They'll kill me if I try. You just said so yourself."

"Katherine is with them. You think she'd let them kill you?"

I thought about that.

"OK," I said. "But even if I made it up the mountain, what's the point? So I can commit suicide with him? All he's got to do is press the button. Wherever the button is." I waved my hand at the screen. "Then everything goes boom."

"Exactly," Hak Po said, and bowed his head.

"Exactly what?"

"What Hak Po means," Ambo said, "is that Pitt's been up there for the last four hours. We watched him lay the charges. The bomb is ready. Why hasn't he pressed the button? What is he waiting for?"

I shrugged. "For a signal. Who knows."

Ambo's index finger bayoneted my forehead. "He's waiting for you."

His fingernail dug into the skin just below my scalp. I swallowed. "What makes you think that?"

The bayonet withdrew. He plucked a postcard from his jacket, dropped it in my lap. On the front was a picture of

Mt. Illimani, the extinct volcano that towers over La Paz. I flipped the card over. It was speckled with Ambo's blood. There was no "Dear Dad," no signature, just the words:

Horse was right about us both.

"What did you tell him about me?" Ambo asked.

***

A private room.

Cocaine and *pisco* spread on the table. Brown-skinned girls in matching blue lingerie writhed on our laps.

"Best not grow old," I said, my finger moist.

"Why's that, bro?" He tickled the girl on his lap until she contorted in a mass of giggles.

I reached around a warm tittie for my glass of *pisco*. I drank long and slow. "Wind up like your dad."

"How's that?"

"An old man with a heavy conscience."

***

"Nothing," I said. I tossed the postcard to the side. "Why don't you ram a missile down his throat? You just said you've been watching him for hours."

"Not as simple as that," Ambo said. "Suppose we hit the payload? Suppose we set off the chain reaction? We can't take that chance."

"Or send in commandoes in a helicopter? I got to think up everything for you guys?"

"Pitt sees us coming he'll blow the mountain before we

even get close."

I swore. Why was I getting so worked up about this? Here I had my chance: one little red button. One push and the world and the pain go away.

"Then why didn't you take him out in the desert before he even got to the mountain?" I asked. "Why didn't you guard all the likely volcanoes in the region? You could have picked him up anytime."

"First of all, we only found out about all this from Sergio three hours ago. The full extent of the conspiracy. Second, there are twenty active and semi-active volcanoes in the Salar. Seventeen have weak spots Victor could exploit. The Salar covers thousands of square kilometers. Finding one man in that space, even with all our satellites and drones looking for him, is a needle in a haystack. If it weren't for Sergio, we wouldn't have found him at all."

"But why me? What about his wife? Go get Janine up here. Have *her* talk to him."

Ambo hung his head. "Janine has disappeared. The kids too. No note. Nothing. For all we know, she's part of the conspiracy."

Something nagged at me. What was it? Images flashed through my brain. La Paz, the witches' market, Aurora, that woman, the photo.

The motorcyclist.

"Or maybe," I suggested, "you knew where he was all along, and did nothing."

Instead of the violence I'd hoped for, Ambo sighed and lowered his chin into his palm. "Are you a father, Horace?" he asked. He ran a fingertip across his lower lip.

"That's a low blow," I said.

"Why?" he asked. "Because it's true? Because you're a failure of a father, just like me?"

"You knew where he was all along."

"He was playing a double game. After we had you released from jail, Pitt got in touch. Said he was following you, thought you were part of the conspiracy." Ambo held out his hands, let invisible sand trickle through his fingers. "We thought he was on our side. We were wrong."

I stood, turned my back on him. Clenched my fist, desperately looking for someone to punch, something to destroy. Through a narrow slit of glass I could see the Japanese tourists smoking, wrapped in blankets, hot mugs steaming in their fists. The Frenchwoman said something and the Dutch backpacker in the llama earflaps laughed, mouth wide, shoulders thrown back.

Aurora spotted me. Waved. I ducked sideways. Smacked my head against the wooden wall.

I am such an idiot. All around you people are dying, you yourself want to die, have nothing to live for, your ex-wife is a suicidal environmental terrorist, and all you can think about is this woman. Aurora.

What would she say if she knew? If I told her? My best friend killed your boyfriend. Thanks anyway for the shag in the jeep. I closed my eyes.

"I am dying," Ambo said. Blood pulsed from the wound on his shoulder.

"I can see that."

"No." He looked away. "Cancer. Six months max. Pancreatic. No treatment. Lots of pain."

"No less than you deserve," I said.

He nodded. "Time to reflect on my life."

"Time to relive your sins over and over again, replay them in your mind until you go mad, until the only thing you crave is death?"

He pressed his chin to his chest. "I believe in God, Horace. I believe in America. But that doesn't mean I don't have doubts. Have I always done the right thing? Am I a bad man?"

"Well," I said. "Let's see. No. And yes."

Ambo nodded his head, each downward movement drooping lower than the last. "I loved my wife and now she's dead. Because of me." He looked up at me suddenly. "But what if you could end the guilt?" he whispered. "What if, in one good deed, you could wipe the slate clean? Unburden your soul of its weight, and start over?"

For a time I had thought it was possible. It's what had sent me on this wild-goose chase in the first place. I had closed that door on Isla del Sol when I knelt over a blond-haired corpse. To rip open that wound once more—to be tortured by false hope—it was more than I could bear.

"If only," I said. "If only God existed, and trees were made of chocolate, and the sea was made of beer. And not that crap American dog piss, but decent brown ale." I stood. "But it's not, is it."

"Please." Ambo's outstretched arm was pathetic. "You're the only one who can do this. Anyone else goes up that mountain, Pitt will blow it up."

"So let him," I said. "He deserves it. So do you. So do I. So do we all." I held on to the wooden door handle, like a drowning man groping for a life preserver. "Besides," I said. "It's not my fight. If the world is doomed to end this way, then let it. The human race has made its bed. Now let it lie in it."

Hak Po spoke. "Chinese state pay much your help. Much you like. Never work again."

I laughed, let go of the door handle. "You think this is about money?"

He took a small plastic bag from his jacket pocket. "All cocaine you want. Lifetime supply. No charge."

It was tempting. Never have to worry about nightmares again. Spend the rest of my life awake. Able to control the demons that lurked just beneath the surface of the world. I reached for the bag. He drew back his hand.

"Get high and stay that way," I said.

"Exactly. Please." He held it out to me again. "Take. Sniff snort." He tapped a finger against his nostril, grinned.

I held up my hands, stepped backward. Shook my head. "No. That's too easy. A high's no good without the gutter in between."

I opened the door. "Now, if you'll excuse me, I'm off to Lima to look for a new drug dealer, this time hopefully some-one who's not a Chinese spy." I paused. "Oh, and to celebrate the end of the world."

Ambo stood, stretched out a hand to me, but slipped and fell to the ground. He clutched his chest, gasped for air. Hak Po pushed past me, shouting for the medic.

I bent down to where Ambo lay.

His bloody fingers smeared my cheek. "There may be no God," he whispered. "There may be no priest to forgive your sins. But there is one person whose forgiveness you must have. If you are ever to find peace."

"Oh yeah?" I said. "Who's that? Pitt?"

"You," he said, and tapped his finger weakly against my chest. "You must forgive yourself."

THE *FUCK*.

Goddamn fucking *bullshit*. Twist my arm and send me up this godforsaken mountain. And for all I know, I might just help him press that button, blow the world to kingdom come.

Boom.

No more fucking people. Human race dies off, a handful of farmers left to till the soil. Mankind back where it belongs. An end to concrete jungles and the crowds. An end to city living, city morals. An end to all the ugliness.

An end to me.

Would that be such a bad thing? I was half-dead already, destroyed in an orgy of chemical self-flagellation. My organs groaned under the onslaught of cocaine, liquor, junk food. *I know what punishment feels like. I know what I deserve.*

How many people had died because of me? My killing spree hit an exponential curve in the last week. It began slowly, of course. Data point one: my child, last year. What was her name again? I cringe at the thought. I've forgotten her name!

Liliana. That was her name.

Then we pick up the pace.

Lynn. Dead because of me. Because she loved me. Ambo was wrong. It wasn't his fault. It was mine. If I hadn't gotten involved with her, she'd be alive today. True, I didn't strangle her myself. But I might as well have.

Riding in the jeep to the base of the volcano, I asked Ambo, "So why did Pitt kill Lynn? It *was* him, after all, wasn't it?"

The heart meds the medic gave Ambo seemed to be working. *Keep the bastard alive for a little while longer. Let him suffer with the rest of us.*

He nodded. "Went to your apartment. To talk to you. I think," he said, and closed his eyes, "I suspect he wanted to recruit you for his bomb expedition."

I pinched my broken pinkie. The endorphin rush was the only drug available. "He found Lynn there. And something happened. Something snapped. But what? And why? I mean, he killed his own mother, for chrissakes."

"You were a bad influence on him, Horace," Ambo said. "I told you that the first time I met you."

A medic pinned a saline bag to the roof with his thumb.

"Hello?" I said. "Who's the killer for hire? Not me."

"Pitt serves a useful function in society. He makes sure the herd sticks together."

"Oh," I said. "Is *that* what it is."

"You, on the other hand," he said, turning to me, "serve no useful function in society. A conscience like yours in incompatible with life."

"With killing dissidents, anyhow."

"Your sense of moral outrage is contagious, son. He's caught your disease. A fate I wish on no man."

I struggled to process this. "So what are you saying, he broke into my apartment to talk to me, found Lynn there, and was, what? So disgusted at seeing her half-naked ass waiting in lust for my cock that he went apeshit?"

Ambo's head drooped, marking time to music only he could hear. "Something like that. Yeah. You remember how he killed her?"

"You don't mean that—"

But my throat convulsed and no more words came out.

Lynn, strangled on my floor.

Jump.

Pre-dawn glow creeps in the open window. Pitt stands over me, a knife in his hand, staring at my fist as I twitch and spurt. My face is purple. A hangman's noose dangles from my neck.

Jump.

How do I explain all this?

The SUV lurched over a rock. Ambo made a noise. The medic fussed. A diamond-encrusted fist pushed the man away. "That's exactly what I mean," he said. "Who did he learn it from?"

***

I taught him. Showed him. How to wrap his belt around his throat. Just enough to give a boost. To come, but not to kill. Weeks after the Hak Po op he came to me, noose in his fist, begged me for my opening lecture in Autoeroticism 101. I gave it to him. My own form of revenge, or so it seemed at the time.

"It's about getting as close to death as you can without dying," I told him.

"And then what happens?"

"I see things."

"What things?"

"How can I explain it to you? Life looks different afterward."

What monster of the deep had I awoken?

"It's not your fault," Ambo said. "Snap out of it, you hear me? Last thing I need right now is you out there in guilt-trip land."

I stared out the window. Razors of acid slashed at my insides. Pitt had come to confess. But I'm no priest. I'm no saint. And when he found Lynn there, and saw my sin for what it was, he knew the truth: there is no way to end the guilt. At least, none in this life.

"Is that what it was?" I asked the moon, already visible on the horizon. Night was never far off at this altitude.

"He strangled her with his bare hands. You came home before he could escape. Knocked you on the head, called the police, got the hell out of there. The police find a naked woman, dead, the rope in your bathroom... Sex play gone bad. That's what Villega thought, anyway. Until I set him straight."

"Villega thinks?" I said. It was such an absurd thought, I laughed out loud. I might never see his pimply jack-o'-lantern face again. Grade his ridiculous English homework. Then I remembered those photos he'd shown me, and I stopped laughing.

Lynn dead. Because of me.

Who else?

Who was next?

The train. The Chinese vendor Red Cap murdered.

"He very good agent," Hak Po said. "Family get big pay for loss of husband father. So sorry."

So sorry.

Who else?

The dead monk in the back of the van. When they kidnapped me, his corpse leaking all over my pants.

The unnamed spy at the mine Ambo and Pitt were after, the whole point of the Hak Po op. Tortured and murdered by the DSU because of me.

Paco, skull bashed in by Umlaut while the cops looked on. He was a pickpocket, but he had never hurt anyone. Just a little kid.

The innocent guests at the Hotel Finski. I could still feel the dead flesh under my fingertips, Sven melting in the noonday sun, the shark-tooth necklace burned into the skinless meat of his neck.

***

"You come back now, you hear?" Aurora cried, her arms around my neck.

"Back in a jiffy," I said, turning my lips away for her to kiss my cheek, all the while thinking: *maybe never. Maybe I'm the one who'll push the button, not Pitt.*

Then Victor's massacre on the lake shore. Old men. Children. The little kid with the soccer ball, those empty eye sockets. When Will Be The Leave-Taking, the volunteer who'd volunteer no more. Michael, the CIA tool. And a score of meditating monks, fugitives from the First World, seeking no more than a decent mantra and a well-earned peace, plus a chance to blow up the world. If I hadn't sent Pitt their way, none of those deaths would have happened.

And Kate.

Oh, Kate.

The SUV zipped its way across the salt flats toward the mountain. The early afternoon sun glared through the smoked glass. The medic jabbed Ambo with a needle.

A walkie-talkie crackled. "You there, sir?"

Ambo picked up the radio. "Talk to me."

"Missed the *banzai,* sir," a gruff voice said.

The radio hissed. "Come again?" Ambo said.

"*Banzai,* sir. Dozen men in robes just went over the top. Suicide charge."

"Survivors?"

"Negative, sir."

Ambo and I exchanged glances.

"Casualties?" he asked.

"Two down, nothing serious. Shit."

A loud popping noise in the background.

"What's that?" Ambo shouted, fighting off the medic.

"Got one taking potshots at us, sir!"

"Is it a woman?" I asked. I grabbed the walkie-talkie from Ambo's hand. "I said, is it a woman?"

There was a pause. "Affirmative. Sniper is female."

"Don't shoot!" I shouted. "Hold your fire!"

Another pause at the other end. "Those your orders, sir?"

Ambo held out his hand. I gave him the walkie-talkie. He said, "Hold your fire. Keep your head down and wait for us." Ambo looked at me, eyelids drooping heavy over his eyes. "Repeat, hold your fire."

The rocky four-wheel-drive track wound upward. We lurched along in the backseat. I turned to Ambo. "Something I have to ask you."

"So ask."

"I may not come down off the mountain."

He shrugged. "In which case none of us will either."

"That's not what I mean. There's something I need to know."

Ambo waited.

I took a deep breath. "Lynn," I said. "Was that on purpose?"

"Was what on purpose?"

"The whole thing. To seduce me."

His face went blank. Motionless. "What do you mean?"

"Was that part of your plan?" I said. Still he didn't answer. "Do I have to spell it out for you? Did you order her to sleep with me?"

He looked out the window at the volcano rising huge ahead of us. His lips moved several times before the word slid from his lips.

"No."

We continued in silence.

The salt flats petered out, replaced by rocks piled high by ancient volcanic belches. In the distance a path zigzagged up the side of the volcano, the dusty trail pounded flat by decades of tourist traffic and, before that, centuries of human sacrifice, Incan priests leading their victims to the slaughter.

The road ended. We dismounted from the jeep. A soldier ran toward us stooped over. He wore camouflage with a Bolivian flag on the shoulder. The rest of the soldiers huddled behind car-sized boulders, their rifles aimed at an unseen enemy. Up the hill lay the scattered corpses of the brown-skinned, shaven-headed monks. Their robes fluttered in the cold breeze.

"They die long way from home Tibet," Hak Po said. He spat.

A rifle shot rang out. The dust at my feet puffed in a cloud. "Get down!" the soldier shouted. We crouched low and ran for cover.

Ambo struggled to keep up. He rested against a man-sized

boulder. Panted for breath. An American soldier wearing captain's bars crouched at his feet.

"Who the hell is this guy?" I said. "American troops in Bolivia?"

"Military advisor," Ambo said. He addressed the captain. "What have we got here?"

The advisor gave me an ugly look. "Single shooter, sir. Not a very good shot. Female. Dressed in black. Not like the others, sir."

"She most certainly is not," I said.

Ambo held out a hand. "Why did you attack?" he asked. "My orders were, I wanted them all alive."

The American straightened, shoulder against the rock. He put his thumbs in his belt. Nodded his helmeted head in the brisk movement of a construction foreman. "Scattered across the hillside in sniper formation, sir. Very clever. Would have had to dig them out of their foxholes one by one."

"So you attacked," I said.

The captain ignored me. "Would have meant high casualties, sir. Decided to show them the chopper."

Ambo said, "You didn't."

"It was a bluff. Those missiles look pretty scary, I guess. Instead of coming out with their hands in the air, they grouped together and did a suicide charge."

"Except the woman."

The man shrugged. "Except her. Funny thing, though. Didn't scream. The monks, I mean. Just ran toward us silently. Not a sound."

"Except for your gunfire as you shot them down," I said.

Ambo stuck two fingers into the breast pocket of the

captain's fatigues, pulled out a pack of Hamiltons. He put a cigarette between his lips. The medic had confiscated his un-filtered Camels in the jeep. He glanced at the captain. "You mind?"

"For a living legend like yourself, sir?" The captain lit the cigarette with a plastic lighter. "They teach your exploits at Langley."

Ambo took a puff, held it in his lungs, let it trickle out. He offered the pack to me. I waved it away. I expected suffering in my immediate future. I was probably going to die. I wanted to experience it raw and unadulterated. He handed the pack back to the captain.

"My fault," Ambo said at last.

"How is it your fault?" I said. "Sounds to me like your overeducated grunt here fucked up."

"He doesn't know what's at stake."

"He knows how to follow orders, doesn't he?"

The captain said to Ambo, "Sir, I got to put up with this? I don't need a disciplinary problem on the line."

Ambo dropped his hand on the captain's shoulder, gripped the man's flesh like a basketball, his thumb along the man's collarbone. "Friend, this disciplinary problem, as you put it, is about to save the world. Isn't that right, Horse?"

"Or destroy it," I said.

Another shot rang out, and by instinct we ducked lower, even though we were fully protected by the boulder.

"Gimme your bullhorn," Ambo said.

The captain held it out.

"It's for him." He jerked his head in my direction.

The captain held the bullhorn out to me grip first, with

elaborate ceremony, as though it were a weapon. I took it. It sagged heavy in my hand.

"What do I say?" I asked Ambo.

Smoke swirled from his nose. "You want her to come out of this alive? Maybe you should tell her that."

I swallowed. Tiptoed to the edge of the rock. Put the bullhorn to my lips. The sudden squawk made two nearby soldiers flinch away from me. Another bullet pocked the side of the boulder. I pointed the bullhorn at the sky.

"Kate!" my voice blared through the bullhorn. "It's me!"

Three gunshots in succession smashed against the opposite face of the rock.

"It's me!" I shouted again. "Horace! Horse! You know." I felt like an idiot. "Me!"

The voice came clear, if faint, from several hundred meters up the mountain. "What do you want?"

"I don't want you to die!" I shouted through the bullhorn. "Why don't you come down here? We'll talk about this!"

There was a long pause. I looked at Ambo. He looked at me. The captain put his hands on his hips and looked at both of us.

The voice floated down the mountain, the voice of heaven taunting those in hell. "Why don't you come up here?"

Ambo pursed his lips. Shook his head. The captain raised his eyebrows.

"Ex-wife," I said.

The captain whistled. "Were my ex-wife, I sure as hell wouldn't go up there."

A burning cigarette floated at my ear. Ambo leaned heavily on my shoulder. He smelled like smoke and antiseptic and old man. "Can't let you go up there, son."

"How's that?"

"You're our secret weapon. She kills you, we got nothing on Pitt. No one to talk to him." He patted my shoulder. "Stakes are too high. You understand?"

He pointed his chin at the captain and lifted it an inch, and I knew that slight movement was as sure a death sentence for Kate as any judge and jury could provide. The captain spoke in rapid-fire Spanish to the Bolivian sergeant at his side. I couldn't catch what was being said. But I could guess.

I vaulted a prostrate Bolivian soldier and ran up the hill.

"Goddammit!" the captain swore.

"Horace!" Ambo called out. "Horse, please!"

I clambered across the rocks. A long string of oaths followed me. "Fuck's sake, man!" Ambo shouted. "Don't you realize what you're doing, what you're risking?"

Where was Kate hiding? I headed uphill and toward the right, where it seemed I had last heard her voice.

"Come back, you asshole!" the captain cursed. "She's going to kill you, can't you see that?"

Another shot rang out. Something tugged at the skin on my left bicep. I reached up, found my hand covered in blood. I flexed the muscle. Just a graze. Another shot splintered a shard from a nearby boulder.

I stopped running, pulled my shirt out of my pants and lifted my sweater to expose my ribs, then rotated in a full circle, a fashion model exposing his unarmed navel to a freezing, high-altitude runway. I let my sweater drop and held up my hands, fingers spread wide, and walked toward the source of the gunshots.

"Don't come any closer!"

I stopped. Her voice came from nearby. I scanned the rocks, looking for movement. She peeked from behind a boulder, her rifle pointed at me.

I took another step. "Let me come and talk."

Bullets skittered and pinged off the rock I was standing on.

"I know how you feel!" I shouted.

"You know nothing how I feel!"

"I know because I feel the same." The cry died in my throat, came out more like a moan.

"You always were a touchy-feeling bastard!"

There was a silence. I took another step.

"Please!" she shouted. "Tell me about your feelings!"

My hands out, arms high in the sky, Moses commanding the waters of her heart to part, I, the jury, delivered the verdict:

"Guilty!"

She withdrew behind the boulder. Long seconds passed. The frozen wind whipped through my sweater. I took another step.

I pounded my fists against my chest. "Guilty!" I shouted again. "I am scum!" My voice screeched high, verging on falsetto. "Scum! And you know what?" I shrieked at the rocks, not caring who heard. "I deserve to die! I do! Me!"

A sniffle. In the distance. I stepped forward. No response. Her sobbing grew louder. I put one foot in front of the other, climbing toward her.

Twenty meters.

Ten.

Five.

Her head popped up from behind the rock, her face red and inflamed, tears glinting on her cheeks. She pointed the rifle at my chest. "We all deserve to die."

"Yes," I said. "We do."

"I mean all of us. The world. The human race. This infection that's destroying Gaia."

I shook my head. "It's not their fault."

"Isn't it? You said so yourself."

"I did. That's true."

She sniffled again. I doubted my ears at first. In all the time we'd been together I had never seen her cry. Not even at our loss. She had been dry, impossibly dry, unbelievably dry for a woman who'd just lost her child.

I took another step. She stopped me with a movement of the gun. "What changed your mind?" she asked.

I hesitated, but told the truth. "I didn't."

"What do you mean?"

I let my shoulders droop and hung my head. "I am tired, Kate. I am so fucking tired."

"Tired? Of what?" The outrage mounted in her throat. "Of grieving for our child?"

"Of everything," I said.

She stood, exposing herself from waist up to the snipers below.

"Are you crazy?" I said. "Get down!"

"Fuck them," she said. "And fuck you!" The rifle shook in her hands. "We are poison! Don't you understand that?"

"You want to shoot me?" I said. "Go ahead."

She sighted down the barrel at my heart. Her finger pulled back on the trigger. I closed my eyes, prepared for impact. I hoped her aim was better than the captain suggested. How long would it take to die? An abrupt thought: was there an afterlife? What if I was wrong? I discarded the notion but it lingered, an unwelcome fungus in the dark corners of my brain.

It happened so fast, I couldn't believe there was no pain. A gunshot exploded in front of me. I patted my torso for wounds, but found none. A firecracker went off behind me, and I opened my eyes. Kate stood there with her mouth open. The gun dropped from her hands with a clatter, and she disappeared behind the boulder.

I ran to her. She lay draped across a rock, her back arched against the smooth stone, her face contemplating the sky. She gasped for breath. Clutched her black robe, now sticky and wet.

She lifted her eyes. "Horse."

"Here, babe." I squeezed her hand. Memories of the day she gave birth, her hand in mine. She hadn't cried then either. Now her tears came in rivers, a lifetime's supply demanding to be shed.

She said, "They killed me, Horace."

"No," I said, and stroked her hair. "You killed yourself."

She looked up at me, her eyes so green, flickering as they studied mine. She touched my face, and I realized that my cheeks were dry. She smiled. Her lips fluttered. She laughed, went rigid with the pain.

"Don't," I said.

She looked at the sky. "Will we see each other again, do you think? Will we see," and she coughed up blood, "will we see Lili?"

I clasped her hand to my chest. "Lili is gone," I said, "and we have burned in hell for long enough." I kissed her bare knuckles. "Go and find your peace."

Her fingertips were icy rose petals on my cheek. Her hand quivered with the effort. "Peace," she said. "I—"

But I will never know what she wanted to tell me. Her hand fell back and her body convulsed and the life went out of her, a rasping breath from deep inside her lungs, and she was still, a smile on her face, perhaps the first real smile she'd had in years.

And for the first time since our daughter died, I wept.

A man is not supposed to cry. A man should be hard, should endure, should be a rock, a stoic who soldiers on no matter what the cost.

But I was none of those things. I had never been. I never would be. I was a failure of a man.

As I looked down at her automatic rifle and wondered if my toe would reach, I felt a hand on my shoulder, lips on my cheek. Kate's ghost brushed past me, a final peck on my wet cheek before beginning her eternal, unhappy wanderings. I jumped to my feet, slammed my shoulder into a headful of blonde hair.

Aurora stood there, her hand to her nose, blood trickling down her upper lip.

"Goddammit," I said. "I can't fucking do anything right, can I."

She put her arms around me and held me tight. She pressed her face to my neck. Her blood dripped into my shirt. My arms stuck out straight like some fucking robot. I bent my elbows at right angles, and felt her spine under my fingertips.

Her blonde hair tickled my face.

"Hush now," she said. She rocked me from side to side. "Shh."

Time took pity on us, and galaxies gave birth and died in the time we stood there. At last, in a distant, faraway land I heard footsteps approaching. They stopped. A gun clacked against the rocks. Knees creaked. Coins jingled. I took a long shuddering breath, and pulled away.

The captain squatted over Kate's body. Checked her pulse. Took out two Bolivian coins and laid them over her eyes, crossed her arms over her chest. He kept his eyes on the ground. "I'm sorry," he mumbled.

I think he actually meant it.

I turned to Aurora. She'd unbraided her hair. Curled it, even. Put on fresh makeup.

"How—" I said, but my mouth refused to work. "How did you—"

She smiled, wiped tears and blood from my neck. "How did I get here?"

She jerked her thumb sideways. Ambo stood there, leaning against a rock, studying the snowcapped crater in the distance. Another SUV was parked below.

"One more chore before we're done," he said, not to us, but to the clouds that encircled the mountaintop.

"Then we can rest," Aurora said.

Ambo lowered his head. "One way or another."

26

THE SHALE SLIPPED UNDERFOOT. I LOOKED UP
at the crater. It didn't seem to be getting any closer.

Somewhere up there Pitt was waiting for me. Pacing back
and forth. Wondering when I'd get there. If I'd get there.
Wondering, perhaps, even, if he shouldn't just push the button and be done with it.

I struggled for breath. I looked back. Far below, Ambo
and Aurora and a group of soldiers huddled, awaiting the
fate of the world. No doubt they were watching me this very
minute. Satellites from above. Binoculars from below. Pizza-
eating Langley analysts in polyester trousers ogling me on a
scrambled satlink. Or were they using drones? I had a worldwide audience. I unfurled my middle finger and saluted the
men below, the sky above.

"Mount Testimony," Ambo had declared with a broad
sweep of his hand. "Five thousand, four hundred and sixty
meters."

"How high are we here?" I'd asked.

"Four thousand and a bit," the captain had answered.

The cold wind slashed through all my layers. I had long
since lost sensation in my ears. Pins and needles jabbed my

toes. When they went away, I knew, I would be at risk of frostbite. I laughed at the thought. Toeless Boy Wonder, English Teacher Extraordinaire. My laugh grew into a cough and I spat on the rocks.

I hefted the backpack Aurora had given me. It was time for a rest. No good breaking a sweat. It'd just freeze to the skin. I sat on a nearby rock.

"Snacks!" she said, held the bag aloft.

"What for?" I asked stupidly.

She unzipped the pack and rummaged around. "Long climb up the mountain. You need energy. Got you a couple of tuna-fish sandwiches, fruit, plenty of water. Some cookies. Homemade, too." She held them out: oatmeal raisin, they looked like.

I looked at the bag, then at her. The blood streamed down her nose, formed a red goatee around her lips. "You'd make a helluva mother, you know that?"

She laughed. "What, you think I did this?" Her laughter echoed on the rocks, a foreign sound in this place of death, Kate still warm at my feet. Aurora's green eyes danced, bittersweet emeralds tempting me, defying me.

Reminding me of Lynn.

Reminding me of Kate.

Of all the women I had ever loved and lost, and would never see again.

"No, of course not." Brain not functioning. Query: why not? Altitude? Or those eyes? *Damn it. Wipe drool.*

"Ambo and his crew fed us when they picked us up. This

one's for you." She zipped the backpack shut and held it out. Lowered her voice. "Except this one has a gun in it, just in case."

I took the bag. I could think of nothing to say.

"You coming back?" she asked casually. More words bubbled out of her before I could answer: "You coming back to me?"

My hand stroked her hair, her ear cold under my fingers. Some primal impulse took hold of me, short-circuited my usual fail attitude, and I pulled her lips down to mine.

When we broke away, her face was covered in blood. So was mine. I wiped my lips with my sleeve.

"Better get that looked at," I said.

Her smile quivered. "I will."

I shuffled my feet, preparing to go.

"Yes." The word erupted out of her, aimed at my back.

"What's that?"

"I would make a helluva mother." She waved at me, an awkward twitch of her hand, then knotted her fingers together.

I headed for the trail. I didn't look back.

Ambo shouted after me. "Horse!"

I kept walking.

"Horse!"

The bullhorn squawked, amplified Ambo's voice. "What's more important?" He paused, as though waiting for an answer. "Pitt? Or the world?"

I didn't stop. I didn't turn.

"My son is dead, Horse! You understand that? He is nothing to me!"

I walked quickly toward the trail.

The voice faded in the distance. "He is nothing to you!"

I flipped up the hood of my borrowed anorak. It muted the howl of the wind. And Ambo's voice.

Hak Po's plastic baggie rested in my palm. How did that get there? I fumbled with it, couldn't get it open. I took my gloves off, set them down next to me. A gust of wind seized them, dashed them into the air, two black specks fluttering far in the distance. I unzipped the baggie, took a pinch in my fingers.

Last time, I thought. *Really the last time.*

Last burst of energy. Get to the top. That's all that matters. What happens after isn't life. Life as you know it is over.

I jammed my frozen fingers up my nose and snorted as hard as I could. *Numb. Numbness. Come on. Do your job.* Another snort, and another, and another, until the bag was half gone. I was as high as I had ever been, but it was not enough. It would never be enough. I could never mourn her as she deserved. I could never make right that wrong. I would go to the grave with that sin on my conscience.

A photo fluttered in my hand. Liliana. My baby. Frozen in time. Wrapped all in pink. Mouth open in surprise. When she was born she weighed six pounds, seven ounces. Now she felt like a ton.

The breeze whipped at the picture. I held it out, tight between my thumb and forefinger. All I had to do was let go. That was all. So simple.

And so impossible.

The backpack sat open at my feet. I reached under my sweater, put the photo back in my shirt pocket, over my heart. I fished around for a bottle of water. Cracked the seal, drank a mouthful, then poured the rest onto the ground. I didn't need it. Just more baggage to weigh me down. Where I was going, water would be the least of my worries.

I unwrapped the sandwiches and threw them out across the rocks. I crushed the cookies, shook the crumbs on the ground. The apple and banana I hurled into the air, as high and as far as I could. I watched as they came down, smashed against the rocks. At the bottom of the backpack I found the gun. Heavy pistol. Automatic. I threw it sideways, like a boomerang. It clattered hundreds of meters below me, disappeared into a deep crevice.

The cocaine was still in my hand. I hesitated. I turned the open baggie upside down. The cocaine never hit the ground. The wind blew it back in my face, stinging my cheeks with frozen granules. When the storm had passed I opened my eyes. The baggie was empty.

I left it there on the mountainside.

The afternoon clouds rolled in, surrounded me in mist. I could see the trail in front of me but that was it. I was free of the watchers, but at what cost? A misstep, one wrong turning, and I would be lost for good. The world would be lost for good. They must be holding their breath down there, I realized, waiting for me to come back down the mountain.

Damn them, I thought. *I didn't ask for this. I am not ready. Who am I to do this thing?* It should be Ambo. It should be

Pitt's wife. Wherever she'd gone. It should be a professional negotiator. Anyone, really. Anyone but me.

I took long, slow, deep breaths, filling my lungs with the thin air. The cocaine helped, but not much. Each step was a labor: lift foot, move foot forward, put foot down, press upward. Repeat.

Step by step I crunched my way up the trail, studying the ground before me, following in the footsteps of centuries of murderous Incan priests and their human offerings. Usually children.

Kate had explained it to me once.

"The Incas didn't torture or disembowel their sacrificial victims. Nothing so primitive. They simply left them on top of the volcano. Tied them up. They'd die of exposure. That's why there are so many mummies there. The bodies freeze solid and stay that way." Of course, the mummies had long since been put in museums or sold to necrophiliac pimps in Lima.

The trail got steeper. I stopped, unable to go on. I peeled off my anorak, threw it aside. The wind seized it, flung it into the void. A bitter mountain wind slashed through my sweater, froze my sweaty T-shirt to my chest. The pain woke me. I was alive. I had things to do before I died. I knew that now. Even if I wasn't sure what that thing was.

Footsteps had worn a path across a steep pile of rocks. I climbed across them, my gloveless fingers giving me a shock of pain at each touch of the icy stone. My broken pinkie had swollen three times its normal size. I ripped off the tape that bound it to my ring finger. Pity I didn't have a knife. It would be easier to just cut it off and be done with it.

A sheer rock wall loomed before me. I craned my neck, trying to see the top.

The final assault, bucko, Ambo had said. *Better hope that rope's still there.*

I bent my frozen fingers, felt in the cliff face for a hand-hold. There were none. No chalk, no rope. Nothing. A red dot of light danced across my hands.

"There you are," called out a voice from above. "I've been waiting for you."

It was Pitt.

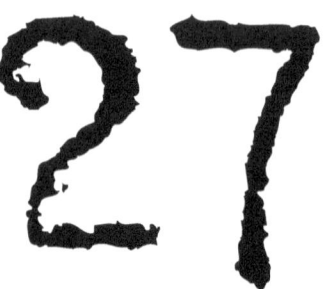

A ROPE POOLED IN CIRCLES AT MY FEET. I
picked it up. Tried to tie it around my waist, but my fingers
were too stiff. My left hand was useless, my pinkie kinked
to hell and back. The cliff was twenty meters high. At least.
What was I supposed to do, pull myself up, hand over broken
hand?

Pitt answered the question with a sharp tug. I curled the
rope around my left wrist, hooked it under my elbow, and
behind my back, where I held it with my good right hand. I
flexed my arms, felt my weight on the rope. I scrabbled at
the rock face with the toes of my boots. Inch by inch I rose
into the air. Twice my footing slipped and I hung in midair,
the mist thick on all sides, unable to see above or below. Each
time the rope inched upward once again, my boot found another toehold, and I lunged ahead. A final surge and I lay on
my stomach, gasping for breath, my legs dangling over the
edge of the cliff, Pitt's polished leather hiking boots at eye
level.

"Wicked view," he said, his smile all teeth. "Enjoy the
climb?"

There he stood, the blond god in all his glory, on top of

that mountain of fire. Multiple layers of wool showed at his throat, underneath a motorcyclist's black leather jacket and pants. He looked warm, comfortable; unconcerned. I crawled farther onto the ledge, pushed myself to my feet. I shoved my naked fingers into my armpits, trying to get some feeling back into my hands. The cold whistled through me now, as though I wasn't even there.

"Dude, you look frozen." He rummaged in a green rucksack at his feet. "Put this on." He held out a puffy anorak and a pair of fluffy knitted mittens. I had barely put them on before he crushed me against his chest, pounded my back so hard my lungs echoed like a drum. His breath stank of booze.

"You've been following me," I managed to chatter.

He held me at arm's length. "Hey, someone's got to be your guardian angel."

"Is that what it was?"

"Wanted to make sure you got here safely, bro."

Like when you whacked me on the head after killing Lynn? I wanted to say. *No. I came all this way. Hear him out first. He could be right.*

"What for?" I asked.

"What *for?* Today's our day of victory!" He shook me, raised his clenched fists in the air. "The most important day in human history!" He spun in a circle, whooped a wide receiver's touchdown triumph.

I stood, expressionless, looking at him.

"What's the matter, dude? Show some enthusiasm already."

My teeth chattered in the cold. "Forgive me if I'm not excited by the deaths of billions of people."

"Who deserve to die." A finger out in warning. "I am

merely the avenging hand of God."

I walked away from him. The patchy mist came and went, giving glimpses: distant mountains, the *altiplano,* more mist. A trail led down into the volcanic cone. The opposite side of the crater was barely visible. Sulfurous fumes belched from below. Patches of snow clung to the rocks.

"Dude," he called after me. "What's wrong?"

"You fucking think?"

"Horse," he said, grabbed my arm, this time gently. "Don't tell me you're on their side."

"I'm on no one's side but my own."

He laughed, threw up his arms again. "That's the Horse I know and love."

I realized with a start that he was drunk.

He darted about in tiny circles, his arms held out, a little kid making airplane noises. "Wanna help me make the world go boom?"

"Where *is* the bomb, anyway?" I asked, noticing the small black device he clutched in one hand.

He grinned and pointed into the crater, at a crevice twenty meters down. A bundle of plastic and duct tape stuck out of a gash in the rocks.

Pitt burst out laughing at my expression. "How about a drink?"

"What's the occasion?"

"Since when you need an excuse?"

He dragged a half-full bottle of *pisco* from his rucksack. Unscrewed the top and poured a long swig down his throat. He grunted, held the bottle out to me. "Don't look so glum," he said. "This is a celebration!"

"What are we celebrating?" I asked.

"End the guilt, baby!" He leaned into me, his breath over-powering. "An end to suffering, an end to sin!"

He had me there. I lifted the bottle. "I'll drink to that."

Pitt laughed, pointed at me with a drunken index finger. "I knew they'd send you up here. Victor said so."

The liquor tasted sour. It went down the wrong way, and I coughed. "You wanted me to come?"

"Of course!" he shouted over a sudden howl of wind. "That's why I came back to Lima. To tell you. To share this with you."

"Then you found Lynn in my bed, waiting for me," I prompted, and drank again.

He hung his head. "That was fucked up, dude."

"You're telling me." I put the bottle to my lips.

"Yeah, but hey." He lifted his shoulders, let them fall. "Easy come, easy go."

I hacked liquor from my lungs.

He slapped me on the back. "Besides, who wouldn't want to share this with a friend?"

My breath returned. "Is that what I am to you?"

"There's no one else I'd rather have here with me." The clouds parted, and he gestured with a sweep of his arms at the view: crater yawning deep before us, salt flats distant far below, the mist a blanket of frozen wetness, snowy ground beneath our feet. "Front-row seats to the end of the world."

I fingered my swollen pinkie through the mitten. "Is this the right thing to do, I wonder."

Pitt laughed, a bright, melancholy sound. He took the bottle from my hands. "That is so like you. Always doubting.

Never sure. You think too much, you know that?"

"Guilty as charged," I said. "But is it?"

He paused, the bottle at his lips. "Is it what?"

"The right thing to do."

He drank. "It's what we deserve. All of us. You know that."

"It *is* what we deserve," I said. "But who died and made you God?"

He turned to me, excited. "But don't you think I'm right?" He pointed an accusing finger toward the west. "Wipe out Lima. All the Limas of the world. The cesspools of humanity. A clean slate. The cities, the pollution, the crime. Back to a state of nature."

"Hobbes would be delighted," I said. "No laws. No medicine. No food. A billion people feeding on each other as the population dwindles, worldwide cannibalism, dog eat dog."

"That's somehow worse than what we have right now?" He snorted and spat a bloody loogie on the summit marker. It squatted there like a red medallion, frozen to the painted white rock.

I was so tired I didn't know what to think anymore. "Maybe you're right," I said at last.

"Of course I'm right. We're both right. Here."

He lay the detonator on the ground at my feet. It looked like a toy remote control.

"Is this for me?" I asked.

"What do you *think,* dude? That's why I wanted you up here. To do the honors. I knew you'd want to be part of this."

I filled my mouth with *pisco.* Swallowed. It was no use anymore. The liquor did nothing for me. I picked up the detonator. Flipped off the safety. Caressed the button with my thumb. All I had to do was press this little piece of plastic and the nightmares would end. I'd get the punishment I deserved. I'd even be doing humanity a favor.

"Put them out of their misery," I mumbled.

"Exactly. End the suffering. You ready?" He knelt, gripped the other side of the detonator with his thumbs.

The liquor made me woozy. I gulped great lungfuls of cold air. "But people will suffer because of us. It will take years, decades even, before they start to die off."

"It's like spaying a stray dog," he said. "You cut off its nuts so the kids won't suffer."

That snapped my head around. "What about your kids?" I asked. I thought of Janine, her little black space fighter, the cat. The baby whose diaper I changed.

Pitt bowed his head. "They have gone where life can no longer hurt them."

I frowned. "Why? What happened?"

"Janine thought it for the best. When she heard of our plans."

"*Our* plans," I said. "What have you done?" Already knowing.

"Put them out of their misery. Like you said."

"Even the baby? Even Esmeralda?"

"Especially Esmeralda. Did a DNA test. She's the only one that was mine."

"You killed your own child?" I said. "On purpose?"

He grinned at me, like he had in the surf. "Snapped her neck with a noose. For her own good."

For a long moment I was speechless. Spittle froze on my

lips. That little baby. Dead.

Pitt put his thumb on the button. He picked up my limp hand and put my thumb next to his. Closed his eyes. "On the count of three. One. Two. Thr—"

"Wait." I jerked away.

"What? What is it?"

I shivered in the cold. Swallowed hard. "I can't do this."

"Don't be such a wuss, man."

"There must be some other way."

"To end the guilt? You got something else, you tell me. I'm all ears."

I thought of Esmeralda again, the way she had gripped my finger, waved her hand at me. She looked so much like Liliana. "Maybe there is no way out," I said.

"Duh. Of course there's a way out, dude. It's called death."

I chewed my lip. "It's too easy. You're admitting failure."

"It's not a question of failure."

"But isn't that what you're doing here? Saying, you can't cope?"

He whispered, "You have no idea what I've been through."

"What *you've* been through?" I said, and stood. "Well boo fucking hoo. Poor little Pitt had a rough time, killing all those dissidents. You joined the fucking CIA, dude. What did you expect?"

"I don't know what I expected," he said. "All I know is that ever since I met you, I can't stop thinking about the people I killed." The words seemed to stick in his throat. "Innocent women and children, dead so that large corporations can 'maximize shareholder value.'"

"And your own mother, Pitt. How could you do that?"

He looked at the ground. "I'm not proud of that, either."

"Strangled with your own bare hands. I saw the bruises. I saw the photos."

His answer came slow and late, his tongue thick in his mouth. "What photos?"

"The police photos, dude. Ones they showed me? Thought I did it."

Pitt chuckled. "You?"

"Why is that funny?"

"You couldn't hurt a fly."

I crossed my arms. "That's what Villega said."

He half stood, then sat down again. "How is the good ol' major these days, anyway?"

"Fat rapacious prick doing his best to survive. Which is more than I can say for you."

Pitt screwed the cap back onto the bottle of *pisco,* lowered it to the ground. "I'm sorry," he said.

"No you're not," I said. "Since when are you sorry for anything?"

He scrambled to his feet. He held the detonator out at me, as though it were a knife. "When I say I'm sorry, I mean I'm fucking sorry!" His thumb twitched on the button.

"OK," I said. "You're sorry."

"If I wasn't sorry, would I fucking be here right now?" he said. "Don't you think I know what I have done?" He paced the precipice, shouting at the plains below, then into the silent volcano. "To watch my own hands, these hands, again and again. Like some bad movie. Not able to stop myself. Squeezing the life out of her. Out of Lynn. My own mother. And you know the worst part? The worst part of it all?" He waved the detonator in my face. His breath was foul. "Her body tensed. She bucked her hips. And she came. She came! In some sort of death orgasm. And then—" he stepped back, wiped the back of his wrist across his nose, "and then—"

"Coming so hard you thought you'd die."

His head whipped around. "How did you know that?"

"That's how it feels when I do it to myself."

Pitt stood over me, chest to chest. "There's guilt enough to go around, you know."

I couldn't meet his eye. I struggled to control my voice. "You can't pin this on me."

"Your room. That morning? Found you in the bathroom, with—"

"Enough!"

"Well," he said, and drew himself up straight with the dignity of a drunk. "I tried it. Like you showed me. It was as good as you said. No, better." His shoulders slumped. "And then something happened. It was like wearing sunglasses all your life, and suddenly you lose them." He swept a hand at the cloudy vista. "There was my life. Spread out before me. Everything I'd ever done. I saw the world for what it really was. Myself. Mom. You. Ambo." A bitter laugh. "Human filth, all of us." He chewed a fingernail so hard it bled. "It hurts, Horse. It hurts, it hurts, it hurts."

The cold wind knifed through the jacket he'd loaned me. I staggered on the edge of the precipice. "And that's when you called Kate," I said. "The postcard I gave you. Went to the ashram, found your way to end the guilt."

The bottle of *pisco* was halfway to his lips. He laughed. He drank again, long, slow, luxurious swallows. He poured the remainder of the bottle down his throat, and I realized that, instead of being jealous, instead of having to resist the urge to rip the bottle from his hands and drink it myself, for the first time in my life I no longer wanted a drink.

"End the guilt." He held the bottle upside down, shook it. He threw it over his shoulder into the crater. It rattled once on the soft shale, then—nothing. I waited for the crash. No sound came from below. "Not yet, but I'm working on it."

"So, what?" I said. "End the world and your guilt goes away? All your sins magically disappear? How does that work?" All of a sudden it sounded ridiculous.

"We are sinners in a world of shit," he said, and slid to the ground against a rock, his thumb barely missing the detonator button. "End the world. End the shit."

I sat down and huddled beside him, in the lee of the wind. "They sent me here to stop you, you know."

He bumped his shoulder against mine. "Sure fooled 'em good, eh?"

I put my arm around his neck, pulled his forehead down to mine. The detonator was within reach. "That doesn't mean I'm going to help you either."

Pitt went still. He pulled away. He ripped off his woolen hat. His dirty hair stuck to his skull in matted tufts. I saw his face then, as though for the first time: skeletal, emaciated, skin stretched tight across bony Nordic cheeks.

"What did you just say?" The tone of his voice made me shift sideways.

"You want to end the world," I said, "you can do it by yourself."

He stared at me, then slumped against a rock. "You're just

pissed 'cause I killed Mom, is that it?"

"No. It's not." I could still smell Esmeralda's diaper in my hands. But Pitt would never understand that.

He laughed again, slapped his leg. He wiped tears from his eyes. "I can't believe you were screwing my own mother—"

"—I didn't know she was—"

"—and no one knew a thing!" He punched the air with his fist. "Hurt the bastard where it counts."

"Who?" I asked.

"Ambo, of course. Who else?"

"I didn't do it because I hated Ambo."

"Oh, so you were head over heels in love with a fifty-year-old woman with fake tits?" He cackled, head thrown back. "Christ, Horse, you're more fucked up than I am."

"Quite likely," I said.

Pitt leaned forward and exhaled in my ear, the smell of the liquor fumigating my face. "Want to know why I did it?"

I didn't answer.

He panted his barroom breath against my neck. "Kill her, that is?" he added, suddenly unsure of himself.

"Why did you do it, Pitt," I said in a monotone. "Please tell me."

"Well there she was," he said. "Down to her bra and panties. In your bedroom. She reeked of sex. Bitch in heat. Door was unlocked, I walked right in. She must have thought I was you. When she realized whose cock she was grabbing, she started to babble. Tried to explain. Wasn't what it looked like."

He paused and spat again, a second medallion of red on the rock. "It was disgusting," he said. "My own mother." He snorted, sat up straight. "She had to die. Simple as that."

"Don't we all."

Pitt put a hand on my shoulder, pushed himself to his feet. The detonator swung back and forth in his hand. "I'm glad you see it that way," he said thickly. "Any world that could produce a man like me does not deserve to continue." He held his hand in front of my face. The detonator lay flat on his palm. "You deserve a clean slate, too."

I shook my head. "There is no clean slate."

Pitt crouched. "But there is! Mother Earth, the world spirit. Gaia forgives us. Will forgive us. If we do this one thing."

I nodded my head, not looking at him. "That we are an infection," I said at last.

"You feel it too? We're a disease, a cancer, and—"

"—the only cure is death. Yes," I said. "I got the lecture at the ashram."

Pitt rested the detonator on my knee. He held out his gloved fist. "Bros forever?"

I left my hands in my lap.

"Dude." The fist trembled in midair. "Bros forever?"

"Maybe our only task as human beings is to survive." I put my hand on his shoulder. "To survive and endure."

Pitt's eyes plummeted to earth. I will never forget the look on his face. He growled at me from deep in his throat, "Who would want to live on this vile, pus-filled canker sore of a planet?"

I pushed him away. "I would."

Pitt stood, the muscles in his face contorting and twitching. He spat at me. The loogie landed on my cheek, slid down to my chin. "Then you are my enemy. And you must die."

He lifted the detonator to waist height. Checked the safety. Off. Where I had left it. His thumb descended to the button. I slashed my legs around, slammed my shins into the backs of his knees. He toppled to the ground. The detonator fell from his hand. It landed a few meters away. He reached for it.

I leaped on top of him. Curled my fist tight and crashed it into his face. His nose snapped against my knuckles. My broken pinkie collided with his teeth. I screamed. Clutched my injured hand.

He put his hand to his face. His fingers came away covered in blood. I thought for a moment he was going to punch me back.

Then he laughed. "I deserve that," he said. He held out his arms wide, palms open. "Well? What are you waiting for?"

I sat back on my heels. Shook my head.

"Fucking wuss," he said.

His fist crunched against my jaw. I fell off him onto my side. A loose tooth rattled around on my tongue. He climbed to his feet, stumbled to where the detonator lay. I shook off the punch, stood up. I ran the few steps between us and threw myself at him. He tumbled backward, with me on top. I wrenched the detonator from his hand. Snapped shut the safety catch, threw it over the ledge into the volcano.

He rolled over on top of me. Gripped my throat with his hands. Thumbs pressed down on my windpipe. I grabbed at his wrists, but they held me tight. I squeezed his throat shut, blocking the lungful of air inside his chest.

Seconds passed. Long, painful, dreadful seconds. I felt faint. Pitt's face went red.

His hands weakened. Loosened their grip on my throat.

Air surged into my lungs. Pitt pulled away, but I got back on top of him, my hands still tight on his throat.

"Do. It," he grunted.

His eyes wobbled back in his head. I let go. His body shuddered with an intake of breath. He lay there, fighting for air.

"Finish it." His voice was hoarse. He tried to sit up but couldn't make it. "Damn you, finish it!"

I stood. Stumbled and nearly fell into the crater. My lungs fought for oxygen. Black spots swam in my vision. I teetered on the edge. "Do what you have to do," I said. "I want no more deaths on my conscience."

The icy mist stung my cheek. The black spots disappeared. I stood up straight, still gasping for air. Stepped over Pitt's prostrate figure. Forced my feet to walk the dozen meters to where the rope lay spooled. My mashed pinkie pulsed with pain. I put it in my mouth and bit down. The pain eased. I spat the useless finger over the cliff.

I turned back. Pitt stood at the edge of the crater, peering into it. I looped the rope around my waist, prepared to rappel down. When I looked back again, Pitt was gone.

I took Liliana's photo from my shirt pocket. One last time. My lips moved.

"Goodbye."

I parted my fingers. The wind whipped her from my hand. She danced and floated between the clouds, like a dead leaf, or a bit of ash. Then she was gone. Where? Would I ever see her again?

Who knew? There was nothing more that I could do.

Go down the mountain, I told myself. That was all. After that? No idea. There was Aurora. No guarantees. There never are. But worth the risk? Maybe she could love me. Maybe I could even be worth loving.

Yes, I thought, as I descended the cliff, banging against the sheer granite wall, I would go down the mountain. But I would not go back to Lima. Not that far. Not that low. I wasn't dead yet. Not by a long shot. I had things I needed to do. Risks I needed to take. Pain remaining yet to suffer.

One man can save the world. One man can destroy it.

Now I knew which man I was.

Maybe even, I thought, as I landed on both feet at the base of the cliff, *maybe even, a placard in my hands and a protest on my lips, a cop's billy club crushing my skull, maybe even joy.*

ACKNOWLEDGMENTS

Thanks go first, as always, to midwife/editrix Alison Dasho, who patiently coaxed this one into the light.

Derek Murphy's fine artwork adorns the cover.

Michael Mandarano copyedited.

Derek Murphy pulled double duty as proofreader.

Kevin Glidden laid out the innards.

Many people read and commented on various drafts. Thank you!

Y finalemente, y mas importante que todo, gracias a mi conejita y ladybug girl. Te amo y te amo.